The Northern Keep

Book 2
of
The Master of Fate

William Price Jr

To Ma,
    For, well everything, I guess.

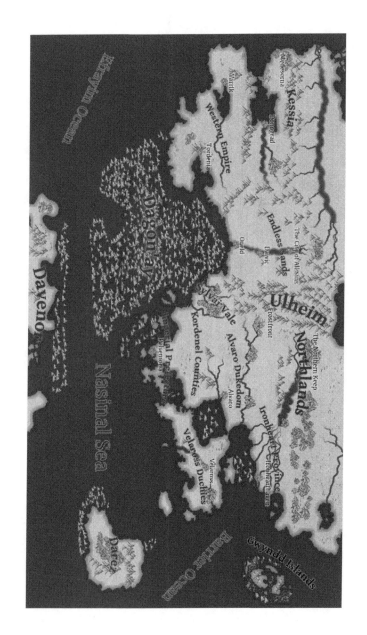

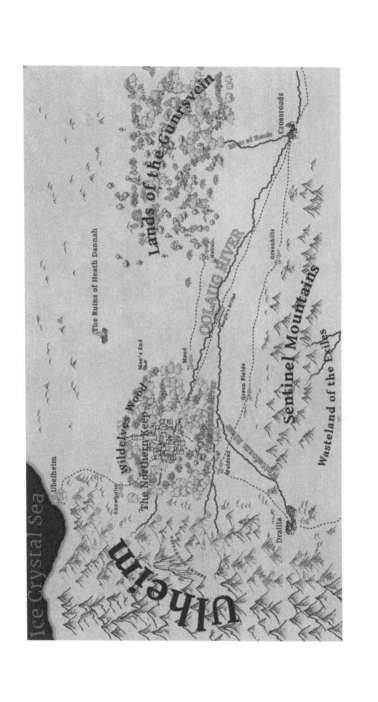

I

Winter

Chapter 1

Spring had come to the Northlands at last. The sky, so long burdened by an obscuring grey blanket, was letting go of this seeming-comfort. Patches of soft blue had begun to show through, with the renewing sun even peeking out with its promises of warmer times to come. The frigid air, unrelenting and unforgiving, had shifted, just a bit. This new, gentler breeze from the south brought with it the scent of flowers and birds and a season of renewal. Despite the scattered patches of snow still clinging to the soul of the land, the thaw had begun. The Northlands' grudgeful winter must inevitably relent, even as the frost has at last given way to a return of life.

Tomas Fidelis closed his eyes and lifted his chin as a patch of warm sun broke through the canvas overhead, letting a gentle radiance warm not only his face, but his soul as well. Months and miles ago, far to the south when he had first begun his quest, he had met a woman named Palsilyagathalexia. She was a sylva, a female of the strange elder race that had once ruled Lanasia. In only a few short weeks, Alexia had become a dear friend to Tomas. So often, in the months since, when he could bare to think of this wise older woman, the young man's mind would inexorably drift to her tragic, violent death. She had given her life to heal him after a mob's brutal attack. She had spent what little remained of her strength to restore his. She had died with his head in her lap, singing a lullaby to Tomas. In the months of travel since, months spent mostly in the company of a hated enemy, the young man could not separate that tragic death with Alexia's loving memory, and so tried to avoid the pain of recall altogether. But now, in this warming light and for the first time in months, when his thoughts drifted towards his dear friend, they were not pulled to her death, but to her life.

So many times, in their brief journey together, Alexia had turned her own gaze upwards, eyes closed and a soft smile on her lips. When a gentle mist fell from the heavy sky, she would whisper a thanks to her sylvai gods, or perhaps to the world itself. When a warming breeze briefly pushed back the winter cold, the sylva breathed deeply of the gift. When a winter flower or berry peaked through slumbering Nature, Alexia would pause and whisper a gentle prayer for the delicate birth, gently encouraging the emerging life. She found joy in life, in all life, even in an undeserving shepherd's.

Tomas' journey has been a hard one. Born into the wealth and privilege of Pelsemoria, once-capital of the Lanasian Republic, his life should have been one of research and philosophy, of poetry and art. As the son of a Praetorian officer, sworn to the defense of the Imperial Family, Tomas and his small family should have enjoyed all the privilege and luxuries available within the great city and heart of lanasian culture. Benefitting from the best education the Repubilc could provide, and the tempering of all the benefits of wealth and status, Tomas should have been Fated for a noble place in history. Instead, the Black Duke had come.

With the tyrant of the Northlands came his unholy daughter, the dark priestess Kyla, and her mercenary husband, Rogan Eigenhard. Facing charges exposing his villainy within the Elector Council, Cylan Calonar should have finally faced justice for his brutality, his treachery, and his vile heresy. Rather than risk the judgment of the Republic's greatest nobility, the Black Duke slaughtered that sacrosanct council. In the carnage, when the Praetorians desperately tried to save their Emperor, Tomas witnessed his father, leading those great warriors, being cut down by Rogan Eigenhard himself. The death of the city's defenders, the leaders of the Republic, and the Emperor himself, should have been vengeance enough against his accusers. But the Black Duke was not one for mercy. Instead, his twisted daughter had brought her infernal magic to bear.

Kyla's Madness swept the city. In a single night, with the Emperor's blood still wet on the ground, Pelsemoria, the great metropolis that had stood for ten thousand years, burned. Chaos reigned in an orgy of lust, betrayal, and slaughter. Tomas' own mother fell victim to Kyla's Madness; still dressed in deepest mourning for her fallen husband, the infant boy was forced to watch as his virtuous mother indulged the most blasphemous carnality with his father's best friend. In the wake of Kyla's Madness and the ruination of the city, life had become hardship, bitterness, and suffering. The Legions, leaderless and fearing for their own homes, abandoned their duty and the city. Most survivors of the Madness fled. Supplies no longer made their way to the capital. Starvation and disease claimed many as those who remained desperately eked out a crop from the unyielding land. Xeshlin slavers took advantage of the helpless survivors, claiming hundreds. Warlords emerged to war with each other, carrion-feeders squabbling over the dying Republic. And always, there remained the threat of the Black Duke's return.

House Calonar and its horrid master had destroyed Tomas' world and slaughtered everything he knew. The shepherd's heart had hardened long ago against the unending torrent of deprivation and death. But Alexia had changed that.

She did not heal his soul as she had his body, in one burst of loving magic. Instead, she had merely formed a crack in the ice wherein his heart once beat. Like so many of those who suffered under the predations of House Calonar and its Black Duke, Tomas felt a reasonable hatred for the Sylvai, the Halvans, and the other Inhumans who served the menacing Lord of the Northlands. But Alexia was sylva herself, and through a kind, forgiving example, showed the virtue of her race. As he had journeyed north, Tomas had seen, time and again, the evils of Humanity, the brutal horror of his own race as Lanasia tore itself apart amidst the Republic's death throes. Former allies conspired against one another. Brother lords mustered their peasants for pointless wars over arbitrary lines on new maps. Warriors who should have united in defense against the growing threat of the marauding Xeshlin slavers instead preyed upon those whom they had once sworn to defend. Humanity seemed determined to end itself. Alexia, in sharp contrast, stood as compassionate, forgiving, charitable, humble, and honest; she embodied all the virtues the Church claimed for Humans alone.

So many times, during their brief journey together, Tomas had seen Alexia close her eyes and raise her chin, even as he did now. So many times, her tiny fingertips caressed the golden rose pinned to her dress, even as his own fingers traced the tiny metal ornament now resting on his collar, a final gift to him before her passing. So many times, she had seemed to reach out with her very soul and embrace the world around her. Tomas reached out now, not with his soul, but with… something. His fingertips traced the golden rose, its tiny petals just beginning to open. He closed his eyes against the grudging retreat of winter. He heard the spring breeze dancing amidst the branches far overhead. The fragrance of new life, of flowers and leaves and grass teased him, not present just yet, but close. He felt the new sun shine down a rejuvenating baptism, the promise of the summer to come. He felt something stir deep in his soul; not awake, not just yet, but close.

"You going shiny-eyed on me, kid?"

Tomas eyes snapped open and a familiar grimace returned to his lips. Rogan Eigenhard. The young man often had to remind himself of just who it was now traveling with him. No longer a soft-spoken sylva priestess, but the gravelly-voiced heir to House Calonar. Not a woman of spiritual magic, but a warrior with the blood of hundred, perhaps thousands on his soul. Not a friend who taught him of the kindness of others and the virtue of forgiveness, but the man who murdered Tomas' father.

"Remind me again why I don't kill you?" Tomas asked with only partial sincerity.

Rogan shrugged, his grey cloak stirring slightly in the breeze. "Which answer do you want?" he asked mildly. "You tried and failed," he ticked off the reason on a finger of his thick-gloved hand. "You'd be stuck in the Northlands alone," another finger. "And, oh yeah, there's Cyras' geas."

"I guess there's a reason he's called the Trickster Mage," Tomas grumbled.

His unwanted companion snorted. "And you only got a day or two in his company," Rogan pointed out. "Imagine what long-term exposure would do."

The shepherd shuddered and rubbed his head, even the memory of his labyrinthine conversations with Cyras Darkholm bringing on another headache. The Trickster Mage, so legend said, never told a lie. What the legends did not mention, however, was that his truths were so twisted, so bent within themselves, that they may as well have been lies. Tomas had believed the legends, that Cyras Darkholm would grant a wish to anyone brave enough, lucky enough, and foolish enough to seek him out.

Rogan ducked under a low branch, weighted down with melting snow. "Did you ever get around to making your wish," the knight asked. "You never did say."

Tomas blinked. "Son of a..." he muttered darkly at the memory. "He never let me. Every time I started talking, every time I said anything, he..."

"Changed the subject?"

"More like ignored the subject. He just had a conversation with himself; you could go along for the trip or just..."

"Get trampled?"

Tomas shook his head. "Well," he added, "there was also that little distraction that came up."

Rogan glanced at Tomas. "Are you talking about my arrival, or the Druug attack?"

The shepherd glanced down at the shield hanging from the saddle of his father's killer. During most of their magically-mandated trip north, Rogan had kept his shield covered, trying to obscure his identity. Upon their arrival in the Northlands, though, the knight had removed that covering. The broken beams of sunlight often caught on the shield, shining a flash of light that kept drawing Tomas' eyes to its heraldry. A field of blue and grey with two crossed, four-sided diamonds center, one silver, the other pure white. The sigil of House Calonar.

Rogan followed the young man's gaze and snorted. "Yeah, I guess that would have been distracting." A thought occurred to the knight then and, as often happened, he quickly gave it voice. "Was that the first time you'd actually seen our heraldry?"

Tomas turned his head away, a shameful memory bringing a flush to his cheeks that burned even more than could the spring sun. "No," the shepherd nearly whispered. "There was one before."

"The Madness," the knight guessed. "One of our House Guard?"

Tomas shook his head. He drew a waterskin and drank, drying to flush away the guilty dryness from his throat. "I didn't see any Calonar House Guard that night," the young man grumbled. He then cast an accusing look at Rogan. "I was busy hiding in a closet and watching my mother shame herself."

His unwanted companion sighed. "Would another apology mean anything?"

"No." Tomas returned the skin to its place in his saddlebag. "I saw the sigil on a… soldier."

Rogan thought a moment, his gaze lost amidst the evergreen trees among which the road they followed traveled. The road, though not as good as a Republic one in the south, was still of fair quality, Tomas had conceded. Well-maintained stonework and a wide avenue offered a reasonably comfortable and efficient path through the dreaded forest. The young man had noted in surprise just how many travelers they had passed in the days since their entrance to Wildelves Wood. The reputation of this cursed forest was legendary; the Sylvai tribes within were the most savage, the most predatory of their race, not like the more pacified who lived in their Vale, far to the south. Entire armies had vanished upon entering these trees. Church officials, determined to sanctify the unholy place, returned to Velaross broken and mad, if they returned at all. Despite this, as Tomas and Rogan made their way deeper into the fearsome Wood, the travelers they met were content and friendly.

Time and again, as the unlikely companions led their horses at a canter further into Wildelves Wood, they were warmly greeted. More accurately, the merchants, villagers, tradesmen, and commons warmly greeted their Prince, the heir of their Black Duke. Cheers and waves and hails greeted Tomas and Rogan. Many people, even those clearly of ungentle upbringing, seemed to recognize their prince on sight, not needing to see the heraldry of his shield. There was no hint of fear in the Humans they passed, despite the imminent threat of the savage Sylvai all around.

"The scouting parties," the knight nodded, finally realizing where Tomas could have encountered the warriors of House Calonar.

"The raiding parties," Tomas corrected.

"We've talked about that," Rogan sighed with a roll of his blue eyes. "House Calonar knows exactly where your people are. If we wanted to attack you, to raid you, to do *anything* to you, we could have... easily."

"But instead, you've been protecting us," the young man added sarcastically. "From Xeshlin slavers, from the worst of the warlords, from all the horrid monsters in the dark." He snorted his rejection of Rogan's explanation for the presence of House Calonar soldiers near the ruins of Pelsemoria. "Sure."

"Believe it or not, kid," Rogan grumbled. "I'm done trying to convince you the truth." He pointed his chin further down the road, though only a few dozen feet were visible before the twisting path was swallowed by the trees. "Be in the Keep in another week or so. You can actually meet the people you've been told are all demon-worshipping, Human-sacrificing, blood-drinking monsters. You can actually see the city you've been told is a dark bastion of whatever." The knight paused and glanced over with a wry grin. "And you can actually meet the 'Black Duke, vile Lord of the Northlands.'" He chuckled at the thought.

Tomas said nothing, he only stared at the road ahead.

Although there was no sign of any Sylvai during the long days of travel through Wildelves Wood, Tomas' increased nervousness allowed him to sleep for no more than a few minutes, perhaps an hour at most, each night. As they moved ever-deeper into the cursed forest, the young man began jumping at every shadow that crossed his path. Every snap of a branch was a Sylvai trap. Every bird was a spy. The rustle of leaves in the wind signaled an attack. Everywhere the shepherd looked, he saw another place a Sylvai archer could hide, waiting for just the right time to strike.

"So," Rogan began as they sat around their campfire on their fifth night, "just what is it you think you'll be seeing in the Keep?"

Tomas barely glanced at the knight as he spoke, his eyes moving instead to try and penetrate the darkness. Night was far worse than day, he realized. The sun could, occasionally, penetrate the heavy evergreen shield, but the moon and stars had no chance. Only their pitiful little fire offered any relief against the omnipresent shadows. "I know what you're going to say," the shepherd replied. "Every story I've been told is wrong, and the Northern Keep isn't the den of evil it's been described to be."

"Pretty close," the knight conceded. "Why don't you tell me some of those stories?"

"They all say the same thing. The warlocks serving the Black Duke are the darkest of their kind, leeching the souls of countless victims to increase their power."

Rogan nodded. "The Keep does have some pretty powerful wizards."

"The priests of the Northern Keep," the young man continued, "they're all under the dominion of the Black Duke's daughter. They still practice the pagan rites of the old religions: Human sacrifice and carnal celebrations, everything that's long since been abandoned by the civilized peoples of Lanasia."

The knight poked a long stick into the fire. "Actually, if any one person in the Keep could be said to have the most influence over the various temples, it would've been..." A strange look came over Rogan's face, a brief shadow he quickly suppressed with a shake of his head. The knight's blue eyes very briefly, almost guiltily, passed over the golden rose pinned on Tomas' collar. "The Queen probably has the most influence now. She's the one who ordered the city open to all the old beliefs, after all."

By now, Tomas had stopped his constant scan of the trees. Although the small voice in the back of his head insisted he was worried for nothing, the young man's entire upbringing had been filled with stories of the terrors of Wildelves Wood and its cursed Northern Keep. The shepherd leaned close over the fire, his eyes locked on Rogan and his mind filling with every childhood story. "The armies that call this place home are the worst sort of assassins and brigands that have ever blighted the face of Arayel. Most of their officers are men who were expelled from the Legions for war crimes."

"We do get a lot of former Legionaries."

"I notice you're not denying any of what I'm saying," Tomas said in an accusatory tone.

Rogan shrugged. "Can sit here and tell you the stories are wrong. Doesn't seem much point to it, though. You've made up your mind about everything and everyone. Just curious about what you think you'll see.

"Come to think of it," the knight said suddenly. "What do you think the King himself is like? What do the stories say about him?"

"The Praetorians always said he was sired from the unholy union of a sylvu mercenary raping a human noblewoman."

"Close," Rogan corrected. "Actually, his father was the noble and his mother the common."

"Sylvai titles mean little," Tomas objected automatically. "He could still have been a mercenary."

The knight nodded. "From what I understand, the King's father *was* a soldier. His mother was a priestess, if you're curious."

"But human?" the shepherd asked.

"Oh, yes. His mother was human."

"You see? A sylvu warrior ravishing a human priestess! No man could be born from something like that and not be tainted by evil."

Rogan shrugged. "Well, that's for you to decide, I suppose. And, from what I've been told, his parents were married a long time. What else do you know about the horrible Black Duke?"

"The current Duke of Calonar was schooled in the dark magic of the Sylvai."

"Again true," the knight confirmed, casting another brief, veiled glance at the golden rose pinned on Tomas' collar.

"As a young man, Calonar had been trained at the Imperial War College and been given command of those forces responsible for policing Wildelves Wood."

"From what I understand, that's true. After the Siege of Velaross, when the rogue priests Leria and Lar Nenic were defeated by the Heroes of Fate, Cylan Calonar was admitted to the War College, and he did eventually take responsibility for the Northlands, especially this forest."

"Of course, he eventually betrayed the Republic and assumed lordship of the area, reforming the old alliance with the Sylvai."

"Kid, as far as I know, half the King's ancestors are Sylvai. He's got family down in the Vale, the ones who were aristocracy in their Empire, and he's got family up here in the Wood. I don't know you if you can really call it 'reforming the old alliance,' when it never really broke."

"The Black Duke is a man of infinite ambition and infinite evil," Tomas continued, regardless of Rogan's attempts at clarification. "History has proven, time and again, that any man bearing the name Calonar is willing to go to any lengths to achieve his insidious goals." And now, the young man thought, he was heading straight into the Black Duke's seat of power.

"Would it do any good if I told you how kind he is to animals?" Rogan asked. "He has a real soft spot for dogs."

The young man laughed at that. It was a fearful laugh, one tinged with a gnawing uncertainty, but a laugh nonetheless. In truth, Tomas did not know what he was expecting of the Northern Keep. Beliefs of a lifetime, however, were difficult to abandon.

"Kid, whatever you're expecting to see, whatever you're expecting to find, nothing can compare to the reality. When I first came to the Northern Keep, none of it seemed real. Nothing I say will prepare you for tomorrow. If I had the power to undo what Cyras did, I would, and make sure you didn't have to come with me into the city. This is going to be strange to you. It's going to be difficult and probably painful.

"If there's nothing else I can say that'll give you some peace, let me say this: I swear to you, by God and everything holy, that I will let no harm come to you. At least until we've gotten you a new sword."

Tomas' hand began reaching towards his pack. He pulled the hand back before it moved an inch, though. The young man did not need to feel the broken hilt again. He did not need to see the shattered blade. That sword, with its gold-etched eagle, was all that remained of his father. It was the traditional symbol of Praetorian honor, passed to him only a few months ago by his mother. And Tomas had allowed his father's blade to be broken defending his murderer.

"Or," Rogan said softly. "Better yet, we'll get your father's blade repaired."

For some reason, as Tomas sat there, the knight's words did bring him a sense of calm. If, he thought, Rogan would keep a promise of mercy to a child murderer; if he could show concern for the safety of a thief; if he was the man of honor who Tomas witnessed during their long journey north, then the young man knew Rogan Eigenhard would die before violating his oath.

"Well," Tomas said, "I guess that will have to do."

Chapter 2

Something woke Tomas. It was night, that dead
part of the night when the world was trying to decide whether today
had become tomorrow, or remained yesterday. Even those handful
of stars normally visible through the heavy evergreen canopy had
been lost to inky darkness. Even the wind had retreated, leaving
lifeless air to press down upon the shepherd's chest. He glanced
over, blinking, to their campfire, but saw the embers collapse, as
though twisting into themselves in retreat from some horrid cold.
The forest had gone silent. The birds and bugs, having begun rising
themselves, had fallen still. Tomas' breath frosted in the night air, as
though dead winter were forcing itself back into the newly-awakened
Wildelves Wood.

Tomas tried to breathe, to steady his thumping heart. He shifted
in his field blanket and adjusted his shirt. Alexia's pin, the golden
rose gifted to him months ago upon her death, rested as always on
his collar. No matter the situation, Tomas always kept the pin as
close as possible to where his dear friend had pinned it, at the pulse
of his neck. Now, in his lose undershirt, it rested against his heart.
The pin felt warm, the only warmth to be found as, somehow, the
night's chill had found its way under the shepherd's blanket. Tomas
put a hand on the golden rose, caressing it, as though to draw some
of the warmth of his best memories of Alexia.

A sound. Not a whisper, not a moan, not a chime or a chirp or
anything else natural. It was the last breath of a dead body, forced
from its cooling board, sitting up to face its still-living family.
Something awakened amidst the dark trees. Something moved, just
outside the edge of living sight. Not a form, but just the movement
of a form. And then another.

The horses, tied up but not hobbled on Rogan's direct
instruction, snorted. Stick, the knight's own brutish warhorse, began
stomping and pulling on his lead, disturbed by something in the air.
Tomas, his eyes wide and his heart hammering in his chest, looked
to Rogan. The knight was also awake. His blue eyes were open and

steady, catching the sparks of their dying campfire. His hand was moving, sliding like a predatory serpent creeping upon ignorant prey. It moved to his side, to the short arming sword the knight called Fang. His fingers slowly constricted around the hilt… and waited.

Then, a sound, a true sound. From the forest came a twisted moan, like the warping of lake ice in a brutal winter. Tomas yelped and rolled out of his blankets, to crouch at Rogan's feet, the experienced knight already standing with sword raised in one unwavering hand. Then there was another moan from behind, answered by more and more, all around. The last pitiful embers of their fire flickered once, then died. There was no moon, no stars, no light of any kind. The moans fell silent. The whole world slipped away, with only Tomas' panicked breathing and Rogan's unmoving body remaining.

Their dead campfire erupted then in a ghastly blue roar. No heat came from this ethereal fire, but rather seemed to pull at what little heat their bodies struggled to produce. A baleful cackling, like predatory birds chirping wrathfully whilst rending their still-living prey, emerged from the un-fire. Tomas and Rogan backed away uncertainly, not knowing whether safety lay in the oppressive darkness. Then, white bits of the blue un-fire pulled free. Rather than natural smoke, these bits twisted and stretched, growing rather than fading. They tumbled, as though caught in a horrid gale only they felt in the still air. Impossible faces emerged from the white forms, twisted mockeries of faces with extended chins, gaping holes for mouths, deeply-angular eyes, and ears that seemed as though pulled back into knife-like points.

"Lamashti!" Tomas gasped, his own eyes wide and his whole body trembling in mortal terror.

"What?" Rogan demanded, snarling and raising Fang in readiness to fight the unreal things.

"Spirits! Ghouls! We can't see them! They can't appear! They aren't real!" The shepherd's mind raced, twisting against madness at the sight of impossible nightmares.

The horses reared and broke their lines, fleeing into the forest. All but Stick. Rogan's warhorse of midnight black snorted and snapped his line, moving forward. The beast thrashed his head and tail, digging up the earth and snorting his fury at the ethereal threat.

The Lamashti rose higher, twisting against the intangible winds, howling despair and wrath and pleas and envy all at once. They swirled out, away from the blue un-fire, growing skeletal, distended arms that ended in claw-like hands. Hands that reached towards Tomas and Rogan, though perhaps more towards the cringing young man. Seemingly unable to move of their own, the Lamashti were caught in some unknown tide, an irresistible current known only to them. They circled the blue un-fire, slowly moving further and further from that eerie light. Each orbit let them reach further away, closer to the mortals. With each trip around, the Lamashti lashed out, swiping their immaterial claws at the two men.

"Don't let them touch you!" Tomas yelled, ducking behind Rogan.

"Yeah," the knight grunted. "Figured that." As one Lamashti came within reach, Rogan swung his sword, aiming to carve the thing in two. However, Fang passed through with no effect. Instead, the gnashing spirit reached out and raked its claws along Rogan's arm. The knight screamed and dropped Fang, stumbling back against Tomas and falling to the ground. In the blue un-light of the Lamashti bonfire, the shepherd looked and saw Rogan's wound. The sleeve of his undershirt was in tatters. Purplish lines ran the length of the warrior's arm. The flesh around these gashes was turning blue and white, as though the worst icy blight of Underworld itself had been used to slash at Rogan. Stick lunged, but not at the Lamashti. Instead, the warhorse moved to his knight, standing between his fallen rider and the lashing spirits. "Stick, no!" Rogan barked, too late. The Lamashti swiped at Stick, ethereal claws carving frozen gashes on the animal's hide and sending him squealing to the ground.

Rogan snarled and clenched his teeth, staring hate towards the nearing Lamashti. His eyes then darted to the side before snapping to Tomas. "The shield!"

Tomas moved without thinking, obeying immediately the snapped command. The young man dove around the small camp, desperately avoiding the lashing arms of the Lamashti as they hungrily, angrily, enviously reached for him while twirling helplessly in the unfelt gale. He tumbled into Rogan's bags and ripped free the shield with its flashing blue and grey heraldry. A Lamashti reached out, able at last to lunge for the shepherd. Tomas ducked whimpering beneath the large shield. There was a thump, as though a playful child had thrown a large snowball that impacted harmlessly on the steel barrier. Tomas looked up and saw the Lamashti spinning away, back into the swirling vortex of its kind. He looked in wonder down at the shield but saw nothing, only the hated sigil of House Calonar: two crossed, four-sided diamonds, one silver the other white, on a field of blue and grey.

The young man shrugged away his hesitation, though, seeing that the Lamashti vortex had spread far enough away from their un-fire to reach Rogan. Tomas lunged, holding the shield between himself and the grasping Lamashti, diving onto the man who killed his father and covering them both with the shield of the heir of House Calonar. Again and again, Tomas felt the Lamashti hurl themselves onto the shield, clawing and beating upon the smooth metal. The creatures, though, could gain no purchase. They slipped from the shield as raindrops slip from a well-oiled sword.

The face of a Lamashti appeared over the rim of the shield, its gaping mouth growing hideous fangs. It hissed at the two men, staring envious hatred at Tomas, and reared back as though to strike. Then, a silvery bolt slashed through the face, dispersing the Lamashti like mist waved away. Tomas and Rogan looked at each other in confusion, then carefully pulled back the shield. More silvery bolts filled the air, as though the moon had shattered into a thousand, thousand shards and rained into their campsite. The two men started at the whooping cries now filling the woods. Echoes of that strange, almost joyful near-laughter harmonized with themselves, as though the whole forest had joined in the chorus. As the Humans watched, the trees themselves seemed to lean in, and upon each branch was a Sylvai warrior.

The Sylvai did not conduct war as did Humanity. They wore no true armor, but rather leather vests dyed a riot of naturally-blending colors. Their long manes of brown and blonde and red, some reaching past the neck and some spilling past the waist, were tied into lose braids and whipped about in the focused-frenzied of the sylvai wardance. They did not stand upon the swaying branches, but leapt among them, passing one another in midair and never resting in the same place for more than an instant. They were all small, androgynous things, indistinguishable from each other and uniform in their snarling hatred for the Lamashti.

The Sylvai whooped their bizarre warsong, and spun in their alien wardance, letting fly with bolt after bolt, fired from shortbows that held no arrows. Each Lamashti hit by a glowing missile was dispersed, but only for a moment. The creature reformed quickly, drawing more blue and white essence from their un-fire. Despite the intervention of the sylvai warriors, still the Lamashti vortex expanded. The warriors made no move to retreat, though. Nor did they try to extract the disabled humans.

At last, a shining light emerged from the surrounding Wood. Tomas blinked as his eyes struggled to adjust. The trees seemed to withdraw, as though to bow, in the presence of this newest arrival. The sylvai warsong did not stop, but it did shift, as though now singing a hymn. The young man saw a woman, no, a sylva. She was short, like all their kind, but carried herself like an empress: chin lifted, gaze unflinching and unforgiving, her gait steady and sure. She was beautiful, as all sylva were, despite what seemed great age. Her verdant, opalescent eyes glowed emerald with the use of her magic. A crown of silvery holly encircled her head, holding back blonde hair streaked with grey, a thick mane that spilled down in a very lose braid, falling past her knees. The Sylva held high a staff made of the same wood as the surrounding trees but that bore no sign of toolmark, as though it had been grown, rather than carved. The staff was twisted into a perfect mirror of the Sylva's braided hair, with the same light coloring streaked with grey. At the tip of the spear was a hollow point, with parts of the staff grown up and around, like a hand gently clasping something. In the center of this hollow point shown the mystical light, a light from which the Lamashti retreated.

Words of magic filled the small clearing. The sylvai warriors had ceased their missile fire and their wardance, shifting their warsong to join in the sylva's chant. She marched forward, the light from her raised staff seeming to enhance the song of the Sylvai, flickering a counterpoint, a harmony, with the song. In response, the Lamashti howled their renewed frustration, desperation, and pleas. They lashed against the sylvai light and chant, but were forced back. The vortex and the blue un-light retracted, twisting in on itself, and dragged the Lamashti with it. Further and further, the vortex collapsed, with the elder Sylva never hesitating in her march, walking straight to the former campfire. There, with the Lamashti wails a bare whisper and the blue un-fire nothing more than a flicker, the Sylva raised a foot and stamped the vortex out.

All was silent then, save only for the fading echo of the sylvai chant. The elder kept her staff raised, illuminating the clearing. She looked at where the two men lay, still cowering behind the shield, with a half-smile and a slight tilt to her head.. "I am *Ayatorcelasi*, Speaker of the *Lankystoshama*." Her opalescent eyes sparkled with suppressed amusement. "Welcome home," she said, "Heir of Calonar."

Chapter 3

Rogan woke with a start, bolting upright and jerking his head around in confused anger. Tomas, sitting on the opposite side of their shared tent, held up his hands and spoke softly. "It's ok. We're safe."

"What?" the knight asked, still obviously trying to orient himself. "Where?"

Tomas stood slowly and pulled back the tent flap, exposing the camp outside. "Same place," the shepherd told his unwanted companion. "They didn't bother moving us, just set up their own camp."

Rogan groaned and pulled aside the heavy fur blankets still covering his legs. He stood and stretched his back, grunting at the series of pops and cracks. "How long?" he asked.

"Two days," Tomas replied. The young man handed over a waterskin. "It's not water," he cautioned. "The Sylvai filled our skins with... something."

"Vinari," the heir of House Calonar noted after a testing sip. He then took a much longer drink, grimacing at the taste. "Wine, spring water, some herbs. The Sylvai say it restores the soul."

"Does it?"

The knight shrugged and took another drink through his grimace. He replaced the stopper and handed the skin back, then moved to the flap. "Anything happen while I was out?" he asked.

Tomas joined Rogan and the two stepped outside. "Just them," the young man replied.

The Sylvai had set up a half dozen tents. Unlike those of Humans, which tended to be angular, these tents were all small domes. It looked as though a field of giant mushrooms had sprouted in the forest. The Sylvai tents were all dyed green and brown, and the tops of each released small streams of smoke. A larger campfire burned where the Humans' once had, though this one had a haunch of fresh meat roasting over it and a few bubbling pots.

"They healed your horse, too," Tomas noted, jerking his head to the side. Rogan looked, and could not fight the relieved smile on his weathered face. Stick, as healthy and frolicsome as a colt, stood with their other horses, retrieved by the Sylvai. A group of the small Inhumans were gathered around the brutish warhorse, petting him, brushing him, offering him treats, and generally offering unquestioning admiration of Rogan's mount. Stick accepted this adoration with magnanimity.

Nearly as one, the Sylvai stopped in their tasks and turned to look at the Humans. A sea of opalescent eyes regarded them, the only sound in the camp the crackling of the fire and the discontented snorts from Stick, unhappy that the devotion showered on him had paused. Their faces carried no overt hostility, but neither any particular welcome. One of them stepped forward. It (Tomas could not tell if the Sylva was male or female) was a head shorter than the shepherd, and far leaner. It had a pair of Sylvai blades sheathed at the hip and long, dark hair was bound in a tight braid that fell just past the narrow shoulders. "The Speaker rests," the Sylva said in a light, almost feminine voice. "She wakes soon. She... asks you stay in tent until she calls." The sylvai's voice was thick with the inhuman accent, and its words were broken, signaling its unfamiliarity with Velish, the common tongue.

Rogan nodded and turned back, jerking his head at Tomas to follow. With a nervous glance around the silently starting Sylvai, the young man obeyed. He returned to his blankets as Rogan sat down on his own with a grunt. "Take it you've been under house arrest?" the knight guessed.

Tomas nodded. "They're polite about it, but yeah. They bring food and drink, they let me go to the treeline to relieve myself, but that's it."

"Don't take it personally," Rogan advised, pulling his saddlebag over and reclining against it. "The Sylvai have good reason too mistrust strangers."

The shepherd grunted. Humans in general, but Adamics in particular, had spent the thousand years since the collapse of the Sylvai Empire returning the myriad cruelties of their former masters in kind. Centuries of pogroms, incarceration, subjugation, and forced indoctrination were the legacy of Human-Sylvai relationships through the history of the Lanasian Republic. "Are they your border guards?" Tomas asked. "They protect the Keep?"

"More like the whole forest, which includes the Keep." He absently scratched at his arm, then pulled up the sleeve of his mended undershirt. "Good," he muttered, noting the marks left by the Lamashti attack were gone. In fact, little remained of the unearthly incursion. Even the stitching on Rogan's shirt was so vague as to be nearly invisible.

"The Speaker healed you," Tomas confirmed. He then glanced towards the loose tent flap. "They spent the first day doing some kind of ritual," the shepherd said somewhat nervously. "Chanting, dancing. It lasted a while."

"Purification," Rogan noted. "Cleansing the Wood of those... what'd you call them?"

"Lamashti; dark spirits. Damned souls deprived of bodies for some ancient betrayal." The shepherd squinted out the small parting of the tent flap. "They're supposed to be a fairy tale."

"Apparently not."

Wanting to change the subject, and sensing Rogan's similar inclination, Tomas glanced again out the slightly-parted tent flap. Beyond, he could see the Sylvai going about minor tasks, preparing food, mending clothes, chatting in their musical language. The scene was disturbing, given its banality against the alien appearance of the Sylvai themselves. "Why are they all so young?" he asked.

"What?"

The young man jerked his chin to the scene outside. "They're all kids. Infants. Do the Sylvai make their children do their fighting?"

Rogan chuckled. "Those 'children,' are probably centuries old."

"But..."

"Never learned much about the Sylvai?" the knight asked.

Tomas shook his head. "Pelsemoria's enclave was forbidden unless you had a pass. And the local Sylvai were only allowed out on specific business. There wasn't a lot of... interaction."

"I'm not clear about it all myself," Rogan admitted. "The Sylvai don't talk about their... biology with other races. As I understand, they all look the same until puberty. Same body, same voices. Different faces, of course, but other than that..." He nodded outside. "That's why they all look so similar; none of those Walkers have gone through..." the knight paused in thought. "Damn, what was that word? *Shey'iel...* something or other. When that happens, then they look more..."

"Normal?"

Rogan glanced at Tomas. "Might want to rethink that word," he advised. "You'll find up here that there isn't much of what you'd call 'normal.'"

The tent flap was pulled aside then, and the Speaker entered with a much younger Sylva. The elder Sylva was dressed in a loose, flowing gown of almost incandescent white. The gossamer cloth was almost like mist made solid, but only partly so, flowing along the matron's body thinly enough for the eye and the mind to note the generous, feminine lines, while opaque enough to conceal any specific detail. A thick, intricately-embroidered golden ribbon was tied about her generous hips, spilling down the front between her legs. The Speaker regarded them calmly with her verdant, opalescent gaze. Tomas was reminded then of Alexia, and how his dear friend would sometimes have a nearly identical expression on her kind face when looking at Tomas; at those times, the young man recalled, it was as though Alexia was not looking at him, but rather at something within and all around him. The Speaker stared at Rogan, inspecting him from the safe distance of their tent's entrance, then nodded and pulled back an errant strand of her grey-streaked blonde hair. Although the circlet of silvery holly still adorned her brow, her thick mane nonetheless moved slightly as though swaying to some invisible breeze.

Apparently satisfied with her inspection of Rogan, the Speaker cleared her throat. "You are cleansed, Heir of Calonar." The Sylva's voice was almost like a chorus of perfectly synchronized members. Her command of Velish, the common tongue, seemed perfect. She harmonized and nearly sang the words with no hint of accent.

Rogan stood and bowed deeply to the Speaker. He ceremoniously placed his right hand to his heart, and then to his forehead as he maintained the bow. "Thank you for your help," he said.

"Our duty is to protect the Wood," she replied with the slightest of shrugs. "Even had you been intruders, still we would have dispersed the *La'ma'shti*." She cocked her head a bit at another thought. "Though, had you not been of House Calonar, we would most likely have just killed you and burned your bodies, rather than bother with the cleansing."

Tomas skin crawled at how casually, almost indifferently, the Speaker considered the invalue of Human lives. He looked to Rogan for some reaction, but the knight seemed unaffected by the sylvai willingness to slaughter people.

"You have experience with those... creatures?" the knight asked.

The Speaker nodded slightly. "Though the ages, we have dispersed these incursions, banishing the betrayers back into the Winds." A look of concern drifted across her timeless face. "Though, the number of these has grown distressing of late."

Rogan leaned forward. "How many?"

"Many," was the Sylva's terse reply. "For a quarter year, since winter's beginning, our Walkers have reported increasing incidents of the *La'ma'shti* finding ways into substantiality. Our Speakers have been hard-pressed to address the increasing threat to our Wood."

"Why haven't any other attacks been reported?" Tomas asked.

The Speaker regarded him. Her opalescent eyes burning into him, unblinking, unwavering. "Sometimes they are," she finally replied. "But your kind tends to dismiss the extraordinary, or cast it as... what did you say before? Fairy tales?"

The shepherd blushed.

The sylva turned back to Rogan. "We have intercepted these incursions as quickly as possible, and... purify those tainted by exposure to the Lamashti so as to prevent further corruption. However, these attacks have scattered us, and place a great strain upon our people. There are a few among the Speakers Circle who fear these incursions may be a prelude to something worse." She glanced at Tomas. "Thus our need for more... expeditious methods of purification."

Another Sylvai, this one quite clearly a male and showing similar signs of age as did the Speaker, entered the tent. Although he was lean, as were all his race, he was well-muscled with an athlete's physique. Numerous scars adorned his face and hands, though did little to detract from his aesthetic quality. He had a thin beard that ran along his jaw, and a glyph of Sylvai writing tattooed on his left cheek. This sylvu said nothing, nor even glanced at anyone in the tent besides the Speaker. He set down a small chair, into which the Speaker sat. The male then placed a footstool for her and arranged the voluminous gown around her. Neither the sylvai females nor Rogan gave an indication of surprise at how servile the male was. "What do you remember of the *La'ma'shti* attack?" the Speaker asked, almost ignoring the male's arrangement of her dress.

Rogan sat back down on his blankets, reclining again on his saddlebags. He nodded at Tomas to do the same. "Not much," the knight admitted. "I think the kid here faced the worst of it."

The Speaker glanced her verdant gaze at Tomas. "Yes," she nearly whispered. "Interesting that he faced the worst of the *La'ma'shti* and yet required no cleansing." The sylvu finished arranging his mistress' gown and turned, retrieving three small wooden cups. He distributed these among the Speaker and the two Humans, then filled the cups with wine from a small skin at his belt. The Speaker waited until all three had their drink before raising her cup and intoning a few words in the Sylvai tongue. They all drank. The sylvu refiled his Speaker's cup when she held it to him without a glance. Rogan and Tomas were not offered more wine.

"What were they?" Rogan asked. "Ghosts?"

The Speaker hesitated, but only for a heartbeat. "As the youth told you," she replied. "Spirits without flesh. Cursed by the *Sa'kai* for their service to *Ethroi'sa'kai*. Once, they were flesh, and lived with the *Sy'lva'n*. For their betrayal, however, they were stripped of form and cast into the Winds, the storm of magic, separate from both this and Otherworld."

"But why attack us?" the knight asked. "And how?"

"You assume the attack was directed at you," the younger sylva noted with a hard look at Tomas. She wore a loose shirt identical in material and design as the Speaker, and her hair was the same color, though lacked the grey and only barely reached her shoulders. She had a single Sylvai blade at the small of her back, the curve of the flawless blade concealed by a sheathe adorned with glyphs of their language. Her small body had hints of emerging adolescence, the slightest swell of the breast and curve of the hips. Her opalescent gaze, as brightly verdant as the Speaker's, was filled with suspicion.

"My daughter," the Speaker noted with a slight smile. "*Komalan.* It is for her sake that I and my Walkers have traveled here, despite the urgency of suppressing the *La'ma'shti*."

"She has begun her Search?" Rogan asked in a very polite tone.

"Indeed," the Sylva answered. "You are quite fortunate at our presence, as we have traveled to the villages. Most of their Walkers and Speakers have dispersed to address the *La'ma'shti* incursions. I do not believe the local tribe is even in this area at present."

In response, Rogan nodded his head to the younger sylva. "Our thanks, Daughter of the Speaker," the knight said formally. "And our best wishes on your Search."

The Speaker's daughter dismissively sniffed at Rogan, instead focusing her intense gaze at Tomas. Her manner suggested hostility, suspicion, and an almost predatory hunger. Noting this, Rogan cleared his throat meaningfully. The Speaker held up her hand, and the younger sylva bowed her head. Still, though, the young Sylva's gaze burned at Tomas. "My daughter's point is an important one," the Speaker conceded, glancing towards Tomas. "This one has the mark of Fate upon him." She sniffed the air. "And also, the taint of the Trickster."

Rogan sighed. "We ran into Cyras Darkholm some months ago," he admitted. "He put a geas on Tomas here, forcing us to go to the Keep. We're not sure why."

"Of course not," the Speaker agreed. "The Trickster is never one for explanations. However, "she leaned slightly closer to Tomas. "There is something... some*one* else." Her verdant gaze again seemed to pierce beyond the young man, deep into his very soul. Her opalescent eyes then fell to the golden rose pinned, as always, on Tomas' collar. "*Palsilyagathalexia*," she whispered.

Tomas started, recognizing his friend's true name. "You knew Alexia?"

"Knew?" the Speaker said with the barest hint of sorrow in her choral voice. "You speak of her in the past."

The young man nodded slightly. "She died."

The young Sylva behind the Speaker gasped and made an odd gesture. Her went up, as though grasping at something and pulling it down to her heart. The Speaker made an identical gesture and looked to Rogan.

The knight sighed. "I wasn't sure, but seeing the pin..."

"You did not investigate?"

"The geas," he explained. "Events moved too fast. Also I..."

The Speaker regarded him through flat, emotionless eyes. "You did not desire the answer," was all she said.

"Excuse me," Tomas interrupted. "May I ask for an explanation?" Although his tone was even, the young man was battling to maintain his composure as this group loyal to the Black Duke spoke of his dear friend.

The Speaker regarded Tomas for a moment. "He does not know?" she asked Rogan.

The knight shook his head. "He's from Pelsemoria. He was there during... the Madness."

"Your shame is unbecoming, Heir of Calonar," she said reproachfully. "And also unproductive. Atone or ignore."

"We're trying," he insisted.

"Excuse me!" By now, Tomas' patience was wearing thin. "I would ask for an explanation!"

The Speaker returned her gaze to the shepherd. "Palsi... Alexia is known to us. She is... honored. I will say no more, for such a revelation is not my place." She stood then, and the sylvu took the chair outside. "The Matriarch gifted you her golden rose; we will honor that gift. You may go in peace as soon as you are ready." Without another word, the Speaker exited the tent. From outside, sounds of activity drifted in. The Sylvai were breaking camp.

"What was that all about?" Tomas demanded of Rogan.

The knight sighed. "I knew Alexia," he admitted. "You'd have a hard time finding someone in the Northlands who *didn't* know her."

"Explain."

Rogan thought a while, his eyes lost to time and memory. Finally, the knight shook his head. "No, I'd better not. There's something strange going on, and that conversation is likely to take a while." He glanced around the tent. "I think we need to push on to the Keep. There's too much weirdness going on."

"What do you mean?"

Rogan stood and started collecting his things. "Xeshlin slavers, rampaging warlords, imminent civil war, these Lamashti-things. All at the same time? And don't forget that Nekalan we found in Alvaro."

Tomas shuddered, not wanting the memory. The creature had been hiding within the royal court of Alvaro, twisting minds and manipulating the city towards war. "Why the sudden urgency?" the young man asked. "You've been getting hints our whole trip about some growing problem."

The knight paused, looking up, his eyes lost in thought. "This forest is protected," Rogan finally continued, pulling on his clothes. "Attacks here, where Sylvai magic is strongest?" The knight shook his head. "The Speakers understand the spirts, the threats from Otherworld. They know how to fight them and how to keep them out. But now there's attacks here, ones that're scattering the Sylvai. I'm not a believer in coincidence to start, and there's way too many coincidences happening." He stopped and glanced at Tomas. "Not to mention Cyras' little warning and his interest in you."

Tomas paused in his own preparations and stared at Rogan. "The Speaker, that young Sylva, did you get the impression they thought the Lamashti were after *me*?"

Rogan nodded. "Yeah, I noticed that." He shrugged slightly. "It could be Cyras' geas. It could be they were attracted by his magic."

"Or?"

The knight shook his head. "No idea, kid. This is far over my head. We need help."

"From the Northern Keep," Tomas snorted.

Rogan smiled slightly. "It's the only place in the world you're going to get answers."

Chapter 4

Three days later, Tomas was confronted with the reality
of the Northern Keep: the Black Duke's seat of power and heartland
of House Calonar. The shepherd's first glimpse of the cursed city
came as a light shining through the trees, like sunlight sparkling off
a clear forest lake. As always, the road he and Rogan took through
the forest did not follow a straight line, instead winding around the
large trees, causing the light to appear and disappear. Finally, the
woods parted and Tomas saw without interruption the evil that was
the Northern Keep.

The city rested amidst a series of hills sitting in the center of
Wildelves Wood. The forest had been cleared well away from the
walls; however, as best as Tomas could tell, there were no signs of
the trees being cut down or the plants uprooted. They simply did not
grow within a mile of the city walls. The walls themselves seemed to
be made of both dark marble and quartz, seeming as though the
starry night had descended and solidified, forming an impenetrable
barrier to the community within. Unlike every other city Tomas had
heard of, there was no gloomy cloud of chimney smoke and
burgeoning industry above the Northern Keep. Instead, the air was
fresh and clean, free of any pollutants except the scent of bakeries
and perfumeries drifting on a gentle breeze.

Rising above the city, visible to all from even beyond the walls
of the Keep to the very edge of the treeline, was a castle so grand it
could very nearly be called a palace. Huge windows, sweeping
balconies, and in place of the traditional gargoyles were simple trees
and other plants highlighting the beauty of what had to be Castle
Calonar. As best Tomas could tell, there was very little gold or
stained glass incorporated into the construction of the fortress as
was so popular in the homes of most of the other high ranking noble
families of the Republic. Rather, as was the custom to all the
buildings visible upon their approach, the simple grey stone
common in the Northlands formed the castle, broken only by
unadorned glass windows. Blue and grey banners fluttered in the

light spring breeze and the sound of music drifted through the air. wood shutters were opened to welcome spring's arrival. The sky had cleared, with only a few tatters remnants of winter grudgingly holding on.

"Beautiful," Tomas breathed.

Rogan smiled. "In all the years I've been traveling, I've never found any place that makes me feel so much at home."

The pair galloped to the city gates. Although manned by House Calonar's blue and gray liveried House Guard, all of whom wore chainmail and bore the Northland poleaxe, the massive gates nonetheless stood open in welcome. Traffic flowed steadily through this gate, an assortment of clerics, peasants and villagers, tradesmen, and others. Curiously, there were few obvious merchants or caravans of trade goods. This despite Tomas having seen such on the road from Crossroads.

When the shepherd mentioned this, Rogan shrugged. "They usually use the northeast gate. The mercantile district is there, with most of the warehouses and workshops. It's easier to go through that gate rather than entering here and circling through half the city."

As the two travelers approached what Rogan called the eastern gate, the soldiers standing guard immediately recognized their prince and gently, but firmly, redirected traffic to clear a path. The sergeant of the guard stepped forward with an overly-deep bow and said, "Welcome home, Prince Rogan." Tomas noticed that the sergeant seemed to put unusual emphasis on "Prince." He was an older man, thick of build and with a weathered face. He moved with a grace that belied his years and his mass, to say nothing of the weight of his polished breastplate.

Rogan just grimaced. "Thanks for reminding me and everyone else for a mile around who I'm married to," the knight grumbled. "Now, would you do me a favor, Sergeant Rainer?"

"Of course, great prince!" the sergeant roared, obviously enjoying Rogan's discomfort.

"Good; get out of the way so I can go see my wife."

The sergeant bowed again, quite a bit lower than protocol really required, and moved out of the way. As Rogan and Tomas passed, Rainer said, "Yes, my prince. Please give the Princess my best. Or better yet, give her *your* best."

Rogan rode through the gate, muttering, "Smartass."

After Rogan and Tomas passed through the gates, Sergeant Rainer climbed to the battlements and, using his best parade ground bellow, cried, "Make way! Make way! Prince Rogan, hero of the Northlands and heir of House Calonar has returned! Make way!"

Rogan stopped Stick, looking for a moment as though he might go back. Fortunately for Sergeant Rainer, Rogan resumed the ride to the castle. Much to the knight's irritation, however, the word was out, and the citizens of the Keep flocked to cheer the return of their prince. People from all the surrounding buildings pressed in, despite the wide, open street. They cheered at the return of their prince, waving whatever makeshift banners they had, and shouting their praise of Rogan and House Calonar. Although the knight was less than thrilled by the impromptu parade, Stick reveled in the adoration of the masses, the warhorse picking up a kicking trot that emphasized each step. Whenever the children of the Keep shouted, "Hi, Stick!" the proud warhorse would toss his head and neigh.

"Glad someone's enjoying this," Rogan said sourly, wincing from the pain lancing though his still-healing wounds with each step. Stick ignored his rider and continued prancing.

"Your people seem to have a lot of love for you," Tomas noted dryly.

"Yeah," Rogan agreed sourly. "Aren't they swell?"

"You could at least wave."

"I'm not some country bard who needs the adulation of the masses," he snapped. Nevertheless, Rogan did raise his free hand, and unenthusiastically waved to the people.

Castle Calonar sat in the northern district of the city. Rogan turned them off the main boulevard that, the knight informed Tomas, joined with the seven other major streets at the city center. Rather than endure an extension of his welcome from the people, the heir of House Calonar instead turned them right, through the smaller, but still pleasantly spacious side streets. The knight led them around the edge of the mercantile districts and through several residential neighborhoods. As they rode, Tomas could not differentiate poor home from more affluent. There was, if not a uniformity, a strong commonality among the houses of the Northern Keep. They were all built of stone and wood, with high angled roofs. Shops typically made up the ground floors, with living quarters on the floors above. Most windows had planters filled with flowering plants, herbs, and small vegetables. Small drainage channels passed through the middle of each street, large and small, and these ran full with the spring melt. Small stonework fountains were on every corner, running with clear water. At the intersection of any two larger streets, a space in the center of this crossing was occupied by a fruiting tree. People chatted with their neighbors and turned aside from their day's labors to wave and cheer the passage of the champion of the Northlands. Children laughed and played.

As they passed through one residential neighborhood, a young girl, overcome with enthusiasm, ran out in front of Tomas and Rogan. Lost as he was in the bewildering banality of the Black Duke's capital, the shepherd did not notice the small child and would have run her down had Rogan not yanked back on Tomas' reigns. "Pay attention!" the knight snapped. Dismounting quickly, Rogan picked up the little girl. "Are you alright?" he asked.

With a look of wide-eyed adoration, the girl wrapped her arms around Rogan's neck and kissed him on the cheek. With a delighted squeal, she slipped out of the knight's arms and ran back to her waiting mother, demanding to know if she had seen. Rogan, blushing furiously, remounted and continued to the castle.

During their ride through the Northern Keep, Tomas could not help but notice how peacefully normal the city seemed. Men wore shirts and long vests, woolen breeches, and leather boots; women wore woolen dresses in the traditional Northlands style, with low necklines, long sleeves, white aprons tied in simple bows at their back or on their hip, and simple leather half-boots. Children played in the streets while the elderly sat on wooden benches talking calmly about unimportant things. The few House Guard and City Watch they encountered all went about their duties, stepping aside for ladies, lending aid to workmen, and generally making themselves as unobtrusive as possible. At one corner, Tomas saw an Adamic priest having a light meal with a pagan priestess. Down a side road, two young lovers walked hand in hand, casually wishing good day to others and passing through a few shops, many of which were owned by non-Humans. Tomas felt nearly overwhelmed by this impossibly mundane city.

Noticing the look on the young man's face, Rogan grinned. "Not what you were expecting?"

Tomas could only shake his head.

"While you're here, you may find that a few of the stories you've heard about our little corner of Underworld have been exaggerated."

Tomas stared in open-mouthed shock as a human soldier of the City Watch helped an old sylva reclaim some packages she had dropped. Once the sylva had reclaimed her things, the soldier nodded his head, politely tipping the blue cap all watchmen wore, and wishing her well before continuing on with his day. "What in God's name am I seeing?" the young man demanded.

"The truth," Rogan replied.

Chapter 5

After nearly an hour of riding, the pair finally approached Castle Calonar. Once clear of all obstructions, Tomas could see that the Black Duke's imposing home had been built on a large outcropping of rock. Less than a mountain, but much more than a hill, the castle's foundation seemed as though Arayel herself had raised stone from her very core, just for the placement of the castle. Cliff faces more than a hundred feet high added to the already impressive battlements. A tributary of the Oolaug River, one several the city employed, ran around the base of the stone foundation forming a wide moat. The water was not stagnant, nor overly-fast, but rather moved with a steady, almost graceful current. A family of geese, no doubt having only recently returned from their winter migration, swam along the stream under the grumbling care of the mother. The only visible means of crossing the moat and gaining entry to the castle was a stone bridge, formed from a series of arches laid together so tightly there appeared to be no mortar, and leading up along a narrow path of switchbacks. On the near side of the bridge was a large gate house composed of two opposing towers and a pair of open iron portcullises. The soldiers in blue and grey who manned this defense stood at rigid attention as Rogan and Tomas approached, presenting their arms in salute. Like those House Guard at the city gate, these warriors all carried the Northlands poleaxe and wore chainmail and helmets. Rogan returned a military salute to the men as they rode past.

The climb up was not exhaustive, but Tomas could easily see how deadly such an attempt would be for any attacker. The entire road was visible to the castle above, and the switchbacks would allow access for no heavy siege equipment. The path was well-constructed with a gentle slope, and the view of the city as they road upwards was increasingly impressive. At the top was the massive gate to Castle Calonar. Like every other portal so far, the castle gates stood open. The two doors were made of layered wood more than three feet thick, with alternating horizontal and vertical lines and steel reinforcements. Another system of iron portcullises could further protect the gateway, though these stood open.

Rogan let out a sigh of relief once the crowds that had followed them on their ride through the city returned to their homes and businesses. This was emphasized all the more when the pair passed through the final entryway to the castle's courtyard. The knight's shoulders seemed to slump a bit, as though he was shedding the pressure of the outside world. Several stablehands approached as the two entered the courtyard and bowed. "Welcome home, your Highness," one said, taking Stick's reigns.

"Hello, Roderick," Rogan said as he dismounted. "How have you been?"

Roderick smiled. He was a young man, much the same age as Tomas. He wore the simple tunic and trousers that seemed popular in the Northlands. He had sandy hair and a pleasant attitude as he directed his people to take charge of the horses. Unlike the servants of the other great Houses of the Republic, which were traditionally required at all times to wear the livery of their lord, Roderick's clothes were brown, rather than the blue and grey of House Calonar.

"Aside from Princess Karen causing all kinds of mischief, things have been fairly peaceful," he answered as he took Stick's reins.

"That bad?" Rogan grinned.

"She takes a great deal after her sister, I think. Though, Princess Karen seems more… introverted. Less inclined towards… public displays, I mean."

"Don't remind me," the knight said, rolling his eyes.

"Courage, my prince. Many of us are hopeful that one day soon you and Princess Kyla will have a little one of your own running around causing mischief."

"Roderick."

"Yes, your Highness?"

"Go away."

"Yes, your Highness." The stablehand turned back to his stables.

Tomas spotted an older man walking up from the servant's entrance who, though weighted by his many years, nonetheless carried himself with a quiet confidence and steady stride marred only slightly by a limp that spoke of an old wound. "Who is that?" the shepherd asked.

The knight smiled. "Roland, our chief butler."

"Little old to be a servant, isn't he?"

"Roland's a good man, one of our best in fact. He's already dedicated more than thirty years to House Calonar. At first, he was a soldier in the House Guard. After being wounded in battle against a Xeshlin raiding party, Roland was transferred to the castle for lighter duty. Once he reached retirement age, he became one of the castle's many butlers and even helped raise Kyla."

"That must have been interesting," Tomas noted.

"Roland calls them the anxiety years," Rogan laughed. "He's slowed a bit by that old wound of his, but he sees it as his duty to look after Kyla's sister until she gets safely married off."

"Sounds like a good man."

"The best working knowledge of the people and facilities of the castle. Couldn't imagine trying to work in this place without him." Smiling warmly, Rogan took the old soldier's hand in greeting. "Hello, Roland. Has the King improved?"

Bowing briefly, the butler shook his head. "I'm afraid not, your Highness," he replied in a surprisingly soft voice. "The King's condition remains unchanged. His Majesty sends word that he would like to have dinner with you and his daughters tonight if you are able. He wished to meet you personally but remains weak. Besides, the Queen thought it best if you had some personal time with your wife first."

Rogan nodded. "How is Nora?" he asked, heading towards the grand double front doors. Tomas followed behind. The doors themselves, although large, contained little decoration, just simple carvings in an intricate pattern, representing what the young man thought he recognized as scenes from Northland fairy tales.

"Her Majesty is well, your Highness," Roland was saying. "The Queen is currently dividing her time between caring for the King and overseeing the festival preparations."

"Has my wife been informed of my return?"

Before the butler could respond, the great doors were yanked open despite their great size. A divinely beautiful young woman nearly flew down the enormous staircase. Her very long blonde hair whirled about her head and shoulders like a writhing halo. She wore the traditional dress of the Northlands, dyed in the blue and grey of House Calonar, but altered in what Tomas though were shocking ways: the already low-cut blouse was cut lower still, offering any casual viewer an ample sight. The grey embroidered bodice did little to restrain either the woman's enthusiasm or her chest, both heaving as they came down the large stairs in a dead sprint. The high-waisted skirt, long believed to be inappropriately-short in the minds of the conservative south, had a long slit cut in one side; although this made her long strides easier, Tomas was taken aback at how much of her legs were on display. Shocked as he was at the sudden and scandalous sight, Tomas found himself frozen.

Roland wisely stepped out of the way, guiding the shepherd to safety. The young woman crossed the distance between the huge doors and the courtyard in the blink of an eye and hurled herself into Rogan's arms, wrapping her legs around his waist and her arms around his neck. Rogan tried his best to lean into the collision, compensating for the woman's constant writhing as best he could and supporting her so she would not fall.

"I believe her Highness has, in fact, been informed," Roland said evenly.

Despite the constant stream of kisses Rogan's wife was placing on his mouth, neck, shoulders, and elsewhere, the knight tried to shift in Tomas' direction. "Tomas," Rogan said, sometimes with a full mouth. "This is my wife, Kyla."

Dropping to the ground, Kyla spun around and pressed her behind into Rogan. "Hello, Tomas!" she said brightly, her hips writing against Rogan's.

"Uh, hi," Tomas replied his mind blank in a riot of conflicting ideas. Here was Kyla, blasphemous daughter of the Black Duke and mistress of infernal magics. Here was the bringer of chaos, feared and cursed by all honest folk of the south. And yet, here was a beautiful young woman, sparkling with joy at being reunited with her husband.

As the princess and jewel of House Calonar climbed back up her husband, the knight desperately tried to use what reason he had left. A losing battle, Tomas guessed. "Kyla, hang on a second," Rogan tried to say through his often-full mouth.

The priestess continued her sensual movements, this time facing her husband. "Kyla, seriously, we have to take care of something first." She began tearing at his traveling clothes, trying to reach more skin. Tomas silently speculated if the reason Rogan had set aside his splitmail that morning was in anticipation of this reunion and his fear of the damage his wife might cause to the expensive amor. Calonar's beloved daughter began digging her fingernails into the back of

Rogan's neck, somewhat savagely biting him on the shoulders, lips, and ears.

"Kyla, for God's sake!" Rogan's eyes had rolled back into this head by now, his hands almost involuntarily moving across his wife's body and producing moans of pleasure and shudders of sensual joy in her.

"KYLA!!!"

"What?" she asked innocently, confused by her husband's reaction.

Breathing heavily, sweat rolling off a face that betrayed a war against every natural instinct, Rogan fought to focus on the task at hand. "Kyla," he said through clenched teeth, "Cyras did something to Tomas; I need Esha to break the enchantment before we can..."

Smiling a sweet smile Kyla said, "Esha's at her tower, but I can fix it!" She licked Rogan on the cheek, causing the knight to grit his teeth and shake with barely controlled desire, and skipped over to Tomas. Stepping right in front of the young man, the High Priestess of the pagan Goddess of Pleasure clasped her small hands over her heart and looked deep into Tomas' eyes. As Kyla stood there, her enchanting fragrance overwhelming the young man's senses, the shepherd could not help but notice the gleam in her soft, pearlescent blue eyes. Although not as pronounced as the opalescent eyes of a Sylva, Kyla's did carry the gentle glow of a Halvan. She was one of that mixed-breed race as was her father, long despised and hunted throughout Lanasia.

Again, fear intruded on Tomas' consideration of the beautiful woman before him. Here was Kyla, priestess of a pagan cult, inductee of the blackest secrets of House Calonar, insidious sorceress, and daughter of the dreaded Black Duke. Here was the terror who had wrought her Madness upon Pelsemoria. Here was the woman who, the stories said, could use her enchantments to force a man away from his lawful wife and seduce him into the worship of dark gods. Here was the spawn of the Northlands, whose magic could twist a man's mind, break his spirit, and devour his soul. And she had now turned her full attention on Tomas.

The moment her magic was unleashed, Tomas knew. Kyla looked into Tomas' eyes and blessed him with a bright smile. A rush of unwanted joy flowed over the young man, banishing all thoughts of fear and intimidation from his soul. A thrill of nearly-painful bliss charged through his entire body, rising to an almost intolerable height until the shorter princess reached up and placed a light hand over the shepherd's heart, releasing a tension Tomas was not even aware had been present in his body and leaving behind only a soft glow of golden joy.

Lowering his head with her hands, the priestess stood on the tip of her toes and kissed him lightly on the forehead. Afterward, Tomas could never articulate the intense happiness that flooded through his soul at Kyla's lightest touch, happiness that turned to joy at her lightest kiss. Gasping and staggering back, Tomas' eyes filled with wonder as he could not help but stare into Kyla's pearlescent eyes of shining sapphire.

"I believe the spell is broken," Roland noted evenly.

"Good," Rogan said through clenched teeth. "Roland, please see to it that Tomas is made welcome. He'll be staying for a while."

Roland bowed, "Yes, your Highness."

"Kyla," the knight said, quivering with intense need.

Kyla threw her husband a wicked glance over her shoulder. "Yes?" she purred.

Dropping all pretenses at control, the prince grabbed his beautiful princess and, throwing her over his shoulder, charged into the castle.

Trying to put the situation into words, all Tomas could manage was, "Wow. She certainly seems..."

"Enthusiastic?" Roland suggested.

"Enthusiastic," Tomas agreed.

Signaling a servant to take Tomas' few possessions, the head butler motioned Tomas towards the main doors and said, "This way, Master Tomas. I'll show you to your rooms."

Tomas followed behind as Roland made his way into the castle. Upon entering, Tomas was shocked by the beauty within. Beautiful carpets lined the floors and exquisite works of art were everywhere. Every piece of wood was intricately carved into beautiful designs. Gold and crystal chandeliers hung from the high ceilings, and tasteful candelabras gave off a cheery, inviting glow. At the top of the grand staircase hung a life-size painting of the Calonar family. Tomas paused in front of the painting, looking up at the man often described as the greatest evil in Lanasia.

Cylan Calonar was as common looking a man as Tomas had ever seen. The Black Duke stood straight, but not rigidly so. His iron-grey hair was cut close, reminiscent of a military style. He had a plain build, neither overly muscled nor overly thin. The lord of the Northlands was dressed in the same long vest and undershirt Tomas had noted most men of the Keep wearing. He had no ornamentation, other than a small signet ring. The eyes were what startled Tomas the most, though. Pearlescent Halvan eyes served only to reinforce his obvious lack of noble breeding. Somehow, the artist had captured the soft glow of the Black Duke's Halvan eyes, as though to emphasize a quality any other rational person would hide. Those were the eyes one would see in a kindly grandfather's. A smile danced on Calonar's lips; a smile that, while just as soft as the eyes, held in it the sense that this person spent a lot of time smiling, that it came easy to him.

Beside the Black Duke stood Kyla, looking just as bright and beautiful as she had in life only minutes before. The princess of House Calonar wore a traditional Northlands dress, like the one Tomas had just seen her wearing, with similar modifications to accentuate her generous feminine attributes, and dyed in the same blue and grey of her Noble House. The jewel of the Northlands had her hands clasped behind her back and her head slightly lowered, with a mischievous grin dancing on her sensuous lips. Calonar's hand was placed upon his daughter's slight shoulder, almost as if the man was at once trying to hold her back and encourage her further. On his other side, that hand about her full waist, had to be the Black Duke's wife, Nora. It was easy to see that Kyla was of Nora's blood. Looking past Nora's wrinkles and the ever-so-slightly graying hair, one could easily see beauty that easily matched Kyla's, perhaps even surpassed. The same smile could also be seen on both mother and daughter, but while Kyla's conveyed exuberance and joy, Nora's was one of a loving mother. Tomas finally noticed, in his detailed examination of the painting, the artist's signature on the bottom. "Roland," Tomas called. "Did Rogan do this painting?"

"No Master Tomas," the butler replied. "That particular work was completed nearly twelve years past. The Prince did not arrive until ten years ago."

"But the artist' name was Eigenhard," Tomas said, pointing to the signature.

"This painting was done by Derrik Eigenhard, the Prince's third cousin."

"So Rogan really is a blood member of House Eigenhard?"

"He is, though he is estranged from that family. As far as I have been informed, out of the entirety of House Eigenhard, only the Prince and a single uncle did not take up some form of art as their trade, and both were ostracized. We have repeatedly asked Thane Eigenhard to send an artist for an updated portrait, one with the Princess Karen and his Highness in it, but from what I have gathered, there is a great deal of unresolved enmity between the Prince and his House."

Turning back to the painting, Tomas stood at it for some time. "An interesting family," Roland said evenly. "Many interesting events for one small group."

Tomas grimaced. "Hard to believe such an ordinary-looking family could be responsible for the destruction of Pelsemoria," he said.

"That is probably because they are not responsible. Contributive, certainly, but not singularly responsible. Contrary to what many would have you believe, young master."

Tomas turned, facing the butler. "Rogan admitted his culpability in the Madness. Him and his wife. If House Calonar isn't responsible, then who is?"

"I wouldn't know," Roland replied coolly. "If the good master wishes to know what really happened to his home and about the people involved, perhaps he should ask the people who were actually there and participated in the events instead of relying on the secondhand testimony of people who have much to gain by House Calonar's destruction."

With that, the butler continued towards the next level, Tomas trailing behind, Roland's words somehow sounding very much like Alexia's had months ago.

The bottom two floors of the main hall, as Roland explained to Tomas, were dedicated to the barracks, training rooms, and offices for the House Guard. The four floors of the southern wing were for the veritable army of serving staff it took to keep the castle working. The northeastern wing held the various supply rooms and quartermaster offices. The western wing of the castle was not open to the public as so much of the rest of the castle was. When asked about that, Roland replied, "Those floors are used by the Baron Rashid Tressalon and his men."

"A criminal Rogan and I encountered mentioned Rashid's agents."

"It is not my place to speak on such a subject, Master Tomas, but one could perhaps say that they take care of a problem before it becomes a problem."

"Calonar's assassins," Tomas noted grimly.

"His Majesty does not condone assassination, nor does he allow it in any organization that serves him."

Unconvinced, Tomas said nothing. As they continued up the carpeted stairs, Roland continued briefing the young shepherd. The third floor of the main hall was dedicated to guest quarters, rooms of various sizes for various types of guests. The fourth floor of the main hall was reserved for only the most important guests. It was to this floor that a suite would be provided for Tomas. The next floor up was dedicated to the Archaeknights, House Calonar's elite bodyguard.

The top floor of the main hall was, of course, where the King and his immediate family lived. This area was guarded day and night by the Archaeknights. "I cannot emphasize enough, Master Tomas, that trying to go there without permission and an escort would result in some extreme unpleasantness. The Archaeknights are an unforgiving group."

This floor held the personal quarters of the Baron Rashid Tressalon, who was Calonar's Chief of Intelligence, and his wife Aebreanna, who was Princess Kyla's principal lady in waiting, and the royal couple themselves. "Odd that a baron and his wife would be quartered on the same level as the Crown Prince," Tomas noted.

"Princess Kyla insisted," Roland remarked, ushering Tomas into his suite.

"What about the big tower at the center of the castle?"

"That is reserved for Master Cyras Darkholm on those rare occasions when he visits."

"No one else goes in there?"

"I have never encountered anyone who wished to."

Seeing Tomas settled into the enormous, eight roomed suite, Roland ordered the rest of the staff out with a single gesture. Before leaving himself, the old butler turned back to Tomas who, at a loss of what to do in such space, simply stood in the middle of what Roland called the receiving room. "I shall see to it that a meal is brought up immediately, Master Tomas." The old butler gestured to a blue velvet bell-pull. "A maid will be assigned to see to your needs, but until she arrives, please don't hesitate to summon the staff should you require anything. I would recommend that the young master remain here until such time as the Prince is done reacquainting himself with his wife and family."

"Am I a prisoner then?" Tomas asked stiffly.

"We are all prisoners of our destinies, Master Tomas. In the meantime, please make yourself at home. Your maid and dinner will be up shortly. If there is nothing else?"

Tomas shrugged, and the butler bowed and left. Tomas poured a glass of wine and flopped into a large upholstered chair. "Well, Alexia," he said, staring out the large glass doors leading to the balcony. "At least it's a comfortable cell." He could imagine his friend laughing at his dour comment and advising patience. Soon enough, the motives of the Black Duke would be made apparent.

Chapter 6

A quarter of an hour later there came a polite knock on the door, and Tomas' maid entered. Curtsying with a fluid poise despite the large silver tray in her hands, the young woman said, "Good evening, my lord. My name is Mary; I've been assigned to see to your needs for the duration of your stay." As Mary moved the tray to the dining room, Tomas marveled at the young lady's grace; she positively floated across the floor, never once catching her small, slippered feet on any of the furniture or myriad carpets. She wore a traditional Northlands dress, with a white, low-cut blouse and short sleeves, and an apron reaching to her mid-calf skirts that displayed an intricate embroidery evoking the forest. Her cheeks had a natural blush to them, matching the bow of her lips, without the need for the cosmetics so beloved by the women of the south. Her long hair was caught in a ponytail by a white ribbon and spilled down her back. This matched another ribbon tied around her waist with a bow on the left side. While Mary was slightly shorter than Tomas and certainly more diminutive, there was a surprising strength in her slight form; she carried the loaded silver tray with ease as she walked to the dining room and effortlessly placed the tray on a side table before setting a single place to eat. The young woman worked and moved with surety, with a quiet confidence.

Sensing Tomas' gaze on her, Mary turned her eyes to him, a concerned look in them. "Are you alright, my lord?" she asked.

Snapping himself out of a near trance, Tomas replied, "Fine, fine; I just didn't realize how hungry I was is all."

Mary laid out the meal on the large dining room table, sparking a sudden, ravenous hunger in Tomas as the various smells wafted over him. The scent of pickled herring and roasted potatoes with peppers teased him. His empty stomach growled in response to the sliced cheese and good, warm bread. Tomas nearly began drooling at the bowl of wild berries and pitcher of ale. Sitting, the young man devoured his first plate in record time before greedily taking more.

"This is delicious!" Tomas said through a mouthful of food. "Would you like some?"

Caught completely off-guard, Mary could only blush. "No, no thank you, my lord."

"Come on, you couldn't have had dinner already. Have some; and the name is Tomas, I'm not a noble."

"It wouldn't be proper for me to address you by name, sir."

After several assurances that she would not get in trouble, Mary finally acquiesced and ate a very small bit of cheese and bread. As for himself, the young man tore into his meal, relishing the joy of the first hot food he had eaten in weeks. Finally pushing his plate back, having eaten much more than was good for him, Tomas realized that he was in the mood for conversation. Unfortunately, Mary rose from the table. "Where are you going?" Tomas asked.

"To draw your bath, sir. I was told you just arrived today, and thought you must wish to bathe."

Tomas had not even considered it, but, suddenly catching his own scent, he realized that a bath was probably not a bad idea. Following the maid to the bathing room, again noting the grace with which she moved, Tomas watched as Mary manipulated the controls of the bathing tub, summoning hot water from a golden pipe. "Did a wizard do that?" the young man asked.

"My lord?" the maid looked confused.

"The water. Did a wizard create that tub?"

Turning back to the preparations, the better to hide her smile, Mary replied, "No, sir. This is not magic. The Uldra have developed a new plumbing system like those used in the old Sylvai Empire, except this doesn't use magic. I'm not entirely sure how it works, to be honest, but the water is drawn from the river and heated in a large tank beneath the castle, then piped up here."

"Amazing. And all without magic."

"Do you not have baths in the south, sir?"

The shepherd shrugged. "Not one that small. Every bath I've ever seen was large enough for several people and meant for communal use. I didn't realize they could be built that small."

Finally seeing that all was ready, Mary stood by the bath expectantly. "Is something wrong, my lord?"

"What do you mean?" Tomas asked confused.

"Did you require assistance in undressing?"

"Of course not!" he sputtered, his face turning bright red.

"Then, why do you delay?"

"I'm waiting for you to leave."

"Why would I do that, sir?"

"Because I'm about to bathe!"

Understanding dawned upon the maid's face. "Forgive me, my lord; I had forgotten you were not raised as a noble. It is customary for a nobleman to receive help while bathing."

"Somehow I doubt Rogan has help with bathing," the shepherd countered.

"Although I would not be in a position to know, sir, I would assume that Princess Kyla offers him whatever assistance he needs."

"Well I don't need help," Tomas said indignantly, his face burning.

Mary curtsied patiently. "As you wish, my lord," she said.

As the maid moved to leave the room, Tomas looked down at the tray resting beside the tub. He grew dizzy at the sight of all the various stones, bottles, cloths, and towels occupying it, to say nothing of the small handles, levers, and knobs controlling the water. "Wait," Tomas muttered, feeling foolish.

"My lord?" Mary answered sweetly.

"I don't know how to use any of this."

"Would you like some assistance, sir?" she asked sympathetically.

"Just keep your back to me until I'm in the water."

"Of course, sir."

Once undressed, Tomas got into the bath, relishing the feel of the hot water on his weary body despite his throbbing self-consciousness. Without a word, Mary rolled the short sleeves of her blouse and grabbed a cleansing stone of some kind, doing little to try and hide the smug little smile she had on her face.

With a calm and casual efficiency, Mary scrubbed Tomas down, cleaning off the months of hard riding within minutes. After finishing with the cleansing, the maid picked up one of the crystal bottles and poured a fair amount of some flowery-smelling oil into her hand.

Desperate to get his mind off the fact that an attractive woman was rubbing her hands all over his nude body, particularly since it seemed to Tomas that she was spending far too much time massaging those oils into his chest, shoulders, and arms, the young man tried striking up a conversation. "So... how long have you worked for House Calonar?"

Mary set the oil she was currently using back on the tray and cleaned her hands with a small cloth. "I have served his Majesty for nearly two years," she replied.

"Are you're duties difficult?"

"Not at all." She gently but firmly pushed him lower into the water. Once there, the maid wet his hair and rubbed another oil into it. "The Queen ensures that none of the staff are overworked or abused," she said while slowly rinsing his shaggy, unruly hair.

Prompted by the young lady, Tomas sat up straight. "What about the Black- about Calonar?" he asked.

Mary selected another of the bottles and, smothering her hand with the oil within, began massaging Tomas' neck and upper chest. "King Cylan is one of the gentlest men I've ever met," she said, careful not to look into his eyes. "His Majesty would die before causing anyone who serves him unhappiness."

As Mary's hands continued to massage Tomas' chest and slowly moved to his shoulders, extreme proximity brought them close enough that the young man was certain he could hear her heartbeat. Much to Tomas' regret, the maid seemed to be going out of her way to avoid eye contact, turning her head when necessary. For some reason it seemed to Tomas that, whenever her eyes did make a very brief contact with his, the water seemed to heat. Indeed, droplets of sweat began running freely from his forehead and neck to merge with the steam from his bath. "So... uh... why do you work as a maid?"

Mary moved her hands down Tomas' arms slowly, still keeping her eyes downcast, away from his. "I wanted to be a scribe and archivist," she said softly, "but my family couldn't afford my living in the Keep while attending school here, and our village is too far away to stay there."

"Women can be scribes in the Northlands?" Tomas asked, surprised.

"House Calonar maintains schools in many villages and towns. All children are encouraged to learn writing and arithmetic, even history and languages. There's a university here in the Keep for anyone who passes the entrance exams, which I did. My mother petitioned Princess Kyla for her help." Mary's hands began massaging the back of Tomas' neck, making the shepherd almost inarticulate with the sensation. "The Princess found me employment here in the castle," she continued, "which also meant that I would have a place to stay while I attend university."

Tomas feared he would soon be at the point of embarrassing himself. "You know," he stammered, "I think I'm clean enough."

"I'll get you a towel and dry you," Mary offered.

Raising his hands sharply, soaking her embroidered apron, the blouse, and the skin beneath. "No!" he nearly shouted. "That is, no thanks; I think I'd like to just soak a while." A long while, he thought, as he noticed the water reflecting tiny rainbow pools above the low-cut neckline of Mary's blouse

"As you wish, sir," she said, rising to her feet. "If you require anything else, I will clean your meal and retire to my room."

"Mary," Tomas said as she was about to leave.

"My lord?"

"You've been here for how long now?"

"Nearly a year, sir."

"Is it hard being away from your family?"

Mary clasped her small hands in front of her green and red apron. "You have traveled with Prince Rogan," she said, "Was that hard?"

"You have no idea."

"Pardon?"

"Uh... Travel with Rogan is tense but in some ways exciting."

"But never dull?" she asked.

"No, never dull."

"It is the same way here, sir. I miss my family and my friends, but I've made new friends. My mother once told me you have to find happiness where you are, not where you wish you were."

"Thank you, Mary," he said finally. "Good night."

"Good night, my lord," the maid bowed and left.

Tomas sat in the warm bath for some time, and not just for the obvious reasons. Lost in his thoughts, he did not notice the passage of time until the water had cooled. Stirring somewhat, the young man dried and made his way to his bedroom. There, he climbed into the ornately-carved wooden bed. The feather mattress was of so soft and the bedding so smooth and warm that Tomas drifted into a deep sleep very nearly as soon as his head hit the pillows.

In the morning, Tomas was rudely awakened by a thunderous explosion that shook the foundations of the castle. Another explosion sent the young man diving for cover under his bed, thinking it could be anything from a volcanic eruption to an attack by a rampaging dragon. Lying there and fearing the end of the world, Tomas suddenly thought of his new maid.

"Mary!" he yelled, rolling out of the bed and heading towards the serving girl's room. "Mary!" he yelled again.

The door to her room opened and the young woman walked out, still pulling on her robe. Her long hair was disheveled, sticking out from her sleeping coif, and she rubbed her sleep-thick eyes with one hand even as she held her robe closed with the other. "My lord?" she asked, stifling a yawn.

"Didn't you hear that?" he demanded, gesturing wildly towards the pre-dawn sky beyond the windows.

Mary tilted her head to the side, straining to hear. Just as she was about to question the nearly hysterical young man, there was yet another earth-shattering explosion. "Oh," she noted. "You mean Parden Esha."

Tomas dived for the young woman and pulled on her arm, desperate to get Mary to some kind of safety. "What is parden Esha!?!" he screamed, pulling at her with the intent of finding shelter.

The maid shook off the nearly panicked young man before he reached the doors leading into the halls outside; she calmly worked to re-cover her exposed body, her robe having been inadvertently pulled open by Tomas. "Parden is a Sylvai word meaning 'master wizard.' Parden Esha is the archmage in charge of the Arcane Guild here. She is also one of the King's senior advisors." Mary took a moment, noticing Tomas' lack of dress, and, without a glance downwards, moved to his sleeping room for a robe.

"What in Underworld is she doing," Tomas demanded, "destroying the city!?!"

"No, my lord. Some experiment of hers is always blowing up; you get used to it." Having retrieved a robe, Mary, tastefully averting her gaze, held it up meaningfully.

Tomas finally noticed he was still undressed for bed and blushed, his entire body burning in shame. He snatched the robe and hurriedly covered himself, desperately trying to prevent his mind's eye from recalling how Mary would be in a similar state of undress beneath her thick robe. "Is there no single sane person in this place?" Tomas grumbled in exasperation, trying to distract from his embarrassment.

Mary could only smile sweetly. "As I said, sir, life in the Northern Keep is never dull."

After Mary served Tomas his breakfast, which was only disturbed once by another cataclysmic explosion, the young woman excused herself.

"Plans?" Tomas asked, leaning back in his chair as he watched the maid repack the meal.

"It's Godsrestday, my lord," she explained. "I wish to go to Church. If that's a problem, I'll stay."

The shepherd blinked. "Godsrestday? I didn't even realize." He paused. "You mean there's actually a house of God in this city?"

"Of course."

"It's a shame I'll have to miss services," Tomas noted. "I really wouldn't have minded hearing what kind of sermon a priest loyal to House Calonar would give."

"Did anyone say you couldn't go, my lord?"

He nodded. "Roland hinted something bad might happen if I left without permission."

"Then why don't you ask permission," Mary suggested. "I'm sure the King wouldn't mind."

Feeling somewhat foolish, the young man nodded and moved towards the bell-pull that would summon the old butler. "My lord," Mary said, intercepting him. "I would be happy to relay your request to Roland. I'll probably see him in the kitchen."

"Right, that's probably a good idea. Could you also ask him if there are some spare clothes I could wear? Mine are a little…"

"Road-weary?" Mary offered. She curtsied and left. Nearly a half an hour later, she returned with both Roland and another woman. This new arrival was taller than Mary, even a little taller than Tomas, with fiery red hair that flowed freely. While Mary was quiet and reserved, frequently adopting a humble pose with hands clasped in front of her waist, this new woman stood defiantly, with a solid stance and steady gaze that did not shy from anyone, least of all Tomas. While Mary wore a traditional Northlands dress so common in the Keep, this new woman wore a short skirt and loose blouse in defiance of the cool weather of the Northlands' spring. At the small of her back was a pair of short blades, sheathed in the same double-scabbard with the hilts facing out, in opposite directions. Of all the features of this woman Tomas noted, the one that stood out most to him was the tattoo across her left eye, the crossed diamond sigil of House Calonar.

"Good morning, Master Tomas," Roland said. "This is Sarah." He gestured to the young woman as she walked across the room and put her back to a far wall, crossing her arms over her chest. "His Majesty has granted permission for you to attend Church today on the condition that Sarah and Mary accompany you."

The young man gestured vaguely at his own left eye, a puzzled look on his face.

Understanding the unspoken question, Roland smiled slightly. "That is the mark of an Archaeknight, Master Tomas. Sarah is a member of the King's personal guard."

"Why do I get the feeling she's not here to be my bodyguard?" the shepherd asked sarcastically.

Roland bowed slightly. "If the young master wishes to attend services, he should probably hurry. They begin in just over one hour, and the church is in the western district, a fair walk from the castle."

"Thanks, Roland."

"My pleasure, sir," he replied as he turned and left.

There passed then an awkward silence. Tomas glanced over at the archaeknight who never broke eye contact with him. "Uh, hi," he said lamely.

The archaeknight raised one eyebrow, the one covered by the crossed-diamonds.

Mary walked silently up to Tomas and put a light hand on his arm. The young man jumped, letting out a startled yelp. The maid fought a giggle by lowering her eyes. "Roland was kind enough to provide these clothes for you, my lord," she said, handing the folded bundle over.

Taking the clothes and trying to feel less foolish, the young man crossed to his bedroom. He stopped at the door when he realized Sarah was standing right behind him. Turning, he looked at her. "Is there any way I could change without an audience?" he asked.

The flat look she returned was answer enough.

Sighing, Tomas opened the door and left it open for Sarah, who entered and closed it, putting her back against the only way out of the room and once again folding her arms across her chest. Blushing from head to toe, the young man stripped and put the new clothes on as quickly as possible. As flustered as the shepherd was at the unwanted audience, he almost did not notice how relieved he was that Roland had not provided a Northlands long vest and shirt. Rather, Tomas had been given a simple wool tunic, the kind often worn in the south. Despite his comfort with the familiar clothes, however, there still remained his discomfort with the audience. Still blushing, the young man stood before Sarah. "Well?" he demanded.

The archaeknight stepped away from the door, never showing her back to him.

Tomas shook his head and muttered to himself about the unfairness of life and the deliberate cruelty of women. Mary was waiting in the outer room, careful not to show her smile. "Well ladies," Tomas said, sticking out his chest and daring anyone to say anything. "Shall we?"

Mary opened the door and held it for Tomas. As the young man passed, she threw Sarah a questioning glance he did not see. Reading the glance, Sarah shrugged a waved her hand in a so-so gesture.

Chapter 7

Stories in the Republic had been told for generations of the evil of the Northern Keep. Tomas never doubted that the Black Duke and his servants worshiped evil gods and practiced black magic. So much evil had been done by House Calonar and in their name that it just made sense in his young mind that only someone who worshiped evil could be capable of such darkness. Since his arrival yesterday, however, the young shepherd had seen things that caused him doubt. The teachings of his admittedly young lifetime were hard to dismiss, though, and he continued to look for evidence of the truth that was somehow being hidden. As with so many other things in the Northern Keep, Tomas was unsure of what he expected to see. What his eyes finally did find, though, was the last he expected.

It was a church. The one refuge of the Adamic faith anywhere to be found within the Northlands was as simple as any other modest cathedral. The wood and stone building was so unremarkable that at first Tomas had trouble believing they had, in fact, arrived at the correct building. The surrounding gardens were lush with the lawns and carefully manicured shrubbery so common to all Adamic property. The marble statuary and cobblestone pathways were a perfect representation of the careful construction that was a hallmark of all Adamic houses of worship. The Pool of the Sacrament with its single brazier in the center, ever-burning as the holiest symbol of the True Faith, rested in the courtyard.

"Is that it?" he asked, somewhat disappointed.

"Disappointed, my lord?" Mary asked.

"It's not that. It's just that the church is a little less... ominous than what I guess I was expecting."

The young maid smiled softly and clasped her delicate hands in front of her small waist. "Is the evil of the Northern Keep once again failing your expectations, my lord?"

"Very funny," Tomas muttered back.

Softly at first, but with increasing volume and power, the bells of the Keep's cathedral began to ring. The joyous song filled Tomas' soul, nearly lifting him off the cobblestone path he and his two escorts followed through the church's gardens. Feeling the first true peace in months, the young man closed his eyes, letting the holy song ring through his heart as he breathed in the delicate scent of the many nearby flowers.

Had Sarah the archaeknight not been so attentive, Tomas could very easily have committed a grievous offense against the Church. As enraptured with the ringing of the church bells as the shepherd was, he had no idea of the distance he and the two ladies had traveled despite their leisurely pace. The red-haired warrior-woman's arm snapped out faster than a hummingbird and forced Tomas back away from the Pool of the Sacrament into which he was about to fall.

Mortified, not over the embarrassment he should have felt, but at the thought of defiling the Pool, Tomas blushed and a slight tremble ran through his arms. It was the greatest trespass, as all Adamics knew, for a person to enter the water. Only the Sisters of Purity, blessed and as free of sin as any Human could hope to be, were allowed to enter the sacred waters resting at the entrance to even the most humble House of God. Their Order accepted the holy task of maintaining the brazier at the center of the small pool as their greatest responsibility.

"Are you alright?" Mary asked, laying a gentle hand on the young man's arm.

"I can't believe I almost..." the shepherd's words failed him.

"It's alright. Sarah stopped you."

Tomas shook his head. "To think," he said. "If I'd gone in, the priests and the Sisters would have had to rededicate the entire church. Weeks of work, all because I wasn't watching where I was going."

"Well, we don't have to worry about that now."

"I wouldn't even know how to apologize to the Sisters."

Mary shrugged. "Well, that at least you wouldn't have to worry about. We don't have a cloister here."

Tomas threw a shocked look at his smaller escort. "You don't? Then who maintains the Pool? The Sisters are the only ones allowed to enter the water."

"Cardinal Tain and his priests use a large poll to pull the brazier to the edge where they add the oil and incense before pushing it back into place."

"Why doesn't the Keep have any Sisters?" The young man demanded. "Is it Calonar's doing?"

Sarah snorted and rolled her green eyes.

Mary shook her head and led their small group around the Pool towards the entrance to the church. "No. In fact, His Majesty made a personal request to the Lords Cardinal that a cloister be allowed to relocate here to the Keep. King Cylan offered to provide any facilities they needed and a detachment of his House Guard to escort the Sisters north."

"So, what happened?" the shepherd asked.

"The caravan was ambushed while passing south of the Desert of the Exiles. We never found out what happened. Only the bodies of the House Guard were found. The Sisters and all their possessions, including the holy books, sacraments, and even their clothing, were taken by the attackers. When word reached the King of what had happened, he insisted that no other Sisters risk the trip until a way could be found to ensure their safety. Cardinal Tain agreed, and the Lords Cardinal sent no others."

"How long ago was that?" Tomas asked.

"Four years."

"So even the Sisters of Purity aren't immune to the fire consuming Lanasia," he whispered, filled with sadness at the thought of what horrors the holy women may have been subjected to at the hands of their attackers.

Wishing to change the subject to one less painful to her ward, Mary gestured ahead of them, and up the large stone steps to the double doors that stood open, inviting all to enter and commune with the Father Creator. "So, how long has it been since your last Mass?" she asked.

"I don't know. Nine months? Ten? What's the date?"

"Ansesen 11th," the maid informed him.

Tomas stopped in his tracks, his eyes lost in the time that had somehow slipped away. "How is it Ansesen already?"

"When did you leave home?" Mary asked.

"Anfaelal 1st," he replied. "I thought it was sort of symbolic to start my quest on Endyear Day."

"Quest?" the young woman asked. "Is that why you travel with the Prince? You're on a quest?"

Tomas nodded mutely, stepping aside as a small family passed by them, looking for a seat inside the church.

"May I ask what you quest for?" Mary asked curiously.

The shepherd put a weary hand to his head, closing his eyes and feeling an enormous weight press down on his shoulders. "I don't even know anymore. As bad as life was at home, it's so much worse out here. All I've seen is war and death and people who don't care that the world is falling apart. I don't even know who I am anymore."

Mary put her hand softly on Tomas' arm, feeling an enormous swelling of sympathy. "Perhaps there are answers inside," she suggested, glancing to the pulpit where the priest was stepping up to begin the services.

Tomas laid his own hand on the maid's smiling and nodding. "Let's find out."

It had been a long time since Tomas had participated in a full Adamic worship service. With the destruction of Pelsemoria a decade ago, the Church had withdrawn its personnel from the city in hopes of consolidating its power and ensuring its survival in the rapidly escalating civil war being waged across Lanasia. Because of this, Father Konrad was left alone to see to the spiritual welfare of those few who stayed within the crumbling walls of the capital. For ten years, the only ceremonies Tomas attended and participated in were those few the old priest could conduct.

The shepherd always had a strong sense of spirituality. Father Konrad had been as much mentor as priest to him, and Tomas sought the will of God in all things. He tried to maintain his faith no matter the suffering he or his friends and family had to endure, trusting that it was all a part of the divine plan. Whilst all the survivors of Pelsemoria avoided the Great Cathedral once it had been nearly destroyed, the young man never failed to spend at least a little time each Godsrestday within the holy walls of Pelsemoria's great church.

It had been so long, Tomas thought as the final benediction was given and the parishioners told to go in peace, since he had sung the songs along with a large group of fellow believers. There was a sense of community within a church. Once again, the young man felt the touch of the divine within his soul while listening to an Adamic priest read aloud from Scripture. It had been so long, and until Tomas had once again reveled in the warm comfort of his Church, he had not realized how very much he had missed it.

But how could such a place exist in the Northern Keep? The shepherd was left feeling even more confused than ever before as everyone around him stood and began to file towards either the confessional or the exit. Most of the Northlands had been declared unholy by the Lords Cardinal centuries ago. The Black Duke was directly responsible for the assassination of the Emperor and his entire family, to say nothing of the entire Elector Council. Calonar allowed the practice of pagan religions within his walls, and his agents and armies even now were spreading across eastern Lanasia like a dark tide. How could it be that a Church located within the cursed walls of his infernal capital could stir within Tomas the same feelings he remembered from his childhood. How could anything in this unholy place be holy?

Mary must have sensed the disquiet within her charge. As the trio made their way to the grand double doors, the polished wood thick and engraved with images from throughout Adamic history, the maid gently led Tomas aside. "Is something wrong?" she asked.

The shepherd looked past her to the church. He cast his gaze at the large stone arches that held up the vaulted ceiling. He looked past the wooden pews towards where the marble altar rested, festooned with candles and the Holy Fire. The young man let his eyes drift up to the stained-glass window standing directly behind the altar, letting the dim light of the spring afternoon filter in to cast its many colors throughout the church. "I don't know what's real anymore," Tomas finally said with the fear and uncertainty he had been feeling since first entering the Northlands.

"I wish I could help you," Mary replied.

"I don't know anyone who could help me," the shepherd noted.

"Perhaps someone can," the young woman suggested. She took her charge by the arm and led him against the far wall back up towards the altar where several priests had gathered. When finally the pair drew close, the clergymen noted their approach and one, an ancient man, withered by uncounted years with a pale face highlighted with an affectionate smile turned to face them. He was a grandfatherly old man, bent with years of life's hardships, yet with warm eyes. His grey hair stood out in whisps and his cardinal's robes, bright red with gold inlay, enfolded his frail body like a cloud. He moved slowly and carefully, discomfort plain on his wrinkled face, and yet somehow also with a power and confidence that belied his weary body. Mary gestured to the old churchman and said, "Tomas, this is Cardinal Alton Tain. your Eminence, this is Tomas, a new arrival to our city."

Cardinal Tain smiled warmly and, after receiving an affectionate hug from Mary, took the young man's hand in his own. His grip was soft, with a slight tremor. "Greetings, young Tomas." His voice, like everything else, spoke of many years, and yet carried those years with authority and grace.

Tomas shook hands in return, nodding his head low in greeting to a holy man. "Your eminence. It's an honor to meet you."

The Cardinal laughed lightly. "The honor may wear off before long, young man. But perhaps it could be replaced with a pleasure."

The shepherd shook his head solemnly as he clutched his arms behind the small of his back. "I'm afraid there's very little in my life now that brings me any pleasure, your eminence."

A concerned look crossed the churchman's face. "That's an odd thing for such a young man to say," he noted. "I see no scars on your face from battle, Tomas, but I sense them on your soul. Have your perhaps been tested of late against God's design?"

"Tested and, I think found wanting, your eminence."

"Please, young Tomas, there is no need for such formality. Many of my contemporaries may revel in the glories of high Church office, but I would still like to think of myself as a simple servant."

"Then what would you have me call you?" Tomas asked.

"If you must use a title, then 'cardinal' would do. Though most insist on 'your eminence.'" He grimaced and rolled his clouding eyes at the unwanted title.

"As you wish, cardinal," the shepherd agreed, again bowing his head.

Cardinal Tain turned to Mary, who was standing as unobtrusively as possible to the side. "Mary," the old priest said with another gentle smile. "Would you excuse us? I think this child of God and I should speak without the hindrance of other ears, even ones as pretty as yours."

The maid blushed and smiled. "I'll be waiting at the front," she told Tomas and walked to the far end of the church.

The clergyman gestured for Tomas to follow and moved to the front row of pews. Once there, the old man sat with obvious relief, though the effort of sitting was clearly great. "Sit, Tomas," the old priest said. "Let us talk of unimportant things."

The young shepherd sat with a puzzled look on his face. "Unimportant things?" he asked. "I thought you'd want to speak of things that were greatly important."

"I've found that the best conversations begin with talk of unimportant things. Once begun, a conversation can lead to many interesting places."

"As you wish, cardinal. What would you like to talk about?"

Cardinal Tain shrugged. "Anything. Mary mentioned that you have only recently arrived. Where are you from originally?"

"Pelsemoria."

"You say that with such gravity," the clergyman noted. "I take it you were there for the tragedy of ten years ago."

"Yes, and all the tragedies that followed."

"Much suffering," the holy man agreed. "Father Konrad does what he can, of course."

"You know Father Konrad?" Tomas asked.

"Of course. Who do you think recommended Konrad as our contact in the capital?"

"The Church...?"

Cardinal Tain shook his head slightly. "No, just House Calonar. I have the honor of sitting on King Cylan's advisory council, and when the plan was formed to send aid to your people, I was the one who recommended we work through Konrad." The old man sighed. "Of course, many of us, myself included, argued for an evacuation. Konrad, however, convinced us that those who remained would not want to leave."

Tomas nodded. "Pelsemoria was our home," he agreed. "We didn't want to leave it." Although Rogan had revealed Father Konrad's collusion with House Calonar weeks earlier, the confirmation from a cardinal was still painful. Of all those who scraped a life together within the ruins of Pelsemoria, Konrad was the last Tomas could have imagined making deals with the Black Duke.

"Was? Do you no longer think of it as your home?"

"I don't know. There are times when I miss it so much, I feel as though my heart will burst. There are times when I can't even remember the faces of the people who live there." The shepherd stared at the stained-glass window. "I'm not sure I even know… anything."

"Such is the way with memories," Cardinal Tain noted. "They come and go as leaves caught in a strong breeze."

"I sometimes wish they would just leave me forever."

"Was there nothing but unhappiness there?"

"No. I had… I have friends there. My mother is there. There are good people who live in Pelsemoria. We built for ourselves a good community despite what's happened to us. We survived."

"That is, after all, the Creator's greatest gift to us," the Cardinal said. "Humanity is capable of surviving in almost any place, any situation."

"Is surviving enough?" Tomas asked.

"From one moment to the next, surviving is all we can do. But as time goes on, greater things can be attempted and achieved."

"Are you telling me to have patience, cardinal?"

The old priest laughed. "I never give advice, young man. Only half the time can I possibly be giving the correct advice, and of those times, the person I'm advising only takes the advice half the time."

"So what are you saying?"

"Nothing of any great importance."

"Then what's the point?" Tomas asked.

"There isn't one. That's my point."

"I don't understand."

"Neither do I, really. So why did you leave home in the first place?"

And on it went. Tomas described to the cardinal his quest in its entirety, beginning with meeting Alexia and mourning her passing. "Death comes to us all, Tomas," Cardinal Tain noted, but there was a clear look of pain at the revelation of Alexia's death. "Though hopefully not in so horrible a way."

"I only knew Alexia a very short time, but she became important to me. To see her killed because of a mob's hatred…"

"Did it make you doubt? Did it make you fear?"

"It made me hate. I hated the crowd for their ignorance, their petty revenge. I hated the warlords for the misery they've inflicted on the people of Lanasia. I think I hated everything." Tomas laughed then. "I suppose that was one of the things that made my first meeting with Rogan so interesting."

Tomas continued in his tale, relating to the holy man his encounter with Cyras Darkholm and Rogan Eigenhard. He spoke of the Trickster Mage's geas, forcing the young man's trip north with the murderer he had hated for so long. Tomas spoke of their encounter with the Nekalan in Alvaro and the child-killer Senen in Crossroads, and the Lamashti in Wildelves Wood. At the end of the young man's tale, Cardinal Tain nodded and frowned. "It is a sad tale, this quest of yours," he said. "But something troubles me. You said that you left Pelsemoria on a quest and that after meeting with the Prince you came north. But after your encounter with Darkholm and Prince Rogan, you never mentioned your quest again. Have you abandoned it?"

Tomas shook his head. "No. But my quest remains unfulfilled."

"What is your quest?"

The young man was silent, his mind going blank while searching for an answer. "I don't know," the shepherd finally whispered. "After all I've seen and experienced. I don't even know what I'm questing for anymore. I don't know where I'm supposed to go or what I'm supposed to do."

"Have you asked?"

"Asked who?"

"Anyone. Is there anyone with whom you feel you can confide?"

Tomas shook his head. "All my friends and family are back home. I'm trapped in the Northlands, surrounded by the servants of the Black Duke."

"Well," the Cardinal said, unruffled at being one of those servants. "Since you feel so alone, young Tomas, let me remind you of one very important truth of life." He gestured to the altar. "No one is ever really alone."

The young man stared at the altar.

"How long has it been since you spoke to God?" the clergyman asked.

"So long I can't remember," Tomas replied.

"Then perhaps there is some good advice waiting for you. Perhaps He has just been waiting for you to listen. You said before that it was while you communed with Him in His house that you felt the call to Quest. Have you since tried to commune with our Father?"

The shepherd shook his head.

Cardinal Tain stood with difficulty, finally needing Tomas' help. "I've made it a point in my life to never tell someone they must pray, Tomas," he said after catching his breath. "But I've also found that when we most need direction in our lives, there is always at least one person who can give it to us."

The old priest walked slowly away, speaking and laughing with a small group of parishioners well away from Tomas. The young man stayed for a little while longer, continuing to stare at the altar. Finally, he climbed the brief stairs that rose from the stone floor to the marble dais. Setting aside the soft cushion placed for supplicants, Tomas dropped to his knees and, clasping his hands over his chest, lowered his head.

Have I strayed? He asked his creator. *I felt Your divine will touch my heart all those months ago and heeded what I thought to be Your commands. Tell me, O Lord, where my path leads now. To You I give glory and praise in the highest. To You, my God, I submit in patient hope that in Your great mercy You will once again lead me to whatever purpose You require.*

Tomas looked up into the stained-glass window and marveled in the perfection of its construction that highlighted the great battle fought between Ramalech and the Creator's Hosts. *Forgive me, Lord,* he thought then. *Forgive me for surrendering to doubt and despair. In my heart I felt Your guidance, but once tested, I faltered. I have let my lust for vengeance consume my soul until Your voice was all but lost to me. I renew my faith in Thee, O Lord, and swear upon all that I love that I will serve Thee in whatever way You wish. I ask only for the wisdom to never again stumble while walking the path You lay before me.*

Guide me, My Creator. Lead me from this place to whatever my Fate is. Show me the path You wish me to tread, my God, so that I may once again walk in Your glory. In Your Name, Your Creation, and Your Holy Church, amen.

Once he was on his feet, Tomas felt as though a great weight had been lifted from his shoulders. He felt renewed. The young man looked around the church. Seeing Cardinal Tain, he nodded thanks to the old priest which was returned with a smile. The shepherd felt as though God had heard his prayer and answered. It would be soon, Tomas thought, when he would again embark upon his path.

At the rear of the church, the young shepherd spotted Mary standing at the center of the aisle. Tomas suddenly realized how long he must have been separated from his companions. The young man stepped down from the dais, walking steadily but not really in any great hurry up the center aisle between the two rows of pews. The shepherd was halfway up the aisle when his pace slowed. A nobleman had approached Mary and was engaging her in what seemed a deep conversation. The noble was dressed in rich clothes layered with innumerable folds of delicate lace, the price of which could have fed the survivors of Pelsemoria for months. Jewels adorned his hands and clothes, and the signet ring of some minor House adorned his finger. His long blonde hair moved with a life of its own, and his perfect face was set in an equally perfect smile.

Tomas tried to be a courteous person. Since it was obvious Mary and the courtier were deeply involved in their conversation, he delayed his approach to give them time to finish. As he leaned against a pew, though, it became obvious from his overly familiar touches and close proximity that the fop had no intention of leaving. As Tomas looked on, in fact, it became clear that their conversation was one of an intimate nature. Mary was blushing. Each whispered remark from the popinjay brought an even deeper blush and an occasional step back. Of course, each retreating step made by the maid was countered immediately by an advance of the predatory nobleman.

It was clearly none of Tomas' business. He had no right to interfere. Tomas had only met Mary the day before, and for all he knew, she and the preening little brat were intended to one another. The shepherd had heard that, in the Northlands, couples would often engage in what would be embarrassing public displays of affection in any of the more civilized southern principalities. It was not Tomas' place to intrude unless the nobleman made an obviously threatening move. Besides, the young shepherd thought, Sarah was still somewhere in the church. The moment anything dangerous happened, she would no doubt put a stop to it.

Then the bastard took Mary's hand and kissed it, bringing a hesitant giggle to the maid's lips.

Tomas sprinted towards the two, stumbling on the way. The nobleman had time enough only to turn a surprised look towards the shepherd before Tomas' fist impacted with his face. The noble's head snapped back, and he stumbled but quickly regained his feet and put a hand to his dagger. In a blur, Sarah was there. The red-haired archaeknight thrust a hand into the nobleman's chest, sending him stumbling several steps away before thrusting the same arm into Tomas' middle. Then she grabbed the startled young man and threw him across the church in the opposite direction as the fop. The noble stepped forward, intent on exacting his vengeance, but was stopped by a single glance from Sarah.

The nobleman wiped the blood from his lip and looked from the archaeknight to Tomas and back. The courtier then let his hand slip away from his dagger. "I'll not forget this insult," he swore, spitting blood at the ground on which Sarah stood. Turning on his heel, the young nobleman strode out to his waiting carriage.

Mary stepped up to Tomas and looked down on his pitiable form. "I'll thank you not to attack anyone I'm having a conversation with, *my lord.*" She then left the church as well, trusting Sarah to escort the shepherd back to the castle.

Chapter 8

Returning to the castle with only the silent Sarah as company, Tomas could not help but feel the entire day had been something of a failure. True, he had no deliberate designs on Mary, but still… The young man really could not give any good explanation for his behavior. It was not like him to lash out irrationally at someone based solely on a first meeting.

"What do you think?" he asked his escort, not really expecting a response. "I suppose you think I was being rude, too."

Sarah did not even glance at him.

"You're probably right," the young man conceded. "I could have handled that a lot better."

The archaeknight continued to walk down the cobblestone street. It was a wonder, Tomas thought in passing, that she did not catch cold. Even in the early afternoon, the light was dimming and the air cooling, more subtle reminders that, although winter had at last relented, the season stubbornly held on where it could. The days were warm, Tomas realized, but a frosty chill was slow to leave and quick to return, finding purchase in the night. The shining sun did what it could, but only with difficulty. Sarah seemed either indifferent or overly defiant to this, however. Her loose blouse and skirt could not offer much protection against the wind, and her arms and legs were utterly exposed. Still, the silent warrior gave no indication, no consideration for any possible discomfort.

What was perhaps most surprising to Tomas, now that he thought about it, was the lack of acknowledgement from the townsfolk. The people of the Northern Keep gave almost no sign of recognizing Sarah. Men and women, soldiers and workers, Human and non-Human alike, all made only the barest nod to the warrior-woman as they passed by. Tomas had thought that her status as an Archaeknight, made evident and undeniable by the House sigil tattooed over her left eye, would have afforded Sarah a measure of fear, or at least respect. Despite this, though, his journey back to the castle had offered no evidence. Either the Archaeknights commanded little respect in the Northlands, Tomas thought, or they were more commonplace than he first suspected.

"No, I don't think I was being irrational," Tomas continued despite his companion's silence. "That guy was a jerk and being way too forward with Mary. It was rude."

Sarah absently scratched her cheek.

"Yes, I know. The people of the Northlands have a different attitude towards how men and women should interact, but that doesn't change the fact he was being impolite to a young woman just because she wasn't noble-born."

His companion sneezed.

"God bless you. I bet if Mary had a title, that jerk would have never had the courage to even talk to her, let alone proposition her like that."

"You're probably right."

Tomas stopped dead in his tracks. For just a moment, it seemed to him that Sarah had spoken. That could not have been, of course, but just the same he thought he heard her speak. He stood there for a moment staring at the archaeknight.

"Problem?" she asked clearly in a voice that was soft, almost more breath than voice, and lacking any emotion. So gentle was the sound that Tomas could not be sure she had even spoken.

"You talked!" he exclaimed.

Sarah rolled her hard green eyes.

"Why've you been silent until now?"

"I speak when I have something to say," she informed him. Now hearing her words, the young man realized that she must be from the Gwynnd Islands. Her voice carried the lilting accent of those strange lands, the rolling harmony of emerald hills and a rugged, half-civilized people.

"Haven't you ever heard of casual conversation?" the shepherd demanded.

She merely shrugged.

"Well," Tomas sighed, "what is it you think is worth saying?"

"You're an idiot."

Tomas paused. "I think I liked you better silent."

The archaeknight walked over to a small fountain and cupped her hands, drinking slowly before turning back to Tomas. Expecting clarification, the young man stood there for several moments before losing patience. "Was there any particular reason you think I'm an idiot," he asked, "or was it just a general opinion?"

"You only struck him because he was showing an interest in Mary," she explained, her Gwynnd accent filling the air, becoming heavy and rich the more she spoke. "Had he tried seducing another woman, you wouldn't have interfered. As soon as you realized he had intentions towards *your* maid, you became irrational."

"That's not true," Tomas insisted. "I've never approved of men who treat women as objects. I've always stepped in when a girl's being accosted."

"Did it look like Mary wanted or needed your help?"

"I was a little distracted."

"By your irrational hatred of a man that hadn't spoken to you."

"He was a jerk," Tomas insisted.

"I'm not arguing it," Sarah insisted. "That spoiled noble brat deserved the bloody lip you gave him. As you deserve the sore shoulder I gave you."

"In what way did I deserve being thrown halfway across the church?" the young man demanded, absently rubbing his still-sore shoulder.

"Because you weren't coming to Mary's defense," she explained. "You were protecting your territory."

"What, are you saying I was jealous!?!"

Sarah continued walking towards the castle. "You only struck that nobleman after he kissed Mary's hand. You tolerated his advances and his obviously condescending attitude with little care. It wasn't until he touched his lips to Mary's skin and she smiled that you felt the need to strike him."

"I wasn't jealous!"

The archaeknight shrugged. "You just felt a moment of irrational anger towards a person who was receiving more attention in a given situation from someone you felt should be giving that attention to you."

"Exactly," Tomas said. "That's all it was."

"That's the definition of jealousy."

They walked in silence for a while. Tomas finally said, "I wasn't jealous."

"Whatever you say."

"I wasn't!" he insisted.

Sarah just shrugged.

"Oh, now I get the silent treatment again?"

She kept walking.

"Fine! I like you better when you're silent anyway."

A deep but friendly voice drifted out from the deepening shadows of the cobblestone street. "I hope that's not the case for everyone around you," it said.

Tomas turned to face the source of the voice even as Sarah seemed to appear before him, turned slightly to the side with her arms held before her in a defensive manner. Though the streets were busy, filled with the bustle of a Godsrestday, with preparations of family meals, greetings of friends, and well-wishes, both Tomas and Sarah had been convinced none of the passersby had given them the slightest attention.

A figure, cloaked in dark blue against the afternoon chill with a hood drawn around a thin but well featured face raised his hands slowly to show his lack of hostile intent. "I mean you no harm, honored Archaeknight," he said softly. "I merely heard what I thought was an argument. It was my hope to assist."

"We have no need for assistance, citizen," Sarah remarked, lowering her arms but still facing the man. Her bearing, as always, communicated the potential for violence, though her face and voice remained neutral. "You may return home."

Tomas walked past his bodyguard/jailor. "It's nice to see you're this rude to everyone," he muttered to the Gwynnd woman. The shepherd raised his right hand in greeting. "I apologize for my companion; she was raised in the mountains by bears."

The stranger laughed softly. Sarah raised an eyebrow and frowned at her charge. "Funny," she muttered.

The cloaked man raised his hands. "Please take no offense, my lady Archaeknight," he said with a slight bow. "Our friend here is clearly from another land and unfamiliar with the ways of your order."

"How did you know I'm not from around here?" Tomas asked.

"Your manner of addressing the archaeknight," he replied. "No citizen under the rule of House Calonar would ever speak to or of a member of the King's elite guard in such a way."

"Fear?" the shepherd asked.

"Or respect," he shrugged. "For the average peasant, they are often one and the same. So, what brings you to the Northern Keep, young sir?"

"Business," Tomas replied carefully.

"I had thought it would be," the stranger laughed. "Few men travel this far north for pleasure."

"It's personal," the young man said.

"I did not mean to pry into something that you did not wish to speak of, young friend. I was merely expressing polite interest. Godsrestday is the time for friendly encounters, is it not?"

"I apologize. I've been a little on edge since arriving here."

"With good reason, no doubt." The man sat down on a nearby bench, a single piece of wood carved into a natural-appearing growth of ivy. He gathered his cloak around him. "These are, after all, troubled times. Differentiating friend from foe becomes difficult. In these days, the two blur together until a person is surrounded by nothing but grey figures that could betray at any moment."

"You have a very dark view of the world, friend," Tomas noted.

"Like you, sir, I have had many difficult trials in my life. I have been betrayed by friends and aided by enemies. I have traveled far to find nothing and have worked hard only to fail. This is a time of such things in Lanasia."

"And what brings you here?"

The stranger looked up, showing his handsome face clearly for the first time. "Like you," he said with a friendly smile that was marred only slightly by a slight twitch in his right eye, "business." He had soft blue eyes and an angular face, with a very thin beard and well-kept hair. His appearance and slight accent suggested an origin of the Gwyndd Islands like Sarah, though his tasteful clothes were of Alvaro design, and his voice carried no hint of accent.

"So, we two businessmen find ourselves in the Northern Keep on different affairs," the shepherd remarked.

"Or perhaps not so different."

"How do you mean?"

"I come seeking answers. You have the bearing of someone doing the same."

Tomas laughed. "It's not the answers I need. It's the proper questions."

The man nodded, closing his dark brown eyes. "That was a very enlightened reply. You are a man of education?"

"Some," the young man replied feeling flattered. "Mostly self-taught, though."

"I have always felt that a man can learn best from himself. No teacher can ever remove their own prejudices from any lesson enough to teach properly."

"You said you've come seeking answers. May I ask what answers you are looking for?"

"Answers to questions and answers to actions."

"I don't understand."

"Perhaps it is not yet your place to understand. Forgive me if I seem overly cryptic, but I have learned over the years to keep my motivations and goals private, especially when I am in a place that may contain enemies."

Tomas glanced over to Sarah, who was idly scanning the surrounding area while listening very carefully to every word exchanged between the two men, no doubt for a later report to her superiors. "As you say, though," the shepherd replied. "In these days, it is often hard to tell friend from enemy."

The stranger locked his eyes with Tomas.' "That is why it is important to see things as they really are, not as others would present them to us."

"Why would someone put on a deceiving performance for only one person?" the young man asked.

"Have you studied history at all?"

"Quite a bit, actually."

"In your studies, you have surly seen that history shows, time and again, that one man can be of such vital importance to events, either ongoing or upcoming, that it would be of vital importance to influence him."

"To what end?"

"To turn him from one side to the other."

"These are dark thoughts to be thinking," Tomas noted.

"Indeed," the stranger replied, standing. "But important ones. I've enjoyed our conversation, Master Tomas. I do hope we'll run into each other again."

"I suppose that depends on how long our respective business holds us here."

"Indeed." He extended his hand, which the shepherd took. "Until we meet again, should Fate decide we do so."

With that, the stranger departed down a side street, disappearing into the crowd. Tomas and Sarah resumed their trip back to the castle in silence. The shepherd's thoughts dwelled on both the scene at the church and the words of the person he had just met.

Later that day, as the sun slipped lower on the horizon, reaching the tips of the great forest, Mary returned to Tomas' rooms. The young woman walked on her silent feet towards her bedroom, making obvious efforts at remaining unobtrusive. Tomas looked up from the book on Uldra language and culture he had spent the afternoon reading.

"Afternoon, Mary," he said suddenly, surprising her.

"Oh, my lord! You startled me."

"Sorry," he replied. "You've been gone a while. I was getting worried."

Mary bowed. "I apologize, my lord, but I was having dinner with some friends and lost track of time."

"Anybody in particular?" he asked.

"Sir?"

"Your friends. Was there anyone in particular who made you lose track of the time?"

"Forgive me, sir," she said somewhat sternly. "But the Queen has commanded the private lives of the servants are to remain private."

Tomas stood and walked around the chair to her. "You're right; I'm sorry. I didn't mean to pry. I was just worried. It's none of my business who you spend time with."

"Very true, my lord."

Fully aware of the dressing down he deserved, the shepherd hung his head and kicked at the rug beneath his feet. "And I'm sorry for how I behaved at the church," he said lamely. "I shouldn't have hit your friend."

Mary smiled. "He wasn't my friend," she consoled him. "As a matter of fact, I've been trying to avoid him for weeks now."

Tomas' head snapped up. "Really!" he exclaimed before regaining control. "I mean, that's none of my business either."

Her smile descended to a grin as she regarded the bumbling shepherd. "Still, my lord. That was very kind of you to come to my defense."

Tomas puffed his chest a little. "Well, you know. That's a man's job, after all."

Mary's eyes narrowed. "Really?" she remarked, the grin turning somewhat cold. "Well, please don't feel like you should trouble yourself, sir. I am capable of defending myself."

The young man chuckled a bit. "Nothing personal, Mary, but maybe someone *should* stay with you. I mean, you are a very beautiful woman, and someday someone is bound to try and take advantage of you when you're alone."

"I think, sir, that I am quite capable of protecting myself," she snapped.

Tomas chuckled, causing a flush of anger to spread across Mary's face. "I'm sure you can, Mary."

In retrospect, Tomas was later surprised that fire had failed to shoot from her eyes. "Would my lord care for a demonstration?"

"Sure," the young man said in the most condescending tone he had. "Go ahead."

The next few moments were forever a blur to Tomas. In one instant, he was standing only two feet from Mary. In the next she seemed to spin and there was a sharp blow to his jaw. Before he could regain his equilibrium, Tomas was flying through the air, finally impacting against something that felt suspiciously like a wall. Lying there, the shepherd collected his thoughts, realizing that a pattern was developing in his life of beautiful women throwing him into things.

"Sleep well, my lord," Mary said softly with a demure smile and polite courtesy.

Chapter 9

Over the course of the next day, there were several more explosions from the local Guild tower. Despite the interruptions, the young man spent most of his time talking with Mary, learning the history of the Northern Keep. The shepherd had been following his maid around during her duties, making idle talk that filled the time and distracted him from the fact that he was, for all intents and purposes, a prisoner of the Black Duke. Tomas often caught his eyes almost involuntarily following the curves of Mary's body as the young woman would reach up to dust the tops of shelves and bend over to fluff cushions and pick up Tomas' clothes.

The original settlement, according to Mary, was long ago. "This was just a small town called Berend back then," she noted as she struggled to move one of the chairs in the greeting room back into place after her altercation with Tomas the night before had knocked it over. "The people mostly traded with the Uldra, buying the metals and stone they mined from Ulheim and selling them to the rest of the Northlands."

Tomas crossed the room and picked up the chair, moving it as Mary directed. "Was it a part of the Republic?" he asked.

"Not really," Mary sighed, removing the kerchief tied around her hair to wipe her brow. Whether from the warming spring air or her light chores or something else, a slight glean of sweat had formed across the young woman's flesh. "No prefect or governor would ever want to be assigned this far north, and the army almost never traveled past the Miryam River." She replaced the kerchief and smoothed her apron. This day, she wore a soft green blouse with a skirt of a slightly darker hue. Her traditional Northlands apron was again embroidered, but this time with a flowing vine of blooming roses.

"Must have been dangerous," Tomas noted, setting the chair in place and consciously trying not to follow the movement of her hands as they ran along the curves of her dress.

Mary, finished in the greeting room, crossed to a small closet in the receiving room. "Actually, thanks to the frequent contact with the Uldra, Berend was fairly safe," the maid replied, giving just the slightest glance back over her shoulder as she gracefully moved. "They tend to be protective of their friends." She picked up a coarse brush and several pieces of cloth and crossed towards the bath.

Tomas joined Mary in the bath, watching as she went on to describe the other events while cleaning the bathing tub. As she spoke and scrubbed, the young woman was kneeling away from him. She continued her story, to which Tomas was struggling to listen. "But a big problem did finally come: a Druug helter." She stood and flushed the tub with fresh water.

"Helter?" Tomas asked.

Mary nodded. "It's our word for when the Druug come together, when several packs join and begin rampaging through the country. His Majesty had no title at the time, and this was just after the Siege of Velaross. You know of it?"

Tomas nodded. Who did not? More than four centuries ago, two rogue priests, Leria and Lar Nenic, had used ancient and forbidden magics to unleash the Plague of Walking Death on Lanasia. More than a third of the Republic's population had been killed in less than a year; the worst of it was that those who died of the plague rose the following night. The priests used their dark magic to control the dead and used them to conquer Velaross. "It was then the Heroes of Fate appeared for the first time and led the Army of the Golden Flame," Tomas noted. "They led all the forces left in eastern Lanasia to liberate the Holy City.

Mary nodded and continued, "Well, his Majesty was there for that great battle. After the war, he moved north. When an emissary from Berend pleaded for help from a great Druug helter, the King gathered some of his friends and destroyed the monsters." Stopping her work for a moment to again wipe the sweat from her brow, she glanced back again at Tomas. Caught looking, the young man made a show of glancing about the room. Mary smiled and resumed her work and her story, leaning a bit little lower in her tasks.

After the destruction of Berend by the grey-skins, Calonar, with the remnants of his people behind him, moved the townsfolk away from the mountains and built a new town of Berend at the edge of Wildelves Woods. "In honor of the efforts of his Majesty," Mary said, "the people of Berend wanted to rename their home Calonar's

Keep. But his Majesty refused, so instead they renamed it the Northern Keep."

After Cylan Calonar's son, Kyle, was born, the mad Vaeyen, Ravana, kept attacking the Keep in the form of a great red dragon. "Why?" Tomas asked.

Mary shrugged. "Revenge. You've heard about their great battle during the Siege of Velaross, right?"

The shepherd nodded. During the great battle, the bad Vaeyen had attacked the Heroes of Fate and been defeated. To avenge this loss, Ravana harassed the followers of House Calonar. Each time the King fought her off. While he was away with several of the most powerful of his inner circle, though, the monster attacked one last time, causing great destruction. After that, Calonar moved the city and its people deeper into the Wood. Mary began sweeping the floor around the tub. "It was at that time the alliance was forged with the Sylvai who live in this forest."

"What exactly is this alliance?" Tomas asked, taking the rugs Mary indicated and draping on the balcony outside the living room. "What are the terms?"

Having finished in the bath, the maid took her broom and joined Tomas on the balcony, beating the rugs in the fresh air. "Well, as you can guess, the alliance is very old. Only a few were there when it was originally made. Our teachers tell us the King agreed to defend the Wood and keep away any Republic expansion. In return, the Sylvai promised to provide him an area in the center of the Wood to build his city and to ensure the safety of travelers."

"What about all the stories of men being attacked in the forest?" Tomas asked, recalling the ominous insinuation of the sylvai Speaker they encountered after the battle against the Lamashti. She had hinted at other incursions, and dire consequences of those travelers unfortunate enough to have suffered a Lamashti attack.

Mary took a moment's rest, breathing in the mid-day air. "As long as a traveler stays on the highways and does nothing to harm or disturb the Wood, the Sylvai promise them safety."

Tomas grunted, unconvinced of this version of the story. He went to a service tray inside and poured two glasses of sweet berry wine. Returning to the balcony, he wordlessly offered one to Mary. She accepted with a slight smile.

"About a century later," the maid continued, "another Druug helter came out of the mountains. The horde could have destroyed every village and town in this part of Lanasia." She sipped the wine and reclined against the balcony railing, an unadorned, low stone wall. Doing so, the young woman pulled free the kerchief to let her long hair flow in the gentle breeze, and wiped some of the sweat from her chest, incidentally tracing her hands along her low-cut blouse. "Historians think the invasion could have pushed in as far as Ironheartshaven or even the Duchies of Velaross before it would have been stopped," Mary noted, sipping again at the wine.

"I think I remember this from my history lessons," Tomas mused, swirling his glass and fighting the urge to follow with his eyes the path of Mary's kerchief. "That was during the attempted coup, when the wizard Tyrus tried to take the Redwood Throne. The Legions and City Watch were too busy stopping a civil war before it started to do anything about the grey-skins."

Fortunately for Lanasia, Calonar and his allies stopped the Druug, Mary reported. Not long after, the Church, in growing fear of House Calonar's growing popularity with the people of the Northlands and its open acceptance of non-Human religions, decreed the Northern Keep to be a den of evil. "When priests from the Inquisition arrived, they demand that all non-Adamic temples and religions be destroyed." The young woman grimaced at the cultural memory. She set down her glass and returned to work.

"Somehow, I doubt he complied," Tomas guessed, taking the glass Mary had set down and returning them to the serving tray inside.

The maid, struggling a bit with the largest of the rugs nodded. "The King went down personally to the city square to try and reason with the Inquisition leaders. The resulting battle of magic caused quite a bit of destruction."

Tomas noticed the trouble Mary was having, and after she put the large rug down to catch her breath, picked it up himself and placed it where she directed. "That was why the Church declared House Calonar unholy?" Tomas guessed.

"Yes," Mary agreed, following behind him. "After their failed attack, the Church leaders realized House Calonar was a direct threat to their power, especially once his Majesty opened the Keep to all peaceful religions."

Tomas returned to the serving tray but this time poured a glass of water, offering it first to Mary. She tried to refuse, but the young man insisted. The maid demurely accepted and sipped. "Something confuses me, though," Tomas said, taking her glass and drinking the remaining water himself before returning it. "Why do you keep referring to Calonar as 'his Majesty' during periods when House Calonar was only a duchy and others when they didn't even have that?"

Mary looked quizzically at the young man. "It doesn't matter what title the King held before, he's a king now, so I refer to him with the proper respect."

"You talk like all those different Calonar's were the same man."

"They were," she replied matter-of-factly.

Tomas sighed and shook his head, tired to his core of this piece of Northland propaganda. For years, perhaps longer, the agents of House Calonar had tried to convince the world that the Black Duke was the same man as his ancestors, that the various men, some quite noble, who served among the Heroes of Fate, were all this one person. "Mary, it's a recorded fact that a Calonar died at the Siege of Velaross. You said yourself, that particular Calonar was a warrior. The one who joined in the fight against the Xeshlin Invasion was a wizard. Halvans may live a little longer than Humans, but being the same man would make him over five hundred years old!"

"Five hundred forty-four, this spring," a deep voice said from the doorway.

Tomas and Mary whirled around. Dressed in rather common Northland clothes, the type any minor merchant or tradesman might wear, his short gray hair unencumbered by a crown and his face still holding the same, if a little more tired smile Tomas had seen on the portrait the day before, stood Cylan Calonar, Lord of the Northlands, flanked closely by Sarah of the Archaeknights. His pearlescent eyes, marking him a Halvan, regarded Tomas without emotion.

"Your Majesty!" Mary said breathlessly, curtsying as deeply as possible without falling.

Tomas simply stood there in shock.

"Hello, Mary," the despot said warmly. "I haven't seen you in some time. Have you been well?"

The maid stood straight again, still not meeting her king's pearlescent eyes. "Oh, just fine, your Majesty!"

"I hear your dancing improves every day."

"I hope so, sire."

"I look forward to seeing your next performance."

Mary could only stand there and blush, at a clear loss for words.

"And you must be Tomas," Calonar said, a speculative look drifting into his halvan eyes. "Rogan spoke of you at dinner last night."

Tomas could only nod, his mouth still agape.

Calonar turned back to the maid. "I'm sorry, Mary," he said softly, "but could you please excuse us? I think Tomas and I need to have a conversation."

Nodding without looking up, Mary started making her way towards her room. "Why don't you take the rest of the day off, Mary?" the king suggested. "I'm sure Tomas will be alright until supper."

"Oh, your Majesty, I couldn't!"

Calonar laughed very gently, "It's alright, Mary go ahead."

She dashed off, nearly forgetting to curtsey to her King and close the door behind her.

Once the young woman left, Calonar turned back to the still-gaping Tomas. "May I sit?" the Black Duke asked his prisoner.

Tomas could only gesture vaguely at a chair.

Calonar sank slowly into the chair, his grayed face showing obvious relief at being off his feet. Taking a few deep breaths, the old halvan reopened his pearlescent eyes to regard Tomas thoughtfully. "Rogan tells me you want to see me defeated and stripped of all power. He also mentioned you probably want to kill me."

Tomas silently sank into a chair across from the Dark Lord of the Northlands. Once her master and the shepherd were both seated, Sarah moved behind Calonar's chair, her gaze steady on the potential threat to her master.

"I can't imagine what must be going through your mind, Tomas," the Black Duke admitted. "You've been raised on stories of the den of evil men call the Northern Keep, yet as I'm sure you've already noticed, the city is somewhat tamer than rumors suggest. Having lived in Pelsemoria all your life, I imagine you've heard nothing but 'Eigenhard the terrorist,' 'Eigenhard the assassin,' 'Eigenhard the murderer;' and yet, after being so close to him for so much time and so many miles, meeting his wife and seeing how the people regard him, I'm curious; what *you* think about him?"

Tomas closed his eyes and took a deep breath. "I'm having trouble believing the stories about him," the young man admitted quietly. "He's a soldier, not an assassin. And yet..."

"And yet, there is what you witnessed, ten years ago."

Tomas' eyes jerked up, to meet those of the Black Duke. "Yes," the shepherd said flatly.

Calonar nodded, a look of apparent sadness drifting across his greying face. "And the people of the Keep?" he asked. "Do they seem to you to be the practitioners of evil so many rumors describe them to be?"

"No. Your people are like any other people in the world. You have the good and the bad mixed together. I'm not sure what to believe anymore, but the memory of... the past..." He straightened in the chair. "Also, I've seen what happens to those who submit to House Calonar. Railing just won't allow me to think you people are the good guys."

The Black Duke gave Tomas a slightly confused look. "What are you talking about, Tomas? What happened at Railing?"

"You mean your spies haven't told you?"

When Calonar shook his head, Tomas relayed, somewhat painfully, what he had witnessed in the village. With a moment's reluctance, he even told the Black Duke how he desecrated the body of the commander of the Calonar soldiers stationed there. After the young man had finished, the Black Duke was quiet, looking at Tomas with his hands steepled in front of him. Tomas returned the look with equal thought, trying to understand the conflict raging in his soul, hoping for something that would decide how he should regard this man before him.

Finally, the Lord of the Northlands spoke. "This is the first I've heard of this. I promised the people of Railing I would protect them, but it's clear now that I've failed. I'm afraid I can't do anything for the people, but I assure you, the men responsible will be dealt with. I am curious, though, did attacking the commander of my soldiers make you feel better?"

Tomas shook his head. "No, not really."

"Did you hope it would?"

"No."

"Then why?"

The young man thought about it, trying to understand. "I guess," he said, "that I just had to see someone punished for what happened."

"Punished more than what had already been done?"

"Punished for causing it."

"Did that man cause the massacre?"

"No. But he was responsible."

"In what way?"

"You put him there. Him and all those soldiers. Had they never been there, maybe Vagris would never have attacked, maybe he still would have. But either way, your soldiers were there, and they were supposed to protect that town. They failed."

"And for that failure you desecrated that man's remains?"

Tomas stood and shook his head, feeling the welcoming anger return to his heart. "What do you want me to say? That I'm sorry for what I did? Well I am!" He began pacing the room, not even looking at Calonar. "You have no idea how much this has torn me apart! Women, children, the old, the infirm! Everyone who lived in that town was butchered! They were terrorized, brutalized, and killed! And it's ALL YOUR FAULT!!"

Sarah moved a few steps closer to the young man after his outburst. Calonar remained passive, only watching Tomas and waving Sarah back. "Was it?" he asked.

"Don't try to tell me it wasn't! If you hadn't forced them into that treaty, they would still be alive!"

"Possibly," he admitted. "Even probably. The treaty certainly was the excuse Vagris used to attack."

"Finally!" Tomas roared. "The Black Duke admits his sins!"

Calonar sighed. "I have more sins weighing down my soul than you could possibly imagine, Tomas," he replied with that damning calmness. "There is much in my life that I regret, and while I regret what happened to Railing, I do not regret signing that treaty with them."

"How dare you!?!"

The Black Duke's face remained passive. "Tomas," he said very softly, "why do you think I wished for an alliance with the people of Railing?"

"The town was prosperous. A great deal of money could have been taken from them."

"You've seen this city, this castle. Does it seem to you that I would need the money I could extort from Railing?"

Grudgingly, Tomas shook his head. "No," he muttered. "I don't know where your wealth comes from, but it's obvious it must be vast to pay for all this. One more town would hardly make a difference."

Calonar nodded. "Then why? Why would I desire a treaty with a town lying so far to the south? Why would I send a part of my army there if not for plunder?"

Tomas' mind raced, searching for an answer. "Railing's strategic," he finally said. "It once sat at the major crossroads of the south. If you one day wish to expand there, you would need to control that crossroads."

"To where do those roads lead?"

"Velaross."

"Which is already allied with me."

"The Sylvai Vale..."

"Which is once again under Sylvai control, and abstaining from the civil war."

"Daivic lies further on that road," Tomas pointed out.

Calonar shook his head. "Duke Parano is trying to reestablish trade across Lanasia. Why would I disrupt that? Even the Republic only offered a token governance of the Endless Sands. House Parano seems the only ones willing to try and rule the Khepri and Shamashi. Where else do the roads from Railing lead?"

"Alvaro and eventually to Ironheartshaven."

"One independent and the other already within my sphere of influence."

"The only other road leads south, to Pelsemoria," he said quietly, finally being forced into the Black Duke's point.

"And the capital has been in ruin for years. So, Tomas, what strategic value would Railing have for me?"

"None," he grudgingly admitted.

"So, if I didn't want the money, and I didn't need the land, what did I want?"

Tomas thought. "The people," he guessed.

Calonar smiled and nodded. "Yes, Tomas. Railing had no value for me except for one thing. I wanted its people."

"You admit that?" the young man demanded incredulously. "You admit you wanted the people?"

"Of course," the Lord of the Northlands replied. "I wanted the people of Railing to be a part of the new nation I'm trying to build."

"What gives you the right?" Tomas demanded.

"Excuse me?"

"What gives you the right to build yourself a kingdom? You may be a nobleman, but you have no right to the Redwood Throne!"

"I have never made a claim for the Throne," he replied. "I have no interest in rebuilding the Republic. I want to try and make something new."

"A kingdom with you as king."

"Who else would you have rule over you, Tomas?"

"There are plenty of men who could make a decent emperor. Duke Edmondo Parano."

"Parano was born noble in a House that has been noble for generations. His family originally comes from Pelsemoria, but House Parano has ruled the Endless Sands for centuries. In all that time, none of them have bothered adopting local customs. Edmondo himself doesn't even speak the Shamashi tongue. He's always stressed the importance of the nobility. The commoners in his lands have few rights, if any, and he actively subjugates the Shamashi and Khepri."

"What of Theodorico Balshazzar? The Emir of the Western Empire?"

"House Balshazzar has, for centuries, concerned itself with expanding their power, not in actually caring for the people or the land. Theodorico Balshazzar has no idea how to run an economy, and his pride will not allow him to take the advice from those who do. His lands are virtually bankrupt, and the commoners are starving."

"Czar Nicalos…"

"Nicalos is a good man and House Georgios has done a fine job caring for their people. Kessia has prospered under their guidance and been mostly protected from the Republic's collapse. However, Nicalos is a young, inexperienced man, and he has no interest past the plains and mountains of Kessia. His people live very isolated lives, and he prefers it that way. He has not participated in the civil war other than to protect the towns and lands loyal to him, and he has made it plain that his country has had enough of empires."

"Well there's…"

"No one. You have named every noble left who could possibly unite Lanasia. Geraldine Eigenhard can't even control the Gwynnd Islands, and the conservative Elector Lords would never allow a woman on the Redwood Throne. Dignan Sandrine may be Lord Paramount of Velaross, but he has no real authority over the Church and his House is a minor one; the Elector Lords would never bow to him. No one trusts the Frostfront Triumvirate, the Lords Cardinal are forbidden from holding secular authority, and Asmund Hulda has already sworn the jarls of Ironheartshaven to me. None of the minor Houses has a candidate who could possibly make a strong claim to the Redwood Throne. None of the major Houses can set aside their own ambition for another candidate. Each of us has something wrong. There isn't a man or woman among us who should be sitting on the Throne, but someone *must* end the fighting."

"And that someone must be you?" Tomas asked, with much less heat than before.

"A day does not pass in which I wish that it could be someone else," the old man admitted. "I never had any interest in ruling, Tomas. I was born to a noble father, true, but his House was stripped of its title after the Uldra Uprising, and my father himself was shunned after marrying my mother, so I grew up common. Over time, I was granted one title after another as thanks from men who thought all men want power."

"What *do* you want?" Tomas asked. "What desire rests in the heart of the Black Duke?"

Calonar looked out the door, past the balcony, and into the distant sky. "Freedom," he whispered.

"Freedom? From what?"

The Lord of the Northlands gestured around the room. "This, all of it. I live in luxury, with servants and guards and people who love me, but I would trade all of it if I could to take my wife and my children, pick a direction, and just go."

Tomas sat back down, looking into Calonar's pearlescent eyes and hearing the truth in his words. "Why don't you?"

"Who would protect my people if I did?" he asked. The king shook his head. "No, Tomas. My days of adventure and freedom came to an end long ago. I'm no longer Cylan Calonar, Hero of Fate, riding out to protect the helpless and avenge the wrongs done by evil men. I'm no longer even the Duke of the Northlands, member in low standing of the Elector Council, fighting against bureaucracy to try and protect the rights of commoners and non-Humans. Now I am King Cylan, and I am directing the fight from the safety of my city to forge a kingdom I don't want so that no one else may claim it."

"And how will you fight that fight?" Tomas asked.

"Well," the king sighed, "to start with, I'll tell Rogan of the news you bring. He'll most likely be the one to bring Vagris to justice."

"Is that what Rogan's for?" Tomas asked. "Is he the man you send to kill people who anger you?"

Calonar rubbed his pearlescent eyes wearily. "Do you honestly believe Rogan would allow himself to be used as a glorified assassin or bounty hunter?"

Tomas thought about it. He thought about what he had learned of the knight during their journey north. "No," he finally answered. "Rogan is loyal to you, and he would kill someone in battle, but I can't see him as an assassin."

"Not a murderer?" Calonar asked. "Not a terrorist?"

Tomas shook his head, "No. I just couldn't see Rogan killing a man in cold blood for no other reason than he was ordered to."

"What about Senen?"

Tomas thought about it. "At first, I thought Rogan was finally showing his true colors, beating a man who was obviously helpless."

"And then," the old king prompted, "once you had learned what Senen had done? His cruelty to those children?"

Tomas hesitated only a second. "I don't know. Maybe Rogan would have been doing that monster a favor by killing him there. Instead, some bounty hunter will probably catch him and turn him over to the Church. They'll torture him for days before burning him at the stake. By letting him go, Senen will spend what little of his life is left in terror of being discovered. When he is, he'll be killed. He has no future; Rogan just gave him a stay of execution." The young man shrugged. "Besides, Rogan gave the man his word. I don't think he could ever go back on an oath of honor." The shepherd turned towards the balcony and looked out over the Northern Keep, the twilight seeming to emphasize the merry warmth of a hundred hearthfires, glittering lanterns sparkling their cheerful light against the growing darkness, and the sounds of music, merrymaking, and family drifting on the springtime breeze. "The people of your Keep genuinely love this House," Tomas finally conceded. "Rogan tries to hide it, but it's pretty obvious he cares very much for them."

"He'll make a good king someday," Calonar agreed. "You know, Tomas, it can be very hard abandoning one's beliefs. Perhaps the most painful thing you can possibly ask of someone is that they change their mind. So, I won't ask that of you, not now or ever. Instead, I will ask that you make up your own mind about my House and my people. Rogan and Rashid have given recommendations you not be allowed to leave the castle again. Usually, I take their advice to heart; the two of them are both very good at their jobs. This time, however, I must disagree. Go out into the city, Tomas. See how the people live. Talk to them. No one has the right to make up your mind for you or to try and change it. If you must hate us, hate us for who and what we truly are, not for what someone else says about us. After you've seen the city, we can speak again."

"And then what?" Tomas asked.

"You're not a prisoner here," Calonar assured him. "Despite the warning Cyras has given to Rogan, I won't hold you against your will. You're free to leave any time you wish. If you stay, consider yourself my guest."

"What if my wish is to kill you?" the young man asked, not sure if he still meant it.

Calonar smiled that warm smile of his again. He nodded towards Sarah, who had raised an eyebrow at that comment. "Then you should probably talk to Sarah here and the other Archaeknights, to say nothing of Rogan, Rashid, Remm, and just about everyone else in this city. They have a rather annoying habit of trying to keep me alive."

Showing obvious difficulty rising, Tomas helped the aging king to his feet without thinking. After the old man had stood, Tomas realized that Sarah had moved up behind him without making a sound, one hand a breath away from the shepherd's neck, the other resting on the hilt of one of the blades at the small of her back.

"Thank you, Tomas," Calonar said through heavy breath, nodding Sarah away.

When Calonar and Sarah reached the door, the archaeknight opened it for her king. Tomas suddenly asked him, "Are you really five hundred and forty years old?"

The old man smiled a soft smile again. "No," he replied, "I'm five hundred and forty-*four*. Of course, the only reason I know the exact number is because my wife and daughters insist on celebrating my birthday every year." This last he said with a gentle roll of his pearlescent eyes.

"How is it you've lived so long and only now show signs of...?" Tomas' voice trailed off.

"Infirmity?" Calonar laughed softly. "My wife and daughters fear it may be some form of sickness. Rashid thinks someone has managed to poison me."

"What do you think?"

Calonar paused for some time before finally answering. His eyes drifted out the balcony, towards his Northern Keep. "Well," he finally said, "no one really knows how long Halvans live; historically, my kind have been hunted and killed long before they could possibly die of old age. Perhaps this is just my natural life-span. Perhaps Time has finally gotten around to me." He shrugged then, seemingly indifferent to mortality. "Goodbye, Tomas. I'll see you again, after you've had your tour."

The old king made as though to leave but paused, looking back at Tomas. Finally close enough to see details with his clouding, yet still pearlescent eyes, Calonar took a long look at the golden rose that rested, as always, at the young man's neck. "Tomas, may I ask how you came to wear that pin?"

The shepherd's hand went to the ornament. "It was left to me by a very dear friend."

"No," Calonar sighed. "I mean to ask, how did Alexia pass?"

Tomas could not keep the surprise out of his voice. "You knew Alexia?"

The old king nodded slightly.

"A mob in Wignis attacked us" Tomas said in a choked voice, the emotion once more trying to force itself to the surface. "We fought them off; she tried to use her magic to save us. But she died a few days later."

Sadness passed over Calonar's face. His pearlescent eyes teared, and the old man turned to leave. "I see," he sighed.

Tomas was unsure why, but he felt an uncontrollable urge to ease his obvious grief. "Sir. If it's any comfort, it was peaceful, her last day. She died in a small grove of trees and was smiling to the last. She even sang me an old sylvai lullaby."

Calonar turned back to the shepherd, unshed tears glowing in his halvan eyes. "Thank you, Tomas. That does mean quite a bit to me."

"May I ask how you knew her?"

The old man thought a moment before replying. "When we speak again, Tomas. Then, I will tell you of her."

Chapter 10

Obviously in need of a guide, Tomas decided to wait until Mary returned to ask her. Hours passed, however, with no sign of her. His supper was delivered and retrieved and still Mary had not returned. The sun had long set and the sky darkened to full night and still she was absent. The moon and stars were long into their nocturnal dance and still no sign of his maid. Tomas was surprised to notice how increasingly worried he became. He used the bell-pull to summon a butler but was assured that, since Mary had been given leave by the King himself, the time was hers as she pleased. Finally, nearly at midnight, just minutes before the shepherd was about to demand help in organizing a search, Mary returned.

At first glance, Tomas feared some misfortune had befallen her. Mary's face was red and her body trembled with near-exhaustion. Seeing the young woman limping into the suite, her Northlands dress rumpled as if hastily thrown on, Tomas asked, "What happened?"

Mary curtsied, saying, "Forgive my lateness, my lord. I lost track of the time."

"Mary," Tomas said impatiently, "for God's sake, what happened? Are you hurt?"

"I failed to properly stretch, my lord," she replied tightly, limping towards her room and obviously fighting the discomfort. "I lost track of time during my rehearsal, and in my haste to return, I may have pulled a muscle."

Tomas rolled his eyes, throwing his hands in the air. "Why is everyone so desperate to please Calonar? He'd probably be angry at you for hurting yourself for something so trivial."

"My lord..." Mary objected.

"Look, take a hot bath, and then I'll do something about that leg."

"Oh, I'm fine my lord..."

"Go!" Tomas ordered, pointing towards the bathing room.

After a fairly quick bath, Mary returned to the study, her long hair damp and only a light robe covering her body.

"Sit," Tomas commanded.

Mary obediently sat in a deep chair. Tomas knelt in front of her, trying to ignore the fact that, once the woman raised her very shapely leg for Tomas to hold, the robe she was wearing parted, exposing smooth flesh nearly to the hip.

"So..." Tomas felt his temperature, among other things, rising quickly, so he tried to focus on his task of relieving the strain on Mary's calve. "What kind of dance style do you do?"

Mary's eyes were closed, her breathing deep. "I study ballet and religious expressive dance," she said softly.

"Baalay? What kind of dance is that?"

Mary half-opened her eyes, looking down that well developed leg to Tomas, who was so focused on his treatment of the troubled muscles he did not notice her scrutiny. "It's very new. Cardinal Tain talks about it every time he returns from Velaross; the lords there have commissioned several dance companies. Princess Kyla heard about it and attended a performance some years ago. She had a dancing master from Reme move to the Keep and begin teaching. Basically, ballet tells a story. Instead of talking, the people dance to convey their ideas."

Tomas, suddenly sensing Mary's observation, glanced up, his hands never leaving her leg. "Does that feel better?" he asked in a stuttering voice.

"Yes, but the muscles higher up are stiff."

"You've got that right," the young man muttered.

"What?" Mary asked.

"Nothing," Tomas said quickly.

As Tomas worked his hands up Mary's leg, the young woman's eyes fluttered closed. Her breathing deepened and she leaned back. Having been looking into Mary's eyes, Tomas' gaze drifted downward as he noticed that, because she'd leaned back, the front of her robe had opened scandalously wide.

"That sounds great," Tomas breathed. Tearing his eyes away from the front of Mary's robe, he met his eyes with hers again, and Tomas realized she had been watching him looking at her.

"When done properly, it's the most beautiful form of dance in the world," she said in a soft purr. The young woman drew a feather-light touch along Tomas' arm, encouraging him higher. "We perform each season. The King has even commissioned a new theatre, just for our company."

"Beautiful," Tomas echoed quietly, only hearing some of what she said. His hands, under Mary's guidance, slid further up her leg until they were brushing against her robe. The young woman's breathing quickened in response, and a warm flush spread across her face. "I was wondering," he said in a weak voice. "Calonar suggested I take a look around the city tomorrow. I really could use a guide, if you weren't too busy." Almost unconsciously, Mary leaned towards Tomas, making no effort to cover herself. By now his hands were moving beneath her robe, still probing with hungry fingers under her gentle, yet firm, guidance.

With less than a hands-breath between their faces, Mary and Tomas closed their eyes and opened their mouths. "I'd love to," she breathed into his mouth.

There was a thunderous pounding on the front doors of Tomas's suite. Mary and Tomas immediately returned to the reality of the situation and broke contact. As Tomas stumbled across the room to answer the door, tripping over a footstool, Mary quickly closed her robe and stood, making an effort to bring her hair under control.

Opening the door, Tomas had to take a step back. Standing in the hallway was Rogan. The shepherd was used to the knight standing tall, a veritable icon of heroic stamina. The man now standing before him was bent at the waist as though drained of all strength, his shoulders slumped under the weight of the thick wool robe he wore. Rogan's ragged face was pale and drawn, reminding Tomas of a warrior just returned from intense battle. The knight seemed to the shepherd to have somehow withered a bit since they last saw each other.

"What happened to you?" Tomas demanded.

"Kid, I wouldn't know where to start," Rogan replied, pushing his way into the room. Seeing Mary flushed and dressed only in a robe, her hair still wildly disheveled, the knight turned back to Tomas with a smirk on his face. "Am I interrupting?"

"No, not really, not at all," Tomas and Mary both replied, their voices overlapping each other.

"Excuse me, your Highness," Mary said, retreating to her rooms, in her confusion forgetting to curtsey.

"Did she hurt her leg?" Rogan asked.

"I hadn't noticed," Tomas lied. "What are you doing here?"

The knight flung himself into the chair Mary had been sitting in. "Needed some time to relax, and everyone else is either asleep or occupied."

"Nice to know I rate so high," Tomas said going to the pitcher of cider resting on its serving tray. "Want some?" he asked.

"Like some fresh blood, but that'll have to do," Rogan said sourly.

Handing the knight a cup, Tomas walked towards the balcony. "I thought you'd be with your wife," he said.

Rogan let out a breath explosively. "You know, I love my wife dearly, but there are times I wish she wasn't so damned..."

"Enthusiastic?"

Rogan grunted. After taking a long drink, the knight nodded in the general direction of Mary's room. "You and her turning into a thing, or is she just a distraction?"

Tomas opened the wood and glass doors leading to the balcony and the cool yet comfortable night. Stepping out, he leaned onto the stone rail. "I don't know," Tomas admitted. "She seems nice and I like her but... I don't know."

"If you like her, then what's the problem?" Rogan rose from his chair and joined the young man on the balcony, breathing in the cool night air and looking out at the city.

Tomas rubbed the back of his neck, saying, "Well, back home there's this girl."

"Ah," Rogan nodded sagely. "You in love with this girl?"

"I don't know."

"Committed to her? Make her any promises?"

"Well, we did sleep together."

"Not what I asked."

"Cecilia might have taken it for a commitment."

"Still not what I asked.

"No, not really. I just promised I'd come home someday."

"To her?"

"To everyone. I like Cecilia a lot, and we grew up together. Our parents even talked about betrothing us, but I don't think I'm in love with her."

"Sounds like you've already made up your mind," the knight noted, taking another drink.

Tomas shook his head. "But still, wouldn't it be wrong to... you know?"

"Kid, I think you need to straighten yourself out real quick," Rogan said, taking yet another long drink and holding the glass up for a refill.

"What do you mean?" he asked defensively. The young man took both cups back to the tray and refilled them.

"Look, you're starting in on a difficult and dangerous life," Rogan advised him after taking the cup. "That means a life of wandering and fighting and probable death. If you've found a girl who you like and who likes you, don't pass up a good thing."

"I heard you wouldn't sleep with Kyla for weeks during which she was literally throwing herself at you," Tomas said.

"That's different!" Rogan snapped. "Kyla was looking for a conquest, and dammit, I'm nobody's whore!"

"Did I touch a sore spot?" Tomas asked sweetly.

"Hey, I'm trying to help you, kid. If this girl likes you and you like her, then don't live for some childhood sweetheart you may never see again. If you want the girl back home, then go back home and don't lead the maid on. Either way, make up your mind. Life will rarely give you enough time to procrastinate."

"Hey," the young man said defensively, "she's the one making the passes."

"Oh, really? Like what?"

"Well... she keeps... smiling at me and being real... friendly."

"Oh, dear God in Heaven! She's being friendly!?! I say we stone the whore."

"Smartass," Tomas grumbled.

"Dumbass," the knight countered. "Look, I understand you grew up in Pelsemoria and they have a different way of doing things down there, but you're in the Northlands now, kid. People live differently up here."

"What do you mean?"

"Well, for one thing, the ladies up here don't usually go in for all that 'playing hard to get,' that girls in the south seem to do. Around these parts, if a woman wants a man, she usually just comes right out and stakes a claim, so to speak."

"Not a lot of humility in the north, is there?" the young man muttered.

"No time," the knight shrugged. "Winters up here are long and hard. Down south you may have time for all that courtly love nonsense poets and bards love to go on about, but up here we tend to live a little more grounded."

"That's not necessarily a good thing, you know."

"True. But then, who are you to judge?"

"That's been the question of the day," Tomas replied ruefully.

"Had a talk with the King, did you?" the knight guessed.

"Yeah. Things have sort of been put in perspective."

"He does that. So, what's next?"

"Calonar suggested I go into the city and have a look around. Mary said she'd be my guide."

"After that?"

Tomas looked up at the stars. The moon was out, shining free of any clouds. "That's sort of an involved question. I started out trying to find Cyras Darkholm so he could tell me how to stop the Black Duke from conquering all of Lanasia. Well, I found Cyras, and now I've learned the Black Duke doesn't even *want* to conquer Lanasia."

"Feeling a little deflated?" Rogan guessed.

The young man laughed. "You could say that. I had this image in my head of my whole quest. I was so wrapped up in how noble I was being and now..."

"You feel like somebody changed the ending of your story?" the knight guessed.

Tomas nodded.

"Got news for you kid; this isn't the end of your story. Your story has barely gotten started."

"I just don't know where to go from here. I guess I could go home, but I haven't really accomplished anything. If I went back now, wouldn't it be like giving up?"

The knight shrugged. "Guess that depends on what you wanted to accomplish," he replied. "The Black Duke isn't a threat to you or your home, so you could call it a win."

"Doesn't feel like one."

"Well, what do you want?"

"I really don't know. I just don't know what comes next."

"Hit that point a few times," Rogan admitted. "Usually, if you look around a bit, you can find a direction."

"What if I pick the wrong direction?"

"You fall off a cliff."

Tomas looked over at the knight and smiled. "I guess that means I should just start looking around then. I think I'll try to avoid the cliffs, though."

"Probably a good idea." Draining his cup, Rogan squared his shoulders. "Now, if you'll excuse me, I know what my particular direction is; my wife will only wait so long before she starts doing something... odd. Think about what I said, kid." With that, the knight left to rejoin his wife. Before closing the doors, Rogan stuck his head back in. "And remember what I said about procrastinating. You never have as much time as you think."

Chapter 11

Poets and artists have tired throughout history to quantify the town called Crossroads. Many have tried to establish some order to the chaos of the streets and people that seemingly exist only to breed crime and violence. A painter from two centuries ago, Nomar Eigenhard, made his interpretation of the town his masterpiece. Most critics agree that Nomar has been the only artist who has created a true representation of Crossroads. He did so by not painting a single straight line nor a single clear figure. Instead, the renowned artist blurred all the people and buildings together, giving them each a distinct image, and yet all together as a whole.

Most thieves and mercenaries agreed that navigating the alleys of Crossroads was impossible. For one thing, due to the temporary nature of the construction of most of the town, the alleys were constantly shifting. Only those few who made Crossroads their home and made a constant effort to lose themselves in the dark maze of dead-ends and twisted paths could say to have anything resembling a mastery of navigation within the borders of the town.

These facts screamed through Althaea's mind as she ran for her life through the various back alleyways, desperately seeking some means of escape. The former priestess had been living in Crossroads for many years, ever since her falling out with Prince Rogan of the Northern Keep. While many of her old friends among the Sisterhood of the Lady of Light thought she had gone mad to have settled in such a den of evil, were the truth be told, Althaea thought the town had more personality than any other she had ever visited.

The former priestess, occasional thief, and clandestine spy ducked under a tall horse, cutting the saddle strap in the process, and flew down yet another dark alley. The rider's oath and crash were followed by curses from the several men who had been following her, more than enough evidence to satisfy Althaea that her diversion had worked.

Damn Rashid anyway, she thought to herself. It was that smooth-talking son of an Umbral who convinced Althaea that skills like hers would have been wasted on any occupation other than as one of his agents. Just as soon as the spymaster had learned of her imminent departure from the Northern Keep, which was most likely ten seconds before the priestess had even thought of leaving, he had leapt at the opportunity to recruit her. Althaea shook her head as she ran, muttering dark curses to that suave man and his manipulations of her pride and broken heart. He had said such things to her, such wonderful half-truths that she could not help but think he was correct. He was one of only two people who had known of her unrequited love for Rogan, and he had used that knowledge as heartlessly as he could.

"Just take a little trip down to Crossroads for me." Rashid had smiled as he ran a light hand over her cheek and spoke those seductive words. Now, Althaea was a fully trained Sister of the Lady of Light; she knew the art of seduction. But Rashid's skills so surpassed any other's that it was a wonder he had not, as yet, tried to talk the King into giving the spymaster his own crown. Within moments, Rashid had Althaea so tightly wrapped around his finger that had he but asked, she would have gladly disrobed, satisfying his every deviant wish. She had been so eager for any man to love her after Rogan's harsh rejection; it took little persuasion on Rashid's part to twist Althaea to his will. Sneaking into Rogan's bed had not even been her idea. Kyla had convinced her the Prince would enjoy the company of two beautiful priestesses for the night. Althaea knew she could never win Rogan's heart away from Kyla, but she reasoned that if she could not have him to herself, at least she could have him partially.

And then the disaster. The Prince had not only rejected her, but had thrown her out of his bedchambers and forbade her from entering the castle again. Kyla had been abject in her apologies, of course, but the fact nevertheless remained that the only man who had ever laid claim to Althaea's heart had rejected her. It would have been impossible to risk seeing him again. Leaving the Keep was the only response she could think of that would not slowly kill her.

And then Rashid appeared as she packed, and he spoke words of flattery and kindness. Even more than that, Rashid was the first man she could ever remember who had actually spoken to her with respect. Lust was the reaction she most often encountered from the stupider sex. That was what had first attracted her to Rogan; he looked at her with kindness and courtesy. But it was Rashid who treated her with respect.

That devil stoked her ego to ridiculous heights, speaking of her agility, quick mind, and abilities at seduction. If only she was really as good as the spymaster had made her believe she was, then perhaps she would not be in such trouble now. The 'one, simple mission,' soon became two, then four, and so on. Before she realized just how well she had been manipulated, the spy was having the time of her life, reveling in the seedy life of a criminal.

Never could she remember a time when she had so enjoyed herself, manipulating mercenaries and thieves for information and passing that along to Rashid. After several years, she had easily earned enough through her pay from Rashid and the various criminal enterprises she had participated in to retire to some country chateau with a cluster of pretty, brainless men to live out her days in decadent pleasure.

Instead, she had remained in Crossroads, living a life of danger and intrigue... and a lot of fun. *Damn Rashid anyway*, she thought again, *for giving me a career I love*. He had known, that bastard; he had known that this life of excitement and mystery and manipulation was just as addictive as any substance one could purchase in the City of All Sins. Now here she was, being chased down the alleyways of Crossroads for finally asking one question too many.

The mercenary had not looked all that bright. He was just another adorable bundle of muscle that should have been good to pump for information, among other things. If only he had not had sense enough to tell his captain about her odd questions during their lovemaking. But talk he did, to both Althaea and his captain. The information ended up being more than worth the disappointing turn they had in bed; he was such a child in both heart and mind that she actually felt dirty afterwards, a rare occasion to be sure.

She had been warned against moving on information too soon. Move too soon, Rashid often warned, and you risk yourself and other agents. But if even half of what that foolish mercenary had moaned in her ear was true, then Althaea had felt it worth the risk of attempting contact with Esha immediately.

At the very least, she sniffed, that merc could have mentioned he was working for a Death Mage. That blasted spell-slinger blocked her communications and traced her location. Added to that, her "lover" had told the most dangerous man in the world about their conversations. Put together, Althaea had quickly found herself in the unenviable position of having to flee from an entire town full of heartless killers. And the single worst killer of them all.

Xaemus. Why in name of the Lady of Light did it have to be Xaemus? And since when did that Xeshlin monster take jobs leading mercenary armies? Even when she had spotted him in the Tavern, she had just assumed he was passing through, searching for whatever poor bastard he was hunting at the moment on behalf of his dead Dark Empress. Well now that poor bastard was her. Althaea was fairly certain she had never made the slightest remark about Kelinva; why would the dead queen of the Xeshlin's enforcer be so interested in her? Xaemus was supposed to be searching for the return of his Dark Empress. Why would he care about a mercenary army or the Northern Keep?

Well, she knew the answer to the most immediate of those questions. His beloved, dead, Dark Empress, or resurrected or soon-to-be-resurrected Dark Empress, had given him one new command:

Find the spy, Althaea, and stop her.

Well, she thought, *Xaemus may be the most feared hunter in the world. He may have never failed in a mission, and he may have a reputation for being the deadliest man in the world. He may serve and prey to that dead queen-bitch of the Xeshlin. But he's never tried to take on me.*

The spy turned one last corner, seeing her goal in sight: the shop of Gregorios the spice merchant. Only one person in Crossroads knew that Gregorios was in truth a deep cover agent of House Calonar trained by both Esha and Rashid to be the agency's method of rapid transportation and communication. His only duty in life was to provide a quick means of escape for an agent in trouble, which Althaea certainly felt she qualified as.

A thrill of hope surged through the spy's heart when she spotted the wizard walking in front of his shop towards a nearby horse. One shout and she would have one of the four most powerful archwizards in service to Esha at her side, sending her home. And she would go home, the spy decided. No more missions and no more danger. Just one shout and a quick debrief and it was off to her chateau, her peace, and her boys.

A needle struck Althaea in the side of her neck, sending a painful paralysis through her entire body. Not one hundred feet from help, the priestess fell to the street, immobile, as she saw from the corner of her eye two black leather boots step up to her. She tried again and again to scream out in terror as a gag was placed in her mouth and a rope was tied around her wrists and ankles. She could only blink by the time she was lifted off the ground and thrown over a powerful yet lean shoulder that was covered with a black leather cloak.

As her captor carried her deeper into the darkness of the alleys, Althaea was able to shed only one small tear.

II

Spring

Chapter 12

The morning broke clear and bright, and Tomas rose with the sun, eager for his tour of the Northern Keep, and more than eager to spend time with Mary. Although the young man still had not made up his mind about the current situation, he was sure that Mary's company was pleasant. Given all he had seen and experienced since his quest began, Tomas felt he deserved a little pleasant company.

While eating his breakfast, Tomas heard Mary moving in her room doing those mysterious things women must do to get ready. She had gotten his breakfast and served but had then excused herself to change, apparently arranging for another member of the castle staff to retrieve the meal once finished. The young man's impatience had grown to almost unbearable heights as he awaited his escort. He had dressed quickly in clothes Roland had been kind enough to provide, a red tunic in the southern style with Northland half-boots, then was forced to wait, and wait, and wait. Once Mary's door finally opened, Tomas realized that it had been well worth the wait.

Shortly after Mary had excused herself, there had been a knock on the door. Not wishing to inconvenience the maid, and still unused to having people do simple things for him, Tomas had answered before Mary had the chance. The young man had been shocked to see the beautiful Princess Kyla standing in the hallway. She had stood on her tiptoes and given a quick kiss on Tomas' cheek before entering Mary's bedroom. The shepherd had half-expected Kyla to perform some magic on his maid, but the sight greeting him was more than he could have conceived in his most fantastic dreams.

Mary was dressed in a very light green skirt that was loose about her legs, swirling in response to her slightest movement. The white blouse his young lady wore had long sleeves, leaving her slender forearms covered but still slightly visible through the thin material. Her bodice and short apron had detailed embroidery of long stems of red clover. Her long hair was tied into an elaborate braid that spilled over her shoulder, highlighted by the same white ribbon she usually wore in her hair. A thin lace collar adorned her graceful neck, from which hung a small golden pendant of a sitting cat. The collar of Mary's blouse dipped low, though not scandalously so, and a small golden charm, a sylvai glyph, rested in that bare space, as though luring the gaze. With only the slightest cosmetic on her face, Mary's significant beauty was amplified to exquisite perfection.

The young woman stood in the doorway, her hands clasped in front of her and her eyes shyly downcast. Princess Kyla stood behind her with a bright smile. "So how do I look?" Mary asked.

Tomas could only make strange monosyllable sounds in response. The maid blushed, greatly pleased at his reaction.

The Northern Keep was a bustling city filled with wonders that defied imagination. While Pelsemoria, in its greatness, stood as a beacon of Humanity's dominance over the world, with its palaces, monuments, and wide streets, the Keep seemed to go out of its way to blend in with the world around it. What would, in any other city, be a paved street, was here a cobblestone nature path, with trees and shrubs everywhere that would not impede travel. The angular wood and stone buildings, while possessing a graceful beauty in themselves with their shutters and thatched roofs, were highlighted by expansive gardens and wide, open windows.

With the Northlands winter well past, the days were pleasant and mild, with little threat of truly disruptive weather, only the occasional cleansing mist of spring rain. Everywhere Tomas looked were children playing, neighbors having pleasant conversation, and generally peaceful and easy labor. Pedestrians paused to give greetings to passersby while shopkeepers traded pleasantries with their friendly competitors. This was no den of evil.

Mary led the young man to the mercantile district, in the eastern quadrant of the Northern Keep. Their path wound past metal- and woodworks, clothiers, spice merchants, and all other imaginable offerings. Herein also were the largest of the city's marketplaces. Mary had insisted that, if Tomas was to learn of the Keep and its people, he could do so where every citizen interacted in their pursuit of economics. He was, of course, aware that her benevolence was only slightly marred by the fact that this trip allowed her to do some shopping, but Tomas really did not mind, so long as he was with Mary. Within these explosions of commerce, the shepherd was able to spot nearly every race and creed of Arayel. Human tradesmen from all over Lanasia bargained amiably with Sylvai craftsmen from their Vale and trappers from the surrounding Wood. Uldra smiths from the nearby mountains traded gruffly, but fairly, with Khepric researchers, no doubt visitors from the Endless Sands. Tramanese merchants offered their exotic goods with local shopkeepers. Even a handful of that most despised of races, the Halvan, walked amongst the other citizens of the Northern Keep with an easy manner and open friendliness. Wizards and merchants, knights and bards, all manner of men and women mingled freely.

"Is there any race that isn't welcome here?" he asked Mary as she led them into a small shop. "I don't think I've ever seen so many different types of people in one place at the same time when they're not trying to kill each other." Tomas marveled at the variety within. Row upon row of stoppered bottles lined the shelves. Some were of wood, others glass, and some even of metal, both precious and mundane. All, however, were intricately fashioned into trees, animals, stars, moons, and other designs. The fragrance of the shop made Tomas feel light-headed.

Mary spoke softly to the Sylvu merchant behind the center counter. He nodded, reaching into a small cupboard and retrieving something, which he presented to the maid. The young woman turned away, holding a small glass bottle filled with a golden liquid and fashioned into a tree in full bloom. "Well, the House Guard and City Watch are pretty firm with any violence." She nodded out the large front window towards a pair of blue and grey liveried soldiers walking by. The two men, both Human, wore chainmail with blue and grey surcoats, grey caps, and carried the Northlands poleaxes that seemed nearly a badge of office for the soldiers of House Calonar. The men nodded politely and stepped aside courteously for passersby, offering minimal intrusion to the bustle of commerce.

Mary handed a bundle of coins to the shopkeeper and, thanking him, turned to leave. Tomas looked over her shoulder as they exited the shop. "What is that?" he asked.

Mary stopped in the cobblestone street, nearly getting knocked over by Tomas in the process, so close he was following. Glancing over her shoulder with a smile, she leaned back against him when he was about to step away. "Afraid you'll lose me?" she asked sweetly.

Tomas blushed, though he did not break the contact. "Uh, no," he said, though needing to clear his throat first. "I was just wondering what was so special about that bottle. You paid a fair bit of silver for it, after all."

The maid opened the stopper and took a quick breath before hurriedly replacing it. "It's *Sa'va'iel*," she sighed.

"Which is?" he asked, absently running a hand along her arm. The material of the blouse, not wool or linen or any other material familiar to the shepherd, seemed like mist to his touch. As his fingers traced lines along Mary's arm, it seemed to Tomas as though he were touching, not her sleeve, but the soft flesh beneath.

"*Sa'va'iel* is a fragrance the Sylvai of the Vale make," Mary replied, leaning just slightly into Tomas' touch. "They say it's the essence of life and the source of new beginnings."

Tomas caressed Mary's other arm with his free hand, again marveling at how his fingers seemed to pass through the sleeve to make contact directly with the young woman. He leaned over slightly. "What does that mean?" he asked.

"It means," she purred, turning her head up to look into his eyes, "that a girl only wears it when she wants to start something, or when she wants to enjoy something."

"Can't she do both?" he asked, letting his eyes close.

"God, I hope so."

"Excuse me, miss," a slightly accented voice called from the perfume shop's front door.

Mary and Tomas straightened and stepped away from each other a small bit. "Yes?" the maid asked, looking flushed.

The shopkeeper handed Mary a few copper coins. "You forgot your change," he informed her.

The young woman smiled and accepted the tiny coins, depositing them in her purse. "Thank you," she said before turning to continue the tour.

Tomas, a little more clear-headed, caught up to Mary. "So..." he said, feeling more awkward than usual. "You said something about the House Guard and City Watch. Are they separate?"

Mary fell into step next to the shepherd. "Like the other noble Houses, House Calonar maintains a Guard. Since the fall of the Republic, the Calonar House Guard has expanded, becoming the army of the Northlands. Other cities like Drailia and Ironheartshaven have begun offering more recruits. But the Keep still maintains a separate force: the City Watch. The Guard is the military, they patrol the King's territory and enforce his laws. The Watch are responsible for the Keep itself."

Tomas glanced over at where a Sylva tailor was talking with an Uldra metalsmith. The two laughed and seemed to get along despite the legendary animosity of their races. "I just can't get over how everyone seems to get along here," he admitted. "If I didn't know better, I'd say there was some kind of spell at work."

Mary stopped and looked thoughtfully at Tomas. Finally, she took his hand a led him towards the center of town. "Where are we going now?" he asked.

"There's something I want you to see," she replied.

The maid led Tomas through several streets, bypassing shops and houses until finally it became clear they were headed to a beautiful, enormous fountain in the very center of the Northern Keep. Eight wide boulevards led away from the fountain, and the circle was a gathering of street performers, travelers, and townsfolk. Constructed entirely of marble, the fountain itself was an enormous, circular pool with a pillar in the center that rose at least a hundred feet. The column was intricately carved, formed into the five races of Lanasia: Human, Sylvai, Uldra, Khepri, and Halvan. All five figures had their arms raised, supporting a golden model of the world. The figures stood on a pedestal, just above where the water came spilling out into the pool. On the pedestal was engraving that said: "One world for us all, to share in peace."

"Cyras Darkholm and King Cylan conceived it," Mary said, "and the master artisan Remm Stonebearer designed it. The water flows from the river as a gift from the Sylvai, through plumbing built by the Uldra, and the marble came from the Khepri." She led Tomas around the fountain to a small marble podium that stood a few feet from the fountain. On the top of it was a golden plaque facing due south. Upon reaching the plaque, Mary said, "A very long time ago, the noblemen of the Republic challenged *Baron* Calonar's right to open his gates to non-Humans; he traveled all the way to Pelsemoria, stood before the Emperor and the entire Elector Council and said this." The young woman gestured to the plaque.

Tomas leaned in and read aloud the inscription. "To all those who fear change and hold to greed, bigotry, and hatred, I say this: for as long as I draw breath, and decent men fight for the good of others, my Keep will stand as a beacon of hope. Anyone, regardless of blood, color, god, or belief may freely enter my gates, and together we will forevermore stand against the darkness. The Northern Keep will accept the oppressed, enslaved, and helpless, providing them the same chance at happiness every man, woman, and child has a right to, and will defend these people always."

Tomas took a step back, his heart racing and his ears filled with the king's words. "This is pretty much an open declaration of war," the young man said.

Mary sighed, "Many took it as such. The Keep has been attacked more times than anyone but the King himself can remember. Each time we were attacked, the Republic would look the other way. The warlords of Lanasia say King Cylan only wants to build an empire with himself as emperor. In truth, his Majesty has no interest in ruling."

"Why does he do it?"

"Different people have different ideas. I think he does it because he can't sit by and let people suffer when he knows he could do something about it."

Chapter 13

"So where to now?" Tomas asked as Mary took his hand, leading him again through the maze of streets. They left the city center and followed the boulevard stretching southwest, away from the mercantile district. This was, the shepherd realized, the same section of the city housing the Adamic church.

The maid glanced back at him and smiled. "Now that you've seen how all the races live in peace here, it's time for you to see the gods do it, too."

"The gods?" But Mary offered no further explanation as she cheerfully led the young shepherd along.

Mary eventually stopped, standing next to Tomas, hands still interlocked, in front of a building that looked to Tomas as if it would better belong in the ancient Sylvai Empire. There were no walls the young man could see. Instead, the roof was held up by rows of columns. The building rose at least fifty feet above street level, with no one staircase offering access to the top. Instead, the entire structure was sloped and tiered, offering easy steps from any direction to the open building above. Mary led Tomas up these steps, stopping at the top and allowing her charge to see inside.

Past the columns was what appeared to be something akin to the public baths that had been the height of fashion generations ago, before the influence of Velaross ended them. An open, pleasant looking patio spread across the place, with large benches, several tables and plants, and a group of musicians playing soft melodies on pipes and strings. In the center was a large pool, whose crystal-clear water was provided by a large fountain in its center that sprayed gently down, allowing bathers to take advantage without discomfort. Looking closer, Tomas could see that the fountain was, in fact, a sculpture, one of a beautiful young woman endlessly pouring water from an ornate chalice. Even from the steps, the young shepherd could feel the gentle, soothing warmth of the bath competing with the comforting warmth of the springtime air. Everywhere Tomas looked, people conversed, received massages, swam and bathed, or simply lay and enjoyed the peaceful serenity of the place on cushioned divans.

The open-air building and the people within were tended to by a group of women, all dressed in one-piece silken skirts that stopped at mid-thigh and left the arms, backs, and most of the shoulders bare. Thin cords were tied about the women's waists, resting on one hip and drifting down along a leg. Each woman had her long hair tied in a variety of braids in the Northland style. Despite how busy they seemed to be, the women moved about with an air of serenity, seeing to the needs of their patrons without fuss. Everyone received whatever care they desired or needed with a peaceful smile, a friendly hug, and bright conversation.

"What is this place?" Tomas asked as he gazed about.

Mary seemed to be doing her very best to contain laughter. "Well, I'm sure you've been told stories about the black magic of Princess Kyla and her sinister priestesses."

Tomas nodded. "Yeah, the cult of the Pleasure Goddess."

Again the maid seemed just at the point of breaking into laughter. "Well," she said, trying to maintain control. "She is really *is* a high priestess, but they call themselves the Sisters of the Lady of Light, and the Princess is called the Sister Superior. Though I suppose her goddess *would* be considered evil by the Inquisition."

"Mary, what are you getting at?" Tomas asked, still looking about.

The young woman gestured to the entire building. "Tomas, welcome to the Temple of the Lady of Light."

"This is a temple!?!"

Mary nodded. "To properly worship their goddess, the Sisters of the Lady of Light must help to spread happiness to those around them. Believe it or not, all these priestesses are currently at services."

"How could anyone consider *this* a religion?" the young man demanded.

Mary shrugged. "Well, why don't we ask?"

"Like who, Kyla?"

The maid motioned for Tomas to follow and made her way through the temple to a very old man receiving a massage from one of the priestesses, this one dressed in a vibrant purple skirt with a bright red cord tied about her waist. She worked diligently, yet delicately, to relieve the obvious suffering from her elderly patient. Lightly tapping the old man on the shoulder, Mary whispered into his ear. He nodded and sat up, using a towel to cover himself with the help of the purple-clad priestess. "Tomas Fidelis," Mary introduced, "I believe you've already met Cardinal Alton Tain."

"Cardinal?" Tomas asked, looking with obvious disbelief. The ancient priest made no effort to hide his emaciated body, nor the extensive scars it held. Angry lines of white and purple crossed his back, torso, and stomach. Tomas noted these marks had been partially hidden by the scented oil the purple-clad priestess had been rubbing into the Cardinal, though the still ran deep. The scars spoke of suffering, of a rage taken out on the body of this withered holy man. They spoke of a pain Tomas could not imagine.

"What?" the holy man asked. He then looked down and nodded gently. "Ah, I sometimes forget." He glanced at the purple-clad priestess, who wordlessly wrapped a great robe dyed a soft pink around the Cardinal's drooping shoulders. "Thank you, child," he whispered to her, and she smiled in return. The ancient priest then looked back to Tomas and Mary. "I apologize," he said. "I forget how jarring my scars can be to those who have not seen such."

"How," Tomas started to ask, but then bit his tongue. To infringe on what had to be a painful memory, a painful reality, to the clergyman was unthinkable.

Cardinal Tain smiled softly again. "It's alright, Tomas. The story is well-known here in the Northlands. Ten years ago, I was in service to House Calonar as Bishop of the Northern Keep. We had traveled to Pelsemoria for a meeting of the Elector Council. The King's enemies captured me, hoping to ransom me back, or to extract the secrets of House Calonar, or perhaps just to vent their hatred." He shrugged slightly. "I know not. I was in their custody for days," his weak eyes drifted towards the past. "I'm not sure how long, truthfully. I lost track of time as they abused my flesh." He straightened a bit and sighed. "Eventually, Rogan and his team rescued me and brought me home. The Sisters here," he smiled again at the purple-clad priestess, "have worked tirelessly ever since to ease my wounds."

The young shepherd shook his head. "Forgive me, it was just shocking to see a leader of the Church in such a place as this."

The old priest laughed again. "Shocking that a Cardinal of the Church would ever set foot in a pagan temple? Let alone the vile house of the Pleasure Cult?"

Tomas shrugged and nodded.

Again, Cardinal Tain laughed. It was an infectious laugh that soon had Tomas feeling foolish. "I'll tell you what, Tomas," he said. "Why don't you lie down and let the girls try to ease your own pain, be it physical or otherwise."

The young man took a step back. "Thank you, but I'd rather not. This sort of 'worship' is really not for me."

"'Your place is not to judge,' Tomas," the Cardinal told him, quoting the Teachings, "'it is to learn and accept.' The sisters here go out of their way to try and make life better for everyone around them. They sing and dance, they bring water to workmen, tend to the mourning or the hopeless. The girls here even take care of children for those families in which both parents must work."

"They allow children here!?!" Tomas sputtered.

The Cardinal sighed and shook his head. "Not up here. There are chambers downstairs. The sisters play games with the children and tell them stories. They teach arithmetic and reading, as well as useful skills like cooking, swimming, and sewing."

Mary walked up to stand beside Tomas. "I did mention that House Calonar offers free schooling to the children of the Northlands," she reminded him.

Just as Tomas was about to launch a retort, Cardinal Tain raised his frail hand. "I know, I know. You've heard about the kinds of things that happen in these temples. You've been preached to about all the evils of the Pleasure Cult and its succubus-priestesses. Well, let me assure you, if there was an orgy going on, do you really think I would be here? Of course not."

Tain took the hand of the purple-clad priestess. "The ladies who serve in this temple believe in living for the sake of others," the ancient priest continued. "They never try to push their beliefs on others, and they never ask for any donations. Their beliefs work for them, so who are we to judge?"

"But aren't you sworn, as a priest of the Church, to try and bring all people to the one true faith?" Tomas demanded.

"Actually Tomas, the Teachings say to spread the word of our religion, to teach and live a good example, but fundamentally to give people a choice," Tain corrected. "Conversion by force was a commandment of the Inquisition, not our Holy Mother. It was the Inquisition that was so intolerant of other beliefs, so insistent that the Church crush all non-believers." He looked sternly at Tomas. "It was also, incidentally, the Inquisition that captured and... abused me," this last was said with surprising heat.

The holy man coughed slightly, losing his breath for a moment. The purple-clad priestess poured a small glass of berry wine and aided Cardinal Tain in drinking, placing her other hand on his bare chest and whispering something. In a few moments, the old man was breathing easier. "I was not unlike how you are now when I was first assigned to this city," he continued. "After seeing this place, I asked the Lords Cardinal what I should do here, and the answer was always the same. I should follow my heart and the guidance of God. I should listen to the Teachings and my heart. The mission of our Holy Mother since the beginning has been to spread the word of God to all the peoples of Arayel. But in the end, the decision must be theirs. Remember that the core belief of the Teachings is that God gave us free will. Our Lord left the choice to us. Why should the Church act differently?

"Besides, Tomas, don't you think God would approve of a place that goes out of its way to help people, to ease the hardships of life?"

"I still say there's something wrong with you getting a massage from a priestess of this place," the young man insisted.

"Is it because I'm of the Cloth or because I'm old and ugly?"

"... Honestly?"

The Cardinal laughed again. "Well, as far as the old and ugly, that's your problem. No one here has a problem with me." The old clergyman glanced back at the dark-haired, purple-clad priestess tending him. "Do you, Medaka?"

The priestess smiled softly. "Well, I keep telling you to watch your diet."

"Traitor," he grumbled in reply. "As far as the clergy thing, and I have to be blunt here Tomas, which one of us do you think is best qualified to make morality calls based on the Teachings?"

"Are you saying this place is alright because you say so?"

"No," the Cardinal chuckled, "but that's not a bad rationale. What I'm saying is that I have no fear for the souls of women who live only to serve their community with no thought of reward."

Tomas was still shaking his head as he and Mary left the temple. "Now what?" she asked.

The shepherd lowered his head and kicked absently at a loose cobblestone. "I don't mean to…," he said. "I guess I just can't… I dunno, it's just that… It's just so… different."

Mary put her hand on Tomas' chin and raised his eyes to meet hers. "The biggest problem people have is that they never give something different a chance. They just automatically assume that, if it's different, it must be bad."

"Are you telling me to stop being so judgmental?" he asked.

The maid dropped her hand and put both on her hips. "I'm not telling you anything. I'm just asking. Could you please stop seeing only the bad in everything and try to start seeing some of the good? Believe it or not, there is a lot of good to be found here."

Tomas nodded, heaving a deep breath. "No promises," he said, "but, I'll try."

Mary smiled. "That's all I ask. Don't worry, though; the next stop should be easy for you to see some good."

"What's the next stop?"

"The Temple of the Harvest Mother."

Tomas stood outside the building and stared. "It's a hospital," he stated flatly.

Mary rolled her eyes. "I told you. It's a temple."

"There are sick people inside who they're trying to be cured. It's a hospital."

"It's a temple."

"Right there! That guy! He's hurt. He's bleeding all over the place, and he's going inside to get fixed up. It has to be a hospital."

"Oh, for God's sake!" she fumed. "What happened to being open-minded!?!"

"Hey, I'm being open-minded, but I know a hospital when I see one and *that* is a hospital."

Mary shook her head and grabbed Tomas by the arm, half-dragging him into the temple that greatly resembled a hospital. Immediately upon entrance, a young woman, only perhaps fifteen, approached and bowed to them, placing both hands over her heart. Her face was unadorned by cosmetics or jewelry and framed by the hood of the simple, undyed wool robe she wore. The robe had a yellow shock of wheat embroidered over the heart and a simple white linen sash tied around the waist. The young woman smiled and hugged Mary warmly.

Breaking their embrace, Mary turned and gestured towards Tomas. "Ilse," she said, "this is Tomas. He just arrived from Pelsemoria."

Ilse bowed again to the young man. "I am honored to meet you, sir." She pulled back the hood of her cleric's robe, revealing long blonde hair.

"Tomas," Mary said, "this is Ilse. She's been my best friend ever since I moved to the Keep."

"Hello," the shepherd said, nodding.

Mary turned back to her friend when Ilse whispered in her ear. The maid giggled and shook her head. "No," she said. "Not yet."

"Well, can I?" Ilse asked with a twinkle in her dark eyes. In response, Mary punched her friend in the arm.

Ilse clasped her hands in front of her waist. "Welcome to the Temple of the Harvest Mother, Tomas," she said very softly, once again bowing.

"Are you a priestess?" he asked.

"No; at least not yet." The young woman placed a hand lightly on the white sash tied around her slender waist. "We acolytes wear the white of purity," she explained. "Once our training is complete, we wear the green of growth."

"Why the color coding?" Tomas asked.

Ilse turned and gestured for them to follow as she led a tour of her temple. "Just as the leaves of a tree change through the year, we change our coloring. White for the purity of beginnings, green for the growth of the student, red for the maturity of life, and amber for the ripeness of completion."

"So as you get promoted, you wear different colored sashes?"

The acolyte led them into the main chamber of the first floor, which was open and domed. At the top of the ceiling was an opening that let the light of the outdoors inside. Set in the center of the wood floor was a granite statue of a mature woman in a Northlands dress and holding in one hand a shock of wheat, a lamb in the other. As soon as they entered, Ilse clasped her hands over her heart and bowed deeply towards the statue. Rising, she smiled back at Mary and Tomas. "Our Mistress," she explained. "The goddess of all things living and growing, the Harvest Mother."

"Is that what she really looks like?" Tomas asked, looking closely at the statue's face as they passed.

"I would not know," Ilse replied quietly. "Only a few have been blessed with visions of her."

"Who carved the statue?" he asked, noting the flawless work.

"The likeness of our Lady was a gift from his Majesty after this temple was completed."

"Is Calonar a follower of the Harvest Mother?"

"The Queen is our High Priestess."

"Then the statue was really for his wife."

Ilse shook her head. "The Queen knew nothing of the gift until it was shown to the entire temple. His Majesty was clear that it was a gift for us all, not just his wife. Although," the acolyte giggled, "rumor is the Queen was *very* appreciative that night. On behalf of the Temple, of course."

"Ilse!" Mary gasped, to which the acolyte giggled yet again.

Tomas stopped just as they were about to enter one of the many doors that lined the walls of the central room. "Wait," he said, a thought occurring to him. "His wife is High Priestess of the Harvest Mother, and his daughter is High Priestess of the Pleasure... or Sister Superior of the Lady of Light. Is that coincidence or was the price of these temples being allowed into his city their placement?"

Mary laughed. "Actually, the Queen was a priestess of this religion for as long as anyone knows, long before House Calonar became noble again. The temple of the Harvest Mother has been a part of this community ever since it was known as Berend. Even before Nora Calonar was appointed High Priestess, there was never a time when this temple was not a part of the city."

"What about Kyla?"

"The Sisters of the Lady of Light petitioned his Majesty for permission to build their temple nearly a century ago, long before the Princess' birth. Although the King was hesitant, the Queen supported their request and they were allowed in. Very nearly from birth, Princess Kyla has shown an amazing proficiency in the traditions of the Sisterhood."

"There are even some rumors that she was Fated to hold the position," Ilse noted. "The Sisters of the Lady of Light saw the Princess as their chance to reinvigorate their religion, to finally move past the corruption of Kelinva. From what I understand, no woman in history has ever progressed to the position of Sister Superior so quickly."

"And her advancement had nothing to do with Calonar allowing the priestesses to build their temple?" Tomas asked suspiciously.

Mary sighed. "Remember," she murmured. "Open-minded."

"Sorry."

The maid shook her head. "There is the chance that Kyla's position is the result of some secret deal, but you've met the Princess. Is there any doubt in your mind that she wields more power than any other Sister, that she has the blessing of the Lady of Light?"

"She's got something," Tomas conceded, remembering the feelings that flood over the young man's soul whenever he was in close proximity to the princess. Noting Mary's narrowed eyes, he moved past the memory. "It was something, but it could have been faked. I wasn't all that impressed."

Mary snorted.

Ilse smiled knowingly and led the two into a long series of hallways that held various men and women who had an assortment of injuries.

"I told you this was a hospital!" Tomas noted in triumph.

Both young women rolled their eyes.

Tomas looked on as a priest, dressed in another undyed robe but with a green sash, applied a clean bandage to a woman's wounded arm. Turning back to where Ilse and Mary stood, he nodded back to the priest. "I thought the clerics of the old religions had magic," he asked with a furrowed brow. "Why don't you just use your power to heal everyone?"

Ilse walked up beside the priest and nodded a greeting. The man nodded back before applying a strange mixture to the bandage. "It would be wasteful," Ilse explained.

"I don't understand."

Mary walked across to the opposite side of the bed the wounded woman was lying on. "One of the tenants of this temple is that a person must never ask their goddess to do something they are capable of doing for themselves. So, the priests and priestesses never use their powers unless absolutely necessary."

"What's the point of having magic if you can't use it?" the young man demanded.

Ilse put a hand on the woman's brow and smiled. The woman looked up and returned the smile. "The gods did not create us so that they could do everything for us," she explained. "It's up mortals to help each other and work our way through life. The power our Mistress has given us is used, but only when it must be, when there is no other alternative, or in times of great need. We would never think to impose on our Mother more than was necessary. To do otherwise would be to abuse Her love of us."

"Would you ask your mother to do everything for you, Tomas?" Mary asked.

"Of course not," he replied.

"That's how we think of it." Ilse looked back up at him. "Our Mistress is the mother of us all. We use Her gifts when we must, but for the most part we try to do for ourselves."

Ilse led Tomas and Mary through the remainder of the temple, through the wards for the injured and the sick, ending the trip in a large room filled with children on the second floor. There were toys scattered throughout the room and scenes from history and popular fiction painted along the walls, each image comically distorted for the children.

Many of the beds were filled, far more than Tomas expected. Although the clergy of the Harvest Mother were there, Tomas was surprised to notice there were also sisters of the Lady of Light as well, each still clad in the short skirts the young man had seen in their own temple. Noting his surprise, Mary smiled. "I told you," she whispered in his ear. "The priestesses include children in their efforts to bring happiness to everyone."

Tomas turned his face to ask her another question, but he had not realized she had leaned so close to speak. His lips passed ever so lightly across hers. A shock greater than all the lightning of a savage ocean storm coursed through their bodies in that eternal instant when their lips met. Tomas felt as though he were breathing in Mary's soul, and she his. Their hearts thundered, crashing against their chests to try and reach one another. Their widened eyes were evidence of their surprise. They stood frozen, locked in the endless tides crashing back forth. Thought was swept away, their faces as close as possible while only touching in that one tiny, infinitely great location. An impossible closeness separated them, if only they could muster the will to close that aching, intimate chasm.

Ilse cleared her throat, bringing them both back from that wonderous storm they both so eagerly wished to experience. Only the snickering laughs of nearby children was enough to separate them. With terrific hesitation, an almost painful tension that threatened eternal heartache, Tomas and Mary each took a step back from one another, both blushing and finding themselves unable to regain eye contact. Eventually finding his voice, Tomas recalled the question he had originally meant to ask. "So, what do the priestesses do for the children?"

Mary looked about the large room, her face still burning. "Well," she said somewhat breathlessly, "mostly they put on small magic shows or play games." The maid struggled against a writhing sensation deep and low, as though some predator cat, long starving, had scented prey.

"The children also enjoy stories," Ilse added, doing a pitifully-poor job of hiding her mirth.

Tomas walked towards one child, a small boy who had no hair and whose entire body shook with minor spasms. "What's wrong?" he asked quietly.

Ilse and Mary joined the shepherd. The acolyte shook her head and sighed. "We don't know. Some kind of disease is causing them to slowly lose control of their bodies The treatments won't work, and our prayers can't help him."

Tomas looked up and down the row of beds, most of which had other young children with the same illness. "Is it some kind of pestilence?" he asked. "Something that only affects children?"

A sister of the Lady of Light, an older woman with short brown hair touched with gray at the temples, approached the two. "None of our most wise and powerful can discern," she answered softly. "Over the last few months, more and more children have succumbed to this disease. All our efforts to cure it, or at the very least stop the spread of it, have failed."

"And it only affects children?" Mary asked.

Ilse nodded. "Only children of less than ten years have shown signs of illness."

"You keep talking like it's a disease," Tomas noted.

"What else could it be?" the elder sister of the Lady of Light asked. "There is no sign of injury, no evidence of attack, no sense of curse."

"What about poison?" the shepherd asked.

"Who in God's name would poison children?" Mary demanded.

"Someone who wanted to cripple a city."

Ilse and Mary looked at him with confused expressions. The young man shrugged. "It's been done before," he informed them. "Before the horde invaded Velaross during the Plague of Walking Death, the rogue clerics who controlled the dead infected the children of the Holy City with a horrible sickness. The city defenders were so concerned for them they gave little thought to their duties. When the dead army attacked, the Holy City fell in less than a day."

Ilse and Mary were quiet for a moment, exchanging looks of concern with the elder sister of the Lady of Light. Finally, Ilse turned to the elder sister. "Hannah," she said quietly, "has anyone tried to counter possible toxins in the children?"

"No," Hannah replied. "I think perhaps I should speak with Aired about this." The sister turned and walked out of the large room.

A weak voice drifted up towards where Tomas and Mary stood. "Did those people really make all the children sick?"

The couple turned and saw to their dismay that the young boy Tomas had originally noticed had overheard every word of their conversation. Exchanging a quick glance, Tomas and Mary sat on opposite sides of the child's bed. The shepherd shrugged. "Yes," he told the sick boy. "The siblings Leria and Lar Nenic made all the children of the Holy City very sick before they had their dead army attack."

"Did the children die?" a little girl on the next bed asked in a weak voice.

"No," Tomas replied. "The Army of the Golden Flame defeated the dead horde, and the Heroes of Fate defeated the rogue clerics. All the sick children were cured by the magic of the priest Mortimus Dominus Eugenius."

Another boy, further down than the little girl, sat up in his bed. "I heard the King was one of the Heroes of Fate," he said. "Did he fight the bad clerics?"

Mary smiled and nodded. "King Cylan was with the Heroes of Fate at the Siege of Velaross and helped them fight the monsters."

The boy lying on the bed the two sat on lifted his head a little and looked at Tomas. "Wasn't that where the King first fought Ravana?" he asked.

"According to the stories," Tomas replied, "just as the Heroes of Fate entered the Holy City, even as the Army of the Golden Flame was approaching Velaross' walls, Ravana attacked them from above, as always in her favored form of a great red dragon. The battle between the Heroes and the wyrm could be seen from miles away. Some of the men in the army later wrote about what they saw. They said the spells cast by the wizard Tienel Greysoul and the arrows fired by the Sylvu Walker, Khaine would bounce off the Ravana's scales, like pebbles thrown at an angry Uldra."

"My daddy told me that Tienel was a bad man," yet another little girl said as she walked up and sat next to Mary.

"He became bad," the maid replied. "He started as one of the Heroes of Fate, but eventually betrayed them. His thirst for knowledge and power corrupted him."

"If he was one of the Heroes," another child asked, "why did Prince Rogan have to fight him?"

Tomas glanced quizzically at Mary, who shrugged. "Tienel heard Baroness Aebreanna Tressalon had a very powerful artifact, a magical device the Greysoul wanted. He attacked the Keep not even ten years ago and kidnapped the Baroness. The Prince took his friend Beraht and fought the Greysoul, rescuing Baroness Tressalon."

"How did the Heroes of Fate beat Ravana?"

And on it went. For hours the children gathered around Tomas and Mary, demanding story after story. Mary told the tales of the Heroes of Fate and the famous people of the Northern Keep, Tomas told those of the Republic and ancient history. It seemed to the young man that the children, despite the sickness affecting so many of them, had an insatiable thirst for stories. The young man did not mind their questions, though, since his own passion for history was very nearly as great as theirs, and he really did not mind retelling the stories he loved so much.

Mary often caught herself staring at Tomas as he told yet another tale from centuries past, children gathered around him and staring at the shepherd with rapt attention. As she looked, she noted an odd feeling, one that was unfamiliar but not unwelcome. This new feeling competed with that hunger, that thrashing thirst deep inside her. They seemed to struggle against one another until, after a while, they merged. She stared at Tomas and felt...

Despite his well-known prejudices against the legends of House Calonar, the young man never let his own feelings color the stories he told. It even seemed to Mary that, as time passed and Tomas realized just how much the children loved the stories about their king, he even began telling them the stories he claimed not to believe.

It was with some regret when Mary realized the sun was dipping low on the horizon. A whispered conversation with Ilse told the maid they needed to leave. Mary stood and crossed around the bed upon which Tomas still sat, being careful not to disturb those few children who had already fallen asleep. Laying a hand lightly on his shoulder, she leaned in close to whisper in his ear. "They need to eat and rest. We should be going."

Tomas nodded. "Well," he told his audience, "I guess we have to get going."

"You can't!" many of the children insisted.

"You haven't told us how Prince Rogan brought the town back from the land of shadows!"

"And we want to hear more about Sir Talius!"

"And Ravana!"

"And the Uldra Uprising!"

Tomas held up his hands, trying to get a word in edge wise. Mary smiled and leaned over his shoulder. "I promise I'll make him come back," she promised. "But he needs more stories."

As the maid leaned over him, her hand lingering on his shoulder, a thrill shot through Tomas' body. Her soft fragrance filled his soul. The warm radiance of her skin enveloped his heart. Somewhat hesitantly, the young man took Mary's hand in his and stood. The young lady made no effort to free her hand from his, instead leading Tomas slowly out of the room, fending off the children with promises to return.

Chapter 14

The next day, Tomas and Mary again went out to explore the Northern Keep. The young couple often walked with hands clasped, rarely finding a need to separate. The young woman led her charge through the wide streets of the city, pointing out the bustle of the people and the delights to be found in the capital of House Calonar.

As the couple walked away from the castle and into the city-proper, Tomas noticed an addition to the urban chaos of the previous day. He stopped in the street and watched. Three Uldra were directing a large team of Human workmen. They were digging a long and narrow, but surprisingly deep trench, into the side of the northern boulevard. One of the Uldra, older than the rest and wearing a great sash of blue and grey across his massive chest, was moving from shop to shop, apologizing for the disruption to their business. The Uldra seemed to offer money to the shopkeeps, quelling most objections nearly before they were made.

"What's happening here?" Tomas asked.

Mary stood beside him and watched. "I think this is that new light system we've heard about."

"Light system?"

The maid shrugged. "The plan was announced before winter. Remm Stonebearer had returned from Oneld, from a visit with the Khepri. He had plans for some new system that he's installing in the city. Something about lighting the streets at night."

"Magic?"

Mary shook her head. "None of the new Uldra inventions use magic."

Once again, the maid found it necessary for Tomas to tour the marketplaces of the Northern Keep's mercantile district, this time exploring those shops and markets that offered more luxurious items. This area was just to the northeast of the city center, as vicinity to the great fountain and statue seemed to be a marker of status among the city's merchants. Mary argued that the community of commerce was the perfect place to learn of its people. Her pious explanations came up short, though, as the community of commerce she was so insistent Tomas experience comprised dressmakers, perfumeries, cosmetic dealers, and other purveyors of feminine delights. When the various merchants and shopkeepers learned Mary was an employee of the castle, they invariably insisted she sample their wares, asking only that she speak of the quality to others who dwelled with the members of House Calonar. Mary led her charge through a morning filled with fabrics and fragrances, of dyes and delicate pastries. She expressed joy at each new discovery, despite the fact she lacked the funds to purchase any of the rich and exotic items.

"What's the point?" Tomas finally asked as they stood in an Uldra gemsmith's shop.

Mary was examining a series of adornments, each made of the finest precious stones extracted from Ulheim, or so the shopkeeper claimed. "Point of what?" she asked distractedly.

The shepherd leaned in to look over her shoulder. A particular set of earrings had drawn Mary's rapt attention. They were smaller than most of the adornments the Uldra had to offer. Golden pins flowed down and around emeralds fashioned into teardrops. The light caught on the gemstones, sparking as the young woman held them up to a lantern. The emeralds were so flawless, so perfectly set within the gold that they appeared to be green water, like drops from some the divine pool of a forest glade.

"Why look if you can't buy?" Tomas asked.

The Uldra, who had been indulging Mary's inspection of so many of his creations, stiffened, the towering mass of hair and muscle leaning down to gently, but firmly, reclaim the earrings from the not-customer. "Sylvai offer free samples," he said in a voice as unforgiving as mountain ice. He replaced the jewelry in their case. "Uldra do not," he said, closing the box with finality. After that, the young couple was invited to leave.

"Thanks a lot," Mary grumbled, leading Tomas to the next stop.

As they explored in the mid-morning hours, Mary ultimately tired of her not-purchasing and led Tomas back to the temple of the Harvest Mother. On this day, however, the young woman only allowed her charge to tell his stories to the sick children until lunch, after which she took him to a nearby restaurant for their own midday meal.

The eatery was outdoors, along the edge of the city center with an open view of the constant travel through the area. A cluster of tables were enclosed by a low shrubbery, tall enough only to conceal the patrons' legs. Only the kitchen was inside a nearby building. Trees spaced through the dining area provided plenty of cover from the warm spring sun and the odd misty shower, and the tables and chairs were all white wood which the proprietor, a fat Sylvu of advanced years and fatherly bearing, assured everyone who entered was from trees that had died naturally.

"I've never eaten Sylvai food before," the young man confessed. "What should I get?"

Mary put her chin on her hand. "Do you trust me?" she asked mischievously.

"Of course," he replied without hesitation.

A strange danced through Mary's eyes for just a moment. She smiled and signaled to the proprietor, who hurried over despite his girth.

Speaking in the sylvai tongue, Mary made an order. Her use of the complex language came as something of a surprise to Tomas. The young man stared at his guide in wonder as she completed their order.

"*Y'al'eth,*" the old Sylvu replied once Mary had finished before switching to accented Velish. "Excellent choices. And because you speak our tongue so well, I shall even add a bottle of *Way'et'ay'nas'a.* Nothing less for two young lovers."

"Oh, we're not..."

The Sylvu held up a hand, halting Mary's objection. "Some things, young one, you should not question," he insisted. "Never question an Uldra in a drinking contest. Never question a wizard in a library. Never question a dragon at dinnertime. And most importantly, never question an old Sylvu in matters of the heart." Without another word, the portly restaurateur left to prepare their order. Tomas and Mary found themselves trapped in an awkward silence with his departure, both embarrassed with the old man's assessment.

"So," Tomas finally said, "you speak sylvai?"

Mary nodded. "It's offered in most schools here in the Northlands. They don't teach Sylvai in the south?"

The shepherd tilted his head. "It's offered, but not very many took the lessons. Sylvai are…" he lowered his head, feeling a sudden rush of shame.

The maid nodded again. "The Republic didn't treat the Sylvai very well."

Tomas snorted. "Or any non-Human, really. I actually spent a few years learning Uldric, the language of the mountain clans, but sylvai was just too… much."

Mary smiled. "It can be complicated. There's a way of thinking to the Sylvai. They blend a lot of ideas together, emphasizing the feelings of the speaker, rather than the definitions of the words."

"So, what did you order? Or would the question be, what were you feeling when you ordered?"

Mary nibbled at a strawberry she plucked from the fruit basket set at the center of their small table. "A little bit of everything," she replied. "I really don't know what most of it is, but I do know it's delicious."

"If you like it, I'm sure it'll be great." Tomas meant to stretch his legs out under the table, but he accidentally brushed his left foot against Mary's. Even through the thick leather of his half-boot, the young man felt a shock at the contact. Before he could apologize and pull his leg back, he felt the young woman lightly brush her own foot against his leg. Tomas could not tell if he was feeling the brocade fabric of Mary's new half-shoes, purchased the day before, or her flesh itself, but still her touch brought heat to his face and quickened his heartbeat.

"I don't often get to eat here," she purred, learning forward with her chin lightly resting on a hand. Beneath the table, her foot explored more of Tomas' leg, traveling a lazy course northward.

"Why is that?" By now, Tomas' heart thundered against his chest, seeming frustrated with the shepherd's inaction and determined to escape his hesitant chest and embrace Mary itself.

"The food here is the best in the city," Mary replied as she absently traced a hand along the low neckline her blouse. Once again, the maid had worn a set of matching charms, the sylvai glyph at the base of her neckline, and the sitting cat adorning her lace collar. "But it's also the most expensive."

"I hope you're not putting yourself out for my sake." As though the gesture held some arcane quality, some mystical, undeniable control, Tomas found he could not pull his gaze away from Mary's hand as it traced along the low neckline of her blouse. It seemed as though there was some enchantment coming from the golden sylvai glyph hanging there, amidst the gentle swells of Mary's heart. What was more, he was increasingly unsure if he wanted to free himself of her spell.

The maid shook her head slowly. "Princess Kyla has ordered the bill sent to her." Her hand once again brushed against the small golden charm that rested against her chest. She idly caressed it and slid it across her flawless skin.

Tomas could do nothing but continue to stare.

Time continued on for the couple at a different pace than the other diners. Although they thought little of it had passed, if any, they were surprised when, seemingly within moments, their lunch arrived. The waiter, a young Sylvu who looked greatly like the proprietor, set the tray against their table and removed several small plates. As he finished, the young Sylvu stopped and glanced at Mary, inhaling slightly. "*Sa'va'ie?*" he asked in mild surprise.

Mary let her eyes drift up to the Sylvu. "*Hal*," she replied with a winsome smile.

The waiter nodded sagely. "I shall cancel your dessert."

With the waiter gone, Tomas sat up, more than a little reluctantly and surprised how far he had sunk in his chair, drawn downward by the gentle probing of both Mary's hand and her still-exploring foot. Noting the lack of utensils, he looked to Mary in confusion. The young woman smiled. "You eat it with your hands. Just be careful not to get the *me'kasa* sauce on your fingers."

"Will it burn?"

Mary giggled. "No, just turn your fingers purple."

The two began to eat, often sharing long looks and not infrequent brushes of each other's feet. The proprietor came to their table at some point and set a bottle of sylvai wine between them. The Sylvu poured two glasses, smiling as he did so. Without a word, he left the bottle and the couple in peace.

Tomas took a long drink from his glass, noting how smooth the wine was and how rich the flavor. "This is delicious," he noted.

Mary nodded, her own glass in her hand. "I love *Way'et'ay'nas'a*. I've only ever had it once but never forgot the taste."

"*Way'et'ay'nas'a*," Tomas mused. "What does that mean?"

Mary looked over at Tomas through deep green eyes and leaned in, breathing deeply. "It means 'the road to great things,'" she said in a voice dipping low.

"Wow," he croaked in a warbling tone. "You know, I'm not so... hungry, all the sudden." Tomas noted, in fact feeling something else entirely.

"Me neither," Mary replied. "Shall we continue the tour?"

"Unless you'd rather quit for the day," he suggested, very quickly.

The young woman smiled. "We have seen a lot," she agreed, knowing full well they had, in fact, seen very little. "And it's getting a little late," this said without a glance towards the midday sun.

Both stood and Mary spoke briefly with the waiter, ensuring he knew to request payment from the castle. Walking out, again hand in hand, Tomas felt a rush of heat from Mary through their hands. Their heartbeats seemed to feed off one another, each empowering the other. They walked, hands clasped, around the bustling city center, making their way towards the northern boulevard that led towards the distant castle. Their path was halted, though, at the very opening of the boulevard, by another Uldra-led team of workman. Like the one Tomas had spotted earlier, this one was digging a deep, narrow trench. Unlike the work area that morning, however, this one did not run along one side of the street. Rather, now the workteam had blocked off the entire boulevard. Here, the Uldra leader with the blue and grey sash was apologizing and directing traffic to alternate routes. Tomas glanced at Mary. She jerked her head in another direction. The eager maid led her man into a side street, but stopped and uttered a dark curse. A group of wagons had parked in front of a clothier's shop, and the teamsters were in the process of unloading. There was no way through the street now blocked by gangs of workers, the wagons, and the merchandise in transit. Mary growled something blasphemous under her breath and led Tomas along a different side street. In this one, preparations were under way for some upcoming faire, the street so full of vendors and entertainers setting up as to make passage impossible. The two traced their paths back to the city center and around the Sylvu's restaurant, taking another, more tangential street. This too, they soon found, was obstructed by a wine and cheese merchant arguing with a neighboring baker, both of whom had deliveries arriving from opposite directions, and both insisting their products needed to be unloaded first. A pair of men from the City Watch were negotiating the dispute, but the narrow street was so congested as to make passage impossible. Again, Tomas looked to Mary. She tried to stifle a low growl and again jerked her head.

The couple once again found themselves passing through the city center, even past the Sylvu's restaurant. The restauranteur noticed their return with a quizzical look. Now the young couple was heading in nearly the opposite direction as the castle in search of a clear path.

"Hi kid!" Rogan shouted, suddenly appearing behind the pair and smacking Tomas on the back.

Having only recently abandoned his homicidal impulses towards the knight, Tomas was actually surprised when he realized that, at just that moment, he really wanted to kill Rogan. The shepherd emitted a darker, more violence-laden growl than had Mary and took a half-step towards Rogan.

Mary rolled her eyes.

"We're not interrupting anything are we?" Rogan asked slyly.

"Not at all," Tomas replied sarcastically. Looking at the knight, Tomas nearly had to do a double take and could not help but laugh. Rogan Eigenhard, hero of the Northlands and renowned warrior of House Calonar, could barely be seen behind the mountain of boxes and bags he was carrying.

"What are you doing?" Tomas demanded through his laughter.

"Shopping," Rogan sneered.

Tomas blinked. "Why in the world would you be shopping?"

"Hello, Tomas!" Kyla said brightly from across the street.

"That's why," Rogan grunted.

Kyla ran across the plaza, nimbly dodging around and past the many people passing through the city center. Upon reaching their side, she enthusiastically hugged Tomas in greeting. Again, Tomas felt a surge of joy at her touch. With an odd look on her face, Mary stepped between Tomas and the delectable princess, putting some space between them by curtsying. "Hello, your Highness," she said smoothly.

"Hello, Mary!" Kyla said brightly.

"And what brings your Highness here this afternoon?" Mary said coolly.

Completely missing Mary's tone, Kyla replied, "Oh, you know, I just had to pick up a few things."

"A few?" Rogan muttered, shifting his large burden.

"So, how are things progressing here?" the princess asked slyly.

Finding it impossible to remain hostile with the eternally cheerful princess, Mary smiled. "As a matter of fact, Tomas and I were just about to..."

"Of that's wonderful!" Kyla declared, clapping her hands in glee and nearly bouncing in joy, bathing all those in the plaza with her bright emotions. "You just *have* to get new clothes! Something extra special no matter how long it takes to find!"

Rogan groaned, on the verge of tears.

"I could never impose on you, Princess," Mary insisted. "Really, we were just..."

"Oh, don't you worry! Aebreanna and I would be glad to help."

"Aebreanna?" Tomas quietly asked Rogan. "Is Baroness Tressalon with you as well?"

Rogan grunted. "You kidding? Those two are practically attached at the hip. You find one, the other's close by. Here she comes now."

Tomas turned to look for the baroness, and had absolutely no difficulty spotting her. Swaying up the middle of the cobblestone plaza, the crowd reverently making way, came Aebreanna, the baroness Tressalon. Dressed all in black, her skirt stopped well above the knee and framed hips that swayed as though guiding the winds themselves. Her slender yet well-toned legs did not walk so much as slide along the ground, as a dancer would across her stage, and her calf-high leather boots each bore the protruding silver hilt of a sylvai dagger. Aebreanna's black top, which began with a neckline nowhere near the neck and dipped quite low, proudly framed a generous bosom that caught the attention of all those around the baroness. Her slender arms, though visible, were covered with sleeves made of a black material so thin as to be nearly see-through. With every eye on Aebreanna's body, only a very fortunate few were treated to the delight of a sensual smile, enhanced all the further with a slight tuck at the center of her bottom lip, and her heavily-lidded eyes which burned with a verdant, opalescent flame declaring the baroness to be a Sylva. As all the females of her race, Aebreanna's head barely reached the shoulders of the surrounding Humans, and yet her poise and confidence were such that she seemed to tower above them. To top the sight, a mane of flowing, lustrous, honey-blonde hair flowed freely in the light spring breeze, cascading down her body and ending just above her waist. While Kyla had a natural sexuality about her, Aebreanna's was quite blatant, even predatory; her swaying hips and deep breaths were a challenge to every male with a heartbeat.

Feeling Mary's eyes burning a hole into his skull, Tomas shifted his gaze off the baroness and over to a fascinating tree, complete with an equally fascinating squirrel. After freeing himself from the Sylva's figure, Tomas noticed she was being followed by her own stack of packages.

"Is that you, Rashid?" Rogan asked from behind his burden.

The stack of packages waved a hand in greeting.

"This must be Tomas," Aebreanna said suddenly.

Looking back to the baroness, realizing that three sets of female eyes were on him, Tomas could only stammer out, "Uh, hi."

"He certainly is young," Aebreanna purred. The look on the baroness' face brought to Tomas' mind a lioness sizing up her lunch. Her voice carried only a hint of a sylvai accent, more an emphasis of emotion in how she spoke than a difference of language.

Tomas instinctively took a protective step back, behind Mary.

"He and Mary are together," Kyla said brightly.

In an instant, Tomas was positive of this, Aebreanna's face lost nearly all hints of sexual predation and was replaced by a warm, open friendliness. "In that case," she insisted, "we will just have to make you look your best. Nothing less will do for Prince Rogan's new squire. Come along, boys. We have a lot of work ahead of us."

Rogan suddenly straightened. "Sorry, ladies, but Tomas and I have some important business to do this afternoon."

"We do?" Tomas asked.

Rogan kicked him in the shin.

"But who will carry the packages?" Kyla pouted.

Spotting his savior in the crowd, Rogan called out, "Hey, Vincent!"

A man dressed so casually Tomas did not notice him until he was nearly on top of them came walking reluctantly towards them. Vincent appeared only a few years older than Tomas, and had a thin and nimble build. The servant of Calonar used this nimbleness effortlessly as he moved through the busy street without touching or being touched by anyone.

"I'll have the kid with me, so you don't need to follow him." Rogan relinquished his burden to the other man with no small amount of relief. Vincent tried to object, the strain showing from his leather boots to his short-cut hair, but he could not find the words while struggling to balance the various boxes and bags.

Tomas' eyes snapped to the knight and then to the dark-haired young spy. Thinking carefully, the shepherd suddenly realized that this Vincent person had been on the edge of his perception for the last two days at least. "So," he nearly snarled at Rogan, "you're keeping a close eye on me?"

"Nothing personal," the knight shrugged. "But considering the fact you've sworn on more than one occasion to kill me and my king, Rashid and I both thought that you needed a little watching."

"Nice to know I'm trusted."

"Trust is earned, kid; not given."

"Alright ladies," Aebreanna said cheerfully, ending the argument. She linked arms with the beaming Kyla and the reluctant but powerless Mary. "We have work to do." The three women marched stoically into the jungles of commerce. Mary glanced back towards Tomas but was clearing being swept away by the older women.

As the two stacks of packages fell in behind the women, they both threw dark looks at the grinning Rogan. "Have fun guys!" the knight said brightly.

"Bastard." "Burn in hell," the stacks replied.

Chapter 15

"So, is there something specific we have to do?" Tomas asked somewhat sullenly as the two walked casually down an adjacent street, this one another narrow road with lines of shops on either side and missing the pleasant shrubbery of the main boulevards.

"There is one thing," Rogan replied, completely dismissing the shepherd's tone. "Old friend of mine has arrived in town today. Thought we should pick him up before there's any significant property damage."

"What kind of friend is this?" Tomas asked suspiciously.

"Actually, Beraht is one of my best friends. Fought side by side with him more times than I can count. No other man in the world I'd rather have at my back in a fight. Beraht is courageous, dedicated, caring, trustworthy..."

The knight's description was cut short as the front window of a streetside tavern shattered outward due to something being thrown through it, across the street, and into a stack of wooden crates on the opposite side.

The something in question being an Uldra.

"Yes, Beraht is truly a legend of our time," Rogan finished.

The Uldra came trampling out of the boxes unsteadily with a barrel stuck on his head that no amount of prying or hitting could dislodge. Beneath the barrel, Tomas could easily see a heavy scale mail suit of the type so favored by the mountain-men. Thick leather boots were complemented by an even thicker leather belt that could only partially be seen through the thick, braided black beard rolling down the Uldra's massive chest.

"Tomas, meet Beraht," Rogan said brightly.

Blindly reaching for his belt, hanging from which was a heavy uldric waraxe. The blade on one end was etched with the runes of the mountain warriors, and the bunt end flared slightly and had an engraving of the Allfather's Throne, the largest mountain in the known world. More runes marched along the oaken shaft, barely distinguishable from the stained wood.

Beraht pulled the waraxe free and hit himself in the face with its blunt end, destroying the barrel and revealing a face covered in black hair so thick it was nearly fur. The nose seemed much too large to fit on that face, and piercing black eyes shone menacingly from deep within the crevasses. Despite the forcible removal of the offending barrel, a helmet still rested on Beraht's head, solid steel with what appeared to be Druug horns on either side and an uldric rune in the center.

"This place is insane," Tomas said, shaking his head.

"Fun though," Rogan replied. He moved over to help his towering friend extract himself from the boxes. Seeing the knight, Beraht mercilessly pounded him on the shoulders saying, "Ho, Rogan!" he barked with a voice as deep as a mountain lake. He was much taller that Rogan, of course, as all Uldra were, and massive in the shoulders. His arms bulged with more muscles than seemed possible, and thick veins ran the length. Once freed of his wooden prison, Beraht turned back to the tavern. "Excuse me," he said politely in a voice as deep as a mountain crevasse, bending his tall frame back through the broken window. The Uldra's return was greeted by the sounds of a full-blown riot.

"Aren't you going to help him?" Tomas demanded.

Rogan had a seat on a bench across from the tavern. "Trust me, Beraht's in his element."

Tomas, being the protective sort, moved to assist the drunken Uldra, ignoring Rogan's shout of, "Don't go in there, kid!"

The young man was in the tavern for perhaps three seconds before being ejected through the broken window, across the street, and into the stack of crates beside Rogan's bench. As Tomas lay in the street, the knight looked down on him and said, "I warned you."

After perhaps five minutes, the sounds of combat ended. Rogan stood up and said, "It should be safe now."

The knight led them through the door, rather than the broken window. It took a few moments for Tomas' eyes to adjust to the dim light within, and a started "Oh, my God," escaped his lips at the sight. Scattered across the tavern, some suspended from the overhead beams, were somewhere in the area of fifteen men. Nearly every piece of furniture was broken, and anything made of metal bore face-shaped dents. Sitting calmly at the end of the bar, Beraht looked upon his work, drinking and enjoying the sight. The Uldra had taken his helmet off, revealing yet more braided black hair held from his eyes by a thick purple headband, embraided with red thread in a strange, almost hypnotic pattern.

Stepping over a few unconscious people, Rogan approached the bar. "Can you ever drink without getting into a fight?" he asked, reaching behind the bar for a pair of undamaged tankards. The search took a moment. Finally finding them, Rogan poured himself and Tomas some cider.

Beraht took some time to consider the question before finally answering. He swirled the mead in his huge drinking horn before answering, "No. What would be the point?" His voice was thick with the uldric accent, weaving up and down with emphasis on strange syllables and a slight mispronunciation of different sounds.

"Didn't think so," Rogan said with a grin.

Tomas had heard many stories about the Uldra. He knew, for example, they were some of the most fearsome warriors in the world; Beraht's scalemail armor, bearing the scars of battle, along with the waraxe at his belt, gave mute evidence of this Uldra's experience with violence. Of course, the plethora of groaning bodies was more overt testimony. Also, Tomas had heard that Uldra, as a whole, tended to drink too much. Considering Beraht had a drinking horn in his hand, was seated somewhat precariously on a beer barrel, and had a broached cider barrel at his elbow, Tomas had little difficulty believing this fact either. All the stories about Uldra Tomas had encountered, however, could never prepare him for the reality of Beraht. Although the young man could understand the Uldra barbarian's obvious lack of a recent bath, he had apparently just arrived after all, the rather obvious crumbs in the warrior's armor and beard were silent testimony of his breakfast, perhaps even dinner.

"How's Kyla and Aebreanna?" the Uldra asked scratching himself somewhere indecent.

"Fine, just fine," Rogan replied, drinking from his tankard.

"And the little axe-blunter?"

"Destructive. We can't tell if she's clumsy, careless, or clueless."

Beraht chuckled into his drinking horn. "Good, good."

Belching so thunderously that Tomas feared the few unbroken windows left would shatter, the barbarian asked, "So why'd you send for me?"

"Need your help."

"What else is new?"

"Tomas here found out our old friend Vagris attacked Railing. It was ugly, Beraht; Vagris has lost what little charm he had to begin with."

Tomas jumped at the mention of Railing.

Beraht looked up from his horn, pure murder in his midnight eyes. "Vagris, huh? Don't worry; I'll take care of it."

"Get some backup. The King thinks it's time to send a message." The knight set down his tankard and scribbled a note for the unconscious bartender. "See if Esha can arrange fast transport for you; we'd like to catch Vagris before he moves again. Rashid'll have the latest intelligence."

Beraht drained his horn, refilling it from the keg at his elbow and tying it to his belt before picking up his dented helmet. "I'll try to bring Vagris back alive. No promises, though."

Walking out of the barely-standing tavern, Tomas breathed deeply, thankful to be away from the musky Uldra. "How on Arayel could you travel with that brute?"

Rogan laughed. "Easy, just stay upwind."

Tomas just shook his head, bewildered at the knight's affinity for a creature like Beraht. "What will he do about Railing?"

Rogan stopped and looked right at Tomas. "Beraht will take some Uldra warriors and hunt down Vagris' warband. He's has been attacking villages for years, and one of them was an Uldra mining town. He killed all the men and did some really bad things to the women and children. Ever since, the Uldra have been aching to go after him, but Vagris keeps moving so we can never pin down his location. You've given us a lead."

"You might want to tell Beraht to take more than a few Uldra with him," Tomas advised.

"Why?"

"Vagris had Legionaries with him when he attacked Railing."

"Of course he did. He always does."

"How do you know?"

"Vagris used to be garrison commander for a detachment stationed near Frostfront. When Pelsemoria collapsed, Vagris and nearly his entire unit went rogue. They've been terrorizing eastern Lanasia ever since."

Tomas shook his head, stunned at the news.

"Something bothering you, kid?"

"What will the Uldra do to Vagris?" Tomas asked

"They're big believers in eye for an eye justice. All the men in his army will be killed just like they killed others in payment for the Uldra who were murdered. Dead or alive, Vagris'll be handed over to House Calonar in repayment for our own dead."

Tomas did not say a word, just looked down the street.

"If you've got a problem, kid, now's the time to speak," Rogan said.

"If I do have a problem with this, will you stop Beraht?"

Rogan put his hand on Tomas' shoulder. "Like it or not, kid, you told us where to start tracking Vagris, and the King was clear. If you have a problem with how the Uldra are going to handle this, we'll find another way. House Guard, maybe."

Tomas looked at Rogan then turned away. "I honestly wish I did have a problem with it. I saw what that bastard did, Rogan. The fact that he and his men used to be Legionaries makes it that much worse. I want to see him stuck on a pole for betraying his oath. Him, and all his men. Does that make me a bad person?"

Rogan smiled. "Makes you Human, kid."

"What was that note you left?"

"Damages," the knight shrugged. "The tavern-keeper knows to contact the castle; we'll rebuild for him."

"What about the injuries?

Rogan laughed. "Anyone who picks a fight with an Uldra gets what they deserve. Still, they know all they have to do is go to the Harvest Mother temple."

"How do you know Beraht didn't start the fight?"

The knight shook his head. "Beraht never starts a fight. Always does finish them, though."

Remembering suddenly something the Baroness Aebreanna had said, Tomas glanced at Rogan. "Why did Aebreanna call me your new squire?" he asked.

The knight stopped suddenly. "I almost forgot," he said. "Apparently, you impressed the King during your little conversation the other day. That, and the Queen got a look at you while you and your little maid were telling stories last night."

"The Queen was at the temple last night?"

Rogan nodded. "She doesn't like a spectacle, so her time there is kept quiet. She noticed you and the girl telling stories to the kids and didn't want to interrupt." The knight shrugged. "After getting her endorsement, it was pretty much set. The king recommended that I take you on as a squire."

Tomas stopped in the alley. "What," he sputtered. "Why... What... Why?"

"Yeah, that was about my reaction, too." He shrugged. "But, like I said, the Queen took a look at you and she agreed. They both think I should take you on as a squire. Plus there was Cyras' little fortune-telling."

"But..." Tomas searched for words, for a clear line of thought. "What do you think?" he finally asked.

Rogan looked down the narrow street, past the busy marketplace and the buildings beyond. "You're rash, impulsive, judgmental, and impatient. You don't know the first thing about swordplay, and you're just as likely to get me killed as yourself."

Tomas' jaw dropped. "Well, don't feel the need to be gentle or anything."

The knight grinned, looking back at Tomas. "That's what my uncle told me when I asked him to train me."

"Did he?"

Rogan put out his right hand. "It's a crazy idea, but people I trust say I can trust you. I'm not getting any younger, anyway; I could use some help. After all, it can get pretty dull on the road alone."

Tomas looked at Rogan's outstretched hand, a million thoughts flooding his mind at once. Memories and grudges and prejudices warred with recent events. His young soul lashed about, until another brief moment of clarity seemed to dawn. He glanced up, along the street on which they stood. In the distance, Tomas heard the bells of the distant church sounding the new hour. He looked back down at Rogan's outstretched hand. Finally, slowly, the squire took his knight's hand.

"I can't tell you how much you're going to regret this," Rogan laughed.

Tomas grinned. "Somehow, I think you're right."

Rogan dipped his hand into his vest and tossed his new squire a pouch.

"What's this?" Tomas asked.

"Queen told me to give you that. It's an advance on your salary. Just enough to get yourself some new clothes and maybe a present for a pretty girl."

That night, Mary completed her work and retired to her private room, eager for the chance to rest. Despite Roland's assurances that her work in the castle would be covered for as long as she needed during the tours she was giving to Tomas, the maid felt it would have been unfair of her to ask one of the other girls on the staff to do the cleaning she was responsible for while she spent the day shopping with Princess Kyla and Baroness Aebreanna. So, after a pleasant day of shopping and fitting and gossiping, Mary still made sure her work was complete before retiring.

The young woman was so tired, in fact, that it was only after she had undressed for bed and prepared to climb in that she happened to glance at the blankets. Lying on the thick coverlet was a single rose, pure white with the faintest hint of pink at the tips. Beside the rose was a small box. The maid picked up the flower and the box. The rose had a soft fragrance that filled her young soul with a wonderful feeling. Opening the box, Mary's eyes filled with tears, and a smile danced across her face as she looked at the emerald earrings she had so desired that morning but had been unable to buy.

Chapter 16

The Guild Tower of the Northern Keep stood in the far
southern edge of the city with a large complex of storehouses and
dormitories built around it. The tall buildings showed signs of
frequent reconstruction, but its original architecture could still be
seen. The base of the enormous structure was squared off, with eight
sides of roughly the same length and rising more than three stories
high. Various buildings of assorted sizes surrounded it, each with a
solid brick and stone wall facing the tower in the center. Four smaller
towers of stone and marble stood above the main building, rising
more than a hundred feet above the streets of the city. These four
towers, though, were dwarfed by the massive pillar rising in the
center. This, the traditional wizard's tower, seemed to scrape the
cloudy sky, beaten in size only by its sibling in the center of the castle.
Surrounding all the buildings was a large park with gravel paths
twisting along in random courses filled with what appeared to be
stone and wood scattered throughout the entire area.

"Who built that?" Tomas asked as he and Rogan rode up the
cobblestone road towards the home of House Calonar's arcane
adepts. Rogan had ordered Tomas be woken that morning with the
sun. He had greeted his new squire in the castle courtyard, their
horses already saddled and waiting. The knight made no secret of his
disappointment in this, his squire's first day.

"Up with the sun kid," Rogan said. "You're in training, now.
Not enough hours in the day, so we use them all."

Tomas had hoped to spend more time with Mary, but he had
been extracted before she had risen. A summons had arrived from
Esha, the Mistress of the Tower, so Rogan informed his new squire
during their ride. Moreover, the knight decided that, from that
moment forward, Tomas would accompany Rogan on all his official
duties.

The knight shrugged at Tomas' question. "Don't know who
built it. As far as I've been told, the tower has been here as long as
the city. Any time it's knocked down, they just put it back up."

"It looks a lot like the wizard towers that used to be in Pelsemoria..." the squire remarked, noticing the wide windows and intricate stone carvings. "Except for the four smaller towers."

"One spell-slinger's tower looks pretty much the same as another," Rogan shrugged. "But it would make sense. All the senior wizards in the Keep were trained in either the Guild Academy in Frostfront or the University of Pelsemoria. Wizards are real traditionalists; they stick with what they know."

There was a large gap separating the Arcane Tower complex from the surrounding city. The buildings stopped some distance from the low wall marking where the Guild facilities began, with a wide expanse of cobblestone stretching before them. There were no benches, no trees or shrubbery I that gap. The street looked well-maintained, but unused. The stones had no indentations from traffic, nor was there any sign of traveler, vendor, or other inhabitant of the rest of the city. Upon reaching the gap, Stick came to an abrupt halt.

"Oh, for..." Rogan sputtered. "It was one time!"

The brutish warhorse did not respond and refused to go further.

"Will you just go!?! Quit being a baby!"

Stick neighed and looked up towards the tower, then shook his head vehemently.

Rogan growled and dismounted, tying Stick to the last stand before the gap, belonging to a merchant of charms and oddities associated with the Guild Tower. The knight handed a few coins to the merchant and gave a warning about not getting too close to the horse, then jerked his head at Tomas, muttering, "Damned overgrown donkey."

The new squire also dismounted and tied up his horse, hurrying to join the irritable Rogan as he stomped across the cobblestone gap separating the Tower from the rest of the city.

A low stone wall separated the wizards' facilities from the rest of the Keep, but it had no gate, and only stood knee-high. Tomas noted this with some confusion. "I can't see that stopping any thieves or intruders," he noted.

Rogan snorted. "The wall's not for keeping people out."

"Then what...?"

"The King ordered it built after Esha took over. It marks the minimum safe distance."

The squire looked questioningly at his knight. "Minimum safe...?" His question was interrupted by one of Esha's detonations.

The explosion shook the whole area, lighting up the entire sky and sending debris falling from the top of the center tower to the ground below. Once the dust settled, Tomas noticed that none of the falling material had made it past the low wall. "Oh," he said, suddenly understanding.

From behind, they heard neighing that sounded suspiciously like laughter. Glancing back, they saw Stick tossing his head at them while the merchant reorganized his disturbed goods. "Ah, shut up," Rogan grumbled. He shook his head and moved towards the path that led through the only break in the wall to the tower beyond.

Tomas followed but looked nervously upwards. "Are you sure this is a good idea?"

The knight shook his head. "Probably not," he replied. "Not much choice, though." When they reached the wall, the knight waved his arms at a grey-robed apprentice mage standing at the Tower's door. The apprentice waved back, and then yelled up into the tower. The call went all the way to the top before a reply of, "all clear," came back down.

Hearing this, Rogan smacked Tomas on the shoulder and ran to the Tower door just as fast as he possibly could. The squire struggled to keep up, throwing constant looks upward, fearing an explosion at any moment. Once the two gasping warriors made it to the relative safety of the main building, they paused for a moment to catch their breath.

"Welcome, your Highness," the mage said, bowing to Rogan. *"Parden* Esha is awaiting you." The grey-robed young woman walked them in through the narrow hallway that opened to a large chamber made of stone and crafted in the column and buttress style of most Northlands castles. Rows of stone bookshelves lined the walls, and wooden benches and tables were scattered here and there. Throughout the chamber, a number of grey-robed apprentices sat, reading by candlelight and apparently oblivious to the wanton catastrophes their mistress was wont to create.

"If she's waiting," Tomas gasped as much from the run as from fear, "then what was with that explosion?"

"The Archmage is easily distracted, sir," the apprentice explained, leading them to a large staircase that wound around the outer wall of the central chamber. "No doubt she became distracted while waiting and continued with one of her many experiments."

"Does everything she make explode?" the squire demanded.

"We have been taught that the universe was created by an explosion. *Parden* Esha tells us that all other creation must follow suit. Once the pain of birth has been accomplished, the joy of revelation may continue."

Tomas stared at the mage for a moment. "Was that a yes?" he asked.

"Yes," Rogan breathed, wiping sweat from his brow. "Everything Esha makes blows up at least once. It works fine after that. Usually."

Another explosion rocked the tower. Both Rogan and Tomas fought to maintain their balance and remained wary of more debris. Following this latest detonation, Tomas noted that every book and breakable object in the large central room of the tower had been secured in place. The students showed little regard for the chaos, most not even bothering to look up from their studies. No doubt the adepts of this place had long since braced their home against the machinations of their Tower Mistress. "Maybe we should go find Esha before she causes some permanent damage," Tomas suggested.

The knight grunted and followed along with his squire behind the mage towards the stone staircase. As the two men made their way up the stairs with their quiet guide, Tomas took the opportunity to glance in to the rooms they passed on the way. There were many wizards within each, most wearing the robes of the Guild, bent over their labors. Some of the spell-casters were huddled over tomes of arcane lore while others worked on strange devices. The squire spotted a few robed figures on one level working in a large, open room filled with bottles, beakers, and vials of various powders and liquids.

"How many people live here?" Tomas asked.

"*Parden* Esha lives at the top of the main tower," the apprentice explained. "Her personal students have quarters in the levels beneath. The four senior archwizards live in the neighboring towers with their own students. Those of us who have yet to pass the tests to be fully inducted, or who do not have specific mentors, live in the surrounding dormitories. Overall, there are nearly two hundred of us."

"Why a tower?" the squire asked. "Why climb these stairs every day?"

"Wizards like towers kid," Rogan said. "Every spell-slinger I know wants to live in a tower. I guess it's just a thing that comes with blowing yourself up all the time."

"The isolation that comes from living within a tower is appealing to us," the grey robe argued. "It is not from some feeling of tradition or separation. It's just that our studies require a great deal of concentration, and distractions are most unwelcome. In a tower, we usually have little worry of unexpected visitors."

Just as Tomas was ready to demand a rest from the climbing, he saw that the stairs leveled out and led to a door made of a single slab of metal. The mage looked expectantly at Rogan, saying without words that it was too big for her to move. The squire climbed up and stared at the massive thing even after Rogan put his shoulder against it and forced the door open. "What is this?" the young man asked. "It looks like iron."

"Lead," Rogan grunted. "After Esha moved in, the doors were all replaced with solid steel. This one, though, the King ordered be made of lead."

"*Parden* Esha is within, your Highness," the apprentice said, gesturing into the room before turning to walk back down the stairs.

"You're not coming inside?" the squire asked.

The grey robe shook her head. "I have duties."

Once the apprentice was out of ear-shot, Rogan snorted, "Not to mention she doesn't want to be here for the next boom."

Tomas just shook his head and followed his knight inside. The top room of the tower was a single, open chamber, with nothing to block the view all around except the reinforced walls protecting the staircase and the dizzying array of tables, benches, blackboards, and charts that cluttered the entire area. The squire struggled to focus his eyes on any one thing in the room, shifting from a table with various small items to one covered with bottles of some liquid enthusiastically producing smoke. Nowhere in this maze of invention did there seem to be any kind of order, just more and more chaos everywhere onc looked.

"Does she sleep here?" the young man asked.

Rogan nodded. "I heard there's a bed in here somewhere; never seen it, though."

"Where's Esha?"

An explosion answered the squire's question. Both Rogan and Tomas threw themselves to the floor, covering their heads and fearing the worst. For some time, the whole room shook violently, and both men feared the tower would not hold. A huge cloud of smoke and heat beat at them, stinging their eyes and noses and bringing to Tomas' mind an unpleasant fear that they had died and somehow been sent to Underworld.

A tiny figure in robes materialized out of the cloud in front of them, waving a hand in front of her small face and coughing violently. "Well," the archmage noted, "I doubt that was the proper dose."

Parden Esha, Mistress of the Tower of the Northern Keep's annex of the Arcane Guild and one of King Cylan Calonar's most trusted advisors, was a very short Sylva wearing rumpled and scorched robes that looked at least two sizes too big for her. Her shoulder-length hair born the scars of fire and explosion, being uneven and unkempt. The adept was short, even for a Sylva, her whole body was very small and underdeveloped, as a child's would be. Despite her lack of age, however, she nonetheless wore the gold lining and magical runes on her sleeves and hood that marked Esha as an Archmage, the highest rank in the Arcane Guild.

Both warriors remained on the floor, looking up at the tiny wizard with a mixture of confusion and fear. Esha stood where she was as the thick cloud of acrid smoke slowly dissipated, staring down at them in confusion through opalescent eyes that bore the squint of someone who spends too much time reading. "Was there something you wanted?" she asked in a cheerful, squeaking voice.

Knight and squire looked at each other then back at the Sylva. "Esha," Rogan growled, "*you* called for *us*."

"I did? I wonder why I did that." The archmage turned and walked back towards a collection of tables resting in the center of the large chamber. Rather than standing on legs, as was custom, this table hung from the ceiling by a number of thick, carbon-scorched chains at each corner.

The two men stood and brushed the worst of the smoke and dust off themselves. "Well," Tomas said, "at least this wasn't a waste of time."

"Shut up, kid," the knight grumbled.

They both followed Esha deeper into her lair, looking about at the various devices, items, and brews with more than a little apprehension. Rogan glanced back at his apprentice as they neared where the archmage stood, deeply engrossed in some mystical project. "Whatever you do," Rogan warned, "don't touch anything."

Tomas nodded, his eyes still trying to take in everything. Once the two warriors reached the central workspace, the squire glanced around and saw several small rods of copper, spools of gold wire, and large glass jars containing a greenish, sour-smelling liquid. "What's all this?" Tomas asked.

"An Uldra clan has commissioned an experiment; they wish to harness the power of lightning as a power source, rather than using fire," Esha replied while writing notes in a large book. She had a strange wooden frame perched on her tiny nose, containing a pair of thick glass lenses.

The young man looked over the Sylva's shoulder but noticed with regret that she was writing in the arcane language. "I thought wizards could create lightning any time they wanted," he remarked.

"We can. The Uldra have a number of new inventions they wish to test without depending on an adept. Fascinating theories, really. If I am successful, then I will be able to construct a device to absorb an electric charge and store the energy for later use."

"Use for what?" Tomas asked as he absently touched one of the copper rods. A surge of pain lanced through the young man's entire body, tensing every muscle he had. In an instant, the squire found himself on the floor with more than a little smoke coming off his clothes and body.

"Be careful with the rods," Esha warned without looking back. "They each hold a large dose of electricity."

Tomas lifted himself off the floor with Rogan's help, still holding the rod in a tightly clenched fist. "I think this one is dead," the young man noted through clenched teeth and blurred eyes.

"Oh, that is ok. I will recharge it later."

Rogan pried the rod out of his squire's hand and dropped it back on the table. "I warned you," he muttered.

"Can we go home now?" The young man nearly wept.

"Ah!" Esha called out. "Yes, now I recall!" She set down her writing quill and the wood-framed lenses.

"Recall what?" Rogan asked nervously.

"I called you here because I have an update on where I believe Anninihus is operating!"

"Who?" Tomas asked.

The knight nodded. "Good, Esha. What have you got?"

"This way," the archmage instructed as she happily skipped to another area of the chamber.

"Who is Anninihus?" the squire asked again.

Rogan followed behind the small Sylva. "Do you remember Senen? At Crossroads?"

"Yes."

"Well, he said that a wizard led the assassins that freed him from prison."

Tomas nodded. "I remember. He said the wizard was tall and thin. He had brown hair and tattoos and shook when he walked."

"Well, that sounds like a spell-slinger I used to know named Anninihus. When we got back to the Keep, I asked Esha to see if she could find the rat."

"I take it you don't really like this guy."

"Not a fan, no."

The young man glanced at a table filled with glass vials and bottles. "How are these things still here after all the explosions?" he asked.

In answer, Rogan drew his dagger and swung it at the table. Just before the blade stuck, a blue field appeared in the spot where the weapon would have hit, blocking the attack. Tomas saw this and nodded. "I guess she'd have to do something like that."

"Magic can be fun," the knight noted, sheathing his dagger.

"Wait, why doesn't she just do that around whatever she's working on?"

"Don't expect me to explain the why's of wizards," Rogan snorted. "I've never understood them."

The two men reached the spot where Esha stood, gesturing at the floor. Tomas looked down and was surprised to see that the floor of the entire room was an incredibly detailed map of Arayel. Where they stood represented the eastern Northlands. "Did she just do this?" the squire wondered.

"No, it was here the whole time," the knight replied, shaking his head. "We really need to work on that situational awareness of yours."

Tomas just shrugged as Esha's voice interrupted their conversation. The archmage was chanting in the arcane language, calling on her power to cast a spell. As the two warriors watched, the small hands of the Sylva formed intricate gestures that neither could follow, and her lips moved nearly as fast. As she chanted, Esha straightened her hands and arms in front of her, palms facing the floor, and slowly spread her arms out to either side.

A golden light slowly began to radiate from the floor as the entire room went dark. Rogan and Tomas could no longer see outside the windows, nor could they see the walls or tables around them. The only thing still visible was the golden light from the floor, Esha, and each other. When her words ended, the archmage made a raising gesture and clapped her hands over her head.

With an odd ringing sound, as if a chorus of bells were being played in some celebration, the golden light shattered around them, the shards disappearing into nothingness. As the two warriors stared about themselves in wonder, the map at their feet came alive, mountains rising to their knees, forests sprouting around their feet, and cities of perfect detail appearing.

With a curse, Rogan stumbled over the Ulheim mountains, stumbling all the way into the Endless Sands and nearly destroying the City of All Sins. Tomas grumbled more than a little as he was forced to step up out of the Barrier Ocean, shaking his soaked boots off once he reached land. A careless step by the squire caused much devastation in Ironheartshaven, to which the people of that city responded with wails of fear and curses. The young man looked up at Esha in concern. "I didn't really just...?"

The archmage shook her head slightly. "Simply illusion," she said.

Rogan took great care in making his way back across the mountains, trying his best not to destroy any of the Uldra villages scattered throughout them. "How accurate is this, Esha?" he asked.

"Completely," the Sylva replied. "The spell calls on *Ar'ae'el* herself to show what rests upon her. What you see now is a perfect representation of anything and everything in the world in the past."

"Amazing," Tomas marveled, making his own way across the lands of the Gunrsvein before joining Esha in the vicinity of Wildelves Wood and the Northern Keep. "Does this mean we're on this map somewhere?"

"If you were capable of seeing such small detail, yes; we are represented exactly as we are at this moment."

Rogan looked down at the forest. "So, is this how you tracked down Anninihus?"

Esha shook her head. "I did not 'track him down,' as you say. I believe I have discovered his former base of operations and his most recent travels."

"Show me."

The archmage spoke a few brief words of magic and gestured to the map. "As you see here," she narrated as a sickly green light appeared in the center of the Keep, "Anninihus started here under my tutelage."

"Already know that," Rogan pointed out.

"Simply establishing a familiar starting point." The green dot moved east towards Crossroads. "As you also know, once we discovered the nature of his studies, he was expelled from my Tower and the Keep."

"The nature of...?" Tomas asked.

Rogan grimaced. "Anninihus is a necromancer."

"Isn't that allowed by the Guild?"

Esha shook her head. "Anninihus went beyond simple necromancy. A necromancer learns how to communicate with those who have passed beyond the veil, to learn from them and seek their council. The power my former student sought was that of a Death Mage."

"You mean... like Karnat?" the squire asked, suppressing a shudder. The last great Death Mage had helped the Nenic twins to unleash the Plague of Walking Death, which killed more than a third of the people of Lanasia.

Esha nodded. "A Death Mage harnesses the power at her disposal not to commune with the dead and gain some measure of their power, but actually to command them. A Death Mage will raise those enjoying their eternal sleep and force them to her will. Anninihus even attempted to gain control of the White Lady herself."

"Is that even possible?"

"Before Karnat, many thought it impossible to raise the dead at all. He did so, and by the thousands."

"Where did Anninihus go after the King banished him?" Rogan asked.

Esha gestured towards the living map. "He spent several months at Crossroads, indulging various debaucheries in exchange for the employment of his modest powers, I imagine. Something odd occurred while he resided there." Kneeling outside of the cluster of tents and half-finished buildings that represented the den of crime, the archmage pointed to an odd shimmering effect around the town. To Tomas and Rogan, it almost looked as though some extreme heat was being produced without fire.

"What is that?" Tomas asked.

"That is what caused Anninihus to leave Crossroads," Esha replied. "Whatever it was, it appears in the town for only a single hour, then vanishes and my former pupil departs."

"What could cause something like that in your map?" Rogan asked.

"A shield spell, most likely," the Sylva mused. "Some magic meant to prevent scrying or divination. It could even be some kind of evil from beyond *Ar'ae'el*, something that the world herself could not identify."

"Something from beyond Arayel?" Tomas exclaimed. "You mean a demon? One of the Umbra?"

"It really could have been any number of things, including a prisoner of Underworld. In the simplest terms possible, the field would have been generated by anything with a strong, unidentifiable arcane nature."

Rogan nodded. "What do *you* think it was?"

"I am unable to form a plausible theory without more data."

"Could it have been another wizard?" Tomas asked. "Someone who wanted to form a partnership with Anninihus?"

Esha shook her head. "I find that unlikely," she replied. "If it was an adept, then it would have had to be a caster of the highest order, far beyond my abilities; someone who would find Anninihus to be little more than an unworthy pawn."

"Who falls in that list?" Rogan asked.

The archmage thought about it. "King Cylan, Cyras Darkholm, and Fak'Har, of course. Tienel Greysoul, if he was still on *Ar'ae'el*. The sorceress Vara, perhaps, as her powers remain uncertain. The senior members of the Speakers Council, though more collectively than independently. The Tribunal of Frostfront, again, collectively. Kelinva, if she was still alive. Perhaps one or two others."

"Can you track those people?"

"No. Each has the power to be effectively invisible to my searches."

Rogan nodded. "Where did Anninihus go next?"

Esha said another word and the green dot moved south, across the hills and up into the mountains, stopping at Frostfront. "Hey," Tomas remarked, "he's got that same shimmer-thing now."

"Yes," the archmage noted. "Whatever or whoever he encountered left him with some ability to mask himself. His ability to enter the crypts of the ancient Guild masters without anyone detecting his presence is no wonder. Even the Triumvirate would have been unaware of his passage, unless they were specifically looking for him. I am unable to discern what he learned there, but he remained beneath Frostfront for three days before leaving again."

"Rashid," Rogan said. "I'll have him send a team to investigate."

"I will provide an adept as advisor," Esha added. "Rashid's agents will need council on what to look for." The Sylva gestured at the map again as the green dot left Frostfront and traveled to the Khepric city of Oneld. All three of them climbed over the model of the Ulheim Mountains. "As you can see," Esha narrated, "Anninihus took ship at Oneld and traveled south, around Dagon'ay, to Davenor." The marker traveled across the water to the shrouded southern continent. They did not follow, instead watching from the dry safety of southern Lanasia. Even if only an illusion, none of them dared set foot in the forbidden home of the Xeshlin. "Once he entered the lands of the *Xesh'lin*," Esha continued, "he moved very rapidly, probably by horse, to a location with unpleasant connotations."

Tomas glanced back up at Esha. "What is that place?" he asked. It appeared to Tomas as though Anninihus had stopped in the center of the large mountain range in the center of Davenor.

"Mount Godsfire," Rogan said grimly.

Esha nodded. "Center of *Xesh'lin* culture, power, and religion." The tiny archmage looked up at Rogan. "And also, the former home of Kelinva the Betrayer."

"What!?!" Tomas exclaimed.

The Sylva nodded. "Indeed. After her exile by the last Empress of the *Sy'lva'n*, Kelinva went there. She took with her the most fanatical of her followers and constructed a terrible center of power. From this place she launched the Invasion that nearly destroyed us all." Esha stared at Rogan. "There are many amongst the *Xesh'lin* who believe that, when Kelinva is once again reborn, she will rise there, the seat of her power."

The knight grunted, crossing his arms. "What happened next?" he asked.

"Next," the archmage replied, "Anninihus returned to Lanasia." She gestured and the green dot moved back across the Nassinal Sea, landing in the south of Velaross.

"Damaris?" Tomas asked. "Why there?"

"He visited a scene with which you should be quite familiar, Rogan." She gestured again to where the green dot stopped, in the hills to the south of Damaris Castle.

The knight nodded grimly, his mouth twisting in dark memory.

"I don't see any towns or ruins," Tomas noted. "There's just that small tower and that little crater to the side."

"Not so little when you're standing in it," Rogan replied grimly.

"You've been there?" the young man guessed.

He nodded. "Ten years ago. Me, Aebreanna, and Beraht faced down Tienel Greysoul there, where he'd hidden his tower. It didn't end well."

"Was the crater there before or after you fought?" Tomas asked.

"Like I said, it didn't end well."

"A great deal of residual arcane energy remains in that location," Esha told them. "So I cannot say what exactly Anninihus was doing there. However, after spending nearly eighteen days in that same area where you had your confrontation with the Greysoul, he traveled in as straight a line as possible to there." The archmage stood at the edge of the Nassinal Sea, pointing towards Darez.

"Too bad Reydia didn't her hands on him," Rogan grumbled.

"I cannot be sure she did not," Esha countered. A dull red dot appeared in the center of the mountains of the penal continent. The green and red dots both traveled to the western-most edge of Darez, paused, and then separated again. "As best I can determine, Reydia was either warned of Anninihus' approach, or learned of his presence. They most definitely had a meeting, and both survived."

"They made a deal," Tomas guessed.

"But for what?" Rogan asked. "I doubt there's anything that spell-slinger could have offered her that she would have had any use for."

Esha nodded. "Her insanity would have presented a dangerous obstacle to whatever my old student's objective was. Clearly, however, he found some means to sway her."

"What next?" the knight demanded.

The green dot returned once again to Lanasia, just to the north of Pelsemoria. "Once returning to this continent, Anninihus traveled west, past the lands of the Khepri, towards Boric. Once there he again encounters the distortion effect." The same shimmer appeared around the northern-most city of Emir Balshazzar's territory. Once reaching the forest that surrounded Boric, the green dot representing Anninihus disappeared.

"I cannot track him for some time after this," the archmage confessed. "Whether this means he remained in Boric or was further concealed, I do not know. He next appears near the prison of Ubelheim with a large group of Oniwabanshi assassins."

"Where did the assassins come from?" Tomas asked.

"The Oniwabanshi have, for centuries, known how to mask themselves from magical detection. Unless I had their names, faces, or some physical trace like hair or blood, I cannot trace their movements."

Rogan looked off into the darkness. "Alright," he thought aloud. "So Anninihus goes to Frostfront, learns something there from the dead wizards. Then he travels all the way to Mount Godsfire, then to the ruins of Greysoul's tower. From there he heads to Darez and meets with Reydia before heading to Boric where he links up again with whoever or whatever that shimmering is. He drops of the world for... how long?"

"Nearly three years," Esha supplied.

"Did the shimmering effect last that full three years?"

"Only a day. Otherwise, I may have detected its presence."

"So Anninihus goes to Boric for one day and disappears of the face of Arayel for three years. When he reappears, he's got a clan of Tramanese assassins working for him and uses a fortune he didn't have before to free and hire the worst group of cutthroats and brigands in Lanasia. He even hires people like Senen to hire even more mercs and tells him to locate every agent of Rashid's he can."

"When was he at the prison?" Tomas asked.

"Nearly six months ago," Esha replied.

"Almost the same time I left Pelsemoria."

"What?" Rogan asked.

"That's right around the same time I left home on my quest." The squire turned to his knight. "Could it just be coincidence?"

"I don't believe in coincidence, especially where spell-slingers are concerned."

"Those of us possessing arcane power often try to cloak our activities in apparently random circumstances that those around us would otherwise dismiss as coincidence," Esha agreed. "A lesson all adepts had to learn once the Inquisition took primary control of the Adamic Church."

"Where is Anninihus now?" Rogan asked, staring hard at the map.

The archmage gestured and the green dot moved north, through the mountains. "He moved with surprising speed through Ulheim, but he encountered that same distortion effect near Grief's Chasm. That was four months ago, and he has yet to reappear." With that, Esha waved her right arm in a broad arc over her head. The map dropped back into the floor and light returned to the room.

Rogan walked around the cluttered table that had appeared between him and Tomas. "Three times can't be coincidence," he muttered. "Either Anninihus knows how to find this distortion thing or it knows how to find him."

"Or they have prearranged meeting places," the squire added.

"And whatever it is, it helped him amass wealth and power, two things Anninihus has always been interested in. And the last location we have for him is west of here."

Esha rejoined them after nearly losing her way around several tables. "My former student most assuredly has some grand scheme that is only now beginning to take shape."

The knight crossed his arms over his chest. "We really need to find Anninihus, Esha. Whatever he's up to, it can't be good."

The archmage nodded. "Especially considering he swore vengeance on the entirety of House Calonar after his trial and exile."

"The Lamashti!" Tomas suddenly said, the thought appearing in his mind and finding voice seemingly without his awareness.

"What?" Rogan grunted.

The squire's eyes widened as his conscious mind caught up with flash of inspiration. "Remember? When we first arrived in the Wood? We were attacked."

The knight nodded. "Yeah, the things the Sylvai banished. The Speaker said…" His own eyes narrowed as he latched on to Tomas' reasoning. "Damn."

"Following half a conversation is quite thrilling," Esha said happily. "This may be what insanity feels like."

Rogan turned to the tiny Sylva. "Esha," he said, "could Anninihus summon Lamashti?"

The archmage shook her head. "The barriers placed upon those betrayers is far beyond my former pupil's abilities to breach."

"What about the shimmer-thing that's helping him?" Tomas suggested.

Esha thought a few moments. "An adept of that power, that skill…" She looked at Rogan. "Perhaps, though not for any length of time. The nature of their banishment means even should someone call forth the *La'ma'shti*, such an incursion would be brief."

"But long enough to draw the Sylvai," Rogan countered, looking at his squire.

Tomas nodded. "Feints," he suggested. "The Sylvai are your eyes in the forest, right?"

The knight nodded and added, "He's drawing our eyeline. He's keeping the Sylvai occupied, allowing his mercs and killers to move unnoticed."

"Sounds like you should have killed this Anninihus or thrown him in prison," Tomas muttered.

Rogan shook his head. "There's no prison a spell-slinger with Anninihus' power can't escape from, not even Ubelheim. The only real option was banishment or death, and the King doesn't like capital punishment."

Esha crossed to a large bookcase and pulled an enormous, leather-bound tome from it. "I shall assign several of my most promising students to tracing the mercenaries and assassins Anninihus has employed. I will continue to search for the Death Mage himself."

Rogan turned to leave. "Let me know the moment you find him," he instructed. "And be ready to get us there as fast as possible."

The archmage bowed. "I shall make every necessary preparation."

The knight glanced at Tomas. "We've got to get word to the Sylvai. Warn them they're being led by the nose."

Outside the tower, the two warriors crossed the cobblestone gap and returned to the merchant watching their horses. They remounted and rode back to the castle. "So," Tomas said as they traveled, "what's the story between you and this Anninihus?"

"We're both from the Gwyndd Islands."

"Do tell."

The knight rubbed the back of his neck. "Anninihus was born to a peasant mother and a noble father. When he found out about the pregnancy, the father cast out his mother and refused to even acknowledge the bastard. Anninihus had to become a beggar to survive."

"His father sounds like a great guy."

Rogan grimaced and shook his head. "A real piece of work, all right. When Anninihus turned twelve, he developed some magic ability, so managed to get himself inducted into the Guild and trained. After he thought he'd learned enough, he broke from his teachers and returned home. Offering his services, Anninihus' father took him in, finally acknowledge him as a bastard, at least."

"What about the mother?" Tomas asked.

The knight shook his head. "Long dead. Anyway, Anninihus worms his way into the family and starts using his powers to give his father an edge in politics and business. The family makes a huge fortune, but also suffers from several... accidents."

"Anninihus wanted to be the heir?" the squire guessed.

Rogan nodded. "He's smart. He covered his tracks and used his father's wealth to hire the best mercenaries he could find as a personal guard, including some Bellonari."

"Which is how you got into this," the squire guessed.

The knights shifted again in his saddle. "Sort of. Still had a few contacts in the Order at the time. They were the ones who thought like me that the Bellonari needed some serious change, but were too afraid to rebel like I did. Normally, they just warned when one of the hunter teams was tracking me, but every now and then, they let me know when something big was going to happen."

"Why would you care? I mean, good deeds are fine and all, but why would you travel all the way to the Gwyndd Islands, right into where a group of Bellonari are operating, just because of some noble family's squabbling?"

Rogan was quiet for a time before answering. "Because of which family was squabbling," he almost whispered.

"Ah... House Eigenhard?"

The knight nodded.

"Then, Anninihus is…?"

"My father's bastard." Rogan paused and leaned over in the saddle towards a nearby street vendor. He purchased a pair of krapfen, handing one of the sweetbreads to Tomas, before resuming their course towards the castle.

The knight ripped a chunk of the fried dough somewhat viciously with his teeth, licking at the fruit jam within. "Anninihus was using the Bellonari to maintain control over my family's lands," he said through a full mouth. "He also started arranging for a few 'accidents' to happen to the neighboring nobles. It was pretty obvious he had his eyes on House Eigenhard itself.

"I joined up with a small group that was fighting Anninihus and we eventually beat him. We captured or killed most of his allies, but he escaped. I offered to help my family rebuild, but was invited to continue my self-imposed exile.

"Wow," was all Tomas could say. "Why did you? I mean, they couldn't really *force* you out a potential heir after losing so many family members, could they?"

Rogan grew quiet and looked up at a certain set of stars, near the moon. The constellation of the Hunter, the squire realized. "Believe me, kid, I had a good reason for wanting to leave." Rogan shrugged away whatever thought was pressing in on him. "I found out later that, after he was beaten, Anninihus came here to the Keep. He managed to lie his way into the Tower."

"Why?" Tomas asked.

"Big part of the reason we beat him that first time is that he never finished his Guild training. Anninihus isn't the sort to make the same mistake twice. Anyway, when I came to the Keep, I found out Anninihus was here and told the King and Esha. We set a trap, and he fell into it. There was a trial, and you know the rest."

"Sounds like this guy has a lot of reasons to hate you," Tomas noted.

"And I've got more reasons to hate him," he replied with a snarl.

The young man looked carefully at his knight, seeing the hatred in his eyes, the thirst for vengeance. "What in Underworld did he do to you?"

"You mean besides killing hundreds of people, including several of my cousins, and trying to enslave my entire family?"

Tomas stopped his horse in the middle of the quiet street. The shops were closing and the vendors returning home. The squire sat and stared at Rogan for some time before speaking. "There's a difference between vengeance and justice. I've seen both. You don't want to bring Anninihus to justice, you want to kill him."

"You're right, kid. When we track him down, it's not going to be about justice."

"Why? If we're going to be working together, don't you think I should know?"

"Not really. It's personal."

"If it's personal, then why didn't you just kill him ten years ago when you first found out he was here?"

Rogan looked up again at the stars, his eyes misting. "Because she told me not to."

"She?"

"Hannah."

Tomas suddenly understood. There could be only one reason a man would have that much hate for someone over a woman that was not blood kin. "You two were close?"

The knight nodded. "In a lot of ways. We were closer anyone else."

"Does Kyla know about her?"

"I don't keep secrets from my wife. As a matter of fact, it was Kyla who convinced me to honor Hannah's last wish. She helped me through that grief. One of the many reasons we ended up together."

"But this time it's different," the squire guessed.

"Said it yourself, kid. We probably should have killed him in the first place."

Tomas and Rogan continued on, neither speaking for a long while. "So," the squire mused aloud, "do these morality issues come up a lot?"

The knight laughed. "Just wait until the first time Beraht gets us thrown in jail!"

Chapter 17

Days passed and Tomas' training continued. Weapons and tactics, armor and maintenance, ceremony and responsibility. The new squire's time was filled with learning, practicing, failing, and trying again. His time with Mary was frustratingly brief. The squire-in-training's days were so overwhelmed with tasks that he often left his rooms before the sun had risen, and only returned long into the night. Those evenings in which Tomas tried spending a candlelit dinner with his lady were often interrupted at the moment of peek intimacy by an alert, a drill, a new lesson, or a required duty within the city. Even on those occasions when Tomas found empty space in his schedule, Mary would be summoned away by Roland on some important matter within the castle. Their exploration of one another become clandestine, with one or the other sneaking away from their masters, secreting together for a stolen moment, only to be interrupted and separated once again. Days became weeks, and their frustration grew, even as Tomas' skills grew.

Whenever Rogan's duties required his presence, the prince required Tomas to come along, offering practical experience in addition to all the theory, and once again interfering with the squire's desired time with Mary. On one such day, three weeks after their meeting with Esha, Rogan took the opportunity of a scheduled inspection of the defenses to further familiarize Tomas with the Watch and the Calonar House Guard. Standing just outside the city gates, the same ones, the squire realized, he and Rogan had passed through almost a month ago, he had to admit the gates were a marvel of engineering. "Who designed these?" he asked.

Sergeant Klug Rainer, the same soldier who had originally greeted Tomas and Rogan when they arrived at the Northern Keep, stepped up and gestured towards a series of runes carved into one of the foundation stones of the outer wall bordering the gates. "The outer defenses were designed by Remm Stonebearer, that's his name in Uldric, and Cyras Darkholm. Several local Uldra clans came together to build the walls and gates out of friendship for House

Calonar." The veteran was dressed in the same blue and grey as all
the House Guard. His steel breastplate was so polished it seemed to
glow in the mid-morning sun, disrupted only by the bronze chevrons
engraved over his heart.

"Amazing."

"The genius in them lies in the use of a casemate system," the
sergeant said. He led Tomas back inside, to the center of the open
portal, and pointed to a separation between the various sections of
the city's primary defense. "It's similar to how the Uldra once built
their cities," Rainer continued, "or so the scholars tell us."

"Before the Uprising," Tomas nodded. "Before the Sylvai
destroyed all the Uldra cities, when the mountain-clans had their
fortresses across Ulheim." The squire had been surprised to learn
that the Northern Keep's walls followed this ancient design. He had
learned of casemate design long ago, but had only thought of it as a
curiosity of history. The Uldra fortress-cities were all long destroyed,
and after their Uprising, their race had lost the population and
resources to rebuild. Here it was in practice, though: an uldric
casemate wall. Three separate walls, actually; from the outside, the
system appeared to be a single stone barrier but, once inside, the
squire noted that large gaps separated each successive layer. Should
an attacker break through the first wall, they could advance little
more than a few yards before facing the next. Worse, as Rainer had
explained, the inner walls were themselves divided into individual
cells by small, separating interior walls. An attacker who breached
the first wall would accomplish little except gain access to what was,
effectively, an enclosed room.

Sergeant Rainer led Tomas up to the battlements and gestured
toward lines of metal grates that ran along the tops. "Anybody who
manages to break the first wall gets trapped in one of those cells, and
the defenders here can pour all kinds of evil on them." Overhearing
his words, the nearby Guardsmen grinned. Only Calonar House
Guard manned the walls and gates. The City Watch were responsible
for patrolling the interior, maintaining peace, and acting as an
auxiliary for the Guard.

"What're these?" Tomas asked, pointing to a series of arcane
glyphs carved into each section of the battlement.

"Wards," Rainer replied. "Esha and her students maintain
them."

"They stop magic?"

"More like disrupt it, I think. Esha says that they prevent magic from passing across or through the walls. Magic can still happen inside or outside the city, but it can't pass the walls."

Tomas nodded, though only partially understanding. He leaned a bit over the battlement and once again marveled at the genius of the Northern Keep's defenses. The first, outermost wall was that beautiful marble, quartz, and stone mixture commonly used in much of the Northern Keep's construction, heavy and durable. Along the inner wall, facing into the city, was a complex system of small watchtowers from which the Watch maintained a vigil, monitoring for fires. These supplemented the Guard garrison stationed along the battlements, within bastions. These small forts extended out from the wall in angular, almost arrow-head shapes. Within each bastion was a cache of crossbows and ammunition, extra poleaxes and swords, and a dedicated garrison of several Guard and at least one of Esha's wizards. "In times of emergency," Rainer said, walking along the battlement and gesturing back towards the gates, "we engage a pulley system. The portcullis in the center comes down, and on the interior, we close the steel gates. Those have more glyphs protecting from hostile magic." He nodded to the nearest bastion. "The standing garrison is supplemented and the City Watch reinforce."

"Sounds nearly impregnable," the squire observed as the two men made their way down a nearby stair, to the ground level and back towards the gates.

Rainer shook his head. "No such thing, I'm afraid. You do your best and plan for the worst, but if an attacker wants in bad enough, they'll find a way."

Tomas noticed that Rogan had returned from his inspections. The knight was standing at the open gate, speaking to a group of people who looked as though they had walked through Underworld itself. Not one of the miserable-looking group was remotely clean. Few had shoes or even decent clothes. Most of the children were so horribly thin it was a wonder they could stand, let alone look towards the city in open-mouthed wonder.

"What's going on?" the squire asked.

Rainer grinned. "Slave auction."

"WHAT!?!"

"I'm kidding," the sergeant said hurriedly. "Between the growing unrest in the south and the increasing Xeshlin slave raids, there're a lot of refugees, a lot of people being displaced. Rashid's agents and our Guard detachments do what they can when they encounter these poor bastards. They're given food and water and whatever money can be spared, and given the chance to go home."

"Are these people from the Northlands? Have the Xeshlin started raiding up here, as well?"

Rainer laughed. "Oh, no. I'll wager a week's pay that most of those people are from the south."

"What are they doing here?"

"Whenever Rashid's people liberate a Xeshlin slave caravan, or the Guard comes upon refugees that can't return home, the people are given the option of relocating where they want or coming here. Quite a few decide to make the long voyage here."

"Why would they want to come all the way up here?" Tomas asked.

"The chance of a better life." The soldier grimaced, looking at the newest refugees. "There're a lot of noble lords out there who exploit their people in the worst ways." Rainer looked at Tomas. "I heard you and the Prince passed through Alvaro?"

The squire nodded.

Rainer nodded his head towards the filthy, miserable-looking people. "Notice the clothes?"

Tomas looked closer and then started. Both men and women wore sleeveless tunics, the kind most common to the Duchy of Alvaro. "I thought House Calexto was in control of their lands, that the peasants were safe."

"Safe from raiders or warlords, maybe," the sergeant grimaced. "There are a lot of peasants in Alvaro, though. The minor lords have spent years earning extra income, and keeping the population in check, by selling unwanted, unneeded, or just surplice peasants to the Xeshlin." He cast Tomas a meaningful glance. "Didn't you ever wonder why the Xeshlin never bother raiding into Alvaro?"

Tomas could only shake his head, the terrible violation of a lord's sacred duty to protect his peasantry anathema to the young man's sense of decency.

Rainer nodded. "In their minds, it's practical. Easiest thing to do is sell people to the Xeshlin. Those bastards aren't choosey. You get rid of people you don't want, and make money on top of it.

"Slavery is illegal here, or serfdom or indentured servitude, or whatever clever little name you want to put on it. No one person can sell another, not even children. Plus, we always have need of more people. With all the Sylvai in the Wood, Xeshlin can never get close to the Keep. The city's industries have a hard time filling their employment needs, especially with all the new Uldra inventions coming out. That's why I joked about a slave auction."

"I still don't get it."

The sergeant pointed to where a large group of men and women approached the new arrivals. One woman, wearing the blue ceremonial robes of the Guild, walked down the line of the refugees, nodding to one who was then taken by grey-robed apprentices, along with his family. The man, his wife, and their two emaciated children all wept and hugged each other, nearly fawning on the blue-robed wizard. "Those're the real lucky ones," Rainer said. "He must be an adept. The local Guild will educate him and give his family care and employment."

Several priestesses from the Harvest Mother's Temple walked amongst the group, handing out clothes and food, speaking to each person. "The priestesses will make sure that everyone has food and shelter until they can take care of themselves," Rainer explained. He then nodded towards a group of children gathering around a pair of Sisters of the Lady of Light. "Their children will get an education."

Several local tradesmen, smiths, merchants, and craftsmen, among others, walked through the group, looking at hands and shoulders, looking into eyes and asking questions. "The Merchant's Guild will make sure that everyone has a job by the end of the day. People who already have a trade skill will be apprenticed. Anyone who doesn't already have a trade will be taught one."

Tomas was surprised to see Cardinal Tain arrive in the courtyard with a few priests. The old cleric entered the crowd and led several of them in a prayer of thanksgiving for the end of their long journey. Once finished, he then gathered to him the children who had lost their families and a few able-bodied men who seemed to the old priest to be most devout. "The Cardinal always takes care of the orphans," the sergeant said with pride. "The Church never turns anyone away."

"How often does this happen?" Tomas asked.

"We get a new group every few months. Even when Rashid's people aren't liberating caravans, word still spreads. Escaped slaves only have to reach the Northlands. Once they do, they fall under the law of House Calonar and are free." The aging veteran shook his head then. "It's getting worse, though," he sighed. "More refugees all the time. Smaller groups, though. More causalities; fewer survivors." The sergeant looked to the southern horizon. "Whatever's happening out there, it's getting worse."

"Politics," Tomas muttered as the dirty word he believed it was. "War and pride and greed."

"Amen."

A commotion rose from the streets beyond the gates. Tomas looked and saw Esha arrive with a new group of her students. The wizards were hurriedly moving to join Rogan, with whom they shared a brief but energetic consultation. The prince turned then, and barked orders for the City Watch to take charge of the refugees and move them away. Concerned, Tomas and Rainer joined Rogan and Esha as they moved through the gates.

"What's happening?" Tomas asked.

"Esha got word from Beraht," the knight replied grimly. "They're calling for an extraction."

"Extraction?"

"Just watch."

Sergeant Rainer had summoned a small Guard detachment and ordered them to spread out in a half circle. Esha's blue-robed students were using their wooden staffs to draw a full circle in the ground outside the city gates, chanting something in the arcane language. The tiny archmage herself stood outside this new ring, also chanting and making precise gestures in the air. When the circle was complete, the wizards stood back, their staves raised and their chant growing. A barked order from Sergeant Rainer brought poleaxes to the ready, all pointing inwards, to the center of Esha's circle.

A pressure grew within Tomas' skull. Slight at first, but quickly building. A tightness squeezed the back of his brain, as though some force was pressing in from the back, attempting to force his eyes from his skull. A strange buzzing sound, like a thousand, thousand bees cheerfully gathering nectar filled his ears. The young man's heart thudded in his chest and he tasted something metallic.

Within Esha's circle, a blue light was building. It crackled like merry lightning. It danced out from some infinitesimally tiny center point. The light swelled, along with the pressure in Tomas' mind. The light grew blinding, but somehow stayed within Esha's circle, constrained by the tiny archmage's students. There was a crack of lightning then, and the pressure in Tomas' skull was suddenly gone.

The light vanished and in its place was a large group of towering Uldra.

"You alright, kid?" Rogan asked.

Tomas blinked, trying to clear his vision, and worked his jaw. "Is it always like that?"

"The lightshow? Oh, yes." The knight stepped forward, and Tomas noticed Beraht among the Uldra. The bulging barbarian took his friend's hand with an evil grin even his voluminous beard could not hide. Beraht held a rope in one massive fist and, without turning, pulled on it. A tall man, though still dwarfed by the surrounding Uldra, stumbled forward. He had been stripped, his muscled yet lean body showing innumerable bruises, cuts, and other signs of recent violence. One eye was swollen shut, and blood still dripped from his clenched teeth, one of which was missing. Rogan stared at this man as though he could cause the prisoner to burst into flames through sheer hatred.

"Who's the prisoner?" Tomas asked as Rainer stepped forward.

The sergeant nearly growled an answer. "Vagris."

Tomas stared hard at the warlord who had caused so much suffering. His hand went almost of its own will to the golden rose that rested as always against the pulse in his throat. The young squire stared for a long time at the man who was ultimately responsible for Alexia's death. The man who had slaughtered the people of Railing. The man who betrayed the Legions.

Esha's students had lowered their staves and were returning to the city. The tiny archmage herself moved to join Tomas and Rainer, leaving a wide space between herself and the Uldra. "They captured him just outside the Wasteland of the Exiles, in the foothills of the Sentinel Mountains," she said sadly.

"What was he doing in the desert?" Rainer asked.

"Moving his army north," Esha answered. "The Uldra believe he was heading in our direction."

"Well, that raises a few questions," the sergeant muttered.

The sergeant barked orders to his Guard detachment. Four men stepped forward and claimed the prisoner from Beraht. The others stepped back as food and drink were brought forward. The grateful Uldra, their brutish weapons and armor showing signs of heaving fighting, gratefully accepted and greedily consumed the offerings, as though they had not had food or drink in days. Harvest Mother clerics moved up and began tending to the many wounds evident on the mountain-warriors. As this bustle progressed, Rogan stood as silent and still as Death Herself. His eyes never wavered from Vagris. The murderous, traitorous warlord stood tall and stared right back.

Tomas watched this all unfold with a torrent of conflicting emotions flooding through his young soul. Had it been any other man, Tomas would have said that Vagris was the epitome of Legionary training. The warlord never blinked, never wavered while his enemies laughed at him and made light of his impending execution. Though bruised and bloody, his body was muscular and lean. His long dark hair was mussed from his captivity but had clearly been kept neat in the Legionary standard. His chiseled face never betrayed any emotion but for his black eyes that burned with hatred. Even his stance was perfect, straight-backed proud without the slightest hint of weakness.

As the Guard untied the rope from around the warlord's wrists, neck, and waist, Tomas looked on, rubbing the golden rose at his neck and wishing a thousand hateful things on the villain. The soldiers put manacles on Vagris' wrists and tied a chain about his waist. In his mind, he heard Alexia warning him against such thoughts, warning him against starting on a path that could only end in Tomas' self-destruction. The squire did not want to hear her but could not avoid the memories. The scent of her hair and the sound of her laugh replaced his memories of her beaten body and dead eyes when last he saw his dear friend. With a sigh, the young man let the happier memories flood through his heart, banishing the dark emotions that Vagris had brought forth.

Vagris was led by Sergeant Rainer and the detachment of House Guard away from where the Uldra celebrated their return with the surrounding Guardsmen and gathering citizens. When he was brought close to Rogan, the renegade warlord finally pulled at his fetters, not in some futile attempt at escape or even in protest. He simply brought himself to a stop only a breath away from the Prince of House Calonar, staring daggers into his enemy. Rogan stared right back, an entire conversation of hatred passing between them. They stood, perfectly mirroring each other's posture and expression. "Good to see you again," the knight said with a dark smile, "brother."

The Guardsmen pulled Vagris, and the warlord turned his eyes away, locking them forward unflinchingly.

"I take it there's history between you two?" Tomas asked, rejoining his knight.

"That, kid, is a major understatement."

"Tienel Greysoul, Cyras Darkholm, Cylan Calonar. Now Vagris. Is there anyone in Lanasia you don't have a history with?"

Rogan thought about it. "I don't think I ever met the last Adama."

Chapter 18

Rogan released Tomas for the day, having made plans with his wife. The knight encouraged his squire to make similar time for Mary. "This job has a habit of burning time," he warned the young man. "Easiest thing in the world to lose track. A woman'll only tolerate neglect for just so long. Always take advantage of your opportunities."

The squire stared in open-mouthed shock at what his knight just said.

"What?" Rogan asked.

"*You're* the one who keeps interrupting us," Tomas pointed out in a tone of deep accusation.

"Oh, yeah," the noble prince recalled. Then he shrugged. "Well, a clever warrior would've found a way past all the obstacles."

Tomas shook his head and half turned, then stopped. "Wait," he said, turning back to face his innocent-looking knight. "Has this been a test?" he demanded.

Rogan walked past his fuming squire. "Don't know what you're talking about, kid."

During the long walk back to the castle, despite the crowded city streets and the groups of citizens in preparation for the upcoming festival, Tomas realized he was alone. For the first time in the weeks since his arrival at the Northern Keep, he was alone with his thoughts. No soldiers or spies dogged his steps and no Rogan dictated his course. Not even the eager moments stolen with Mary, huddled together in some shadowy corner. Having spent most of the last decade either alone or in the company of a very few, Tomas was surprised to realize that he occasionally missed his solitude and the opportunities for self-reflection it provided.

"Hello again, young sir."

Tomas turned and saw with surprisingly little surprise that the same cloaked stranger who he had met during his walk from the Church those many weeks ago had once again located him. Little had changed about the man. He was still of average build with a confident manner that spoke of a combination of breeding and cultured education. In the warmth of the late morning, his cloak was open, showing clothes that, while very fine, were not so expensive as to be extravagant. He wore no jewelry or adornments on his soft hands or fit body, only a series of small pouches that were sewn into his leather belt.

For the first time, the shepherd was able to clearly see the man's face, marveling that in an age of pestilence and poverty, he lacked any blemishes or discoloration of any kind; indeed, he was exceptionally well-groomed with only that same slight twitch that marred his otherwise fine features. His brown eyes shown clear and bright with only a slight series of wrinkles giving mute evidence of many nights pouring over books. His dark hair had the first signs of grey at the temple, and although he was thin in the face, he was not overly so.

"Hello again, sir," Tomas replied to his greeting, extending his hand.

The stranger smiled slightly and took the squire's hand in his own, not shaking but holding it steady while muttering words very softly under his breath in a language Tomas did not recognize.

"What are you doing?" the young man asked.

Again, the stranger smiled and released Tomas' hand. "Just an old tradition," he explained. "Something of a blessing. I hope I did not offend you with it."

"I'll take all the blessings I can get these days."

"I see you are headed for the castle," the cloaked man observed. "I myself am headed in that direction today. Would you object to some companionship for the trip?"

"No, I suppose not." Tomas gestured ahead, and the two men continued their walk at a very leisurely pace. After a few steps, a chill seemed to hit the older man, despite the growing warmth of the late spring day. A shiver ran through his body, slight, but noticeable. With a sigh, the stranger pulled his cloak closed around his lean frame.

"By the way, you never did introduce yourself," Tomas pointed out.

"Did I not?" the stranger asked. "How unobservant of me. You may call me Aneirin."

"It's a pleasure, Aneirin."

"I certainly hope so, Master Tomas."

"How is it that you know my name? I don't recall giving it to you."

"You will find, young sir, there are very few within this city who have not heard the name Tomas Fidelis of late. The whole of the Northern Keep is abuzz with the news. Prince Rogan has taken a squire; a young man who has come all the way from the ruins of the old Capital to bring down the Black Duke, only to be converted to House Calonar."

"I wouldn't really call it a conversion," Tomas said defensively.

"Of course not," Aneirin agreed. "I am simply relaying what I have overheard. Am I to assume that your business here will take some time longer than you originally thought?"

"It's beginning to look that way. And you; is your business nearly complete?"

"Not just yet, though it does progress well. I'm afraid I will be forced to remain here some while longer."

"You say that as though you wish it were not so," the squire pointed out.

"This is true. Of all the places in the world I could be, the Northern Keep certainly does not rate very high."

"Why is that? This city seems pleasant enough."

"On the surface, young sir. But have you peered deeper into this charming facade?"

"I don't understand. What do you mean?"

Aneirin gestured around. "You look around and you see a citizenry that is happy, well-fed, and living peacefully with all those around them."

"Yes. It would appear House Calonar has managed to build a community that anyone would wish to live in."

"But I ask you, Tomas, where are the poor? Where are those who do not live in plenty?"

"I haven't seen any poor since coming here."

"Precisely. Have you ever heard of a city which had no poor?"

Tomas thought for a moment. "I can't say I have."

"Neither have I. So it begs the question, where are the lower classes of citizens here?"

"Do you know?"

Aneirin sighed. "I suspect, young sir. I suspect, but I do not know."

"What do you suspect?"

"Have you noticed that there seems to be a great deal of wealth in this city?"

"Yes."

"And have you wondered where it all comes from?"

"I honestly haven't thought of it."

"Money does not simply appear, Tomas. It must be coming from somewhere."

"But where?" the squire asked.

In response, the cloaked man gestured to the distant mountains, rising even above the surrounding forest. "It is said that great wealth can be found in Ulheim. Rivers of gold and mountains of jewels rest beneath those dangerous peaks."

Tomas snorted. "And hordes of Druug ready to kill anyone who tries to acquire that wealth."

"True," Aneirin agreed. "It would be greatly hazardous to journey into Ulheim. But what if you had a workforce that would otherwise produce nothing but consume much? Would it not be highly efficient to use them as cheap labor to harvest the wealth of Ulheim?"

"That would be monstrous! No worker who entered those mountains could be expected to survive!"

"No, not for long, at any rate. Perhaps only long enough to gather more wealth than either you or I could imagine and get it back to the safety of Wildelves Wood. Did you have the chance to see the arrival of those escaped slaves?"

"Yes. I saw the Arcane and Merchant's Guilds, Church, and various temples pick out the people they thought they could employ."

"And what of the rest?"

"I was told that they would be taught new skills and given employment."

"Skills such as mining and gold-digging?"

"Are you saying the Black Duke is using those people to expand his wealth in such a horrible way?"

Aneirin shook his head. "I am saying nothing, Master Tomas. I have no proof as yet, only suspicions. After all, a new group of those runaway slaves arrives every few weeks, yet the city does not suffer from over-population. It is a strange thing, one must admit."

"Is that what your business here is? Are you gathering information for one of the other Noble Houses to use against House Calonar?"

"I think I have perhaps said too much, young sir, especially to one now in service to House Calonar." Aneirin stopped and gestured down a side street, away from the castle. "I'm afraid this is where I must leave you, Tomas. My affairs are in that direction."

"Good day to you then, sir. I hope we have the chance to speak again."

"One never knows. I suppose it depends on what duties your new master has for you. Farewell, Master Tomas."

"Farewell," the squire said, looking on as the stranger walked away. Dark thoughts entered the young man's mind, and doubts resurfaced.

Chapter 19

Over the next week, Rogan's suspiciously well-coordinated interference in Tomas and Mary's interludes only increased. It seemed as though each time the young couple found a moment to steal away together, some dark corner or forgotten closet that could provide them some eagerly-desired intimacy, the echoing roar of "Let's go, kid!" reverberated through the halls. The mornings grew earlier and the days grew longer. Spring was drawing to a close and summer looming. And Tomas' exasperation grew almost intolerable. This is to say nothing of Mary's ever-burning interests.

Tomas began developing skills in evasion, deception, and coercion. When a messenger arrived from the Prince, demanding the squire's presence, Tomas would angrily demand why the messenger had not gotten the countermanding order. When Rogan's stomping boots echoed down the hall, the squire would dart behind a large drapery, or contort his young body to match a sculpture or decorative plant. When he and Mary found a moment in a tiny closet and Roland or some other emissary of adult supervision appeared, the pair vanish into shadows just before the moment of discovery.

Somehow, their stolen moments became more precious for their rarity, for the constant danger of interruption. Each taste of Mary's gentle lips was sweeter than the purest nectar. Each caress from her soft hands was like the welcoming touch of a new sunrise. Each instant of contact with her flawless flesh was like the caress of new-spun silk. He found eternal bliss, even if only for a few moments, swimming in the moonlit pools of her eyes. He drank the healing wind of her breath. He hungered for her, and she for him; their snatched moments each more valued than perfect gemstones.

The couple would sneak away together, finding seclusion anywhere they could find. In the castle, they would discover a balcony in an unused guest room. Tomas and Mary would spend hours beneath the stars, lying together in the crisp springtime air. The squire would point out the various constellations and their roots in the ancient mythologies of Lanasia. When they could sneak away from their duties in the city, the couple would meet in a small park or at a shaded bench. Mary would dance for Tomas, her legs gliding as though on glass, no matter the cobblestone and her arms slipping through the air in flawless, continuous movement. As time passed, she would even lift Tomas to his feet and teach him some of the dances, guiding his arms and legs through the spiraling movements.

They reveled in each moment they spent together. Their moments of bliss were made all the more important, all the more treasured, since both Tomas and Mary knew they were limited. No matter their secrecy, no matter their stealth, inevitably a call would come and they would be forced apart again.

For some reason that confounded Tomas, to say nothing of further frustrating Mary, the interruptions for training did not infuriate the squire. He was upset at being separated yet again from his lady, but that feeling was tempered by his enthusiasm for the work. Each day brought new challenges, new skills, new knowledge. His young body was hardening with muscle and knowledge, and his mind was devouring all that Rogan had to teach.

"So, what's today?" Tomas asked as he followed his knight down the main staircase towards the castle's central courtyard on a pleasant morning. Rogan had arrived annoyingly early yet again, intercepting Tomas and Mary's breakfast before the food cold give way to other forms of consumption. Despite this, as was so often the case, Tomas offered only token complaints before eagerly leaning into the day's training.

"Sneaking lesson," Rogan grinned.

"What?"

"You're doing a pretty good job learning the basics. Fighting, working, taking care of armor. You need some work in the sneaky stuff, though. You need to get better at being invisible. Thought it was time we moved on to some hard stuff."

"Oh, I don't know," the squire argued. "I thought I might be picking up a few sneaky tricks."

"You mean like ducking behind that plant?" the knight snorted, thumbing his nose at a small potted tree under the care of Princess Karen that had sheltered Tomas from Rogan's messenger only the day before. "Or that closet?" he added, nodding towards a small closet that had sheltered Tomas and Mary from Roland.

The young man came to a dead stop in open-mouthed shock.

Rogan also stopped and glanced back. "Just remember, kid. I'm older, wiser, more experienced, and more treacherous than you can ever guess." The knight then resumed his course, walking out into the castle's courtyard.

"So, what kind of sneaking lesson," the squire muttered sullenly after catching up to his knight.

The two made their way down the hatchback road leading down from the castle. "Talked with Aebreanna last night" Rogan said. "She agreed to work with you on the quiet skills you lack. Sneaking up on people, getting past them without being noticed, blending into your environment, that sort of thing."

The two passed over the great bridge crossing the castle's moat. "Now look," the knight told his squire. "Aebreanna is just about the best spy in the world. There's a lot she can teach you, so pay attention. Do what she says, when she says, how she says."

"You're not coming?" Tomas asked.

Rogan shook his head. "Got a meeting with Rashid and General Killdare. Try to meet up with you later, but it may run long."

"Where's Baroness Tressalon?" the young man asked, looking around the bridge.

"She's waiting for you in the city gardens. You know where that is?"

Tomas nodded. "Mary's told me about it," he answered. "But from what she said, they're pretty big. How do I find her?"

Rogan laughed. "She'll find you."

The squire sighed and left.

Tomas needed more than an hour to walk to the gardens, located as they were in the far north-western corner of the Northern Keep. No mere stone wall separated the gardens from the rest of the city; instead, a towering hedge more than twenty feet high marked the border. This living barrier seemed to be a complicated network of innumerable plants, and the dahlias and astras made the hedge seems as though a rainbow had erupted in this corner of the city. The vibrant wall opened at several locations into high arches covered in more flowers of all different colors, providing easy access from nearly any direction. Tomas passed though one of these living gateways, looking about in wonder.

A rolling park spread out before him. A number of small creeks, tributaries of the Oolaug River, lazily flowed through the gardens, forming small pools and tumbling waterfalls. Flower bushes were scattered about, providing a beautiful break to the sea of green. Several paths meandered their way through the gardens, crossing the creeks by means of wooden bridges that rose in high arches. Several large groves of trees rested in scattered groups, the flowering of their spring foliage contributing to the near-riot of colors, and everywhere the young man looked, people in both small groups and alone enjoyed the serenity of this reserve.

A voice stabbed at the squire from behind. "Tomas," it said.

The young man spun with a yelp, jumping back and raising his fists in fright. The spy Vincent stood at ease, with no emotion on his common-looking face. The only change to the agent's expression was a raised eyebrows in response to the squire's fear.

Tomas struggled to regain his breath and slow his pounding heart. "Was there something you wanted?" he tried to ask, lowering his clenched fists.

Vincent pointed to a grove of trees resting in a far corner of the gardens. "She's waiting for you," he replied in a voice that was barely a whisper.

The young man glanced towards the grove. Turning back to ask a question, he noted with little surprise that the spy had vanished as suddenly as he had appeared. Tomas shook his head in annoyance and made his way across the expansive gardens to the cluster of trees indicated. Entering the grove, the squire looked about the area, trying to find the Baroness Aebreanna Tressalon. Seeing nothing, he continued in deeper. The young man's search continued; he circled the entire area, looking behind every tree, even going so far as to push through thick bushes in his search.

Tomas was on the verge of overturning rocks when an acorn hit him on the top of the head. Looking up suddenly, the squire finally spotted the baroness, seated sedately on a large tree branch and looking down at him in disappointment. "How long have you been up there?" he demanded.

"Long enough to grow impatient," she replied. "Did it never occur to you during your exhaustive search to even once look up?"

"Well... uh..."

The beautiful Sylva slid backwards off her perch, leaping from one branch to another with grace that shamed the observing squirrels. Her long honey-blonde hair danced about her narrow shoulders, the golden mane now turning a darker hue with the summer so near, and her skirt flaring scandalously as she danced to the ground. She landed in front of Tomas, her descent disturbing not a single leaf nor blade of grass.

"If you are to learn from me," she said in a musical voice, "the first lesson is this: always look in the places unseen. Always search in the places unreachable. That is where you will find your prey."

"I thought you were teaching me how to sneak," the squire grumbled. "Not hunt." Even though he was fully a head taller than the Sylva, still Tomas shrank from the neutral gaze of her verdant opalescent eyes.

Baroness Tressalon led her charge deeper into the grove of trees. "You will find that the two endeavors often share a great deal in common with one another. A successful spy is very much a predator. The only significant difference existing between one of Rashid's agents and a hunter of the plains is that we hunt far more dangerous prey."

"And on that lighter note..." Tomas replied.

The spy stopped and faced him, a deadly serious look on her perfect face and unforgiving gaze in her nearly-hazel, opalescent eyes. "For as long as you serve Rogan, you must understand one fact, if no other. Your knight will never, until his dying breath, allow injustice or villainy to exist in *Ar'ae'el*. Rogan Eigenhard will die in battle, of this there can be little doubt. He will forever seek out those in need, a fight needing a warrior, victims needing a savior, and a cause needing a champion. I have known Rogan for more than a decade, and in that time, I have learned that even on those very rare occasions in which he is not actively seeking out danger, danger is seeking him.

"As his squire, you will find yourself in situations that seem as though to spring from nothing. You are apprenticed to a man incapable of avoiding danger and difficulty. As his second, you must learn his skills. You must move as he does, fight as he does. If silence is needed, you must absorb the sound around you. If stealth is required, you must be less than invisible. All these things I can teach you. All these things I will teach you, no matter how difficult or painful the lessons." She paused. "To you."

Tomas stood in place, staring at the Sylva with an open mouth and beating heart. "And suddenly," he noted, "I'm terrified."

The baroness smiled a sly smile. "That is good," she purred, "Males are most obedient when afraid." She gestured towards an opening in the trees and a large, still figure beyond. Tomas looked as closely as he could without moving and saw, to his surprise, the Uldra warrior, Beraht. "Lesson the first," Baroness Tressalon said softly. "Your target is aware of your presence and stands ready in an open area. You must eliminate the target silently and at very close range." She handed Tomas a small twig. "You must approach Sir Beraht unnoticed and tap him lightly on the shoulder with this."

He took the twig and looked over at Beraht, noting the Uldra's utter lack of attention. As he stared, Beraht absently scratched his nose and then picked it. "You've got to be kidding." Tomas all but laughed. "I have to sneak up on *him*!?! Why sneak? I could walk right up to his face beating a drum and he'd never realize I was there! With all that hair growing out of his ears, I'd be surprised he can hear anything at all!"

Aebreanna never changed her expression. Instead, she just stood, waiting for the young man to execute the task. Tomas rolled his eyes, sighed, and began moving through the woods. Making at least some effort at silence, the squire circled the clearing, making sure to never lose sight of Beraht, until he had a perfect view of the Uldra's broad back. Standing there with his back to a large tree, the young man could not help but chuckle. His target was currently yawning and apparently doing his level best to remain awake. He was having little success.

Remembering Aebreanna's speech to him on the predator mind-set, Tomas crouched low and slowly stalked towards his target. Moving with a stealth that came as something of a surprise to the squire, he moved step by step to his objective. Closer and closer he crept, never once breaking the intense stare that bore into the Uldra's massively muscled back. Tomas held his breath as he drew within arm's reach of Beraht, reveling in the excitement of the moment. The squire could not resist the temptation that crept into his heart; he drew even closer to his target, moving right up behind Beraht until he could count the innumerable hairs on the back of the Uldra's neck.

And then there was an Uldra fist in his face.

Tomas noted with surprise that he was lying on the ground, looking up, through gently-swaying branches into a cloudless blue sky. A very pretty sight, now that he had a moment to appreciate it. The young man also appreciated the blood pouring from of his nose. Beraht walked up and looked down on the bleeding squire. "That was for the ear hair remark," he grumbled with his thick uldric accent. "I'll have you know it's for insulation in the winter."

Aebreanna then leaned over Tomas. In his somewhat concussed state, the young man noticed that her flowing mane almost perfectly matched the brightening flowers of the surrounding woods. "Was knocking him to the ground really necessary?" The tiny baroness asked the towering barbarian.

Beraht shrugged. "It got the point across."

And so, the morning progressed. Again and again, Aebreanna would present for Tomas a scenario that he was to endure, always trying to out-wit, out-think, or out-sneak Beraht. In every situation, Tomas was confounded by the Uldra. Time and again, the squire was frustrated by his target's seeming inattention or stupidity, which would lure the young man into making a mistake that Beraht never failed to take advantage of.

It was during one such scenario that Tomas had finally had enough. The squire was sneaking through the trees, moving in utter silence while hunting for Beraht. He had seen the Uldra briefly leaning against a tree, but once he had finally made his way to where the barbarian should have been, there was nothing, not even tracks in the thick foliage. Tomas moved through the trees, scanning all about for his objective, but could see nothing. As engrossed as he was in his search, he failed to notice the lumbering mountain-man walking no more than half a step behind him, perfectly mimicking his every movement.

"Enough," Aebreanna exclaimed, exasperated beyond all measure.

"What?" Tomas demanded.

In response, the spy merely made a turning gesture with her small finger. The young man turned in response to the silent command and jumped more than three feet in the air with a startled yelp. Beraht thought the situation was more than a little amusing. Hearing his rumbling laughter, even Aebreanna was hard-pressed to fight a smile.

"What's the point of all this!?!" the squire demanded, his face bright red in utter rage.

"Patience," Aebreanna advised through her smile. "For your next attempt..."

"No more!" Tomas thundered. "No more hoops! No more jokes at my expense! I can't sneak up on Beraht! I don't know how, but that lumbering mountain is too damned good! You've known him for a decade, and you damned well knew I couldn't sneak up on him! Now you'll tell me just why in Underworld I've been wasting my entire damned morning!!"

For the first time since the training began, Aebreanna gave the young man a smile and a nod of approval. "The whole purpose of this," she explained, "was not to teach you how to move silently or stalk someone. This was not meant to teach you how to avoid capture or sneak past someone without their noticing. This morning's purpose was only to teach you not to underestimate anyone.

"As you have said, Tomas, Sir Beraht is much too experienced to be caught unawares by someone with your lack of training. But I knew that you would have an ill-conceived preconception of my hairy associate as mentally deficient. While I cannot deny he is Uldra in both his girth and mental prowess, I was forced long ago to acknowledge that approaching Sir Beraht unnoticed is quite nearly impossible."

The Uldra glanced down at his Sylva compatriot, visibly unsure as to whether or not he was being insulted.

"During your adventures with Rogan, you will encounter many strange types of peoples and creatures. In most cases, your natural, overly-Human inclination will be to make an assumption on the abilities of these entities based solely on physical appearance and demeanor. This, above all else, you must avoid. Until you have seen your opponent in action, until you are certain of their exact capabilities, you must remain vigilant. Never assume you have the advantage. Never assume you are unseen. These things will bring your end as surely as any blade."

Aebreanna's words rang in Tomas' mind. He felt their truth, their wisdom. He found himself nodding, even as his anger and frustration drained away as though it had never been.

"Is this a closed lecture?" Rogan asked from the tree line. "Or can anyone chime in?"

"Hello, Rogan," Beraht grumbled. "I was wondering when you'd show up."

"Would've been here sooner, but there's trouble brewing. Just got the latest update from Rashid."

"Serious?" Aebreanna asked.

The knight shrugged. "Could get that way. Apparently Frostfront has refused the treaty with House Calexto. They pulled their forces back to further up the Corona River. Rashid thinks they plan to wait until their full force arrives sometime in the summer and retake Jarek by force. We've dispatched a team of diplomats to Frostfront and Alvaro to try and get everyone to the negotiating table. Right now, things don't look too good, and it's only getting worse."

"Gloomy thoughts," Aebreanna noted, turning and pulling a large basket from behind a tree. "Something I have noted a meal helps alleviate." The spy carried her large basket to a fair-sized clearing, giving brief commands to each of the three warriors in preparation of their lunch. Beraht cleared a few rocks to level their picnic area while Rogan spread out a large blanket for them to sit on and Tomas was sent to a nearby creek for water. Under Aebreanna's careful supervision, each of them received a fair and equal portion of the food, dismissing each of their protests that they deserved a larger share than any other.

When finally the meal was over, and the minor horseplay of the boys was brought to an end, Aebreanna again commanded them in the clean-up, making all necessary preparations for the work ahead.

"More training?" Tomas complained. "Haven't we done enough already."

The Sylva looked at him evenly, her nearly-hazel, opalescent eyes forcing the taller male into submission. "I have been tasked with preparing you for service to Rogan, and I shall do just that. When you have shown ample improvement, we shall be finished."

"Well, good luck," Rogan said, standing and belting on his sword. "Guess I'll catch up with you all later."

"On the contrary," Aebreanna argued. "The next phase of your squire's training requires your presence."

"Oh, well I really have to..."

"Stay here and assist? Yes, I agree."

Beraht stood and grabbed his massive uldric waraxe. "Well, if Rogan here is going to help, I'll just be..."

"Sit," the spy commanded. "Stay. Good boy."

Both warriors sullenly sat back down.

Aebreanna turned to Tomas. "This next lesson will involve moving past two sentries who are unaware of your presence," she instructed. "I will accompany you as you do this. You must move as I do, step as I step."

"I don't think he's got the hips for that!" Beraht laughed.

The Sylva turned very slowly to burn her companion with an opalescent stare. "Did you speak?" she asked evenly.

"Uh... no." A slight sylva frown compelled him to add, "No, ma'am."

"Um, Aebreanna?" Tomas spoke up hesitantly.

"Yes?"

"How are we supposed to sneak past them if they already know we're here?"

"Nothing simpler," she replied. "I will make them start arguing, and then we may proceed."

"You can get them to argue?" the squire asked. "Just like that?"

"Yes."

"Now, hold on," Rogan argued, standing. "As good as you like to think you are, Aebreanna, you forget that Beraht and I have been fighting side by side for more than a decade now."

Beraht stood as well. "That's right. We've been comrades and friends a long while now."

The knight nodded and put his hand up on the Uldra's shoulder. "It would take more than anyone could do to drive us apart," he insisted.

"Friends to the end," the Uldra agreed.

"How very sweet," she mumbled. "Have you perhaps forgotten about Rogan's knighting ceremony? The one in which Sir Beraht and Remm Stonebearer showed up so inebriated that Kyla was forced to employ her magic to sober them and prevent a scene?"

"Now what makes you think that would cause an argument?" the knight asked. "I forgave Beraht a long time ago for that."

The Uldra broke their embrace and took a step back. "What do you mean, *you* forgave *me*?" he demanded. "Don't you think that wife of yours is the one who should be doing the apologizing?"

Aebreanna nodded to Tomas, and the two moved into the trees.

"Why should she apologize?" Rogan demanded. "You two were making complete asses of yourselves!"

"We needed to do *something* to liven up that party! Nothing but yawns and formality before we got there!"

"It was a ceremony! It was supposed to be solemn!"

"Solemn!?! Try stupid!"

The yelling quickly became roaring. The roaring led to pushing which quickly led to hitting. Tomas and Aebreanna moved through the trees, taking full advantage of the distraction. The spy nodded with approval as her student quickly picked up the techniques of combining precision and care to create stealth and speed. Within a matter of only a few minutes, Aebreanna led Tomas in a half circle, moving rapidly from one end of the clearing around to the other with Rogan and Beraht never sensing them. The squire stood panting and glowing in victory, relishing his accomplishment. His Sylva teacher did not have the look of approval that he had hoped for, however; much the opposite in fact.

The young man realized that her look of utter distaste was not directed at him, but at something behind him. Looking back, he could not help but chuckle, seeing Rogan and Beraht lying on the ground, doing their best to choke the life out of the other.

It took Aebreanna only a few minutes of negotiating to resolve the dispute she herself had started. The two warriors sullenly apologized, after being ordered to do so, and made amends. Tomas watched all this with a tightly controlled smile, not wishing to incur the wrath of the beautiful spy.

Once Aebreanna had completed her chastisement, they moved on to what the Sylva assured him would be the final lesson of the day. Before the squire was even aware of his new situation, he found himself hidden in the thick foliage surrounding the trees, staring at Rogan's sword.

"You must reach this weapon," Aebreanna had told him as she drove the blade into the ground.

Seeing her do this, the knight had objected, "What in Underworld...!?!"

"You were the one to ask me for assistance as I recall," she had pointed out.

"You know how much moisture there is in that ground?" he had demanded.

"If your tool is so feeble that it cannot withstand such a minor test of endurance, then perhaps it is unsuitable for the tasks required of it."

Beraht had leaned over to Tomas. "You know," he grinned, "she was really making fun of his..."

"Yeah I got it," the young man had replied.

The knight had stomped off into the woods, muttering under his breath something about giving the Sylva rust poisoning should even one blemish appear on his sword. Following this, Tomas had been commanded to lose himself in the trees and discern some way to reach the blade. The task, though simple in nature, had not fooled the squire. Beraht had given more than enough lessons that appearances could be deceiving. The knight may have appeared to have been disgruntled to the point that he would not be paying attention, but Tomas would not take that chance.

Now, the young man was crouched low, his eyes slowly scanning the trees. He frequently shifted his view to the branches above and the gaps that grew among the large roots running along the ground below. The sword was close enough to Tomas that the squire could very nearly reach out and touch it. Even with his goal so very close, he would not grow impatient, would not underestimate his opponent.

Movement in the branches drew his gaze. It was slight, probably nothing more than another breeze making its way through the thick green canopy that seemed to plunge the entire area into shadow. Still, Tomas' eyes remained locked on the area of the motion. Finally, his mind understood what it was that his eyes were showing him: a straight line. Mixed among the leaves and branches of a tree overhead, there was a straight line. Rogan's scabbard had betrayed his position.

A slight smile crept onto the squire's face. Even through the thick shield of leaves, Tomas could now easily make out his knight's silhouette. Rogan was facing in his general direction, remaining as perfectly still as possible and yet somehow moving with the swaying branches to scan the area. If his opponent had spotted him, there was no sign of it. The squire decided to wait; an opportunity would present itself.

The moments turned to minutes. The minutes grew in number. A small bug crept across Tomas' hand, but still the squire did not move. At long last, an opportunity appeared. Rogan had turned away; slowly, never revealing his position had his squire not already spotted him, the knight turned and looked in a different direction.

Tomas exploded from the brush, sprinting to the sword in a blur. His hand closed on the hilt, and he pulled the weapon free, raising it high in the air and roaring in victory.

Aebreanna and Beraht emerged from the trees, the Sylva clapping her small hands and the Uldra digging in his cavernous ear. The spy smiled and nodded. "Very well done," she said. "You showed discipline, stamina, patience, and observation. You waited until you saw your opponent and waited still until an opening presented itself. I must admit to being pleasantly surprised."

"It was nothing," Tomas exalted. "Just doing what you told me to."

"However..."

The young man's face fell. "However? However what? I got the damned sword; Rogan never spotted me until I'd already reached it. What in Underworld do you want!?!"

She pointed at the weapon in Tomas' hand. The young man glanced down and then did a double take. The sword he held was not Rogan's.

"How? What? Who?" Words came with great difficulty to the young man just then.

Beraht drew his arm from behind his back, revealing the knight's weapon.

"How?" Tomas demanded. "When?"

"While you were so engrossed in observing Rogan," Aebreanna replied, "he signaled Beraht to switch out the swords."

"The movement," the squire noted, cursing his over-confidence.

"Yes. Once again, you assumed your opponent had not spotted you. Once again, you were wrong. As I observed, Rogan spotted you while you were still moving into position. Once you were set, he slowly moved his scabbard around until he was certain you would see it and waited. Once he knew he held your attention, he had Beraht change out the swords."

"I could have sworn he hadn't seen me."

"You forget. Your objective was not to remain unseen; it was to reach the sword. Had you, at any point, leapt from your hiding place, you could have easily reached your goal well before Rogan would have had time to react. This was the lesson for you to learn. Never lose sight of your objective. Stealth is a fine tool, but sometimes boldness may carry you further."

Tomas shook his head. "Is there ever going to be a time when I don't feel like a struggling student?"

Aebreanna crossed and reached up, putting her hands on the squire's slumped shoulders. "Everyone must begin somewhere," she said with a warm smile. "Never lose confidence. You have progressed much today. In very little time you will be formidable in every way."

"Aha!" Rogan's cry echoed from behind. Tomas and Aebreanna looked up to see the knight holding his sword less than a finger's breath away from his eyes and pointing at a spot on the blade so minuscule as to be nearly invisible. "Do you see that?" he demanded. "Well, do you!?!"

"Yes," Aebreanna sighed, "I see. Surely such a blemish will forever hamper your performance."

"You know," Beraht chuckled, "she's really talking about his..."

"Yeah, I got it," Tomas sighed.

"What did I say?" Rogan thundered. "Not my sword. You had another but noooo."

"It doesn't look that bad to me," the squire noted.

"Not now, but this is how it starts. One little spot and the next thing you know, I'm standing there with nothing but a hilt in my hand! Do you know how ridiculous I'd look with just this little nothing in my hand!?!"

"I must admit," Aebreanna smiled, "I find the image more than a little amusing. But you surely must have had this problem at some point in your life; possibly during adolescence?"

"You know..." Beraht chuckled. "She's really..."

"I got it, alright, I got it."

"This is no laughing matter!" Rogan snapped. "Rust is a serious threat in the field."

The Sylvu rolled her opalescent eyes while licking her finger sensuously and running it along the length or the knight's blade, removing the offending spot with a finishing flick of her wrist. "You know," she sighed, "you really must stop trying to make something so insignificant seem so very great and powerful."

Beraht grinned at Tomas.

"Oh, for the love of God, I got it already!"

Chapter 20

The next day, after having lunch with Rogan and Aebreanna following another sneaking lesson, the squire used his new skills to evade the adults, returning to the castle early to see if Mary would be able to escape her duties as he had his. While climbing the increasingly impressive main staircase in search of his lady, the young man was distracted from his search by sounds of fighting echoing through the castle. Looking about, Tomas was surprised to note that the people making their way through that area paid little heed to the raging battle. His curiosity had to be sated. Following the often-times frightening curses and ring of steel on steel, the squire made his way through the many hallways, finally arriving at the training chambers of the House Guard. Sticking his head in the doorway, Tomas was shocked to see Beraht and another Uldra who was, if possible, even larger and thicker, doing their absolute best to behead one another while shouting obscenities back and forth.

"Take that, you drunken horse's ass!" Beraht roared as he swung his uldric waraxe in a mighty overhead blow. The light from the barred windows reflected off the flawless, polished blade of the imposing weapon.

Dodging the attack easily, the other Uldra launched a vicious slashing counter-attack, his own weapon a double-bladed axe with an even longer handle and a hoked point at the tip. The barbarian shouted, "You've used that toy too many times you sickly little Sylvu!" His voice, even thicker than Beraht's with the accent of the mountain-men, was far deeper, like the growling echo of a rockslide from a bottomless ravine.

"SYLVU!?!" Beraht roared indignantly, hopping back and then charging back in. The floor was bare stone, and the steel-toed boots of the two mountain-men scraped sparks from the scared flooring. "I'll make you eat those words and my axe, you old fool!"

The two weapons collided, both Uldra pushing each other in a contest of pure strength. The stone-like muscles of each barbarian twisted and throbbed in overt contest, and it seemed as though the air itself in the large hall seethed in this contest of unimaginable strength.

"Give up!" Beraht growled. "You cannot beat me!"

"Ha!" the other Uldra barked. "Your breath is stronger than your arm!"

"And your backside stronger still!"

Anticipating this contest taking some time, Tomas cleared his throat. The two Uldra, realizing they had a visitor, stopped their battle instantly.

"You're Tomas, right?" the unfamiliar Uldra asked gruffly but amiably. "Rogan's new squire."

"Uh, that's right. What are you two doing?"

"Remm here thought he could take me," Beraht explained, punching his friend in the chest. "I had to teach him a lesson."

Remm punched Beraht in the stomach. "You're the one that needs schooling, youngster!" The young man blinked as the older Uldra finally turned towards him and provided a better view. The old fighter appeared to be divided down the center; on his left side he was a typical Uldra of advanced years, long black hair going to grey, a full beard that matched, and a piercing black eye. On Remm's right was an almost entirely different person; solid white hair and beard were matched to a bright blue eye and strange, swirling black tattoos that covered every inch of his exposed skin.

Noticing the stare, both Beraht and Ream laughed. "I think he's in love!" Remm barked.

"I'm sorry," Tomas said, "I don't mean to stare, but…"

"Let this be a lesson to you, runt!" the old Uldra laughed. "Never make bets with wizards!"

"A wizard did that?"

"Well I sure in Underworld did not do it to myself!"

"Did it hurt?"

Remm shrugged, apparently not noticing Beraht sneaking up behind him. "About as much as having fire poured down your throat while an army of Druug chews out of your stomach."

"Ouch."

"I've had worse." The old Uldra shot a fist over his shoulder, catching Beraht on the nose.

"Now that I'm thinking of it, uh Beraht?"

"What?" Beraht asked, putting Remm in a headlock.

"I meant to ask you yesterday, but I got caught up in the training. How did you find Vagris so quickly?"

Beraht roared, throwing Remm halfway across the room. The older barbarian crashed into a weapons rack, causing an avalanche of poleaxes. "Esha found him and magicked us nearly on top of them," Beraht said. "We spent a few days maneuvering before getting to business. it took a few weeks to hunt them all down, but my people did a thorough job."

"But what was he doing so far north? His territory is down around Railing and Pelsemoria."

"Who knows? Let Rashid worry out the whys. I handle the violence."

"What did you do with Vagris' men?" Tomas had to ask.

Beraht spit on the very expensive blue and grey carpet. "There's a new forest near the Desert of the Exiles, just like the ones they liked to plant."

Somewhat disturbed at the degree of pleasure the news brought to him, Tomas decided to change the subject. "I've heard an uldric waraxe can cut through a steel shield."

"It can," Remm replied, sneaking up behind and kicking Beraht behind the knee. Beraht head-butted his older friend in response. "Especially the one the boy here has."

"So?" Beraht demanded.

"Well, I was just curious how you were able to block each other's strikes."

"Easy," Remm said stomping on Beraht's foot and then punching him in both kidneys, "we didn't."

"Then what did you do?" Tomas asked.

When Remm tried to punch Beraht in the stomach, Beraht spun around and shoved his elbow into the back of his friend's skull. "Deflect!" Beraht barked.

"I don't understand."

The Uldra grabbed each other's shoulders, locked in a stalemate. "Easy!" Remm grunted suddenly spinning around so his back was to Beraht. "Use your opponent's energy!" The older Uldra grabbed Beraht's right arm and shoved an elbow into his gut. "Whenever he attacks, redirect!" Remm threw Beraht halfway across the room where the younger Uldra hit the wall and landed upside down. A thick banner of House Calonar fell free of its post and draped gently over the hulking mountain-man.

"No fair!" Beraht said from under the banner. "You cheated!"

"Ha!" Remm laughed derisively. "So did you. I just cheated better!"

"I think I understand," Tomas said uncertainly.

"I'll tell you what," Remm said, "draw your sword and attack; I'll show you."

"I don't have a sword."

"You don't!?!" Beraht demanded, pulling the banner aside and righting himself through the simple means of falling over.

"Why not?" Remm demanded.

"I used to…" Tomas sighed, reminded of the broken hilt resting in his rooms. "My father's. I carried it north but there was a fight and it… it was broken."

Remm and Beraht gestured in unison, both mountain-men placed a finger on their foreheads and then held their hands to towards the sky. Beraht stepped forward. "You carried your father's blade into battle?" he asked.

Tomas nodded. "Rogan was wounded," he recalled. "He'd lost his own sword so I tossed him my father's. But it…"

Remm walked over and placed a surprisingly light touch on the young man's shoulder. "You honored your father," he said, as though speaking words of holy power, "and your father's weapon." The older Uldra looked to Beraht, who nodded. "Do you still have the pieces," Remm asked Tomas.

The squire shook his head. "Only the hilt. We tried to find the blade but…"

Remm held up a finger. "The hilt will do. Tomorrow, you will bring me the hilt. You will come to my workshop in the northeast corner of the city. I will reforge your father's weapon. I will give it the Allfather's Blessing."

"Oh, I can't…" Tomas tried to refuse.

Remm stood back and held up his massive hands. "You will not refuse this," the elder Uldra insisted. "You will give me great honor in restoring your father's weapon."

"Thank you," was all Tomas could say.

"Now," Remm said, putting his arm around Tomas' shoulders and rubbing his head, somewhat painfully, "you must be worthy to carry your father's blade. You must learn to use it, to protect it, so that it doesn't break again." He gestured to one of the few weapons racks still standing. "Grab one of those training swords, and the boy and I will teach you a thing or two."

"Actually, I had something else I needed to do," Tomas said, trying unsuccessfully to break free of the Uldra's hold.

"Oh, don't worry," Beraht said, throwing the dulled sword which Tomas barely managed to catch. "This won't take too long."

"Are you sure?" Tomas asked uncertainly.

"Trust us," the Uldra said in unison.

Six hours later, Tomas delicately limped through the door of his suite. The squire was moving as slowly and as carefully as possible, his obvious agony displayed clearly on his face. Mary, who had just arrived herself, looked at Tomas with undisguised sympathy. "My God! What happened?"

"Nothing," Tomas said tightly, "just relaxing with some Uldra."

"That Remm is a savage!" Mary said with some heat. "Always starting fights and making trouble!" The young girl took Tomas' cloak and set it in the nearby closet. "Well, go to the bath. I'll be there in a minute."

"That's ok; I'll just go to..."

"Go!" Mary commanded, stamping her delicate foot and pointing imperiously towards the bath. Instinctively knowing better than to argue, Tomas sullenly did as he was told. Upon arrival, though, the squire encountered a new problem. His arms were so tired and stiff he could not get his clothes off. Indeed, Tomas could do little more than stand on trembling legs. Mary, a mixture of amusement and sympathy on her face as she stood in the doorway, moved to help. Tomas was extremely grateful for her assistance, being too tired to argue.

By the time Mary had her young man stripped and in the bath, the squire was nearly brought to tears from the pain. Mary dutifully massaged out every aching muscle and rubbed ointment wherever Tomas needed it. During her ministrations, the maid quietly spoke. "How is it being Prince Rogan's squire?" she asked.

Tomas shrugged, fighting sleep. "I never thought being a squire would involve so much training. All I seem to be doing is learning and practicing."

"So, in other words, you're having a lot of fun?" she asked with a smile of understanding.

The squire laughed and winced from the discomfort. "I never knew fun had to hurt so much."

"Does this mean you plan to stay here permanently? Will you stay the Prince's squire?" Mary asked, trying to make the question sound casual.

Again, Tomas tried to shrug. "There are still a lot of things about this place I don't understand; a lot of questions I have. Everywhere I look I see happy people and a thriving community. But I have to wonder what secrets this place has."

"So, you keep looking for the dark side of things?" the maid asked somewhat whimsically.

"I guess I am. It's just too hard to believe a place can exist without some kind of dark side."

"But you haven't left. There must be something keeping you here. Are you just staying until you learn the dark secrets of House Calonar?"

"No... I don't... I just... I don't know. I'm just waiting until I know what I'm supposed to do next. I'm learning a lot here, and I've met some good people. I just don't know if I can stay forever. I guess the only thing I really need to make up my mind is one really good reason to stay. Until I do make up my mind for keeps, I'll keep training with Rogan."

"I guess that means you'll be traveling with the Prince wherever he goes."

"Part of the job," Tomas replied.

"You'll have many possibilities here at the Keep. Traveling with a prince, being close to a king. It's the kind of life most people dream of."

"Like I said, all I need is a reason to stay," Tomas said again, his voice thick with sleep.

"Do you have one?" Mary asked quietly.

Tomas looked into her eyes. "Just one I can think of," he replied.

Blushing, Mary lowered her gaze, occupying herself with rubbing ointment into his shoulders.

"Traveling with the Prince will be very dangerous," Mary noted.

Tomas closed his eyes and grunted, relaxing with the girl's touch.

"You can't always count on tomorrow," she said. The young woman let her hands drift down Tomas' chest, and from there even lower. "You should never put things off when you could do them right now."

Tomas grunted again.

Mary leaned in closer, closing her eyes. "You can't put off something important, waiting for a better time."

Tomas snored.

Mary's eyes snapped open at the sound. "Tomas," she said loudly. "Tomas!" she yelled, shaking the squire. Realizing it was a lost cause, the maid hung her head. "It just isn't fair," she said. For just a moment, a selfish thought entered the young woman's mind. With undisguised duplicity, she eyed the lever that would fill the bathing tub with extremely cold water. Sighing, Mary shook her head and drained the tub. With resignation, the maid put a towel around Tomas and led him to bed, settling him in under the covers and lightly placing a kiss on his lips before leaving him to his much-needed rest.

Chapter 21

The Uldra workshop was everything, and nothing like, Tomas imagined. Stories abound in the folklore of Lanasia of the reclusive mountain-men, especially of their few remaining master smiths. Giants of stone and muscle, whose bodies alone could deflect a crossbow bolt. Inventors and artisans who created marvels without magic: beautiful artifacts of steam and fire, of gold and gemstone. No living Human artisan had ever been allowed to apprentice to an Uldra master. The barbarians refused to give their secrets to outsiders. To even step foot within an Uldra's workshop was rare, an exclusive honor for one of the smaller peoples.

Remm Stonebearer, longtime ally of House Calonar and crafter of many of their wonders, stood in the center of his workshop. The light of a blazing forge seemed to be absorbed by the strange tattoos covering half his body. He wore no tunic or shirt, but only a thick leather apron that strained against the boulder-like muscles of his thick torso. His unkempt beard, half coal-black and grey, and the other snow-white, would not burn when the errant spark from the forge landed upon it, instead glowing for only a moment. The walls were lined with all manner of tools, from common hammers and pliers to strange devices of unknowable purpose, all sized to fit the massive fists of their Uldra master. An array of devices and inventions, half-completed, abandoned and discarded, littered the metal and oak shelves, and the stone floor. The workshop seemed to mirror the binary nature of its master: at once chaotic while also perfectly ordered.

Remm held up a forge-stained hand when Tomas entered, halting the young man at the entrance. "What you see," he said in his thick accent of the mountains, "what you hear, what you sense, and what you learn… all these remain. Only what I allow may leave."

Tomas nodded. "I understand."

Remm touched his fingertips to his protruding forehead and turned to the west, towards Ulheim. "Swear it, in the name of your fathers," he commanded.

Tomas mirrored the movement, wanting to respect the master-artisan. "I swear," he said, "in the name of my father, Alessandros Fidelis, centurion of the Praetorian Guard, who died defending his emperor at Pelsemoria; and his father, Patrizio Fidelis, optio of the Fourth Legion, who died protecting Railing from the Xeshlin."

The Uldra nodded. "Honorable men. An honorable family. Show me your father's weapon."

Tomas hesitated a moment, feeling a surge of guilt and terrible responsibility. He lifted the hilt, wrapped in a small blanket Mary had provided that morning, and offered it to Remm. The master artisan shook his head, though. "Uncover it," he grumbled. "Never hide your father's history, no matter its condition."

With fingers that would not stop trembling, Tomas uncovered the broken hilt. The ivory, wood, and bronze handle remained, unblemished, as though ready for duty. But only a piece of the steel blade remained. The golden eagle of the Praetorians still shone at its base, glittering in the firelight of Remm's workshop. But the blade itself ended in a jagged stump, only a breath above the flawless bird. Tomas could not help but stare at the eagle, running a light touch along its perfection, and a renewed tide of guilt and loss rising from his heart. Not just for the loss of his father's sword, but for the loss of his father, his city, his childhood, and even his past beliefs.

Remm, who had been watching Tomas, nodded. "This is good," he rumbled.

"What?" Tomas asked, looking at the Uldra through tear-stained eyes.

"Soulpain reminds us of what is important, what is best. You have not forgotten your father, nor your duty to him. This is good."

"I would never…"

The master artisan stepped forward and put two massive hands on the squire's shoulders. "Nor should you. You carry your father here," he pointed to Tomas' heart, "not here," he waved a hand at the broken hilt. "Honor him, honor your family and your duty, and all else may be remade."

Tomas held up the broken hilt. "Then…"

Remm closed Tomas' hand over the hilt. "Yes, it shall be restored. But, not as your father's blade."

"I don't understand."

The Uldra took the broken hilt and set it onto a workbench, then picked up a random iron rod. "Your father's blade is not yours, not yet. It fits his hand, not yours. A man must take his father's weapon, and honor it, but he must also make it his own." Remm stared hard with his mismatched eyes at Tomas. "You have tried to fight only with your father's sword. You must find your own." He tossed the iron rod at Tomas.

Tomas fumbled a bit, holding the metal rod in his hands. "I don't…"

Remm held up a hand. "When I forged my first weapon, I used my father's tools. They did not fit my hands, because they were my father's tools. I needed my own." He nodded around the workshop, at the array of tools and weapons.

"Are you… are you going to show me how to forge my own weapon."

The Uldra shook his head. "No, you deserve… you father deserves, more honor than some Human-made weapon. You will have a blade Uldra-forged."

"Then what…?"

Remm picked up his own iron rod. "Show me how you fight." He swung at Tomas. The squire ducked the swing and assumed one of the defensive postures Rogan had taught him. Seeing this, Remm shook his head. "No," he barked, "that's how *Rogan* fights." He swung again, and Tomas intercepted the attack, deflecting and redirecting the Uldra's superior power safely away. "No!" he barked again, "that's how Beraht fights! Show me how *you* fight!" He leapt at Tomas, swinging the iron rod again.

Occasionally, for the past weeks, in their fleeting moments together, Mary had shown Tomas some of how she danced. Delicate movements with light steps and graceful, flowing swings of the arms and legs. She had laughingly even taught Tomas some of these moves. The squire spun then, as she had shown him, and redirected as Beraht had shown him, and countered as Rogan had shown him.

All at once, without thought, without planning, without intent, all at once, something came together in Tomas' soul. He spun with Mary, he deflected with Beraht, he countered with Rogan. He even moved with Aebreanna and Luigino Mariano, the Praetorian who was first to give him guidance, silently and skillfully. All the instruction came together. His body reacted, responding to Tomas' needs, rather than his commands. Also, deep and quiet, like the ripples at the bottom of a deep well, another teacher added to the dance. A fleeting memory thought lost returned; Alessandros Fidelis, bare-chested and sweating, practicing with his gladius in the small garden of their family home. Tomas, barely able to walk, had absorbed his father's skillful practice. This memory joined all the others.

Tomas spun the iron rod in his hands, deflecting Remm's latest attack. He struck the Uldra's own bar out of his massive hands and reached back, ready to deliver a final strike. Remm laughed then and held up his hands in mock surrender. "Good! The mountain has found its fire."

The young man stepped back and looked at his own hands in surprise. Remm stepped forward and took back the iron bar. "Now, you fight like you do. Not like Rogan, not like Beraht, not even like your father. You."

"But," Tomas objected. "It *is* like all the others. I used parts of..."

"Parts of them," Remm agreed, moving to the workshop on which the broken hilt rested. "Parts of all of them, every teacher. We go through life learning. The mountain is not one stone. We are all our teachers, our enemies, our loves and our hates. We are all our victories and our defeats. We never stop learning, until the Allfather calls us home. We take little pieces of others and make them a part of us. Honor your father, as you honor his weapon." The master artisan picked up the broken hilt. "We will honor your past. This will be a part of your new sword, as your father remains a part of you."

"Honor the past, but don't live the past," Tomas mused.

Remm nodded. "Yes." He turned to another workbench and unrolled a large piece of parchment, using a stick of charcoal to make notes. "This will take time," he grumbled. "A master blade requires patience, time, care."

"How long?"

The Uldra shrugged. "Months. Longer. I see how you fight, so I'll forge it to your style. That takes weeks. I'll use your father's hilt as part of the design, and properly adorn it. That takes months." He turned then, and looked fully into Tomas' eyes. "I'll place the Allfather's Blessing on the blade. That takes as long as it takes."

"You said that before, the Allfather's Blessing. What is that?"

Remm turned back to his new project. "You have work, same as me. Go. Leave what you have seen, but take what you have learned."

III

Summer

Chapter 22

The next two weeks were exhausting even in comparison to his training thus far. Between combat sparring and weapons drills with Beraht, stealth and evasion techniques with Aebreanna, moving into his new set of rooms on the same floor as Rogan and Kyla's suite, being fitted for his new splintmail armor and a full wardrobe reflecting the heraldry of House Calonar, the continued diplomatic meetings which he had to accompany Rogan on, and still trying to find a few spare moments for Mary, Tomas was kept busy. During the early afternoon hours of one such, on the first day of summer, Tomas went down to the stables to begin his training on the proper care and use of a warhorse.

On this day, the stablehand, Roderick, handed the squire over to what he described as "the meanest, most foul-tempered horse to ever walk on four legs. Next to Stick, of course." Urge, as his name implied, was a very muscular horse. His dark chestnut coat shined in the sun like fresh blood and his dark mane and tail perfectly matched his malicious temperament. "He really is a patient horse," Roderick said. "As long as you treat him well, this beast will bring you home every time. The only real problem is gaining his trust."

By then Urge had backed Tomas into the far wall of his stall. The warhorse had, immediately upon the squire's entrance, dominated their meeting. Somehow, the beast had managed to block the only means of escape with his large rump and was now looking at this potential meal with evil eyes.

"Uh, Roderick," Tomas said somewhat shakily, "I could really use some help here."

The stablehand laughed. "Don't worry, he won't hurt you."

Tomas screamed.

"Well, he might bite a little."

"I'm bleeding!"

Roderick laughed again. "It's just a scratch. He could have taken your whole arm off."

"He's going to!"

"Well, I guess you'd better reason with him then. I have to get a brush. Will you be alright here?"

"NO!"

"I'll be right back." Tomas heard his footsteps as the traitor walked away.

Urge threw a glance behind and, satisfied he and his prey were alone, turned back and advanced on the cringing Tomas. The squire searched his soul for any shreds of courage that might be there. "Alright... uh, Urge. We can be friends, right?"

The warhorse snorted.

"Ok. How about you just let me out." Urge remained unimpressed as he searched the young man for the most tender spot. Seeing few, the horse decided to just step on Tomas' foot.

"Ow! That's it! No damned horse is going to make a fool of me!"

What proceed next could best be described as a test of wills. As Urge pressed harder and harder on the squire's foot, Tomas grabbed one of his ears and wrenched, keeping as clear of the teeth as he could given his lack of mobility. They grappled for an eternity that lasted nearly three minutes before the hulking warhorse relented and moved back. Satisfied with his victory, Tomas decided to try and make amends.

"Now, can we just start over?" he asked.

Urge looked away.

The squire walked slowly up and gently patted the horse's neck. "Come on. There's no sense in fighting over nothing."

Roderick returned not long after. "No trouble?" he asked.

"None at all," the squire replied.

While brushing Urge down, Tomas looked over at the stablehand. Soft spoken and kind, Roderick, the squire had heard, had such a calming influence that no matter how angry or frightened the animals may be, a few soft words from the trainer never failed to steady them.

"So, how long have you served House Calonar?" Tomas asked.

"All my life," Roderick smiled.

Finishing the brushing, Roderick guided Tomas through preparing the horse's meal and checking the saddle. "He cares very much for his people, doesn't he?" Tomas asked.

"The King? Perhaps too much," Roderick replied.

"What do you mean?"

"If the King has one weakness, I would say that he cares more about others than he does about himself."

"That's hardly a weakness," Tomas insisted.

They finished and walked towards the large stable doors. "I'm just afraid that someday, someone could blackmail the King into doing something he shouldn't do by threatening his people, or worse, his family."

Tomas caught sight of a pure white mare impatiently moving around her stall. "Whose horse is this?" he asked.

Roderick smiled and put a hand to the rail. The horse immediately moved over and lowered her head to be petted. "This is Hope, Princess Kyla's horse," he said.

"Even the Princess' horse is beautiful and happy."

"And a menace," Roderick added.

"What do you mean?"

"Any time this filly is in heat, I have to drug the stallions. Once one of the other horses kicked through his stall door to get to her. Stick almost killed him."

"Rogan's horse?"

Roderick nodded. "Hope was originally Princess Kyla's fourteenth birthday present. At first, she was a frisky little thing. Right before the Princess married Prince Rogan, he mated Stick and Hope. Ever since then, she won't accept any other, and he attacks any that try."

"Are we talking about Stick and Hope or Rogan and Kyla?"

"As a matter of fact, Urge back there is one of Hope's foals."

Hearing the laughter of children, Tomas stuck his head outside the stables. In the training yard were half a dozen small children playing with Stick. "What's with the kids?" he asked.

"They come here all the time," Roderick replied. "Stick is almost as popular as Prince Rogan, more so with the children. Every day after school, at least a few come by and brush, pet, ride, or sneak treats to that beast."

"It doesn't look like he minds," Tomas noted.

Roderick laughed. "Our beloved Prince may be uncomfortable with his prestige, but Stick has no problems with being idolized."

Shaking his head, Tomas was about to return to his work. However, Rogan intercepted him, jogging out of a side door towards the stable.

"Come on, kid, we've got work," the knight said.

"What happened?" Tomas asked, falling in step with Rogan.

"Rashid's people discovered a tunnel into the city."

Roderick brought out a horse for Tomas and saddled Stick; the hulking warhorse seemed annoyed at being torn away from his adoring public and made little secret of the fact, giving Roderick as much difficulty as possible to the amusement of the children. As soon as Rogan was finally able to mount, the children's cheering encouraged the midnight-black warhorse to rear up, subsequently throwing the knight. The children thought that was very funny. Rogan did not.

"You know," the knight said from the ground, "you'd make good glue."

Chapter 23

Rogan and Tomas rode out to the edge of the mercantile district. They entered a great neighborhood of warehouses that rested against the northeastern section of the city wall. There were no shops, homes, or markets in this section of the district. Few travelers found their way here; instead, cargo from single wagons to entire caravans made their way to specific storage locations under the careful direction of the Watch and the close inspection of the Calonar tax collectors. Rogan had told Tomas that most of the mercantile traffic came through the northwest gate, and it was there that levies were assigned, but still agents of House Calonar made random inspections of this area, just in case a merchant forgot about some merchandise when declaring their goods during a customs inspection. It had been during one such surprise visit that a customs official had found the tunnel.

The tunnel entrance, a simple manhole hidden in the back of a contraband storage area, was surrounded by House Guard, four men dressed entirely in dark grey, a priestess of the Harvest Mother, and Esha. One of the Rashid's agents, an averaged-size man with the dark coloring of the peoples of the Endless Sands, with long dark hair that was impeccably groomed to look at once fashionable and still non-descript, approached the duo. "Rogan," the man nodded without a hint of accent.

"What's the story, Rashid?" the knight asked.

"I had a team investigating a smuggler who's been operating in the area; he finally led them to this tunnel," Rashid replied.

"Where's the smuggler now?" Tomas asked.

"He's being questioned."

"Name?" Rogan asked.

"Jon of Greenhills."

"Is he a member of the Merchant's Guild?" the squire asked.

The spymaster nodded. "He's operated out of the Keep for one month short of seven years."

"Who's in command of the Guard?" Rogan asked.

"That would be me, your most Royal Highness," one of the soldiers said.

"Hello, Rainer," Rogan sighed, rolling his eyes. "Do you have the area secure?"

"Of course, great prince," Klug Rainer said, bowing deeply. "My soldiers are even now acting to round up these senseless thugs who would defy your most royal authority."

"Sergeant Rainer, if I ordered you to, would you stop busting my chops?"

"I am at your command, my liege; but that would be *Lieutenant* Rainer now." The soldier gestured to the braid of yellow cord on his left shoulder.

"God help us," Rogan prayed, "you've been promoted."

"I hope only to better serve you in my new role as an officer, your Highness."

"*Lieutenant* Rainer."

"Yes, my prince?"

"Go away," Rogan said flatly.

"Yes, my prince."

Turning to the wizard, Rogan sighed. "Esha, what are you doing here?"

Looking up from the tunnel entrance, the diminutive archmage stood and folded her looking-lenses, tucking them into a pocket of her over-sized robes. Tomas noticed that Esha's normally-blue wizard's robes were freshly scorched. Dark stains covered the front, the sleeves looked to be recently frayed, and the hood was only hanging by a thread. The Sylva herself seemed unfazed by this most-recent detonation, though her face was soot-stained, her hair still smoldered, and she spoke loudly. Esha moved over to where Rogan and Tomas waited, almost absently falling into the hole if not for the lucky catch of a nearby Guardsman. The archmage's opalescent eyes glowed with almost giddy excitement. "Amazing, Rogan! Absolutely amazing."

"What is?"

"The quality of the spells put on that tunnel is beyond criticism!"

"Esha, focus. Tell me what happened." The knight spoke slowly and put emphasis on each syllable.

She blinked a few times, her oblivious delight at some new near-cataclysm not fading in the slightest. "Well, it really is quite simple!

As soon as Rashid's people found the tunnel, they sent request for a wizard."

Rogan looked questioningly at the spymaster. Rashid shrugged, saying, "Standard procedure."

"I was doing nothing truly important at the moment," Esha continued, "so came myself." The archmage laughed in delight. "Let me tell you, Rogan, my coming was most fortuitous!"

"Why is that?"

"Had any of my students attempted to dispel those symbols, they would have been incinerated!" This she said with disturbing glee.

"So, you didn't set it off?" Tomas asked.

"Oh no!" Esha laughed. "Several of the traps detonated; quite a delightful explosion, actually! Quite invigorating! Fortunately, we had a cleric nearby who is quite proficient."

"Esha, is the tunnel safe now?" the knight demanded.

"Oh yes, completely."

"Who built it?"

"I really have not the slightest idea," she replied happily. "Whoever did so possesses the power to block my divinations."

"Who has the power to do that?" Tomas asked.

"Only a very few," she replied, her opalescent eyes lost in thought. "Tienel Greysoul, Cylan Calonar, Cyras Darkholm. It could also have been the Speaker Council, Fak'Har, or even possibly the sorceress Vara."

"That list sounds familiar," the squire noted to Rogan.

The knight nodded grimly. "I'm starting to see a pattern here. Any sign of Anninihus yet?" he asked the archmage.

"None as yet. I am continuing the search, though. His discovery is only a matter of time."

"You guys said Anninihus didn't have any serious power," Tomas pointed out. "But Esha said whoever put the protection-spells around this tunnel is a master adept. Could that mean somebody recruited Anninihus? That he's a part of some bigger plan?"

Rashid nodded. "It would make sense. Anninihus has 'minion' written all over him."

"What about the wizards Esha named?" Tomas asked. "Do we have locations on any of them?"

"Well, the Greysoul can be taken off the list," Rogan said grimly.

"Why is that?" Tomas asked. "How did you guys beat him anyway?"

"Rogan tossed him into a portal to another world," Rashid responded from where he was leaning over the hole.

Tomas looked at Rogan who just shrugged. "Could he have come back?" the squire asked.

"Possible," the knight grunted. "But unlikely. He had a sword sticking out of him at the time."

"Why'd he have a sword sticking out of him?"

Rogan shrugged. "That's where I put it."

"What about Fak'Har?" Rashid asked rejoining the small group.

"He'd have little interest in smuggling," Rogan replied.

"Who's Fak'Har?" Tomas asked.

The spymaster grimaced. "Another wizard. Shapeshifter; manipulator."

"Spell-slingers." The knight shook his head. "Always more trouble than they're worth."

Esha had a hurt look on her tiny face.

"Present company excepted."

Rashid rolled his eyes.

"I'll continue my investigation, Rogan, rest assured," Esha declared.

"Maybe it wouldn't hurt to start a search for all the adepts Esha named," Tomas suggested.

The spymaster nodded. "I'll put a few teams on it."

"I will assign personnel as well," Esha added solemnly.

"Once we've got locations on each of them," Rogan said, "Think we need to start tracking their activities. Anytime one of them pops up, there's trouble."

Rashid grimaced. "We should have been tracking them to begin with."

"Forget the 'should haves,'" Rogan said. "We've got better things to do with our time."

Tomas looked around the warehouse, noting the stacks of crates piled throughout the building that often reached the ceiling high above. "Has anyone searched these?" the squire asked. "You said it was a smuggler using the tunnel."

Rashid pointed to a group of House Guard and grey-uniformed customs agents who were moving from box to box. "We started just as soon as the perimeter was secured, but it's slow going."

"Why?" the young man asked.

"Well, besides the sheer number of boxes, we have to get permission from every merchant who owns any of these before we open them."

"Why? Wouldn't the threat justify just going through them?"

"King's orders," Rogan told his apprentice. "He created laws protecting private property from casual search and seizure. We can only open the boxes if we know for a fact there's something dangerous or illegal in them, or if we have the owner's permission."

"Sounds like a pain to me."

"There have been times I'd agree with you. One of the major drawbacks of having laws is being forced to obey them. But, I have to admit, I think the Codex has done more good than bad."

"The what?"

"The Codex of Laws," Rogan said. "When the King official formed the Northlands kingdom, he and the Advisory Council drafted a list of absolute laws that everyone, including the nobility, must obey. It includes several measures to protect the citizens of the kingdom from unjust persecution without evidence." The knight started walking towards a group of crates that had been opened and set aside. "How's the search going so far?" he asked.

"Slow," Rashid replied, walking behind the prince. "We've already searched everything we could; now we have to wait until we've contacted the merchants to get their permission."

"What are they doing?" Tomas asked, nodding towards the searchers who still moved through the warehouse.

"They've got some of Esha's people with them; they're using magic to scan the boxes. They're also looking for anything obvious from the outside."

"Find anything yet?" Rogan asked.

The spymaster stepped forward to the opened boxes and picked up from within one with a black-gloved hand a curved sword that had a jagged edge. "About four crates filled with these for starters."

"Nasty," the knight grumbled. "All swords?"

"No," Rashid replied. "Swords, axes, mourning stars, spears. You name it; we've found it. The only common factor is that they all seem to be designed for maximum suffering. Saw-edges, hooks, barbs. Anything that can cause a little more damage and pain."

Tomas glanced into one of the crates and saw a large stack of barbed spears. The squire shuddered. "Who would want to use weapons like this?" he demanded.

"Somebody trying to make a point," Rogan replied. "No pun intended." He looked to the Calonar spymaster. "Any chance of tracing them to their origin?"

Rashid shook his head. "Not by me. All different designs; no heraldry or smith-marks."

"Esha?"

The archmage nodded. "I have had one of the weapons sent to my tower. I will discern its history."

The knight nodded and turned back to the tunnel entrance. "Keep me posted," he said as he and Tomas walked to the hole.

Esha and Rashid both nodded and left to give the appropriate orders. Rogan walked to the front of the tunnel entrance, a simple hole dug into the earth with a wooden trapdoor that showed signs of recent fire. Standing at the tunnel entrance, both warriors saw a cleric of the Harvest Mother in her undyed robe kneeling and praying. "Ilse?" Tomas asked.

As the young woman folded her hood back, Tomas was surprised to note that she was, in fact, the priestess he had met before. The only difference was that she now wore the green cord of an inducted cleric. "When did you become a full priestess?" the squire asked.

Brushing her fingertips lightly over the small embroidery portraying an image of wheat, Ilse softly said, "I was granted status last week."

"I'm sorry I missed the ceremony," Rogan said.

"That's all right, your Highness. I'm certain your heart was there."

"Do you know who made this tunnel?"

"No, your Highness, but I do know what they were bringing in."

"What?" Tomas asked.

A shadow crossed over the gentle girl's face, her blonde hair falling forward as she bowed her head. "The dead. Whoever was doing this was bringing dead bodies into the Northern Keep."

"Why in Underworld would anyone want to smuggle in dead bodies?" Tomas demanded.

"Could be anything," Rogan said. "Illegal necromantic grafts, terrorists trying to cause a plague; it could even be a new death cult.

We just don't have enough facts to even come up with a decent theory."

The squire stopped dead in his tracks. "A plague," he said with wide eyes.

"What?" the knight demanded.

"The kids," Tomas nearly snarled. "I told you about the strange sickness that's hitting the children of the city."

Rogan nodded, his mind moving along the same route as his squire's. "If someone's trying to weaken the city's defenses..."

"The best way would be to start a plague inside its walls," the young man finished.

"Then hire every merc and assassin you could get your hands on..."

"And hide them near enough to attack on a moment's notice..."

"Like in a nearby town already known for having those kinds of people in it."

"And hide your movements by distracting the people living in the surrounding forest."

"Senen warned us that an attack on the Keep was coming," Tomas reminded his knight. Both warriors stood and stared at each other, the implications of their theory causing both an unpleasant feeling. Tomas turned back to Ilse. "Have you had any luck countering whatever is affecting the children?"

The young priestess nodded. "After your suggestion to begin searching for possible poisoning, we learned there was something strange in their blood. Some kind of infection that resisted our normal treatments. We have since turned to our gifts."

"Gifts?"

"She means their magic," Rogan told him. "Did it work?"

Ilse nodded again. "We have halted the spread of the sickness," she said. "No more children are contracting it, and we have arrested the infliction in those who already have it. Unfortunately, we cannot, as yet, cure it."

Tomas nodded. "Well, at least you've bought them more time."

The priestess smiled. "They speak often of you, Tomas."

"Me?"

"Your stories brought the children more joy than I have seen in a long time. They long for your return."

"Well," the squire said, "I guess I'll just have to pay them another visit then."

"Ilse," Rogan broke in, "do you know where the bodies that have been brought in were taken?"

"There is a faint trail, your Highness," she replied.

"Can you follow it?"

"Not I. Perhaps someone of more skill."

Before the knight could speak again, Rashid appeared as if from nowhere beside his prince. "Rogan," he hissed.

Startled, the warrior nearly jumped out of his skin. "Dammit, Rashid! How many times have I told you not to do that!?!"

"Vincent just reported in," the spymaster said very quietly. "We are being watched."

"Where?"

"He doesn't know. There may be more than one. They're using magic to stay hidden. He can't pin them down."

Rogan casually looked around the warehouse. "Where's Esha?" he asked.

"Left for her tower, I think," Tomas replied, feeling more than a little nervous at the thought of some unseen enemy watching them.

Ilse suddenly stiffened and gasped, all color draining from her face and her breath coming fast and short. The cleric's normally soft eyes grew wide and feintest hint of a blue glow appeared in them.

"What is it?" Rogan demanded.

"The dead!" she gasped. "The dead wake!"

Screams tore through the warehouse, screams of horror suddenly cut short. Even as Tomas turned to look in the direction of the search team, the direction the screams came from, Rogan and Rashid were already sprinting that way.

"Rainer!" Rogan yelled. "Seal us in! Call for help!"

Tomas struggled to catch up to his knight, stopping only briefly to grab a short sword with a hooked point and cursing that he had yet to replace his father's broken sword. At the edge of his vision, the squire was dimly aware that the newly-promoted Lieutenant Rainer was barking orders to his men, sealing the warehouse as commanded and moving with a small squad to reinforce his prince.

The young man lost sight of Rogan and Rashid as they turned a corner, but sounds of violence and the knight's cursing informed Tomas what they were doing. Just as the squire approached the same corner an explosion of wood and white sand sent him stumbling to the floor. He lay there, struggling to clear the sand from his eyes and

coughing. The moment Tomas cleared his vision, he almost wished
he had not.

Forcing its way out of the crate, a shambling mockery of a
Human being struggled to free itself of the white sand that poured
out of the container and pooled around its feet. The monster had
once been female. The pitiful rags of clothing did little to hide the
grayish skin and female attributes that hung in folds off jagged bones.
Empty eye sockets and a nose withered to nearly nothing gave ample
evidence that only be magic could be guiding the creature.

Shrieking and cursing in terror, Tomas scrambled along the
ground, trying desperately to escape the sight of the mockery of
nature now shambling towards him, arms outstretched and skeletal
fingers clawing at the air. The squire's hand found the sword hilt
beside him and grabbed it, thrusting the weapon up into the
monster's throat. A strange, hissing moan leaked out of the thing's
mouth as black ichor leaked from the wound down Tomas' blade,
and it continued to claw the air, trying to find Tomas. The young
man flinched away from that awful grasp and jerked the blade back
out, its hook-point taking half the creature's neck with it. Black
blood and the stench of decay sprayed over the squire as the
monster's head fell to one side, only a scrap of flesh keeping it
attached to the shoulders. To Tomas' revulsion, the dead thing did
not die. Instead, it blindly groped about and continued that awful
moan.

Screaming in horror and fury that such a monstrosity could exist,
Tomas continued to hack at the creature, cutting it into ever smaller
pieces until finally it stopped moving. The young man was allowed
no time to breath before more creatures began forcing their way
from the crates. It suddenly seemed as though the entire warehouse
had come alive with the angry dead.

A high-pitched scream tore through the air. Looking back,
Tomas saw that two of the monsters were advancing on Ilse. Unlike
the one Tomas had destroyed, these two moved with an unnatural
energy, like predators move as stalking prey. Ilse was backed against
a wall and had no weapon. Her blue-glowing eyes were wide in
mindless terror, and her entire body trembled.

From across the warehouse, Lieutenant Rainer had heard the
scream and looked back. Despite the monsters erupting all around
him and his men, he roared in fury and obliterated the creatures
blocking him. The normally-jovial soldier hurled himself across the

warehouse, knocking aside anything in his way and felling any dead that foolish enough to block his path with sword and fist. Like a force of nature, the grey-haired soldier moved through the growing crowd of monsters in a straight line, surrendering any finesse in favor brute force as one creature after another in his path was simply obliterated. Rainer's eyes never left the besieged priestess as he charged towards her, intent only on her safety.

Tomas saw immediately the soldier would not reach Ilse in time. The creatures would not die with a mortal wounding, instead fighting on until cut into many pieces. While possessing only the most basic combat capabilities, the sheer numbers of the monsters meant they could slow any movement. The squire also began to notice a change in the monsters as more appeared. Newer creatures reinforcing the first wave moved faster than their predecessors and seemed to possess much more will. The first few monsters moved in a straight line, attacking with their gnarled claws and oblivious of the damage they received. The newer creatures moved with a growing cunning, dodging blind attacks and using their fellow abominations in primitive teamwork.

One of the dead leapt at Tomas, arms wide and toothless mouth agape. The squire ducked and rolled along the ground, dismissing the attack and heading towards Ilse as fast as his legs could carry him. Time and again he was forced to dance past or through the increasingly coordinated attacks of the creatures as he pressed on to the besieged priestess. Glancing over, the squire noted that Rainer was moving, if possible, even faster than he was. It very nearly became a race between the two warriors to see which could reach Ilse first.

A hand shot out from a crate Rainer was running next to, grabbing his ankle and sending the lieutenant to the floor with a curse. Despite the force with which he hit the floor, the veteran never lost his grip on his weapon. Instead, he rolled as best he could and struggled to cut the hand away, even as three more of the creatures advanced on him. Within moments, several Guardsmen had arrived to help the officer, hacking their way through the many dead to reach their leader. Seeing he was relatively safe, Tomas refocused his attention on the two monsters harassing Ilse.

Both of the creatures were trying to attack her, lashing out with fists and teeth, desperate to make some injury, to taste living flesh. As Tomas closed on her attackers, he noted that a soft, golden glow had seemed to encapsulate the priestess. Every attack by one of the dead caused a momentary flash of golden light that repelled the creatures. Ilse had her arms crossed over her heart. Her eyes were closed and gave voice to a gentle prayer. A wind, unfelt by ay except the priestess, lifted Ilse from the ground. Her blonde hair rose as well, fanning out into a halo that nearly matched the golden shield encapsulating the cleric. As she did this, the protective sphere intensified, becoming an almost solid shell that continued to push outwards, away from the priestess.

Step by step, the dead were forced away from Ilse, the golden light proving more than enough to overcome them. Not pausing to consider the situation, Tomas barreled in, throwing his shoulder into the closer of the two dead and swinging his arm, knocking the monster several feet back. The second of the two dead turned and swung a fist at the squire; seeing this, Tomas grabbed the arm in mid-air and swung his sword, cutting the appendage off and throwing it away while continuing his attack. Two more slashes of his weapon and the creature fell into pieces at his feet. A moan brought the squire's eyes around just in time to drive a fist into the face of the oncoming dead. The thing stumbled back a few steps, stunned just long enough for Tomas to cut it to down.

Seeing the immediate threat gone, Ilse dropped her arms in seeming exhaustion. The golden light vanished with the movement. The priestess sank to the floor, gasping for breath. Tomas knelt beside her in concern. "Are you alright?" he asked.

She nodded weakly.

Hearing another wave of dead coming, the squire leapt and swung his blade, severing two arms with one blow. Within moments, Tomas realized he was surrounded, a dozen or more of the creatures approaching from every direction; what was worse, though, was that at least a few of the monsters had armed themselves with the vicious weapons piled only a few feet away. The moments of combat passed and the young man grimly began to realize the dead were increasingly coordinating their attacks, one attacking while another parried and yet another dodged. Within moments, he would be overwhelmed, if help did not soon arrive.

In the instant before he was going to call out, a dagger caught one of the monsters in the head, sending it stumbling into an open crate. The squire noted with great relief that Lieutenant Rainer and his squad had finally reached him. Now reinforced, Tomas and the

Guardsmen fought back, desperate to move the fight away from the collapsed Ilse. The squire beheaded one of the creatures and risked a glance past the still-animate torso, seeing a large group of the dead that were not only taking up weapons for themselves, but also handing them out to their comrades. "We've got problems!" the young man called out to Rainer.

"You only just noticed?" the lieutenant snapped. Rainer cut the arms and legs off the creature before him and kicked the rest of the wiggling monster away before turning to another enemy. "Where's the Prince?" he demanded.

"Busy," Tomas replied, seeing Rogan and Rashid also fighting with their backs to a wall as a horde of the dead assaulted them.

On and on the battle waged, the fighters never stopping their assault for even a moment. But for every one or two of the creatures they cut down, three more would burst from one of the containers. It was only a matter of time before Tomas and the others would succumb to weariness, to the sheer number of their attackers. The dead did not tire, and they did not stop. They seemed to be endless and their attacks increasingly coordinated. First one, then another, and another of the House Guard were pulled down. As the moments turned to minutes, the desperate cursing of soldiers being torn apart and agonized screams of men cut open with vicious weapons filled the air.

Tomas screamed in pain as a strike from a saw-edged saber cut into his left shoulder. The squire parried the following attack and cut down the creature that had wounded him.

"You alright?" Rainer panted, struggling to put another of the monsters down.

"Not for much longer," the young man replied. "They just keep coming!"

A light voice echoed throughout the warehouse, cutting through the chaos of battle. "That shall be quite enough, I think." All heads, be they living or dead, turned as one to the largest of the doorways leading to the streets outside. Standing in the center of the open doors was Esha, her staff held aloft, and words of magic dancing from her lips.

A bright white light glowed from her staff, a light that grew brighter and brighter until suddenly collapsing to the very tip. An arc of blue-white lightning shot from the wizard's staff, hitting one of the dead squarely in the chest and causing the thing to explode. The lightning did not stop, though. Instead, it split into first two, then four, then eight arcs. Each of the creatures hit with the electricity caused the lightning to split again until the entire warehouse was filled with Esha's magic.

In an instant, the light of the archmage's attack was gone, and the charred remains of the dead fell to the ground, leaving the smoking remains of the dead scattered across the building and only the defenders of the Keep still standing. Esha looked about casually, nodding in approval. "Well, what do you know," she merrily laughed, "it worked!"

Chapter 22

Rogan and Rashid emerged from one of the rows of crates. The knight was rubbing his right shoulder. "It's about time," he grumbled.

"I returned the instant I sensed the power unleashed," Esha objected.

The knight looked to Rainer. "How many?"

"Twelve of mine," the soldier replied, his voice terse.

"Three of mine," Rashid added, equally terse.

"And five customs agents," Tomas pointed out, nodding towards where the officials had been torn down while trying to aid in the battle.

Rogan closed his eyes and breathed deeply. "Get the names and start the preparations. We'll pay any expenses to have them buried at home. Anyone with family here in the Keep, I want to know about."

Rainer nodded. "I'll handle it, sir."

"Ilse?"

"She's fine. If you'll excuse me, your Highness?"

The knight nodded, releasing Lieutenant Rainer.

Rashid looked about the scattered corpses that were now burnt to a blackened crisp. "Are any of these not well done?" he asked.

A few of the more strong-stomached Guardsmen searched through the smoking dead. Their negative responses brought a curse to the spymaster's lips. Hearing this, Esha sighed. "I do apologize, Rashid. I feared you were being overwhelmed and perhaps overreacted."

"You could have left me one, Esha."

"Perhaps I should have left them all?" the Sylva asked with wide-eyed, and feigned, innocence.

Tomas dropped the gore-stained sword he suddenly realized he was still holding. "Well," he replied weakly, "I'm not complaining."

"Me neither," Rogan agreed, wiping his blade clean with a small oiled rag before sheathing it. The knight saw his squire's wound and roughly examined the arm.

"Easy, will you?"

"Don't be a baby." He tested the flesh and twisted the shoulder a bit. "It'll heal," he noted, "but get a priestess to take a look at it." the warrior grinned. "Should leave a nice scar."

"Oh, joy."

The knight looked around the building. "Is everyone else alright?" Nods and deep breaths of relief answered his call from the living. Rogan put a hand on Tomas' unwounded shoulder. "How about you?" he asked quietly.

The young man nodded, still shaking somewhat. "Yeah, I think I'm alright, considering. What about Ilse?"

They both looked over to where the priestess was being walked out of the warehouse by Lieutenant Rainer. The young woman appeared quite shaken, and tears flowed down her cheeks. "Take some time," Rogan said, "but she should be alright."

"What in Underworld were these things, Rogan?" Tomas asked.

"Let's find out," he replied. "Esha!" the knight called out. "What was this?"

"A distraction," the archmage replied, "clearly." Esha was standing over one of the creatures. She was holding a small object, a metal cylinder with crystal lenses evenly inserted long its length. The archmage was moving the mystical device over the creature and concentrating. "Whoever created and controls these constructs feared what we would have learned from them and ordered a preemptive attack."

"What about the guy who was watching us?" Rogan asked Rashid.

The spymaster shook his head. "I already sent Vincent to look, but my guess would be he's long gone."

"Can you learn anything from these things?" the knight made it a general question.

"Not by me," Rashid said, kicking a charred piece of something Tomas' mind refused to identify. "There's not enough left."

Esha paused what she was doing and straightened. The archmage looked to the small device in her hand, noting that the crystal lenses had turned darkest black. "Death Magic of the highest order," she declared. "These creatures were taken from their graves and infused with false life. A time was set with the spell that created them, putting them into stasis until specific conditions were met."

"What kind of conditions?" Tomas asked.

"I cannot say. Whatever they were, the spell was activated prematurely."

"How do you know that?" Rashid asked.

"Had the creator of these things waited until they were ready, they would have been much faster, much stronger, and much more deadly."

Rogan looked around the building at the sheer number of dead scattered about. "Esha," he said seriously, "was this all of them?"

"There is no way to know."

The knight turned to Rashid. "I want every crate in this place opened. Don't wait for permission, and anyone with a problem can talk to me. Start here and work your way out. Find out where these things came from, and find out if there are any crates that showed up from the same place at around the same time. Any shipment that may have been from the same source is opened, and I want wizard and cleric support at all times, along with an entire company of House Guard. Tell the jailor to move that smuggler to the castle dungeons, and let that bastard know that if he doesn't start giving answers, I'm sending Beraht and Remm to start asking the questions."

Rashid nodded and moved to implement the prince's orders.

The knight gestured to a nearby Guardsman. "From now on, all personnel are to be armed while on duty." He glanced at Tomas. "That goes double for us." He kicked the serrated shortsword his squire had used during the fight. "We were damned lucky this time. If we'd been caught unarmed…"

Rogan turned to Esha. "So, we get reports that Anninihus may be planning something. You say he may have gotten a serious power boost recently, and now we find a large group of dead creatures already inside the city."

The archmage nodded his agreement. "It should be fairly obvious by now that my former student has some scheme at work. Logically, we can assume this was only the beginning of whatever Anninihus has planned."

"Find him."

"I have yet to learn his current whereabouts, but I believe it unlikely he is within the city. His nature would be to strike at us from a place of safety."

Tomas stood staring down at the desiccated remains of one of the monsters he had been fighting. He stared as his hand absently rubbed the golden rose pinned to his collar. A thought appeared in his mind as if from nowhere, a thought that was not overly pleasant. "Rogan," he called out, "what does Anninihus look like?"

"Tall," the knight replied. "Thin, but not too much. Dark hair, brown eyes. He's got a tick on his left cheek and tattoos all over his face. Why?"

Tomas stiffed at the description as the knowledge of his own gullibility seeped into his mind. He could hear Alexia comforting him against his own thoughts of self-recrimination, but nothing his dear friend could have said would have mattered. "Does the name Aneirin mean anything to you?"

Rogan stood quickly and stared hard at his squire. "Where did you hear that name?"

"A man spoke to me twice since I arrived in the Keep. A noble, I think; maybe a wizard. He was tall and thin, with brown eyes. He didn't have tattoos, but he did have a tick in his left cheek. He called himself Aneirin."

"SON OF A-!!" The prince spent several moments destroying crates with his bare fists.

Tomas moved over to where Rashid had returned, now standing a good distance away from Rogan to avoid any accidental wounds. "What now?" the spymaster asked.

Tomas explained and the spymaster's eyes widened, then narrowed. "Aneirin was the name of Rogan's uncle," Rashid said. "The one who first trained him. From what I understand, he taught the Prince a great deal about fighting and honor. They were very close until Anninihus had him murdered."

The squire could only watch as his knight let loose with more fury than he thought possible. After a few minutes, Rogan finally calmed enough to stop breaking things and speak. "He's here," the knight declared. "Anninihus has been in the Keep under our noses for weeks, maybe months. Find him, Esha. No matter what it takes, find him."

"I will, Rogan. Now that I know where to look, he cannot hide."

"Rashid, the minute Esha finds him, I want him captured alive. Make sure he can't cast spells and bring him to me, alive."

The spymaster bowed. Tomas stepped up and put a hand lightly on his knight's shoulder. "Are you alright?" he asked.

Rogan looked at his squire. "What do you think?"

"I'm sorry Rogan."

The knight let out an explosive breath, clearly struggling against an old rage. "You've got nothing to be sorry about, kid. Anninihus is good at hiding and insinuating himself into places he has no business being. It's no surprise he's got magic enough to hide his tattoos. He's tricked people a lot cleverer than you or me."

"But the things he said to me," the young man insisted. "Things about you and House Calonar and this city. They made sense."

Rogan nodded. "Before he was anything else, Anninihus was a liar and a damned good one. If he'd never learned magic, he'd have probably been a con artist. Or a lawyer. Or a priest."

"I may have some good news," Esha called out. The archmage turned and held her staff over the dead body she had been examining. "I should be able to restore this creature to its appearance prior to my attack and even its transformation."

"You know necromancy?" Tomas asked in surprise.

"One cannot achieve the rank of archmage without having at least some knowledge of every school, to include necromancy." Esha concentrated a moment, "Except the forbidden ones, of course." The Sylva took a deep breath and let the words of magic slip through her lips, a bluish light suffusing her opalescent eyes as she cast her spell. A yellowish-green mist drifted from the tips of her staff and suffused the remains at her feet. The mist cleared away the blackened char and rot, revealing a healthy Human man who looked as though he may have been sleeping.

Rogan and Tomas leaned over the body, trying to find any sign of its origin. The squire spotted a tattoo on his left shoulder and drew his knight's attention to it. "He was in the Legions," the young man said.

"You know which one?" Rogan asked.

Tomas leaned in as close as he could stand to inspect the mark. "It's got the gold eagle that every legion had except the 30th. It's holding a spear instead of the gladius; that was for the 15th through 28th. Red background. That was the units under the second army, which means central Lanasia. See the wavy yellow lines behind the eagle? Those represent the dunes of the Endless Sands. I think he served in the 27th Legion, probably from somewhere around Daivic or the City of All Sins."

Rogan nodded and looked at the white sand that was scattered everywhere. "Well, that figures, I guess."

Rashid knelt and scoped up a handful of the sand, examining it closely. The spymaster nodded. "Yes, I should have noticed. Powdered shale, some limestone and marl. This came from around the Valley of the Sand Lords, west of Oneld."

Tomas looked closer at the body. "This man doesn't have any wounds," he noted. "Esha, you said the spell would restore the body to what he looked like just before he was changed into one of these monsters, right?"

The archmage nodded. "True. The body appears now as it did at the moment of undeath."

"The only thing that should have killed him was what *we* did," the squire insisted.

Rogan grunted. "Meaning he was probably alive and well when Anninihus did whatever he did to him."

"Are we sure it was Anninihus?" Tomas asked.

"What do you mean?"

Tomas pointed to another mark on the dead soldier, this one a black sylvai glyph surrounded by a red circle directly over his heart. "I think this is the mark of the Brotherhood of Saint Valkis."

"Never heard of it."

"The Brotherhood was sort of like a special school that some Legionaries could go to. It trained Humans how to fight and kill the other races. They trained on how to beat sylvai magic, uldric berserkers, even how to fight a Vaeyen."

"So why haven't I ever heard of them?" the knight demanded.

"The only reason I know about them is because my father was offered the chance to go to the school but declined to join the Praetorians instead."

"You couldn't be a Praetorian and join this brotherhood?"

"The whole purpose of the Brotherhood of Saint Valkis was to teach a small group of Guardsmen and then return them to their legions where they could teach others."

"What's so important about this guy having gone to some advanced combat school?"

"The school was run by the Inquisition."

Rogan stiffened.

Rashid nodded. "I've heard of this Brotherhood," he said. "After the death of the Emperor, they were the first who broke their vows of loyalty to the Republic. With the Emperor dead, the Inquisition was the only group strong enough to lead. Reports came in for years that small groups of Legionaries who had attended the school were abandoning their posts to join the Brotherhood and serve the Inquisition."

"Perhaps this man attended the school in the past," Esha suggested. "There is no reason to assume that he served the Inquisition immediately prior to his undeath."

Rogan shook his head, staring hard at the mark on the dead man's chest. "No, I've seen plenty of ritual marking, and this isn't that old. Whoever this guy was, he served near the Endless Sands and joined a group loyal to the Inquisition no more than a year ago. Or at least, a year before…" the knight waved his hand towards the unliving creatures.

"Now he's some kind of monster only a Death Mage could create," Tomas added.

Esha ended the spell with a wave of her hand. "There is more to this plot than we yet know," the Sylva said.

"What does that glyph mean?" Rogan asked.

"They glyph is *dagon'ay*," Esha translated. "According to tradition, it is the ancestral homeland of all races created by the Radiant. We use the glyph not only for the turbulent Dagon'ay region, but also to represent all the races that once lived in that place. Essentially, it means, everyone except Humans."

"You actually have a word for 'everyone except Humans?'" the knight asked flatly.

The archmage shrugged. "We have a glyph for very nearly everything."

Rogan turned the investigation over to Rashid. Once outside, the knight took a deep breath of the cool air of early evening, closing his eyes and letting the horror pass.

"So, what now?" Tomas asked.

Rogan shrugged. "Get that arm of yours looked at."

"I meant long term."

"Trust Rashid and Esha to get some more information. Until they can tell us something definite, we're waiting."

"Is it always like this?" Tomas asked as they mounted their horses and departed for the castle. "Rashid or whoever gets the information, tells you who the bad guy is and you go cut him down?"

The knight laughed. "Only when we're lucky, kid. Rashid and Esha are damned good at their jobs; if the information can be found, they'll find it."

"And if they don't."

"Then we start taking the world apart piece by piece until we find it. Believe it or not, I really hope Esha and Rashid succeed. When they get the answers, it's quick, quiet, and relatively painless. Our method is messy."

"From the looks of things back there, when you get a hold of Anninihus, it'll end up being messy regardless."

"That... man... has done a lot of things that he has to answer for. But for dishonoring the name of my uncle... You're right; it'll be messy."

"How do you know Ilse back there?" Tomas asked, wanting to change the subject to something less gloomy.

"Her father is Klug Rainer."

"The funnyman lieutenant?"

"The same."

"I was kinda wondering why he was so worried about Ilse. For a minute, I thought maybe they were a couple."

The knight laughed at the thought, enjoying the levity after so much darkness. "Met Ilse after her brother died," he said through his laughter. Seeing Tomas' quizzical look, the knight explained. "Her brother, Jayden, was traveling with a group of treasure-hunters who were looking for an artifact we needed. About four years ago, the whole team disappeared."

"You never found out what happened?"

"No. We held a state funeral for them all. Any time I lose someone who was working personally for me, I try to look after their family. Her oldest brother is in the House Guard. Wanted to follow in his father's footsteps I guess."

"This is an interesting world I've found myself in, Rogan."

They looked at each other grinning. "Fun though," they said in unison, their laughter carrying into the night.

Chapter 24

As far as dungeons go, this one really is not all that bad, Tomas thought. Calonar's dungeons were rather small, each cell built with stone and iron, with magical wards carved into the bars and walls. Rogan had told the squire that since their construction, no one had ever escaped from those cells.

"Talk!" the knight barked, his voice echoing from a cell further down the dark hallway. There was an awful screaming and the sounds of tearing.

The young man made his way down the stairs into the dungeon itself. Rogan had told him to stay out, that he was not ready for what had to happen in there, to instead have someone treat his arm. Well, the squire had seen to his arm. The stitches had hurt like no other, and the wound was quickly developing a maddening itch. The clerics of the Harvest Mother had offered to use their magic to fully heal the wound, but Tomas respected their beliefs in only using those powers in emergencies, and hopefully, the emergency was past. He did, however, gratefully accept a minor charm to ward off blood-sickness and a quickly-brewed potion to quell the pain.

With his treatment complete, the young man could not help but let his curiosity drag him to the cells beneath the castle, despite the warning of his knight.

"Talk, damn you!" Again that growl and again screams followed by sounds that suggested unspeakably evil acts.

The squire was surprised to note that the merchant described to Tomas earlier was standing in a cell directly across from the dungeon entrance. The prisoner was as pale as a living Human could become and shaking in terror at the sounds echoing through the vaulted prison. Another long scream rang through the cavernous dungeon, a scream that ended in a gargle that slowly faded to nothing. Tomas found his breath shallow and his heart beating with such force that he feared his stitches could not contain the pulse of blood through his arm. Both squire and merchant looked at one another, sharing a moment of mutual horror.

A new sound could suddenly be made out, a sound that was nearly as horrible as the last. Beraht was laughing. The Uldra barbarian walked up the wide corridor, wiping blood off his thick hands and laughing at something he clearly found amusing. Right behind the towering mountain-man came Rogan, who was shaking his head.

"Keep telling you," the knight grumbled, "start from the bottom and work your way up."

"But I love it when they make that gargling sound," the Uldra chuckled. "I wonder what causes that."

"That would be them drowning in their own blood. That's why you can't cut into the chest. You keep hitting the lungs. If I've told you once, I've told you a thousand times, they can't talk if you puncture the lungs."

By now both killers were standing in front of the merchant's cell. Rogan glanced at the cringing prisoner and sighed. "Alright, let's get this over with. I need a bath."

"*You* do!?!" Beraht snapped. "Look at me!" Tomas did not want to, but some force made him. The squire looked at the Uldra's body and noted the leather apron he wore last. What he noted first were the bits of flesh and viscera clinging to the apron.

A gasp from the young man drew the attention of both warriors. Rogan shook his head. "I thought I told you to stay away. You aren't ready for this."

"Aw, let him stay," Beraht argued. "He's got to learn some time."

"He isn't ready," the knight insisted.

"Who is?"

"Fine," Rogan snapped then turned to Tomas. "But don't say I didn't warn you."

With a casual indifference, Beraht opened the merchant's cell and bent low to enter, followed by Rogan and a shaking Tomas. The cell door was left open until a jailor wearing a black mask entered with a cart bearing the worst tools of the torturer's trade Tomas had ever feared existed. The tools had hooks and spikes and jagged edges. Bits of matter clung to them in various places, and blood covered them all like a coat of fresh paint. The smell was the worst part.

"Please!" the merchant begged. "I don't know anything! I swear I'm innocent!"

Beraht nodded and grabbed the prisoner, tying a rope around his wrists and further looping it around a hook in the nearby wall. He then forced the merchant down onto a stool and returned to the nearby tray.

"Now what?" Tomas asked, fearing the answer.

In response the Uldra picked up a pair of what looked like pliers with barbed tips. The barbarian glanced sidelong at his victim with an evil grin burning through his braided beard.

"You're not going to hurt him, are you?" the squire demanded.

"No, I'm just going to rearrange him a little."

"Oh, no you're not!" Rogan snapped. "Not yet!"

"What?" the barbarian asked innocently. "It always works."

"Forget it. Every time you do that, we're cleaning up the mess for days. Besides, it makes me sick."

"What's the point of bringing in all my tools if I'm not going to cut on him?" The Uldra leered at the cringing merchant. "This time, I'm going to keep an ear."

The knight rolled his eyes. "You keep forgetting the order. First, I question him, then he lies, then you cut on him for a while, then I question him, then he gets brave, and then you get to carve him up."

"But I'm telling you I don't know anything!" the prisoner screamed.

Beraht casually hit him.

"Knock that off!" Rogan yelled. "Both of you! It's hard enough to do this right with everybody going out of order. Now, I'm going to start this over and let's see if we can get it right." He kicked the merchant off the stool and sat down on it himself. "Now look," he said amiably, "we know that you've been smuggling black market items in for a while now. We've got more than enough evidence to drag you in front of a magistrate and have you sent to Ubelheim for a century or two. I know you took a job from Anninihus to move those things in. All you have to do is tell me where you met him and where he is now, and I'll make sure you get a break."

"I don't know anything!" the merchant pleaded.

"Yes, you do," Rogan corrected. "Now, it's alright for you to lie, just make sure you lie to Beraht; he's too dumb to know the difference anyway. But if you lie to me, I have to be mean. Trust me, you don't want me to be mean."

Beraht knelt down beside the cringing prisoner and nodded sagely. "You really don't. It scares *me* when he gets mean," he said while absently playing with the pliers.

The merchant's eyes darted from the knight to the Uldra and back. "You won't do anything to me," he said, gaining some measure of courage. "You can't. Calonar's laws forbid torturing for information."

Rogan shook his head sadly. "Now, you see. That's a shame. You pretty much had me convinced you didn't know anything. But the thing is, you would never have said anything like that if you really didn't know anything, which means you *do* know something. So, what is it?"

"You can't make me talk," he said, trying to stand. "You're the good guys."

Beraht kicked the prisoner's legs out from underneath him. "Well, at least you are, Eigenhard," the merchant grumbled as he sat stood up. "You're too weak to do anything. You're just a coward who hides behind Calonar's power. A coward of a knight who's married to a whore of a priestess! So you can just go to Underworld, Eigenhard." He spat on the Prince who grew very quiet.

"Oh boy," Beraht sighed. "You should not have done that."

"What?"

"When you say such nasty things to him, no big deal. But when you insult his wife... he gets really, *really*, upset."

The knight leaned in very close to the prisoner, never blinking, barely breathing. "Please tell me what you know. I would really appreciate it."

"You can't scare me, Eigenhard. I know you're bluffing."

"Tomas," Rogan said, never breaking eye contact. "Go up to the kitchen. Get me an iron bowl. Get me strawberry preserves. Get me a wooden spoon with a long handle. Get me a peacock's feather."

Beraht gasped. "You're not going to use the peacock's feather. The King said 'never again.'"

Rogan leaned in even closer to his prisoner. "Get them, now."

"Uh, Rogan," Tomas said.

"NOW!!" he barked.

The squire ran up the dungeon stairs and made his way to the kitchen. Once there, he found the head cook. "This is going to sound strange but..."

The cook grabbed a tray from a storage closet and set it in front of the young man. "Iron bowl, strawberry preserves, wood spoon with a long handle, and a peacock's feather."

Tomas blinked. All the items were arrayed neatly on the tray. "How?"

The cook shrugged. "The Prince has been here for a decade. We've grown used to his interrogation technique."

Once the squire returned, he noted in surprise that Rogan had not moved. He still sat with his face hideously close to the merchant's. "Uh, I got the stuff," the young man said.

"Bring it in," the knight commanded, finally leaning back.

Tomas entered the cell and set the tray down. Beraht leaned close to Rogan with a concerned look on his face. "You know, you don't have to do this."

"Oh yes. I do," he breathed.

By now sweat was rolling off the merchant's face. All color had drained as he took in the odd items arrayed on his stone bed. "Look," he nearly whimpered, "maybe we can make a deal."

Rogan shook his head. "It's too late. It's just too late." The knight's face took on an eager, almost hungry appearance of wide, twitching eyes and a hungry snarl.

"You can't do anything to me! It's against the law!"

Rogan took the cup of preserves and dipped the spoon into it, pulling it out and letting the thick fruit slide slowly back down.

"Alright! Fine! It was Anninihus! He hired me! That's it! I brought the crates in and he paid me! Alright!?!"

Rogan looked at the spoon as if noticing it for the first time. "Sticky," he noticed.

"GET HIM AWAY FROM ME!!! I'LL TALK!!! I SWEAR TO GOD I'LL TALK!!! Anninihus has a base set up in Crossroads but he doesn't stay there! He's left some bounty hunter in charge and keeps moving around! I was told to bring the crates into the city and paid a lot of money to do it! For the love of God, I swear that's all I know!"

With regret, the knight put the preserves back on the tray and left the cell. Beraht patted the prisoner on the shoulder and left as well, rolling the tray full of torture tools out of the cell and closing the door behind after Tomas picked up the kitchen tray and followed them both down the corridor, back in the direction the two had first come from. Once the young man caught back up with the two grinning warriors, a nagging suspicion tugged at his mind.

"Were you bluffing?" he demanded.

"I can't believe people still fall for that!" the knight chuckled.

"Wait, there's... What about the blood?"

Beraht tapped the squire on the shoulder and pointed to where two butchers were taking a dead goat out of the dungeon by a side exit. "Thanks, guys," Rogan called.

"No problem, your Highness," one called back.

"It's just a goat?" Tomas demanded. "What about the screaming?"

Vincent walked out of the jailor's office holding a black hood in his hand and gargling water. Spitting it back into the cup, the spy narrowed his eyes at Rogan. "That's the last time," he declared in a hoarse voice. "My throat's going to be raw for weeks." He passed them and followed the butchers out.

"So, was there any reason for these specific things," the apprentice asked, holding up the tray of kitchen supplies, "or were they just random?"

Beraht grabbed the preserves and the spoon. "Actually, I am a little hungry."

Rogan grabbed the feather. "Kyla loves feathers."

Tomas lifted the iron bowl. "And this?"

Beraht took it and, removing his helmet, placed the bowl on his head as though trying it for size. Tomas noted in mild surprise the purple-dyed headband that held still held his black hair in place. The strange cloth with its red embroidery was so out of character for the hulking barbarian. Shaking his head in disgust, Beraht handed back the bowl and replaced his helmet, waving his hand dismissively.

"God, I hate you guys."

The sound of slow clapping echoed off the stone walls of the dungeon. The three heroes turned to look at Vagris, who sat on the stone bench in his cell. The warlord was watching them and clapping in mock approval of their performance. He wore only a simple prisoner's smock, stained and torn. His body was healing from the wounds suffered at the hands of Beraht's Uldra, but the blood remained caked on him. "Amazing," he said in a voice filled with contemptuous malice. "You still use that same, tired show to get information."

"Still works," Rogan replied.

"You know, it's nice to find out that no matter how much time passes, some things never change. You're still too weak to draw blood."

The knight walked up to the bars, staying only a few steps away from them. "And you're still too eager to spill it."

"So," Vagris said, suddenly on his feet and moving to stand an equal distance away from the cell bars. "What now, old partner of mine? A trial? Some grand show to put on for the mewling masses. Something truly momentous to remind your blind subjects of your glorious majesty?"

"There'll be a trial. You'll be found guilty of murder, terrorism, rape, and nearly every other crime we have a name for. You'll be questioned and then sent to Ubelheim for the rest of your life, which won't be very long up there."

The warlord shook his head. "Poor, simple Rogan. Do you really think the Brotherhood will just abandon me? That's the one fact you never really understood about us; we remain loyal to those who remain loyal to us."

"I was wondering if you were still with them."

"Why would I leave?" he asked, raising his arms and smiling. "Look at what they've done for me. I rule southeastern Lanasia, I have an army at my command, and I serve no man."

Rogan leveled his eyes at the warlord. "The land you 'rule' belongs once again to the people who live there, your army has been destroyed, and you will serve the guards of Ubelheim whenever it's time for a meal."

Vagris again shook his head. "Poor, deluded Rogan. You still don't know what's going on, do you? The men you killed were nothing, mere pawns who thought they were worthy enough to serve me. The lands you think have been freed will be mine again, just as soon as our brothers arrange for my freedom. And you and your precious King will be dead by this time next year."

The knight lifted his chin, ever so slightly. "You're a part of all this, aren't you?"

"Why, whatever are you talking about old chum?"

"So, they've decided to join with one of the factions after all. Which one? Balshazzar? Frostfront?"

The warlord laughed. "It really is amazing how you've managed to survive all these years without the Brothers to help you. You never did have much of a mind for the larger picture." Vagris stepped up against the bars, looking intently at his enemy. "This goes so far beyond the factions and their petty wars over a meaningless throne. You should know by now, Rogan; we never fight for such small prizes. Our goddess shall return."

Rogan's hand snapped out in a blur, grabbing Vagris by the front of his prisoner's smock and pulling him even tighter against the bars. "Who are you working for, Vagris? Who have they sided with?"

Vagris grinned an evil grin and grabbed Rogan's hand, twisting it in an unusual place, forcing the knight to his knees before releasing him and dancing back out of Beraht's reach before the Uldra could get hold of him. "You still have a lot to learn, old friend," the warlord grinned. "Now run along and tell the jailor I'm overdue for my portion of bread and water."

Rogan returned to his feet and, rubbing his sore hand, led Tomas and Beraht out of the dungeons. Tomas sped up to walk alongside his knight. "So, do you want to tell me what in Underworld that was all about?" the squire asked.

"Not really."

"Don't you think I should know if it might end up involving me?"

The knight stopped and glanced at Beraht. The Uldra shrugged. "He's going to find out sooner or later. Better to hear it from you."

Rogan sighed and nodded. "Vagris was a Bellonari, like me. Apparently, he still is."

Tomas' eyes widened in revelation. "He was your partner. The one you betrayed and who reported you dead."

The knight nodded. "It's the only black marks on his record with the Bellonari: that he not only failed to kill me but also falsely reported my death. The only way he can make that up is by finishing what we started on that rooftop."

"That move he did to your hand, I take it Vagris has had the same training you've had."

"All the same, kid. More. We trained right alongside each other for years. He's good."

"How good?" Tomas asked nervously.

"Good."

"What about that returning goddess stuff?"

The knight shrugged and shook his head. "Old superstitions. A lot of cults swear their god or goddess or whatever is right on the verge of returning.

A messenger ran up and bowed to Rogan. "Your Highness. Baron Tressalon requests you meet him in Parden Esha's tower immediately."

Chapter 25

Rogan and Tomas hesitantly entered Esha's chamber. Both offered thanks to God for a lack of explosions greeting them in the open doorway.

"Fear not," the archmage's voice rang out from deep in her sanctum. "I have suspended my experimentations during the transmission."

Feeling only a little reassured, both knight and squire entered the chamber and followed Esha's directions, finally finding both the small Sylva and Rashid standing between two large bookshelves. Behind the two was a stand crafted of bronze, formed into the shape of the wind. Resting atop the stand was half a crystal sphere, flatted at the top.

"Are you only trying to see half the future?" Tomas asked lightly.

"This is not a means of divination," the archmage replied primly with a slight roll of her opalescent eyes. "This is a means of communication. Besides, any first year at the Academy knows crystal balls cannot reveal the future. That nonsense is left to festival tricksters."

"What have you got?" Rogan asked.

"A signal from Althaea," Rashid responded. "She needs to talk with us directly, so she had Gregorios contact Esha here."

"Althaea is one of your agents?" Tomas asked the spymaster. "She didn't really seem the type."

"You'd be surprised the types of people who make good agents," Rashid laughed.

"Step forward," Esha said. "I shall open the link."

A few words of magic and several gestures over the half-sphere were followed by a soft blue light that lifted up from the flattened surface of the crystal. The light coalesced into an image of the beautiful Althaea. "Wow," she laughed. "I should have been a wizard."

"Can she hear and see us?" Rogan asked.

"And you never looked more yummy," the spy winked.

"Are you blushing?" Tomas demanded.

"Shut up, kid. Was there something, Althaea?"

"Now, now, your yummy Highness. What did we talk about last time? Something about being nicer to me?"

"In exchange for giving me a break, as I recall."

Althaea nodded. "Fair enough. Sorry. I just can't help myself sometimes. I do have some news that's pretty urgent."

"Talk to me."

The spy seemed to sit down, sighing. "I've been keeping an eye out on all the mercenaries here at Crossroads."

"Are there more?" Rashid asked. "That place was already packed."

"Actually, there were more, to include some Bellonari, but now there are less," she reported. "If I didn't know better, I'd think they all got bored and started to wander off."

"But you do know better," Rogan noted.

"Of course," she said with a toss of her hair. "It was a little too casual. Plus, I spotted an old friend of yours."

"Anninihus," the knight growled.

Althaea pouted. "And I wanted it to be a surprise. Yes, Anninihus. He came through just a few hours ago and left in a great hurry. After that, the mercs started clearing out as well."

"Who's in charge of them?" Tomas asked.

"What?" she looked confused.

"If Anninihus has organized those mercenaries into an army, then *somebody* has to be in charge, right?"

Rogan nodded. "Good point. How about it, Althaea? Anybody running things there?"

The spy seemed uncertain for a moment before answering. "I can't be sure; I haven't actually seen him, but..."

"I don't like the sound of this," Tomas muttered.

"I've been hearing rumors that Xaemus has been operating nearby."

Rashid shook his head. "Xaemus doesn't work with others; he only serves that mysterious 'dark coven' of his, him and every other Xeshlin fanatic who's always going on about the return of their Dark Empress. He's probably just going after another target."

"That's the thing," she argued, "as far as I can tell, he's not hunting anyone. He's just waiting. No targets, no work, just waiting."

"Could be he's organizing," Rashid suggested.

"Could be he's looking for work." Tomas countered.

"Xaemus doesn't look for work," the spymaster argued. "Everything he does is under orders from his Coven or part of his search for Kelinva."

"Something else," the beautiful spy added. "I just saw Anninihus leaving Crossroads. He looked like someone had just killed his favorite pet. He was heading south as fast as his horse could carry him."

"It would appear our battle with those creatures dealt my old student a greater blow than we originally believed," Esha mused.

Rogan nodded. "Good work, Althaea. Anything else?"

A pause. "One other thing. This is just a hunch, but I think I'm right about this."

"What is it?"

"I think that whatever Anninihus is doing, he's not the one giving the orders."

"What makes you suggest that?" Rashid asked.

"When I saw him, he had another person with him."

"A wizard?" Rogan demanded.

"No, not a wizard. At least, I don't think so. I think he was a noble. Whoever he was, he seemed to be the one giving the orders."

"Can you tell us anything about him?"

"Nothing special. Average height, kinda fat but not too much. He carried a sword, but I don't think he really knew how to use it; he kept tripping over the scabbard. Plus, he had that look like he'd never done a day's work in his life."

"And you think he's in charge?"

"At least giving the orders. Could be he was just relaying them. I do know one thing. He had the Balshazzar crest stamped on a ring he wore."

"And the plot thickens," Tomas muttered.

"Great work Althaea," Rogan said. "You've done enough, though. I want you home."

"If you only knew the mood that puts me in," she purred. "But alas, my duty to Prince and kingdom forbids it just yet. There are still some mercs here in Crossroads. I might be able to learn a bit more."

"At the first sign of trouble, I want you out of there," the knight insisted.

"I am the first sign of trouble," she replied archly. "Bye-bye, your yummy Highness, and take care of that adorable little squire of yours."

Althaea blew her prince a kiss as the image faded and the light flowed back into the crystal.

"Balshazzar," Rogan growled. "I've been meaning to hate him."

"The good Emir seems ready to make a move against the King," Rashid noted.

The knight turned to Esha. "Does Theodorico Balshazzar have any magical training?" he asked.

"No," the Sylva replied. "He was tested as all children once were in the Republic, but showed no signs of arcane ability."

"Could he somehow be that distortion that Anninihus kept encountering?"

The archmage shrugged. "In a multiverse of infinite possibilities, that is possible."

Rashid rolled his eyes. "Couldn't you just have said you don't know?"

"That is what I said."

"Anyway," Rogan snapped, heading off any arguments. "What does Althaea's news tell us?"

"Well for one thing," Rashid noted, "whatever Anninihus and whoever he's working for had planned, we thwarted it tonight."

Esha nodded. "Also, we can now reasonably assume that the distortion cloaking my former apprentice is of his creation or discovery. If he is in the service of Emir Theodorico Balshazzar of Tordenia, then his master cannot be its source."

"What about that?" the spymaster asked. "Balshazzar dabbling in forbidden magic to further his own agenda?"

"What about it?" Rogan demanded. "He did the same damn thing ten years ago when he joined up with the Greysoul. Same tricks, different day, different spell-slinger. Same Balshazzar."

"I guess that means you'll have to pay the Emir a visit."

The knight nodded. "That matches up with what Cyras told me when I met Tomas. He said I'd go to Tordenia and meet with Balshazzar after the kid and I came to the Keep and Tomas here got to meet everybody."

"And I've met just about everybody," the squire added.

"I guess that means it's just about quest time."

Esha cleared her throat. "Might I suggest delaying your departure? Summer is now under way, and the Druug will be quite active. Spring is the only time of relative safety in Ulheim."

"Why go through Ulheim at all?" Tomas asked.

"Either that," Rogan shrugged, "or sail around the whole damned continent. There are Uldra paths through the mountains. Beraht can make arrangements with the various clans, get them to ready us a path.

"That'll take time," Rashid pointed out. "Why not follow your squire's advice? Go by sea?"

The knight thought about it, but shook his head. "There's still a big mercenary force near the Wood. That's an active threat to the villages in and around our forest. We'll send out units to patrol, but I want to take a little time to make sure everything's secure here before I head out again." He glanced at Tomas. "Besides, some of us need a little more seasoning, first."

"What?" the squire asked.

The light of the spell faded, and with it, the magic that animated her body. Althaea's face went slack. Her breathing stilled and she felt her heart slow to almost nothing. The dominating force controlling her mind and manipulating her body withdrew. Her consciousness, what remained, slipped back into the darkness that had claimed her. Her eyes and ears still worked; she saw the tent and the monsters within, and she heard their words. Her skin still felt the stifling air of their meeting. She felt and saw and smelled and heard, but she could not climb out of the darkness, not even to scream with a limp tongue

A figure hooded and cloaked in the blackest leather stepped only partially into the faint candlelight of the tent. Two blood red eyes stared out from the deeply cowled hood. "Now what?" a voice asked, coming as much from the darkness of the hood as any mouth and heavily layered with the accent of Davenor.

Anninihus stepped around the crystal and grinned. "That will cause more than enough distraction while I move into position," he hissed. "You will continue your preparations. Everything must be ready on time."

"I do not like having my name mentioned," the predator hissed.

"It was necessary. They needed a name that would inspire enough respect to make them fear what the mercenary army could do. Rogan cannot leave the Northern Keep just yet."

"Was it wise to implicate Balshazzar?" the assassin asked. "The Emir may object."

"Don't forget whom you serve," the thin wizard snapped. "Your questions suggest I don't know what I'm doing."

"I serve only as long my search is aided. My devotion is to my Dark Empress, not your master's designs. I will only remain so long before my search must resume."

The shadows behind the Death Mage seemed to thicken into a deep black robe. "Yes," a voice of utter evil said, "and, as I swore, I will reveal your Dark Empress' new incarnation in return for your service." The words, ominous in themselves, seemed to cause the heat in the tent to retreat, bringing a horrible chill to the air. The figure carried no staff and did not summon magic as wizards do with words and gestures; despite this, and even from the prison within her own soul, Althaea could not help but feel the power emanating from this creature.

"Master." The Death Mage turned and bowed deeply.

"Anninihus, is all prepared as I have commanded?"

"Yes, my master. My attack will come without warning even as they are at the height of their celebration."

"And you, seeker?" the shadows asked. "Are your own tasks proceeding?"

"They are," the cloaked killer replied. "All will be ready according to your schedule."

"Good. I will not tolerate failure at this juncture."

"My questions stand," Xaemus insisted. "Implicating Balshazzar was foolish. Implicating me was dangerous. The Emir provides support that you require, and disrupting my quest for the Dark Empress is suicidal." He turned to stare at Anninihus.

"Do not question me, Xaemus," the shadows warned. "And do not threaten my apprentice. My plans are complex and not for you to know. Balshazzar's name was given to Calonar's servants at my command, as was yours. I have need for Eigenhard and his associates to be in a certain place at a certain time. My apprentice is simply obeying my commands."

Anninihus looked at Xaemus with a smug grin.

"And you, apprentice. Why did you attack Eigenhard and his whelp without my permission?"

"They discovered my creatures," the Death Mage replied, trembling slightly and the twitch on his cheek jumping nearly out of control. "I feared what they could have learned from the constructs."

"No more or less than what I wished them to," the shadows replied. "You thought they could discover anything for which I was unprepared? You were wrong. Do not make the mistake of thinking again."

"Yes, my master."

"Esha's probes are growing more powerful. As juvenile as her power is, I cannot risk detection. Above all else, Eigenhard and his lackeys must not discover my actions or involvement; they would alert my brother. I will, therefore, inform the Emir of what has transpired here and return to the project. I leave affairs here in your hands, Anninihus. Do not disappoint me."

The Death Mage bowed. "I would sooner die, master."

"That was my intention." The shadows dissolved, leaving the wizard and the bounty hunter alone.

Anninihus took a deep breath. "Did you dispose of her partner's body?" he asked.

"The wizard will not be found," Xaemus replied. The hunter turned and pointed a gloved finger at the still body of Althaea. "And that? Do wish me to dispose of that as well?"

The Death Mage walked up to the beautiful spy and ran a hand through her long brown hair. "Oh, heavens no. My attack will not be until the very end of their festival, months from now. I have time and need entertainment. I can find many interesting things to do with such a body as this in the interim."

If Xaemus felt any disgust at the Death Mage's comments, he displayed none. Althea, trapped in the darkness of her own mind, could only scream soundlessly and beg for uncaring gods to kill her.

Chapter 26

Mary said nothing when Tomas finally returned to the castle late that night. She had been napping on the balcony, enjoying the cool night air after the warm day. At the sound of her young man's entry, despite his attempts at stealth, she had nearly leapt from their often-shared divan, and ran to the receiving room. The sight of Tomas brought Mary to a standstill.

He tried to hide his discomfort, but she knew. He deliberately concealed his wounded shoulder, but she knew. He tried lying about his involvement and injury in the warehouse battle, word of which had long spread across the city, but she knew. She concealed her gnawing worry, her almost desperate fear, with a venomous berating of her young man.

The scolding for his utter lack of regard, his cold indifference to her, lasted nearly an hour. She berated him as she washed his battered body, pointed to every spot of dried blood, every bruise, every caustic example of his idiotic need to prove himself in defiance of danger. She did not, though, mention the deep gash in his shoulder; Mary only finished cleaning it and saw that the stitching was secure before moving on to another minor example of Tomas' stupidity.

"And when will you find proper clothes?" she demanded, wrapping a light robe around Tomas' weary body. "You're squire to the Prince of House Calonar! You look like some vagabond!"

"Well-" Tomas had made the mistake of attempting an answer to her obviously rhetorical question.

That required another round of chastisement, while Mary led her man to the bedroom. By then, the food she had ordered from the kitchens arrived, and she forcibly made Tomas lie in bed while she made sure he had a proper meal before being tucked in for sleep.

The following morning, Mary woke before her exhausted man and ensured he had another meal ready for when he woke. When a messenger arrived from the Prince, intent on dragging Tomas out for another absurd day of so-called training, Mary sent the poor page whimpering back to his master with instructions that Tomas was, under no circumstances, leaving their rooms for at least a day.

When her foolish man finally rose, Mary sat with him and shared a meal. During this, Tomas broached a subject that was finally of some interest to her. "I was thinking of something you said last night," he noted through a mouthful of sausage.

"Oh?" she said after finishing her small bite of fruit.

"I think you're right. I'm Rogan's squire; I should have proper clothes."

"What were you thinking of?" she asked indifferently, her mind already making selections, color arrangements, and a compilation of possible styles.

Tomas shrugged and wisely said, "I don't know. I'm not good at fashion or color or anything. You should pick."

That had been a week ago. Now Tomas stood, modeling the work Mary had commissioned on his behalf, with his wages. "Trust a *Sy'lva* in manners of fashion," Velaera insisted after yet another of Tomas' objections. "We alone, of all the races of *Ar'ae'el*, have a true appreciation of style." The matronly sylva was one of the finest tailors in the Northern Keep. Normally, an appointment with her had to be made weeks, sometimes months, in advance. Mary, however, had challenged the fashionable mistress of threads with the opportunity to cloth Prince Rogan's new squire. Velaera had been unable to refuse.

And so, the squire had been forced to stand on a low pedestal for what seemed an eternity that morning. Mary had, once again, informed Prince Rogan that Tomas would be unavailable for the day, and, after quite nearly cramming food down his throat, had marched him to the exquisitely-appointed shop of the Keep's most renown seamstress. He stood, staring into a set of uncanny Uldra triple-mirrors, the newest design of an old Khepric concept, offering an almost flawless reflection. His mirrored-self looked almost as sullen as Tomas himself, a fact of which Mary was utterly indifferent.

"I don't know," the young woman mused, "I'm not sure of the material."

Valaera pulled off the small string she had draped over her broad shoulders and measured the young man's waist. "There is nothing wrong with the material," she assured Mary, ignoring yet another of Tomas' sighs. "My only worry is the muscle he has acquired over the past weeks." She held the measured string out to Mary, noting the change from the last fitting just three days prior. "His waist shrinks as well. A full wardrobe may be impossible until his body stabilizes." The master-tailor pursed her lips in concentration. "Do we have any notion as to when his training will be complete?" she asked.

"Rogan says..." Tomas tried to answer.

"At least another month," Mary replied, the women continuing to ignore their subject. "Though," she added, "his Highness has said that the worst of the physical training is over." She glanced up and along her man's body, not for the first time appraising the physical conditioning she often mocked. Tomas was still standing atop a small platform, which, though it only raised him a few inches from the floor, still allowed a better view of many interesting qualities.

Tomas turned a bit, trying to get a better view of himself in the triple-mirror. "You really think I've put on some muscle?" he asked, appraising the trio of warriors standing within the mirrors.

Both Mary and Velaera rolled their eyes

The sylva absently moved an errant lock of her braided brown hair away from her face. "Yes, young Master Tomas. You recent training has made you into a solid mass of virile power. Your lady shall surely swoon when takes her pleasure from you."

This brought a slight pursing to Mary's lips.

The master-tailor shook her head and muttered, "If I am able to properly adjust your clothing, that is." She made a minor adjustment to the linen trousers, dyed a light grey.

"Tighter, you think?" Mary asked.

Velaera briefly turned her opalescent eyes to Mary. "We must leave something to the imagination," she murmured. "Besides, these are yours, and you alone should enjoy them." The Sylva stood back up and went to a nearby counter. "The color, though." Like most of the counters in her large shop, these were covered with a variety of fabrics dyed in a great variety of colors.

"Blue and grey are the House colors," Mary pointed out, joining the master tailor.

"Yes, but the tone," Velaera insisted, "the tone is everything."

Both women turned back to view their project. Tomas was absently curving his arms, appreciating the results of his many weeks of training and physical conditioning. The long tunic Velaera had designed was a rich royal blue, and somehow both conformed to the new lines of the squire's thickening torso, while also allowing him freedom of movement. The linen undershirt was of a very light grey, nearly white, and so thin yet sturdy Tomas had noted he felt like he was not wearing a shirt at all. "It needs something," Mary mused.

"Indeed," Velaera agreed. "Headgear?"

"Ew," the maid objected. "Those duty caps the soldiers wear?"

"Of course not," the Sylva laughed. She then snapped her fingers and moved to a row of rounded boxes lining one wall. She retrieved one and returned to Mary, glowing with the pride of accomplishment. "A Tyrolean," she said in triumph, producing the hat. Mary considered the traditional Northland headgear. It was the same very light grey as the undershirt, with the brim folded slightly down in the front and turned up in the back. A red cord was tied around, which would nicely set off the blue of the tunic, Mary noted. She picked up the hat and crossed to Tomas, placing it on his head, cocked just slightly to one side.

Velaera joined Mary as both women considered their work. "A set of wool to replace the linen when the weather turns," One said.

"And a thicker tunic, but with room for padding, of course," another added.

They added a leather belt, "for that dagger the brute Remm Stonebearer gave him," Mary noted.

"Perfect," Velaera breathed, then paused. "Nearly, anyway."

There was a heavy knock, nearly a pounding, on her door. "And that would be the final touch," she said happily. The matronly Sylva nearly glided across the wide room and opened the door. Outside was the bottom half of an Uldra, the top half obscured by the building. Mary joined the master tailor. The maid noted in surprise the new arrival was the same gemsmith from whom Tomas had purchased her emerald earrings, the same ones that even now decorated her.

The Uldra also recognized Mary. "Make sure she's paying," he grumbled, recalling the maid's propensity for browsing.

Velaera just made a shooing motion with one hand after taking the small box from her irritable neighbor. The seamstress showed Mary what was in the box and the young woman nearly swooned. They indifferently closed the door on the Uldra, his purpose fulfilled, and returned to their project. Velaera held the box to Mary. "If you would do the honors?"

Mary smiled and lifted the contents of the box, pinning it on the left beast of Tomas' new long tunic. The squire regarded the final touch in the triple-mirror. It was large for a pin, nearly a brooch, and made of solid silver. The pin itself was gold, and fashioned into a stylized sword, a gladius, the traditional sword of the Republic Legions. He stared without comment at the crossed diamond heraldry now riding against his heart.

"Well?" Mary asked.

"It looks," Tomas struggled for a word. His eyes traveled up and down, taking it all in, but then lingered on the emblem of House Calonar. "It looks... right."

Chapter 27

"Get him chained down," Rogan ordered. "I don't want Vagris to be able to move at all."

The transfer was going smoothly, Tomas mused. The squire had stood beside his knight as the prince supervised the preparation of the convoy to Ulheim. Vagris had remained silent as his prisoner's smock had been replaced with a thicker one of burlap, the heavy material stretching across his broad chest and the bright yellow stripe running the length of his back. The warlord had watched with calm detachment as the dungeon guards had chained his wrists and ankles to the heavy metal belt he would wear for the rest of his life in Ulheim. He had offered the two crossbow-wielding soldiers outside his cell the briefest flick of his dead eyes before raising his proud southern chin in defiance of his captors. Even encumbered as he was, the former nobleman had managed to retain a sense of grace as he was escorted out into the courtyard, marching with his back unbent and never a single misstep. Surrounded as he was by the security detail that would accompany him all the way to the infamous prison and remain his keepers once there, Vagris made the jailors appear more as an honor guard than a prison detachment. Rogan, upon seeing the prisoner appear, could not prevent a low growl of disappointment from escaping his lips at the unbroken appearance of this enemy of his prince.

The traitorous warlord looked calm and even somehow content as he was chained into the caged wagon that would take him north. Vagris regarded the wizard that continuously scanned the area and the people in it for any mystical threat with mild interest. Even when the mutinous former Legion commander was forced to sit on an unpadded wooden bench with his hands and feet shackled first together and then to the wagon floor, the warlord seemed, if anything, mildly amused at all the trouble his enemies were going to.

Rogan stood just outside the wagon, never breaking eye contact with Vagris as his security detail locked the murderer down. The gaze of the former warlord was disconcerting, Tomas silently admitted to himself. One had the feeling of looking into pure evil.

"Just so you know," Rogan told the prisoner, "these men are some of the best we've got. They can't be bought, and they won't ever quit."

Vagris just stared at his former brother-in-arms.

"Take a few weeks to get to your new home, and preparations have already been made for you there," the knight continued. "On the way, if anything happens, if it looks like you *might* escape, these men have orders to put you down."

The warlord glanced dismissively at the soldiers chaining him down then back at Rogan. Vagris glanced over the knight's shoulder and smiled as wax plugs were inserted into the warlord's ears and a sack pulled over his head.

"*Rogan Eigenhard!*" the shrill voice of Princess Kyla came stabbing from behind.

"Good morning, my dearest," he said in nearly genuine-sounding enthusiasm. The knight and his squire turned and were confronted by the seething jewel of House Calonar. The princess' pearlescent eyes flashed in righteous fury and her tiny body nearly spasmed in outrage. Beside the indignant Kyla was a calm-faced Aebreanna, who's banality was marred by the smug self-satisfaction the Sylva made little real effort to hide.

"What are you doing to that man?" Kyla demanded.

"That *prisoner* is a mass murderer," Rogan pointed out, obviously trying to maintain his composure in public. "He's led his mercenaries in the burning of at least three villages and one major town *that we know of*. He's being treated as he deserves to be treated."

Kyla drew herself up to her full height, which would have worked a little better, Tomas mused, had she another few inches. "Prince Rogan," she commanded, "you will remove those ridiculous bindings."

Seeing the futility of arguing his own opinions, the knight decided to switch tactics. "Kyla," he said patiently, taking her hands in his, "shining star of my night sky, comforting summer wind of my world, delight of my entire life." The seething princess seemed unmoved by Rogan's attempts at submissive assertion. "These precautions are for everyone's safety," the prince continued. "Also, don't forget that your father placed me in charge of the military."

Kyla narrowed her pearlescent blue eyes at her beloved husband and let a chill that froze the pleasant summer air. Tomas tried to move, to pull his knight away from the growing danger, but found his body frozen in terror, much as any prey animal becomes when faced with their imminent doom. "Prince Rogan Eigenhard," Kyla said in a tone that caused Tomas and every other man within sound of it to take a step back. "Hero of the Northern Keep, defender of the Northlands, heir of House Calonar, and champion of the common people. Is what Vagris did moral?"

"No," Rogan sighed.

"Were his actions moral, his behavior, or especially his treatment of helpless people?" she asked.

"No," the knight sighed again.

"How are you behaving right now?" the princess demanded. "Like Rogan Eigenhard, or like Vagris?"

"But..."

"You are either a hero or a villain," Kyla said with finality. "Now, release those bindings, chain him properly, and take that ridiculous hood off!"

"Of course, my princess," Rogan replied far too quickly.

Sensing her husband's duplicity, Kyla looked around the detail of men and found the highest-ranking Guardsman. "You there, Sergeant."

A red-haired man stepped down from the wagon and drew himself up to stand stiffly at attention before Kyla. "Yes, ma'am?" he asked.

"What's your name, sergeant?" the princess asked.

The veteran paled and glanced at Rogan. The prince stepped up behind Kyla to speak softly in her ear. "My dearest, the guards never reveal their names either to or in front of their prisoners," he whispered.

"I asked your name, sergeant" she repeated imperiously.

With a resigned nod from Rogan, the sergeant replied. "Gregor, ma'am."

Kyla smiled her most male-dominating smile up at the uncomfortable soldier. "Gregor," she said, "I am ordering you to escort the prisoner Vagris north to Ubelheim and treat him humanely during the trip. He is to receive the basic courtesy that any person deserves and allowed some measure of dignity."

Gregor looked as though he had swallowed a baby wolf, and said animal was now trying to claw its way out. "Ma'am?" he asked, clearly of two minds.

"What about my orders are unclear, Sergeant Gregor?" Kyla asked sweetly.

"Those orders are in direct conflict with our standing instructions on the treatment of Tier One prisoners, ma'am."

The princess threw a look of shock at Rogan. "We treat all our prisoners this way?" she demanded.

"Just the Tier One prisoners," the prince replied evenly.

"Well, that stops now," Kyla declared. "From now on, you will not treat any prisoners in this manner as long as they maintain good behavior. Is that understood?"

"Yes, ma'am," Lieutenant Gregor replied after a quick glance to Rogan and seeing only a brief nod.

"Good," Kyla said. "And you!" Tomas realized the fury of the princess of Calonar was now directed at him. The squire noted that Rogan was whispering to Sergeant Gregor an assurance that the revealed family man would be transferred as soon as possible.

"Me?" Tomas squeaked.

"You are his squire, correct?" the princess demanded.

"I… uh… that is…"

"And you are responsible for seeing to his needs, correct?" Kyla continued, obviously indifferent to anything the squire might say.

"Well, y-…"

"So how is it you let him do this?" she demanded. "Your knight needs more from you than just oiling his armor! You have to keep him…"

"Enough, Kyla!" Rogan barked.

The princess rounded on her prince, but Rogan was like stone. "Enough," he repeated. "You're mad at me, fine. You don't like my orders, fine. You will *not* berate my people for following them."

Kyla seemed to swell, her fury very nearly igniting the air. Aebreanna leaned in and whispered something to her friend. Whatever the baroness said seemed to mollify, or at least slightly temper, Kyla's outrage. The princess turned to leave. "Come along, Rogan," she commanded over her shoulder in an even voice. "We need to have a long discussion on the treatment of prisoners in my father's kingdom."

Once the sack was pulled from Vagris' head, the warlord again locked eyes with Rogan. The knight could only emit a low growl of frustration when the criminal gave him a knowing smile.

Chapter 28

"Morning, kid," Rogan greeted Tomas as the young
man entered the prince's dining room. "Eat something; going to be
a long day." The knight paused then, and took in his squire. Days
had passed since they had last seen each other. Rumor within the
castle spoke of disharmony between the prince and princess of
House Calonar. Living on the same floor as the couple, Tomas had
heard yells and crashes, oaths and curses. Initially, the squire had
thought to intervene, but Mary had held him back. Finally, on the
third day, all had gone quiet, which caused an even greater fear
amidst the denizens of Castle Calonar, but that silence was soon
replaced by a rather raucous rekindling of marital bliss.

In the days of Tomas' effective release from his responsibilities
as Rogan's squire, Mary had completed her project in remaking her
man as she pleased. A final trip to Velaera's shop saw Tomas
burdened with boxes and packages, which he dutifully lugged up to
the castle, after arranging a final payment to the Keep's mistress of
threads. The squire's entire wardrobe was remade, rearranged into
something more pleasing to Mary's sensibilities. When, on the
morning of the fourth day, summons arrived from Rogan, the maid
was nearly giddy in anticipation of her Tomas' grand reveal to the
prince.

Tomas stood in the center of the dining room and sighed. He
held out his hands and said, "Go ahead," anticipating the comedy to
come. Rogan's squire was dressed in another long tunic of royal blue,
with a very light grey undershirt and matching linen trousers. In his
hat he carried one of the several Tyrolean hats Mary had purchased
with his money, this one blue with a nearly-white cord. The Calonar
pin was once again on his left breast and Alexia's golden pin was on
his collar, against the pulse of his neck.

Rogan was sitting at his breakfast with his squire entered. He
took a long look at his squire and then sat forward, taking another
piece of bread and applying a spread of wild berry preserves. "Do

you remember how I told you about the first time Kyla and I were together?" he asked with a grin.

Tomas dropped his arms and walked to the table, taking a seat. He still struggled a bit with the long tunic, specifically how to sit on it. "Sure, the night of the Madness."

"Well," the knight added, taking a bite. "After that, we all returned here to the Keep. I thought I'd get some time to rest, repair my equipment, maybe get shown around." He leaned back in his chair and savored the bread and fruit. "Well, Kyla had other ideas. She took me to a local seamstress to get outfitted in new clothes."

"Wait," Tomas started. "Velaera?"

"Guess I should've warned you," Rogan admitted through a full mouth. "Velaera's sort of a rite of passage for the men of House Calonar."

Tomas shook his head. Saying nothing while he helped himself to some sausage. "Where is Kyla?"

"Temple." The knight washed his bread and fruit down with some cool berry wine. "That last batch of refugees and a few kids. The Sisters are assessing their education so they can figure out where to start the schooling."

Tomas glanced at his knight. "Is everything... ok?"

Rogan nodded. "You'll learn," he said. "Boundaries are important in a marriage. We try to keep our duties separate, but sometimes there's... overlap." His tone said better than words could that the matter was still a sensitive one, and best left alone.

Rashid entered the room without knocking. He was wearing a tunic of deep grey, an odd color that was very dark and seemed to suggest hints of blue as he walked. His trousers were purely black and he wore a dark grey leather vest with a silver insignia of House Calonar pinned over his left breast. "Good morning, Rogan, Tomas," he said.

"Rashid," Rogan said.

"Breakfast?" Tomas asked.

The spymaster shook his head. "I already ate. I just stopped by to go over the new security arrangements."

"Have a seat," the knight offered.

Sitting down, Rashid raised the parchments he had been carrying. Despite his prior refusal, the spymaster nonetheless took some fruit and nuts. "I've got three companies of House Guard on random patrol to supplement the Watch," he said. "They'll keep changing their routes and times. Esha has assigned a team of her students, so that a wizard will either accompany each patrol, or be on ready-standby should something happen." He handed a sheet of parchment to Rogan. "I've scheduled a series of drills to test response times and readiness. They'll be spread out over the next few weeks."

Rogan cleaned his hands and then took the parchment. He studied it for a moment before saying, "You should make some of these unscheduled, unannounced. Surprise to simulate surprise."

The spymaster nodded. "I'll see to it."

"What about the investigation in the warehouse," Tomas asked.

"Ongoing," Rashid replied. "I have an appointment with Cardinal Tain this afternoon on the Brotherhood of Saint Valkis. He may know something."

"Unlikely," Rogan muttered. "You know Tain won't have anything to do with the Inquisition after what they did."

"It's still worth a try," the spymaster argued. "My people have quarantined the warehouse and begun a systematic search of the contents." He handed over a large stack of parchment sheets. "These are some of the protests. There are more coming."

Rogan grunted and accepted the formal protests. "Anything else?"

Rashid shook his head.

"How're the twins?" Rogan asked.

"Twins?" Tomas asked.

Throwing his squire a surprised look, Rogan asked, "You haven't met Rashid and Aebreanna's children yet?"

"I'm so sorry that I haven't been introduced to the whole of House Calonar," Tomas replied smartly.

"Aebreanna and I have spoken with them after the latest... incident," Rashid said. "Esha has once again offered instruction, or at least consultation. Aebreanna still wants to wait, though."

"What do you think?" Rogan asked.

The spymaster looked, for the first time Tomas could recall, uncertain. He leaned back in his chair and stared at the ceiling. "This isn't a problem that's going away," he finally said. "Sooner or later..."

Rogan nodded. "The King said it's your choice. Yours and Aebreanna's. The Queen doesn't seem worried so..."

"That's really the only thing that offers me any comfort," Rashid admitted.

The two men were silent then. Tomas, increasingly uncomfortable, spoke. "So, am I going to join this conversation at some point," he asked, "or should I just wait outside?"

Rogan and Rashid looked at one another, as though they shared a silent conversation. Finally, "Your kids," the knight said.

To which, the spymaster countered, "Your squire, your choice, your Highness. You have time now," Rashid pointed out. "The King sent word that he wouldn't be ready for another hour."

"Alright," Rogan said, standing and adjusting his belt. "Guess it's time for Tomas to meet the rest of House Calonar."

In deference to Rogan and Rashid's insistence on tight security for the royal family and those very close to them, the floor that would ordinarily be dedicated to only Rogan and Kyla was instead split into three areas. The northern section held the personal quarters and rooms in which the prince and princess lived. The southern area housed Rashid and Aebreanna, as well as their children. The final wing, in the east section, housed the serving staff permanently assigned to the couples and, of course, Tomas' own private quarters. Since they lived on the same floor of the castle, it took only a few moments to walk through the hallways separating the various wings.

Rashid nodded to the two Archaeknights who stood watch over his family, and the two men, after bowing to Rogan, opened the doors. Inside, Tomas was startled at the sight of Aebreanna. He had read of the Wyrdmark, of course, and seen some evidence of it in his time with Alexia. The old sylva's eyes and hair reflected the winter through which they briefly traveled. Their time together, however, was too short to witness the changing of the seasons. Now that Tomas had been in the Keep for months, and been present in the change from spring to summer, he was amazed at the visible transformation in Aebreanna, who clearly also shared the Wyrdmark.

The Sylva was, of course, still beautiful. But much of her had changed with the seasons. When Tomas had first arrived and met the baroness, her hair had been the color of warm honey; now, it had darkened to a vibrant cedar. Her opalescent eyes had glowed with a verdant power before; now, they bore a hazel sheen. Even her complexion had darkened slightly, with the cool ivory of spring now replaced by the warmth of summer sand. The change was so subtle, yet a startling reminder of her inherent mystical ability.

"The young squire seems enchanted," Aebreanna said in her deep, sultry voice. She leaned back in her deep chair, letting her silken robe of very light blue fall aside as she rose a perfectly-sculpted leg to cross it just over the other knee. The baroness ran a light hand down the gown's front, pulling the front aside just slightly, just enough to reveal that she wore nothing beneath.

"As so many men are in your divine presence," Rashid noted, crossing the room and kissing his wife, letting a hand drift along the bare skin she had just exposed.

"I.. I'm sorry," Tomas stammered. "I've just never seen the Wyrdmark before... the change."

A cloud passed over Aebreanna's beautiful face. "Yes," she said flatly, in a tone that pushed Rashid away. "An unwanted inheritance."

Rogan stepped on his squire's foot, communicating the need to change the subject. "Where's the kids?" he asked, helping the young man who was clearly on dangerous ground.

Aebreanna adjusted her robe. "Children," she called.

A side door was nearly pulled off its hinges, and two engines of chaos and destruction stormed in. The twins, a brother and a sister who could not be more than eight or nine years of age, jumped up and down, running to Rashid and Rogan, yelling in enthusiasm, demanding hugs and engaging in light rough-housing.

"We were just hoping you and Uncle Rogan would come and play with us, Daddy!" the little girl said.

"And we wanted to meet Uncle Rogan's new square!" the boy added.

"Squire," Aebreanna corrected.

Catching both children in a hug, Rashid turned, holding the two in his arms. "Well, here he is," the spymaster said. "Tomas, these are my children, my daughter Rasha, and my son Jalad." Nodding and putting his best smile on, Tomas felt his eyes blur as he stared at the twins. They were so alike in looks that if not for a difference in dress and hair style, the young man would have been unable to distinguish them from each other. The children greatly favored their father, with darker olive-toned skin and nearly midnight-black eyes and hair. The twins were lean and athletic, and they nearly vibrated with contained energy. However, their mother's blood could not be denied, for each of the siblings bore the pearlescent eyes of Halvans.

Despite their physical similarity, though, their behavior demonstrated notable differences. Rasha struck Tomas as the rough and tumble type. The Tressalon daughter was obviously just as nimble as her mother, but flaunted that dexterity by climbing up and staying on Rashid's shoulder only through a perfect sense of balance. Jalad seemed incapable of such dexterity, though, for such would require him to hold still for more than a moment. The boy moved constantly, diving between his father's legs, running around behind where Aebreanna sat, only to zoom back again.

"It's nice to meet you," Jalad said seriously, seeming to have lost no breath at all in his constant movement.

"You're cute!" his sister declared from her perch atop Rashid.

"Rasha," Aebreanna said in a serious tone, "what have I told you?"

Sighing, the little girl said, "Never tell a boy what I really think since that will only scare him away."

"Correct."

Tomas cleared his throat. "Excuse me Aebreanna, but you tell men what you really think all the time."

Shooting the squire a look that could have frozen lava and in a voice recognizable to anyone who had ever been a child, the mother said, "That is different."

"Thought you'd be helping Kyla," Rogan said, moving to save his newly-endangered apprentice.

"I wanted to spend time with my children first. Events have been so chaotic of late that I have seen less of them than I prefer," she replied.

The spymaster, with his children still tangled in his arms and legs, again kissed his wife. "My Sylva goddess detests chaos," he smiled.

Aebreanna looked up at her husband through her perfect opalescent hazel eyes and smiled back. "Only because my Human lord causes so very much in my life."

Rogan and Tomas looked at each other with undisguised nausea. "If this keeps up," the squire whispered, "I'm going to be sick."

Aebreanna turned to throw a cool look to the young man. "Then perhaps you should excuse yourself, Tomas."

Rashid cleared his throat and put the twins down. "Alright you two, go get dressed."

"We are dressed," they said in unison. Looking at them, Tomas realized they were, in fact dressed, although he could have sworn that they were still in their sleeping clothes just a moment ago.

Aebreanna took each of them by the hand. "How many times must I tell you not to do that?" she demanded in exasperation.

"We're just trying to help, Mother," again in unison. Tomas now noticed that the Baroness was also dressed, although in some rather mismatched clothes.

Her voice dropping to nearly a whisper, a sure sign of danger in any mother, Aebreanna leaned in close to her children. "If you two will not mind me, you will stay in your rooms all day."

"We're sorry." The speaking in unison thing was becoming unnerving, Tomas thought.

"You know that there are bad people who want to take you from us. If you keep... doing these things, you'll make it much easier for them to find you. Do you want that?" Rashid asked.

"No, Daddy," they said.

"Good," the baroness said, rising to her feet. Crossing her arms, Aebreanna said, "Children, go and dress. Look your best, and I will be in to check on you in a few minutes. Do you understand?"

"Yes, Mother," they said together, retreating back to their rooms. With the younger children seen to, Aebreanna turned back to Rogan and Tomas. "Do you two not have something you should be doing besides standing about looking foolish?"

Grabbing his squire, Rogan used that as his cue to leave. On the way to the royal apartments, Tomas couldn't help but mull over what he had seen. Sensing this, Rogan asked, "What's the matter, kid?"

"I just never met two children who could use magic like that," the squire replied. "Is it because Aebreanna has the Wyrdmark?"

Rogan stopped quickly, making sure none of the staff could hear them. "Look, as far as anyone is concerned, you didn't see anything, and you sure as Underworld don't know anything."

"What do you mean?" Tomas asked.

"First of all, do yourself a favor and *never* mention the Wyrdmark around Aebreanna." Again, Rogan glanced around, though mostly towards the Tressalon quarters. "She inherited it from her father and that is one subject you never, NEVER talk about."

"But.."

Rogan held up a hand. "Not my story to tell, and I like my skin right where it is, thank you. Don't bring it up. Ever.

"As for the kids," the knight sighed deeply. "There were some very special circumstances surrounding the birth of those twins," the knight replied. "While she was pregnant, Aebreanna was attacked by Tienel Greysoul."

"You told me about that," he replied with a shudder. Every child in the world had heard stories about the Greysoul. His status as a boogeyman was so deeply ingrained into the minds of the children of Lanasia that even mentioning his name was considered by most to be inviting bad luck.

"Well, I left a couple things out. After what happened in Pelsemoria, we lost track of him. Didn't really matter, though, since he found us. He wanted something from Aebreanna and tricked us into letting him have it. Didn't take him long to show his true colors, though. That damned spell-slinger kidnapped her while she was pregnant and did something to either her or them. We managed to save Aebreanna and defeat the Greysoul, sort of, but we were afraid there may have been some harm to her children. Eventually, Aebreanna delivered and everything seemed normal.

"After about a year, we started noticing that the twins always seemed to get what they want. Did you notice that when we entered, they both mentioned they wanted to meet you?"

"Not really," the squire replied.

"Well pay more attention next time. When those two are together, and both want the same thing, it happens."

"The clothes," Tomas guessed.

Rogan nodded. "And your visit, and Aebreanna's change of clothing, and a thousand other things we couldn't ignore. By themselves, we don't have to worry, their power only manifests when they're together."

"Rashid and Aebreanna must be very proud," the squire said sarcastically.

"They're scared to death," the knight replied in deadly seriousness. "There've already been attempts to kidnap those kids. Everyone who knows about them wants to use that 'probability influence,' as Cyras called it, for their own ends."

"If the Trickster Mage knows about the kids, why not have him teach them how to control it so that it would be impossible to take them?" Tomas suggested.

"Aebreanna and Cyras don't exactly get along," the knight snorted. "You might say they had a falling out a few years ago and nobody, and I mean nobody, can hold a grudge like that woman."

"What about Esha?"

Rogan shook his head. "The only one with the knowledge is Cyras Darkholm. He tried to teach them behind Aebreanna's back, but that was a big mistake. She's even angrier at him now than before. Until she allows it, the twins will just go on learning what they can from Esha, and we'll go on protecting them and trying to keep the secret."

"Sounds like the hard way to do things," Tomas noted.

"With women, it almost always is," the knight laughed. "Now come on, the King's waiting."

Chapter 29

It took Tomas quite some time to adapt to the opulence of the suites inhabited by Rogan and Kyla. Seeing the quarters of the King and Queen, however, the young man realized that his knight had been living sparsely. Every seat and couch was trimmed with gold. Beautiful vases and other priceless works of art stood in every corner and place of prominence. Tall windows with velvet drapes provided a spectacular view of the city below. Carpets of the finest silk covered the floor while all pieces of marble and wood showed the most meticulous master craftsmanship. "Do you know what the real irony of all this is?" Rogan asked as if reading his squire's mind.

"What?"

The knight grinned, "Almost everything in this room was a gift. The King could never refuse a gift, so they all end up here. Every piece of art, furniture, carpeting, sculpture, everything finds its way up here. In fact, the only uses for this room are to greet visitors and display all this junk." Rogan gestured to a set of double doors. "Those are the real living areas of the royal family. In there is probably the simplest decorations you'll ever see in a castle."

"What's in there?" Tomas asked, pointing to the doors opposite the royal apartments.

"That's the King's private study. Come on," Rogan said, heading for the King's study. "I want to show you something."

Passing through the doors, Tomas entered a large antechamber with the doors to the King's study off to the right. Within this room were several display cases, each one made of perfectly clear crystal with a bronze identification plate set at the base. Tomas moved from one case to the next, each captivating him in different ways. Rogan simply stood at the doors watching his squire.

One case, in particular, caught Tomas' attention. It was one of the smallest cases, and yet, the crystal, which was no more than a hand's length on each side, held a place of utmost prominence, set in the exact center of the room with no other display within four feet of it. Within the case was a lock of vibrant red hair. The plate read only, "Samantha, never forgotten."

"What is this?" Tomas asked.

Stepping up to the case, a somber expression on his face, Rogan grunted. "Never told the whole story. Way before my time. Apparently, Samantha was the King's first love. They traveled together for a lot of his earliest adventures, long before he became a nobleman. I've heard she saved his life more than a few times."

"Wait," the young man stared at the name. "Samantha? As in, Samantha of the Hill People? Warrior-woman of the Gunrsvein?"

"The same," Rogan shrugged.

"What happened to her?" The squire asked. "Stories talk about her at the Siege of Velaross, but that's it."

"That's the subject of a lot of debate here in the Keep. Some people say she died in battle, others that she died of old age. Only thing everyone agrees on is that at some point, Cylan Calonar had to make a decision between Samantha of the Hill People and the priestess Nora. One would marry him and share in his long life, the other would leave forever."

"So he chose Nora, the woman who is now Nora Calonar, High Priestess of the Harvest Mother and Queen of the Northlands," Tomas noted. "I guess he chose the right one."

"I like to think so." The sudden voice startled both knight and squire. Spinning around, they found that the King had quietly entered. "But then, in my mind, there really was only one possible choice."

"So, your wife is the High Priestess of the Harvest Mother, and your daughter is the Sister Superior of the Lady of Light?" Tomas asked, somewhat bewildered. "Does religion run in the blood of the women in your family?"

The king smiled softly. "It very well may. Nora's mother was a priestess, and my wife has felt the calling for as long as I have known her. Very nearly from her birth, Kyla has been the happiest, most joy-inspiring person I've ever encountered, making her own choice of vocation an obvious one. Interestingly, the ladies of House Calonar, for most of the history of the Sylvai Empire, were Truthseers."

"What about your other daughter?" the squire asked.

"Karen is still a little young yet to choose her life's path. However, there can be little doubt that whatever her choice, my daughter will excel."

"How is it that Kyla chose the Lady of Light?" Tomas asked. "I'd think that, with her mother being the High Priestess of one religion, it would have been natural for the Princess to follow suit."

"Her mother and I have made a point of not making our daughter's decisions for her," the king replied. "It was her choice to serve her goddess, and we supported her." He stepped forward to join them. "True courage is not just facing one's opponents, Tomas; it is also having the strength to trust those you love."

Tomas turned back to the case with the lock of red hair. "What happened to Samantha?"

Looking at the lock, King Cylan's face, already lined with the worries of an entire world, briefly took on the manner of deepest mourning, though the shadow quickly passed. "We lost Samantha to the darkness. She fought all the way to the end, but sometimes, sometimes evil wins no matter how hard we fight."

Tomas turned to another display, eager to change the subject from one that caused the king such obvious discomfort. The case that he approached held a large steel shield, the type the Holy Knights carried into battle. "What is this from?" he asked, marveling at the bright red field, broken only by the silver lion with blue claws and tongue.

Walking up beside Tomas, the king smiled, his blue eyes dancing with old memories. "That is the shield of Sir Talius Ironheart, Holy Knight of the Order of Justice, hero of the Army of the Golden Flame, and icon for entire generations of paladins."

Rogan cleared his throat. "Don't forget to mention he was also excommunicated twice times and expelled from the Order three times."

"He was a little unconventional for a Holy Knight," the king laughed. "But no matter how often he found himself at odds with his superiors, Talius always found forgiveness and reacceptance amongst his brother knights."

"He and the King here traveled together for... how long was it?"

"Years," Cylan supplied. "We were together for so many years I have long since lost count. We stood side by side at the Siege of Velaross. We battled the Xeshlin Invasion. Finally, we both retired, he to Ironheartshaven, I to the Keep."

"You never fought together again?" Tomas asked.

"Only one last time. When his city came under attack, I raised an army and went to his aid with Mortimus, Khaine and Cyras. That was a fight to end them all; between Mortimus and Cyras, there was enough magic flying through the air to tear the world asunder. Talius and I fighting side by side once more. Even Tienel made an appearance."

Tomas looked at the king, marveling that such an obvious bloodbath brought a smile to his lips and set his eyes to sparkling. "What happened to them all?" he asked.

"Well, I returned to the Keep and found out Nora was pregnant with my son. Mortimus returned to the Church and eventually fell to the Inquisition. Tienel made a point of not being noticed as much as possible considering every government in the world had a price on his head. Khaine and Cyras stayed with me for a time before returning to their own wanderings."

"What about Sir Talius?" Tomas asked.

"He took his proper place at God's right hand."

"He fell in battle?"

Cylan nodded. "He died defending his people. He died a hero's death."

Tomas turned to a row of swords hanging along the wall. There were eight of them, of various types, from all over the world. Each of the blades bore the crest of House Calonar and were unique in design. One blade was long and deeply curved. Another was the type of saber used by the light horsemen of Varrik. There was even one of the blades the squire had heard was used by the warriors of Tramaya, with a long hilt and a slightly curved blade sharp on only one side.

In the center of the display was an odd sword of indistinct design. Something about this blade drew Tomas' eyes. Calonar and Rogan said nothing as the squire lightly ran his fingertips along the weapon. Nothing about the sword seemed at first to be extraordinary, and yet its strange shape, its uncommon design and construction, called to the young man. It was a little shorter than the common longswords of Lanasia, though larger than a typical shortsword, a little less than the length of Tomas' arm. The crosspiece was diamond-shaped and seemed almost to glow, it so caught the light from the distant window. The grip was textured and solid black, not made of wood or metal, but of some undefinable material. The pommel was the greatest adornment the squire could make out, with a small pearl imbedded in the very tip and surrounded by silver; this gem was so perfect it seemed as though a Sylva's eye stared back at the young man. Upon closer inspection, Tomas realized that the pearl had etched within it, seemingly beneath its surface, the crossed-diamonds of House Calonar.

The squire glanced back at King Cylan. "May I?" he asked.

The aging man smiled slightly and nodded.

Tomas reverently lifted the sword off its rack, feeling the weight in his hands. Holding it with great care, he examined this weapon that seemed to radiate a history of honor and glory. The squire stared at the blade, marveling in the perfection of its construction. But then he looked closer. "Uldric steel," he mused, "but in the Sylvai design."

Rogan chuckled. "No Sylvai would ever admit it," he said, "but they stole that design."

"Indeed," the king added. "The Uldra has mastered this forging technique long ago, before their Uprising. When the Sylvai destroyed the Uldra cities, they... acquired the technique. Now, aside from a handful of master smiths amongst the Uldra, the Sylvai metal-shapers alone know how to forge steel in this way."

The minor sunlight peeking through the open windows was caught immediately by the sword, highlighting the bands that drifted across the metal, like ripples on a forest stream. In modern days, the squire had read, only Sylvai blades showed this craftsmanship, and they refused to share the secret. The fuller that ran two-thirds of the blade's length was almost lost in the dancing pattern of the steel. The blade seemed, as Tomas held it, to be so perfectly balanced as to be nearly weightless; such a weapon could easily be wielded with only one hand.

"This is no common blade," the young man breathed.

The king stood forward and smiled as he ran his eyes along the weapon. "That, Tomas, is Steelheart, a gift to me from Talius Ironheart, forged by one of the last Uldra master smiths. Talius presented it to me just before the Siege of Velaross."

"What enchantment was put on it?"

"What makes you ask?"

"A weapon like this... it's perfect. It must have magic."

"Actually Tomas, Steelheart has been hardened against the arcane. Remm forged it using a process he shares with no one, and placed upon it what he calls, 'The Allfather's Blessing.' It is not steel, as you noted, but an alloy of steel and starfell. The blade is impervious to any form of magic."

"Starfell?" Tomas gasped, looking at the flawless sword in near-reverence. "I thought it was lost."

"Some remains," king Cylan noted. "A very few stones still exist, hidden by their owners."

"The firestones that destroyed Nassinalia," the squire marveled.

"Not quite," the aging king disagreed. "Partly, but there were other contributing factors to the Disaster."

"Was this your first sword?"

"No, I had a blade before this one. But I carried Steelheart through my battles with the Heroes of Fate. After Velaross, I carried it against the Druug in defense of this community and through the Invasion of the Dark Empress, Kelinva."

"And it's rested here ever since?"

"Oh no," the king replied. "My son, Kyle, wielded it as well. When he heard of a kidnapping in a nearby village, Kyle insisted I send him to investigate. I agreed and gave him this sword. He carried it through his adventures, giving it up only after he died."

"So, you intended to pass this blade on from father to son through your family line."

The aging man nodded. "That was my original intention. However, Kyle died before having a child, and my daughters have expressed little interest in swords."

The squire replaced Steelheart at its position of honor. Cylan laid an affectionate hand on the sword and smiled. "Each of these blades has served me over the years. Each of them has a story. But of them all, this one means the most to me."

"Then you're waiting for Kyla or Karen to have a son?" Tomas asked. "Another male Calonar?"

"Not at all," he nodded towards Rogan. "My other son carried it."

The squire looked over at his knight, who shrugged. "When the Greysoul kidnapped Aebreanna, Fang and Talon were damaged," he explained. "Remm eventually repaired them, but I needed a weapon right then."

"Rogan agreed to carry Steelheart into battle," Cylan said with a fair amount of pride. "He continued its tradition of honor."

The knight crossed his arms over his chest. "The King here wanted me to keep carrying it, but I disagreed. That sword is for young men just starting out. I already had my uncle's weapons, and that blade is meant for someone new."

"Remm mentioned something," Tomas recalled. "Something like, a man must have his own tools."

"So now I wait," Calonar said, nodding. "I wait for the day the next hero in our line steps forward. But there is something else that you should see, Tomas."

"What is that, sir?"

The old king gestured to another section of the room, where a large diagram dominated the wall. Calonar led the other two heroes to the display and pointed towards it. "The entire history of House Calonar, all the way to the founding of the Sylvai Empire."

Tomas stared up at the family tree, open-mouthed in awe at the history it contained. His eyes traced along the various bloodlines that were all interlaced with the Imperial family of the old Sylvai Empire. "Amazing," he whispered.

"Actually, Tomas, there was something specific I wanted you to learn from this." Calonar pointed to his own entry and traced his finger back to his father Selendurn, the captain of the House Guard for the Northlands Prefect in the early years of the Republic. From that entry, the old king traced his finger up to his grandfather, the legendary General Naronor Calonar, commander of the Sylvai armies during the Uldra Uprising, and then back down along a different matriarchal line to a name so familiar the very sight of it caused a shock to run through the squire's soul.

The entry read: Palsilyagathalexia of House Calonar. Daughter of Naronor and Sayantia. Sister of Selendurn. Mother of Falkepel. Truthseer. Priestess and Teacher of House Calonar. Companion of Aebresephravaasya.

"My God," Tomas gasped. "Alexia was your aunt."

Cylan nodded. "And the only remaining member of my family. Look carefully at this genealogy, Tomas. Every line of my family has ended. Most during the Uldra Uprising and then the ascension of the Republic. The few surviving lines were cut during the Xeshlin Invasion. Only I remain; I and my children. Alexia was my last link to my family's past, and now she is gone as well.

"You once asked me how I knew her. How Rogan knew her. Now you understand. Alexia midwifed my mother on the day of my birth. Her hands brought me into this world, just as they brought all my children. She was a part of my life for as long as I walked Arayel, and the teacher of my family for generations. She and Raven together kept me sane when my parents were killed. They aided Rogan in his mission to rescue Aebreanna from Tienel Greysoul. Their influence, their example, made me the man I am today."

Tomas looked to Rogan, who sadly nodded. "We had a funeral," he said softly. "A memorial, after you and I arrived."

"I should've been…" the young man nearly snarled.

"We didn't yet know you, Tomas," Calonar objected, raising a hand. "And our mourning was of a family." He turned back to the family tree. "Alexia meant a great deal to us all," Calonar nearly whispered. "I think you can understand this, if only partially."

Tomas wanted to object, to be angry, but he did understand.

"There is a memorial," the king said then. "A shrine rests in the heart of the gardens. We set a memory of our friend there."

The squire turned to his knight. "I want…"

Rogan nodded. "Mary's waiting. Kyla talked to her this morning before going to Temple. She's waiting in the gardens."

Chapter 30

"Why doesn't anyone talk about her?" Tomas asked. "Why can't I find any sign of her?" The young man had his hands clasped in front of him, his head slightly bowed. His eyes were locked on the memorial, a small sculpture of two birds, one white and the other black, rising together in a spiraling dance.

Mary stepped up to him, putting an arm around his back and resting her head against his shoulder. "Well," she said, "Alexia and Raven were a couple of the most unassuming people you've ever met. They never attended any meetings, never stood for portraits, never attended any formal occasions, and never performed any diplomatic missions. In fact, unless you were closely associated with House Calonar, or worked in the castle, you'd never know who Alexia and Raven were."

"But everyone's been saying they were a large part of the House."

"They were. Alexia handled the education of not only the King's children, but the King himself when he was young. Also, she and Raven were representatives to and for the Sylvai of the Wood," Mary looked around the ancient Sylvai shrine, its design clearly dating to the ancient Sylvai Empire, with the tight-fitting stone floors, the intricately-carved columns, and the glyphs carved into the hollow dome above. "Alexia was one of the last survivors of the Sylvai nobility. The people of the forest... she was the closest thing they had left to royalty. They treated her like a queen. Despite all that influence, though, she never put on airs, never had the slightest hint of anything but friendly humility."

Tomas recalled the behavior of the Speaker he and Rogan had encountered months ago, after their encounter with the Lamashti. He nodded. "So, she was an ambassador?"

Mary shook her head and looked up. The domed shrine was open to the air, with only marble columns breaking the view, and even then, only eight to hold the dome above. The ceiling itself had a great hole in the center, deliberately part of the construction to allow natural sunlight to enter. "Alexia was… it's hard to explain."

Tomas glanced at Mary. "What?" he asked.

The maid looked past the marble columns, out into the gardens. A stream ran around the shrine, making it a small island. High arched bridges of red wood offered access. The shrine was empty, though, save for Tomas and Mary. The visitors to the garden kept a respectful distance in their enjoyment of the gardens.

"She was," Mary struggled for a fitting description. "She was like an over-priestess."

"A what?"

The young woman knelt in front of the memorial. A patch of summer flowers had blossomed in front of it, bathing in the sunlight that shown down, from the center opening of the dome. "The Northern Keep has an Adamic Church," she finally said. "There's a Temple of the Harvest Mother, and one for the Sisterhood of the Lady of Light. The Uldra have their… I don't remember their word for it… their 'place of gathering.'" She breathed in the gentle fragrance of the summer flowers. "Many religions that have hated each other forever. But here, they exist in peace."

"Alexia?" Tomas guess.

Mary stood, looking at the memorial, and nodded. "She maintained the peace. She was the arbiter, the neutral authority. Any time a dispute appeared between two religious groups, they went to Alexia and she led the mediation."

Tomas walked forward and put his arm around Mary's shoulders. They were careful, nearly by instinct, not to let their shadows fall on either the flowers or the memorial. "Did you know her?" the young man asked.

"I met her once," she replied. "She was with the Queen, and they greeted me with a group of new workers at the castle. She stared at me for a few minutes, and then she… suggested, but not really suggested, to the Queen that I should be a maid and what duties I should have."

"I thought Kyla got you your job."

"She did, but the Princess only arranged for my employment in the castle. Alexia's… kind-of suggestion to the Queen was why I became a maid." Mary started and tilted her head in sudden realization. Then, she softly laughed. "You know, she's the reason we met."

Tomas looked at her. "What? How?"

"Alexia's suggestion was that I act as a maid for the quarters you were assigned when you first arrived. If I had any other posting, we may never have met."

"Huh," the young man softly chuckled.

Mary nodded. "It's a mystery why she and Raven went on that last mission. The Princess doesn't know, and she says the Queen doesn't either."

Tears welled in Tomas' eyes. "She knew," he whispered.

"What?"

The young man took a deep breath. "She had a... vision, or something. She knew she was going to die." Mary stared at him. He blinked back the memory, refusing the tears that accompanied it. "She didn't know how or where, exactly, I don't think. She knew her time was coming though. She said that Raven liked to travel." Tomas tilted his head, taking in the dark bird. "I think they wanted one last adventure together before..." He took a shuddering breath.

"It's ok," Mary said, putting a hand to his cheek.

"All those times," Tomas sighed. "All the times I spoke ill of House Calonar. The evils of the Northern Keep. The vile Black Duke. The barbarism of the Northlands. All those times trying to convince her all of you were evil. God, I feel like a fool. All that wasted time."

Mary again placed her head on Tomas' shoulder. Her eyes fell on the golden rose pinned, as always, on Tomas' shirt. "She gave you that rose, right?" When he nodded, the maid continued. "If Alexia passed her rose to you, then she must have thought very highly of you. She wore it everywhere. Any time anyone saw here, she was wearing that pin. The Princess said it was a gift from her son, the only thing she had left of him. And she gave it to you."

Tears fell then. The first drops landed on Mary's upturned face. More followed, and she held her man tighter. His breathing was steady, though. These were not the tears of despair or loss or misery. They were not memories being let go or lost or cast aside. What flowed from Tomas' heart was a renewal of faith and friendship. Alexia had placed him on this path, had guided him in the most subtle, loving of ways. His eyes expressed the purest gratitude for his friend and mentor, recognizing one of her first lessons.

Death is not something to fear or bring sorrow. The White Lady comes for us all at some point. She is the destiny of all things living.

Everything that lives must eventually die, but when it does, all that energy and life does not simply vanish. Nothing that lives can really die. It simply changes.

From somewhere deep, in the back of his mind and soul, though now growing close, just beneath the surface, Tomas could almost hear Alexia's gentle laugh and loving voice say, "Well, finally you listen."

Tomas and Mary stood for a time, in no hurry to move. After a very long time, the maid cleared her throat. "The Princess gave me something I'm supposed to pass to you," she said.

"What is it?"

She reached into her dress and pulled free a piece of parchment, folded and sealed with wax. The seal was in the sigil of House Calonar, but overlaid with a blooming rose. "I'm not sure what it means, but the Princess said Alexia gave it to her before she and Raven left. Princess Kyla was supposed to pass it on…" Mary looked into Tomas' eyes, "to pass it on to the young man who accompanies Prince Rogan home."

Tomas took the parchment, holding it lightly, as though it were made of spiderweb. "Before…?"

Mary nodded. "That's what the Princess said. Alexia gave this to her and told her to keep it until summer, then pass it on to 'the young man who accompanies Prince Rogan home.'" She looked from the parchment to Tomas. "You said she… had a vision?"

Tomas nodded dumbly. With shaking hands, he broke the wax seal and unfolded the parchment. The young man stared at the few words in open-mouthed shock.

"What?" Mary demanded. "What does it say?"

He only handed it over. Mary looked and also stared in shock.

"Summer is upon you, silly boy," it read in flowing, perfect script, "and winter will come all too soon. Take the pretty girl for a swim while you can."

Chapter 31

Midsummer was upon them. The days were bright
and cheerful. Birds sang their joy of the season. Wildelves Wood had
settled into its greenery. Commerce and labor were in full force. No
other signs of attack or threat had manifested since the warehouse
battle, and peace settled upon the Northlands and its capital. Serenity
and industry were the norm of each day.

"Don't fight him!" Roderick yelled, an instant before Tomas was
once again flung from the saddle.

The grassy parade field was expansive. It lay outside the barracks
of the Calonar House Guard, a complex of several buildings, training
fields, barracks, and even a smithy. An entire battalion could muster
on the parade field, with their supporting pack animals and all their
wartime equipment, and there would still be room to spare. The area
was kept immaculate by a near-legion of tenders. The grass was full
and soft, yet firm enough for parade drills. Stones were removed as
quickly as they were identified. This was an ideal location, Roderick
had informed Tomas, to learn the art of battle horsemanship.

Despite these comforts, Urge had an uncanny ability to locate
the hardest, most unyielding spots of stony rigidity. He mercilessly
flung his unwanted rider to those spots again, and again, and again.
After this most recent forced dismount, Tomas sat up, spitting turf
and glaring at the beast. Urge stared right back and neighed his
amusement.

"You're fighting him," Roderick repeated, not for the first or
even the fifth time that day.

"Of course I'm fighting him!" Tomas roared. "That damned,
Underworld-spawned, malicious, murderous, spiteful, jackass of a
horse hates me!"

Urge tossed his head in agreement.

Roderick walked forward and offered the seething squire a hand
up. "Look at it this way," the stablehand said in the same soothing
tone Tomas had heard him use on frightened horses. "If you can
ride Urge here, you can ride any horse in the world."

"You're enjoying this, aren't you?" Tomas asked suspiciously.

The stablehand brushed off some of the clinging grass and mud from Tomas' riding clothes. The smock and trousers were stained, torn, and held more than a little of the squire's blood. "I'm just fulfilling the task my prince laid out for me," Roderick said innocently. "Now, one more time, let's try to mount."

Tomas sighed and approached Urge. As he had been instructed, the squire walked slowly, making sure to remain in the chestnut stallion's sight. He spoke calmly, steadily, but firmly. The beast eyed him wearily, but did nothing, just waited. Tomas walked to the side and took hold of the saddle with one hand, again moving with a steady slowness to avoid causing any possible uncertainty as to his intentions. For the first time, Urge stood still. The squire shifted his weight and raised a leg to the stirrup.

Urge took five steps forward.

"Wait, wait, WAIT!" The squire hit the turf again.

Tomas leapt to his feet and stomped forward, again intending to mount.

Urge took another five steps forward. This continued for some time. The animal would take a few steps forward and stop, looking back to see if the human still wanted to mount. Tomas would move up and try, only to have Urge walk further. They had completed almost a full circuit of the parade field before the squire changed tactics.

Tomas looked around, pretending to be ignoring Urge. He casually strolled near to the horse, without actually moving beside him. Without warning, the squire then leapt to the animal's side, grabbing the saddle and hauling himself up. Urge shot into a run, half dragging the cursing squire. Tomas wrenched himself into the saddle, desperately trying to get his feet into the stirrups and his hands onto the reigns. The chestnut monster beneath the squire bucked and leapt, spun and kicked. He snorted his fury and tossed his head. Tomas held on; he tried moving with Urge, feeling the direction of the next leap, leaning into each buck and kick, and used every muscle in his body to retain his dominant place on the horse's back. This lasted a few seconds.

Roderick walked up to where Tomas was once again laying in the turf, a mouthful of grass and a fresh cut on his forehead. "You're still fighting him."

Laughter not from a horse drew their attention away from Urge. Rogan was approaching, wiping his eyes free of his enjoyment of his squire's misery. The knight walked up and looked down, his grin wide and obvious. "How's the training?"

"He is improving, your Highness," Roderick said.

"This isn't training," Tomas insisted from the ground, "this is bad comedy."

Rogan reached down and pulled Tomas to his feet. "Believe it or not, kid, this is good training."

"Color me skeptical."

The knight put his arm around his squire's shoulders. "Look at it this way. If you can ride that animal, then you can ride anything. Not to mention, mounted combat is all about maneuvering, about twisting and dodging, going from full charge to a hard stop, turning, and charging again." Rogan slammed his fist into his open palm to emphasize the impacts. "You need to learn how to stay mounted, even while the battle is doing everything it can to toss you off. The only real way to do that, is by doing it." He nodded at Urge, who was grazing while keeping a wary eye on Tomas. "That horse is giving you a real sense of how tough it can be to stay mounted in a fight."

Tomas grunted, his understanding sullen and nearly as sore as his body.

"Come on," his knight said then. "I think that's enough bad comedy for one day. Besides," he turned them both and started walking off the field, "you've got something important to see."

"What's happening?" Tomas asked as the two men made their way towards the city center.

"Something of particular interest to you, kid," the knight replied. The Keep was decorated for the midsummer celebration. Bright ribbons danced in the wind, and gaily-festooned wreaths adorned every door. Large bonfires were set up at many intersections, awaiting the dusk when they would be lit. Large areas had been cleared in the center of each neighborhood with large tables for the evening banquets. "I finally got the resources together to take care of a little problem you've had," Rogan was saying.

"What... problem?" Tomas gasped, struggling to keep up. The last week of horsemanship training had been exhausting and brutal on his hardening body. Each night, he returned to his rooms and Mary's tender ministries, but the growing weariness was beginning to take its toll. Although the squire felt he was mastering the basics of riding, of mounting and dismounting, of steering and managing the animal, still the heavy work and his frequent mistakes were bruising.

Rogan slowed as they neared the great plaza at the heart of the Northern Keep. Like the rest of the city, its center was decorated for the week-long celebration. Yet what drew Tomas' eyes was not the riot of colors, the flowers, or the brightly-colored people. An entire company of Calonar House Guard, their blue and grey uniforms and pristine equipment contrasting sharply with the holiday atmosphere, occupied the plaza. With the soldiers were dozens of loaded wagons; each of these carried boxes, sacks, tools, and more equipment for the Guardsmen.

"What's all this?" Tomas asked.

"Dry goods, supplies, clothes, seeds, tools. Everything a group of desperate survivors might need to restart their community. Including protection." Rogan eyed the assembled resources with undisguised pride.

The young man needed a moment to understand. "Pelsemoria?" he demanded. "You're sending this caravan to Pelsemoria?"

"I talked with the King about it," Rogan answered happily. "Our plan of smuggling in supplies through Father Konrad isn't enough. Your people need more direct help."

Tomas walked out, among the waiting wagons. He took a mental inventory of the supplies, realizing how much help they would be to his people, how desperately they needed the aid. Hope swelled in the young man's chest, hope for his people. "Tonight's the end of Midsummer," Rogan said, following behind his squire. "They celebrate today and leave tomorrow."

For a moment, a perfect moment, Tomas felt as though he might have finally achieved his quest of helping the survivors of Pelsemoria. He might, at last, have saved his people. But then his eyes fell to one of the waiting House Guard. His eyes locked on the blue and grey uniform, the Northland poleaxe in the soldier's hand, the crossed-diamond heraldry of House Calonar. "It won't work," he sighed, shaking his head.

"What won't," Rogan asked. "Why?"

Tomas gestured around, to the gathered forces of the Black Duke. "The Praetorians will attack this convoy on sight," he said sourly. "One look at that heraldry," he pointed to the Calonar banner waving in the air, "and it'll be a bloodbath." The squire walked away shaking his head.

Rogan hurried to catch up. "Wait, kid," he insisted. "You've said yourself that your people can't survive the warlords, the Xeshlin, hell, even the weather. They *need* these supplies!"

The squire turned back. "I know!" he barked in frustration. "I lived it, Rogan; I know! They're dying while I'm up here playing squire! You think I don't know!?! You think I don't lie awake thinking about it? Wondering if my mother has been taken on the latest Xeshlin raid? If the people will starve with the next winter?" He shook his head. "I know."

The Prince of House Calonar turned back, staring hard at the assembled caravan. "There has to be a way," he demanded. His voice betrayed an urgency, a near-desperation.

Tomas looked at his knight, realization dawning. "You're trying to atone," the squire said evenly. "This is about the Madness, about what you and Kyla did."

Rogan could not meet his gaze, instead turning and staring at the fluttering Calonar banner. "We..." he tried to say. "I..."

This time, Tomas stepped forward and placed a comforting hand on his knight's shoulder. "You can't make it up in one gesture," he said. "You're risking hundreds of men, all these supplies, on something that can't work. Even if the soldiers got through to our settlement, and that would take killing all the Praetorians. Even if they made it, the people would never accept anything offered by the servants of the Black Duke. Don't you remember how *I* behaved when we first met?"

"Yeah," Rogan said grimly. "But..." He paused, his head cocked with an idea. "What about the Church?"

"The Church?"

"Velaross. One of the orders of Holy Knights. What if *they* delivered the supplies and offered protection?"

"But how?"

The prince shrugged. "Easy. Instead of taking ship in Clayton, the convoy goes to Ironheartshaven. They pass the supplies to the Knights of Justice, who deliver..."

"No," Tomas objected. "We heard the Knights of Justice had sworn faith to House Calonar."

"Alright, what about the Knights of Mercy? The convoy sails to Reme with a letter from the King, explaining the situation and asking them to act as intermediaries. Will that work?"

Tomas considered. "They are neutral," he conceded. "They never take sides in any war."

"And the tradition of protecting pilgrims, hospitals, churches..."

The squire nodded, sighing. "Maybe. It might..." He thought, letting his eyes play over the caravan and his mind through the possibilities. "It just might work." he looked to his knight. "Worth a try, at least."

"Exactly!" Rogan turned and gestured to the Guard commander, giving orders they stage at the city gates. The knight then turned and slapped his squire on the back. "Let's go get the King to write a letter."

Learning King Cylan was resting in his quarters, Rogan led Tomas up to the royal apartments. Their attempts at disturbing the King were cut short, though, by the Queen's maid. "Absolutely not, you Highness," the girl, little more than a child, said with unbreakable iron in her voice. "His Majesty is resting, and the Queen has ordered no disturbances under any circumstances."

"But..." the prince tried to object.

"No buts!" the maid insisted stamping one imperious foot.

Rogan growled and loomed over the girl, but she was a mountain of purpose. He finally backed away, grumbling, "What makes the women of this House so damned stubborn!"

"It's all about love, Rogan," the Queen said suddenly, her voice of summer clouds and hearth fire drifting up from behind them.

Queen Nora, High Priestess of the Harvest Mother and Lady of House Calonar, had once been described as one of the great beauties of Arayel. Having lived in what was once the capital of the Republic, Tomas had seen what magic could do, emphasizing natural beauty beyond what nature intended. The squire had once heard that this trend of using magic began after Calonar, at the time a baron, visited the capital with his wife. The other noblewomen, after seeing the natural beauty Nora had been given, very nearly turned green with envy. Until this very day, Tomas never really thought that story was true; it was probably just the propaganda of House Calonar at work.

Looking upon the Queen, Tomas realized the tales of her grace were, in fact, understated. There could be no doubt as to Kyla's parentage, for as Tomas could not help but stare at the queen, he was shocked at the uncanny resemblance between the two. The same luminous beauty; the same golden hair, the same lack of height and perfect build; every physical aspect of mother and daughter seemed to match exactly. After a moment, though, Tomas began to notice subtle yet profound differences.

The eyes were what Tomas noticed first; while Kyla had inherited her father's Halvan pearlescence that sparkled with loving, mischievous light, Nora's Human eyes held an inner power that seemed to calm and soothe anyone who fell under her gaze. While the princess' hair was bright golden, eternally flowing as if the sun itself graced her head, her mother's braided locks, despite extensive graying, seemed like golden wheat. The same feminine curves that were the temptation of ages on the princess, somehow on the queen seemed to convey a woman's maturity and matronly comfort. Most of all, though, was the sense of her. From Kyla, one is immediately attracted to the simple joy and exuberant delight the princess generates; from the queen, it felt as though one is in the comfort of a mother seemingly lost a lifetime ago.

Queen Nora stood with her head slightly tilted and a smile of warm indulgence on her lips. She had entered without sound, and obviously overheard the confrontation between her maid and her son-in-law. She wore an ankle-length dress of purest blue, as though the summer sky had wrapped itself around her. The neckline was typical in the Northlands, low but not scandalously so. The silver embroidery swirled around the waist in a series of overlapping diamonds. Long sleeves flowed down from her hands, clasped in front of her waist. The Queen of the Northlands wore no jewels or other ornamentation, only a single brooch of polished silver that gathered her dress at the shoulder, fashioned into her House's heraldry.

"Excuse me?" the knight said respectively, bowing slightly.

"I said it's all about love," the Queen said very gently, taking him into a hug that reminded Tomas of how his own mother used to hold him as a child. "Kyla and I and all women of our House have discovered within ourselves the ability to love. We care about you boys more than you care about yourselves, so we give you the care you refuse to give yourselves." She looked up at him with a knowing gaze. "Much the same as how you care for the people of my husband's kingdom," she said pointedly. "As much as you like to profess being annoyed with your position as our heir, you still have a deep love for the people of this land."

Rogan huffed a bit at that, trying to find the words to object.

Nora held up her hand. "Don't try your objections with me, young man. I know, just as Kyla knew from the moment she met you, that you are a man of deep compassion. No matter how hard you try to hide it, you will always be a source of inspiration to the people because they all know that you will never fail to put yourself at risk for them, out of love."

Tomas chuckled, unable to resist his mirth at the knight's discomfort.

"Well now," the Queen said, turning her gaze on Tomas, "I don't think I have had the pleasure of formally meeting you as yet, Tomas." Nora turned her full attention on the young squire, her soft eyes at once comforting him and at the same time making him think of several excuses for everything he had done wrong over the last few months. Something in her gaze saw past the young man, past his flesh and his thoughts. This gaze, the squire recalled, he also saw in Alexia and the Speaker at the edge of Wildelves Wood. Nora Calonar seemed to look into Tomas, into and through his very soul.

Finally, after what seemed an eternity of waiting, the Queen smiled softly, but with the barest hint of sadness. "I can see what Mary finds so appealing about you. You will make a fine apprentice to Rogan, Tomas. Welcome."

Tomas had not realized that he was so eager for the queen's approval until she had finally given it; Nora's gentle blessing filled him with a deep feeling of warmth and welcome. When the queen enfolded him in the same gentle embrace in which she held Rogan, Tomas' soul was filled with peace.

Rogan cleared his throat, snapping Tomas from his near-revelry. "We actually need to talk to him," the knight said in a deeply humble and apologetic tone.

"He is resting," the queen replied, "and will continue to do so. You may give me your request and I will discuss it with him."

"But…" A single look from the Lady of House Calonar, not one so stern and unyielding as the maid, but rather as undeniable as the seasons, silenced any possible objections. Rogan quickly outlined the plan he and Tomas had hastily created.

The queen considered. "Hmm," she said. Tomas realized he was almost holding his breath, waiting for her approval. "I agree with young Tomas," she said then, filling the squire's heart with pride. "His people will reject any aid directly from us. Your notion of the Knights of Mercy is a good one, but their order is not large enough to dedicate a protective force. Your initial idea of the Knights of Justice was partially correct as well. We will have the Knights of Mercy make the first open contact, with Father Konrad's assistance. They will offer the initial aid and then, gradually, be relieved by the Knights of Justice."

She stepped forward, moving towards the bedrooms. Pausing at the door, she glanced back. "You'll have your letter before sundown," she said. "Is there anything else?"

"No, ma'am," the two warriors said in unison.

Chapter 32

Althaea had always loved Wildelves Wood in summer. The entire forest was in full bloom; it nearly vibrated with the hope and joy of sensation. The wind danced through the branches. Birds sang their joy. Deer and bears and boars and wolves all roamed in contented freedom. The streams drifted wherever they wished, pooling and running however gave them the most joy. The former priestess, former spy, had heard a great many legends from the Sylvai about their Eternal Forest, the paradise consumed by the Disaster at Nassinalia. Surely, Wildelves Wood had to be as close to that paradise as could still exist.

This was a bitter contrast against the pit in which Althaea's mind had been imprisoned. Her body was little more than a plaything, a puppet for the Death Mage. He had spent weeks using her; Althaea's entire existence had become nothing but an unending damnation in which she felt every touch of trembling fingers, every taste from his wretched tongue, every hair on his emaciated body as it pressed into hers. This was part of Anninihus' enjoyment: she was forced to act out his sick fantasies, forced to express pleasure and lust, all while endlessly screaming from that pit in which her mind was jailed. That should have been the worst of her damnation before death.

Now, she realized the violation of her body and her soul were not the worst acts the Death Mage would inflict upon her. She sat in the beautiful Wood. He had placed her here, on a fallen log. He had forced her to dress, his leering eyes taking in the sight of her slow, lithe movements, as she wrapped herself in the black velvet and leather that had been a gift from Rashid when he had recruited her. Althaea wanted to sob, to pitifully object, when the Death Mage had even pinned the silver sigil of House Calonar on her breast, his touch lingering. "There now," he had said hungrily. "The perfect distraction."

Althaea sat on the fallen log with her legs crossed, a look of patience on her face. The road diverged here, in the place selected by Xaemus for the ambush. One branch of the road led north, through Snowholm and far into the eternal cold of Ubelheim, on the coast of the Ice Crystal Sea. This was where House Calonar imprisoned the worst threats to the Northlands. The other branch of this peaceful forest road led to Man's End and the northern villages. A trace of that long-unused road was even rumored to reach as far as the ruins of Heath Dannah. Here, Althaea would damn herself for yet another time since her enslavement to the Death Mage.

The convoy arrived precisely when Xaemus predicted. Twenty House Guard made their way through the Wood. Their polished breastplates had been left behind, replaced with the dull chainmail the warriors of House Calonar used in the field. Their blue surcoats were dark, nearly black, and the grey of their undershirts and trousers was mottled, like moving shadows. Each man had a shortsword riding on a thick leather belt, and a heavy spagenhelm protecting his head, its long nose guard partially obscuring the face. Even the heraldry of their House on their surcoats was subdued, the normally vibrant white and silver instead dull variations on grey. The men were professionals, their eyes missed nothing, and their reaction to Althaea's presence triggered an immediate response.

Five of the Guardsmen rode forward, the sergeant in command drawing his sword while his four men leveled their poleaxes. The remaining fifteen arranged themselves without orders needed, forming a perimeter around the two cage-wagons. Inside the first, the three prisoners turned ahead to watch the new event, clearly relieved at even a momentary reprieve from their journey to the dreaded prison in Ubelheim. The lone prisoner in the second cage, though, remained calmly seated, as though he was unsurprised by anything.

The Calonar Guardsmen drew only to within twenty feet of Althaea, keeping a distance and eyeing her wearily. The spy desperately tried screaming from the prison of her mind, tried gesturing or leaping or anything to give warning to the men. Her body remained passive, smiling with hands clasped over her crossed knees. "Hello, boys," her mouth was commanded to say.

Althaea saw what the Guardsmen did not. At the very rear of the small convoy, two of the loyal, professional men were cut down. One of the shadows had detached from a nearby tree and slid through the air. In the space between two heartbeats, two throats were opened and the shadow had returned to its fellows. None of the others saw or heard anything, not even the strangled final gasps from the two murdered warriors, as their throats had been cut so deep that the only sounds blended into the summer breeze.

"Move aside, citizen," the Guard sergeant said calmly, but firmly, his sword at the ready.

Althaea's mouth was ordered into a wider, more welcoming smile. "It's alright, boys," her mouth was commanded to say. "Rashid sent me to join with you. I need to travel to Ubelheim." The lie was simple and direct, drawn from Althaea's mind as the most likely to succeed.

Two more Guardsmen in the rear of their convoy died soundlessly as the sergeant shook his head. "We have no orders," he replied. "You'll have to return to the Keep and arrange another escort."

Althea's body was made to stand, stretching to accentuate those traits the Death Mage found most pleasurable. "Now, why should I travel all the way home, just to turn around and come back." Her head was forced to lower, looking at the soldiers with upturned eyes through long lashes that nearly curled in invitation. "Especially when such strong men are already here to help me." This, at last, had been something Althaea could do. Anninihus' perverted mind only saw women as objects of his lust. He assumed all men believed as he did, that women were only ever whores or suppressed whores. Althea knew better. By leaning into the Death Mage's own perversion, she could alert these professional warriors of House Calonar.

The sergeant did not disappoint her. "To arms!" he barked.

His Guardsmen snapped to action, and shouts of alarm echoed from the rear, where the four dead men were finally discovered. The shadow had again detached from the surrounding trees and was nearly upon another two men when the sergeant had been alerted. Their upraised poleaxes deflected part of the attacks aiming for their throats; their chainmail absorbed what little remained of the attack's damage. From the left and right side of the road, men appeared with shortbows already knocked.

Arrows flew, filling the air. The majority of these missed, were intercepted by raised weapons, or caught in the Guardsmen's' armor. Only two Calonar soldiers fell, and only one of these died. The mercenaries one either side drew a riotous assortment of blades and charged.

The mercenaries' threat had lain mostly in surprise. With this spent, they crashed against the Calonar Guardsmen like a feeble wave splitting upon an unyielding beach of stone. One man with the coloring of a Gwyndd swung his straight sword in two hands, but this was parried by a Guardsman's poleaxe. Another mercenary, likely from Eastern Lanasia and swinging a curved blade more suited to mounted combat, was stabbed through before he could reach an arm's length of his intended target. The mercenaries fought as individuals, each one selecting a Guardsman and attacking. The warriors of House Calonar, though, fought as a team. When one blocked, another parried. When one deflected, another countered. When one stabbed, another sliced. The screams of mercenary dead and dying filled the air. Limbs were severed, weapons broken, and organs impaled. The ten remaining House Guardsmen, including the wounded man who fought on with his comrades, slaughtered the nearly three dozen attackers, their numbers counting for almost nothing.

Althaea had desperately hoped the Death Mage was finished forcing her betrayal. But this hope was soon dashed, as all her hopes had been. Her body was commanded forward. It slid under the sergeant's horse, slicing the saddle strap and sending the Guard leader cursing to the ground. She was then made to send her two daggers flying, each finding their targets in one eye each of two different men. When a poleaxe was thrust at her, Althaea's body twisted, leveraging the attack to pull the Guardsman from his saddle. With the newly-acquired weapon, her mind once again found purchase against the Death Mage's control. She held the poleaxe and tried to use it to attack another mounted warrior. The Guardsman easily deflected the untrained strike and spun his own poleaxe, bringing the axehead down towards Althaea's unprotected neck, a strike she desperately yearned for.

"I think not," a hissing voice said calmly through her lips. The poleaxe froze in midair, caught in Anninihus' magic. A mist of toxic darkness leaked from Althaea's fingers, grasping up at the weapon and tracing along it. The Guardsman's eyes widened and he tried to release his poleaxe, but the tendrils of vile magic had already reached his hands and locked the muscles. It pierced into his flesh, despite the heavy gloves, and bored through his body. The doomed man tried to scream, but could only offer a gargling whimper as his organs were devoured.

The sergeant had regained his feet and his sword, and was roaring his fury, swinging for Althaea's head. No one heard her desperate prayer for the success of that attack, though, and the Death Mage nearly giggled his glee at her despair. The once-spy, once-priestess turned her gaze to the attacking sergeant, letting the previous target finish dying on his own. Her arms were made to lash out, along with more vile Death magic. Insidious darkness, like the tentacles of some Underworld monster, flew from Althaea's fingers, wrapping themselves around the necks of all the men nearest her. The warriors were lifted off the ground, their limbs twisting and their desperate, horrified screams reduced to pathetic whimpers.

No! Please no! she tried to scream. Her mind begged Anninihus, pleaded. She offered anything, everything, if only he would relent just this once. Instead, the Death Mage giggled again. The men were turned in mid-air, to face their compatriots. By now, the mercenaries were all cut down. They looked on at the wretched display of death magic. The four upraised men were further twisted, and the snapping of bones and the tearing of flesh replaced any screams or whimpers. Bloody bags of meat that had once been the warriors of House Calonar were dropped to the ground. They twitched before lying still.

Althaea was made to step towards the men, a smile of cruel pleasure, of nearly-lustful anticipation of the torments to come lighting on her beautiful face. The once-priestess had never known such rancid glee, such infernal delight in suffering. She had not realized, even as he had violated her in the most abhorrent ways, the depths of Anninihus' cruelty. Now, she knew.

"Stand firm!" one of the Guardsmen snapped, raising his poleaxe. His fellows hooahed their agreement and formed a spear line against Althaea's body, weapons firm and unyielding.

In the depths of her mind, Althaea felt a brief rush of joy, of hope, of the same inspired confidence the people of the Northlands so often felt when witnessing the bravery and dedication of the warriors of House Calonar. This, of course, was just more delightful torment from her owner. Althaea's face was made to smile again. Her hand was made to reach out, and gestured as though calling children from their sleep.

The mercenaries and the murdered Guardsmen stood. Then, at a soundless command from the Death Mage, they attacked.

Althaea's eyes watched as the last of the Guardsmen stood back up, having been beaten to death by the bodies of his comrades. Now, all the men, mercenary and soldier alike, stood silently and beyond living concern. She had given up on her silent screaming. She just huddled without form, forced to observe the carnage she had been forced to help wrought.

Xaemus was surveying the carnage. Once the Guardsmen had been alerted, the Xeshlin had ceased his attacks. Althaea had lost track of him until after the slaughter was complete. Now, the cloaked and deeply-hooded thing seemed to be counting. His eyes of burning blood passed over mercenary and Guardsman with equal disinterest. The Xeshlin moved as though made of water. He did not walk so much as flow, his every movement as graceful and dispassionate as a changing tide, with all the potential for destruction.

The monster of Davenor paused then. His hood turned this way and that, his eyes of burning blood seeming to search and not find. The shrouded Xeshlin moved to the second wagon and a curse of hissing silence drifted to Althaea's ears. Her body was forced to move, to join the Xeshlin. She saw what had drawn Xaemus' ire. The cage was open. The body of a Calonar Guardsman lay just outside, its neck twisted to an impossible angle, and its keys resting in the cage's lock. The soldier's weapons were also missing.

The Xeshlin spun his double-bladed sword over his shoulder an instant before the strike Vagris had launched would have separated Xaemus's head from his shoulders. The hunter spun and threw a quick jab with the heel of his left hand, missing his target's chin by only a breath and spinning his weapon up into a close guard.

Vagris spun away from the Xeshlin and brought the Northland shortsword and quillon dagger he had clearly taken off his guard into his own defensive posture, facing the hunter with a blank expression. The two killers regarded each other with deadly preparedness. They each read the other's stance and slight movements, looking for any opening but finding none.

Vagris darted forward and thrust the rounded tip of his sword toward Xaemus's face in an obvious feint. The Xeshlin swung one end of his double-bladed weapon up, deflecting the strike and, stepping forward, launched the other tip toward the warlord's leg only to have that end of his weapon caught in the s-shaped quillon of Vagris' dagger. The warlord rolled his sword arm and brought the weapon over Xaemus's head and down toward his shoulder and neck, but the bounty hunter blocked the strike only a hair's breadth from landing. Xaemus pulled his weapon free and spun away from Vagris, obviously trying to gain some advantage of range while bringing his weapon to a low ready position.

The warlord was too experienced a fighter to allow this, however, and closed quickly with the hunter. Once again using his dagger to trap the edge of Xaemus's weapon pointed toward him, Vagris twisted the blade away from his body and swung his shortsword down once again toward the Xeshlin's torso. Xaemus intercepted the strike with the other end of his weapon and spun away again, wrenching his sword free.

Rather than retreating again, Xaemus spun all the way around, struck his opponent's sword with one end of his weapon, and then brought the other down in a blur of hostility, striking the large fuller of Vagris' blade, and forcing the sword from Vagris' hand. A second quick strike toward the warlord's face was intercepted by the warlord's dagger.

"Enough!" the word thundered from Althaea's mouth. Anninihus unleashed a quick burst of his vile death magic, separating the two warriors. His concentration diverted, the dead that had been standing lifelessly fell to the ground.

"I suppose I should be flattered that I've gained enough renown in the world that I warrant a visit from the monster of Davenor," Vagris said, breathing heavy but still in a defensive posture.

"I am not here to kill you," Xaemus replied in his hoarse voice, thick with the accent of his race.

"Interesting way of starting a conversation," the warlord replied.

"You attacked," the Xeshlin pointed out. "I defended."

"Quit the bickering!" Anninihus ordered through Althaea's mouth. "Time is short and there is work to be done." Her head was made to scan the area. "The Sylvai will have sensed my power. They will investigate. I think we should be gone before their arrival."

Vagris considered that a moment, never letting his guard down. He glanced at the bodies, then back at Althaea. "Death magic," he grunted. "Are you my contact?" He then narrowed his eyes. "Where are you, anyway?"

"I am as close as I need to be," Anninihus replied haughtily.

Vagris lowered his guard, just slightly. "If you're not here to kill me," he said, "then what's your purpose?"

Mirroring the warlord, Xaemus answered. "I am charged with freeing you and tasking your service for our employer."

"Well, as for the first, I've managed to free myself, thank you very much. Had you not come along and killed all the soldiers, I would have been able to slip away, quietly. They wouldn't have noticed I was gone until morning."

"My plan was for a silent assault while most slept," this the Xeshlin said with a glance towards Althaea. Although Xaemus wore as always a cloth of midnight black across most of his face, making his expression unreadable, his tone made his displeasure unmistakable.

"I decided to move sooner," Anninihus said imperiously. "Remember who our master left in command."

Vagris narrowed his eyes at the unlikely pair. "I have friends nearby," he said in an even tone. "I'll rejoin them and we can meet later."

"The Bellonari have been contacted," Xaemus replied. "Their contingent is already in our camp, outside the forest."

The warlord said nothing, his eyes narrowing.

Xaemus slowly shifted his double-bladed weapon to one hand and reached into his vest. Producing a small box, the Xeshlin tossed it to the ground at Vagris' feet and backed several paces away. The warlord carefully crouched to pick up the box, maintaining his fixed gaze on the threat.

Flipping the box lid open, and with one eye on Xaemus, Vagris retrieved a piece of folded parchment. He broke the wax seal and read.

Vagris shook his head in disgust. "The fool actually put this in writing, under his name and with his seal."

"As you said," Xaemus agreed, "Theodorico Balshazzar's greatest weakness has always been his arrogance. Nevertheless, the Emir of Tordenia offers a sum far in excess to what the Bellonari typically demand. Are his instructions clear?"

Vagris lowered his blade and narrowed his eyes at the deeply-cowled Xeshlin. "So, who are you really working for, Xaemus?" he asked. "You're supposed to be searching for your Dark Empress." His eyes drifted from the signed, sealed parchment and back to

Xaemus and Althaea. "Now you serve the Emir of Tordenia, along with a Death Mage." The warlord shook his head.

"My holy quest continues," the Xeshlin replied. "Another has offered the revelation I have spent centuries seeking. Activate the crystal within that box, and more will be revealed."

The warlord retrieved a black stone from the box, tiny and with a flattened side. He placed it in the palm of his hand and activated the magical device. The stone grew warm, and a soft red mist rose from it, coalescing in a deeply hooded head whose face was lost in shadow. Vagris stared at the figure saying nothing. The figure raised its head slightly, letting the red light shine into his face.

"*YOU!*" Vagris' roar was enough to disturb the branches overhead. Without realizing, the warlord moved his hand as though to draw his blade. "Why would the Brotherhood agree to serve you?" the warlord demanded.

"I know of the Bellonari's ultimate goals, and I don't care," the figure replied. "Your designs and mine currently overlap, so I offer my assistance in return for yours. This is much the same offer I made to secure Xaemus' temporary service. The other Bellonar Generals were willing to volunteer you for service readily enough."

"In return for what?" the warlord demanded. "What was the price of my sacrifice?"

"Don't be so melodramatic, Vagris. You were promoted to be one of the Twelve Generals ahead of many others; did you not think that there would be a price for that elevation?"

"Why should I trust you?" Vagris muttered.

"Because you've been ordered to. You could defy the other Generals and see how far that gets you." The amusement rolling out of the stone in Vagris' hand only served to increase his obvious fury.

"I will obey the Brotherhood," he said stiffly. "What is my mission?"

"Balshazzar's letter spelled it out," the figure replied. "I have only two additions. First, when you lay siege to the Northern Keep next year, whether you take the city or not is immaterial. I want you to capture the daughters of Calonar alive and relatively unharmed."

"Why?"

"For my own reasons," the villain snapped. "Once you have delivered the girls to me, your service will be complete."

"Why wait?" Vagris asked.

"There are other things I'm working on Vagris," the figure replied. "My disciple is preparing his own attack on House Calonar." Althaea felt the swell of pride and anticipation within Anninihus. "I will tell you when the time is right for your attack," the shrouded figure continued, "and that time is not yet here. Calonar and Eigenhard are moving too quickly, I need them slowed a bit. This is my disciple's immediate purpose. You will take advantage of the delay he creates to prepare your siege on the entire city."

"This had better not be a set up," the warlord muttered darkly.

"My dear General," the figure said with equanimity, "even if it is a setup, there's nothing you could do about it."

With that, the stone in Vagris' hand went cold, and the red mist dissipated. The Bellonar looked at Xaemus and Althaea. "Alright," the warlord said, straightening his back. "Let's see about this army of yours."

Chapter 33

During the exhaustive training that occupied so much of Tomas' days, he and Mary eventually settled into a routine that maximized what time they could find to spend together. Roland had wisely reassigned the maid to duties in another part of the castle, despite the young woman's protests; the old butler felt it would be inappropriate for her to be in service to a man with whom she was romantically involved. Tomas and Mary would both continue their separate duties and try their best to at least have lunch together eating in some quiet corner of the castle. Every evening, she would bring Tomas his dinner, relieving the squire's new maid for the night. They would sit together, most often talking of their experiences, sharing histories, and just enjoying one another's company.

Despite Mary's insistence that her own life was uninteresting, Tomas still wanted to learn everything about her, including and perhaps especially the uninteresting parts. "Well," Mary said, one peaceful afternoon, "like I said, there really isn't anything special. My father was a soldier in the Legions. His family had a farm outside Snowholm and a long tradition of military service." The two had managed to break free of their duties that day, fleeing their respective masters to the safety of the city's gardens where they lounged together, sharing a pleasant meal on a small hilltop. "He was eventually recruited into the Calonar House Guard."

"What about your mother?" the squire asked, laying back on the large blanket he had brought.

"She was originally from the Gwyndd Islands." Mary set the remainder of their lunch into the large basket she had carried and lay down beside Tomas. "Her village sold her to a traveling merchant when she was very young. She was taken to the City of All Sins. When she was fourteen, some men who worked for House Calonar freed her and several other slaves and brought them back here to the Keep. My mother was trained as a dressmaker and given work in the city."

"I heard that some of the escaped slaves were used as miners in Ulheim." Tomas said, putting one arm around her slight shoulders. Mary had worn another of the traditional Northlands dresses as she customarily did, but with summer in full force, like most of the women of the city, she had changed to the lighter summer dresses of the north. These left much the arm bare and were made of lighter linen, instead of the heavier wool. Tomas enjoyed these lighter dresses his lady wore, as he reveled in tracing his fingers along the bared skin of her arms.

Mary sat up and stared at him in shock. "Of course not!" she insisted. "Who would suggest something so horrible?"

"It's just something I overheard," the squire replied guiltily, suddenly remembering that it was Anninihus in disguise who had told him this. "You have to admit there are an awful lot of immigrants, and the city doesn't seem to have a population problem."

"That's because a lot of the people don't stay in the city." She leaned over and sipped from her wine glass.

"Where do they go?"

Mary shrugged. "Wherever they want. There are many small towns and dozens of villages throughout King Cylan's lands. My mother only stayed in the Keep for a year or two before she met my father. He was serving here in the city, and she was apprenticed to a dressmaker. They fell in love and moved back to Snowholm. Many people in the Northlands prefer village life to living in the city."

"I guess that makes sense," Tomas admitted.

"I don't know why you listen to these ridiculous rumors," she sniffed, finishing her glass of wine. "The King would never allow forced labor in Ulheim. He even stations soldiers in large forts in the foothills to safeguard anyone who does try to work near the mountains."

"But how does he pay for all that?" the squire asked. "Where does the vast wealth of House Calonar come from?"

"Do you remember when I gave you that first tour of the city? When you noticed there were merchants from all over the world there?"

"Yes."

"This city has trade rights with nearly every other city and kingdom in Lanasia, and even some in Tramaya. Do you remember that fair in the spring, when hundreds of merchants from all over the world come to the Keep?"

"But why come all the way here? Why not hold such a fair somewhere like Velaross or Alvaro?"

Mary smiled. "Because the Uldra clans that live in Ulheim trade with House Calonar for whatever they need. *Only* House Calonar. The Uldra produce gems, gold and silver, all their strange inventions, and other goods, but they only trust the King, and won't do business with anyone else. The merchants are all selling their wares to the Uldra and to each other, but House Calonar acts as an intermediary between the groups to keep the peace. The King takes a very small tax from each merchant which, considering just how many of them there are, produces a great deal of wealth.

"Once word spread through Lanasia that House Calonar and the Uldra were holding the fair, other merchant princes started attending, and it became the single largest gathering of trade in the world."

Tomas laughed a bit ruefully. "How disappointing," he said.

"What do you mean?" his lady asked, setting aside her glass and leaning towards him on one elbow.

"For years, people have spoken of the hordes of treasure hidden somewhere in the Northern Keep, and it turns out the merchant lords of House Calonar are just good businessmen."

"The Merchant Guild even relocated here," Mary pointed out. "After the Republic collapsed, they needed somewhere stable. That brought even more commerce to the city and the Northlands."

"You knew each other since you were children," the young woman marveled, "and you never once got curious? You and Cecilia never once...?" The two had retired to the balcony after their supper, lying together and watching the gentle path of the moon across a cloudy sky, feeling that contentedness that only comes from full bellies and good company. Most often, Tomas and Mary would spend much of their time outside, either in the gardens or on a balcony, to escape the stifling heat the castle retained, even into the night. They would spread out on a divan and watch the stars, continuing their exploration of one another's lives.

"After the night of the Madness," he said grimly, "we all had more than our fill of debauchery. We were best friends as kids, but when we huddled in a corner that night, watching our parents..."

An odd feeling came over Mary while she listened to her young man talk about his childhood friend. It was clear he held no great love for her. Still, there was something in his voice that told the young woman that this Cecilia would always hold a place in his heart, a place that perhaps she could never touch, nor ever should.

"So, do you think that, if you hadn't left, you would have married her?" she asked. Lying together on the uncovered divan, she did not look into his eyes, for they were upturned to the sky. Instead, the maid turned her own gaze lower, to his chest. Not for the first time, Mary marveled at how much stronger her young man was growing through his squire's training. Tomas was putting on a layer of muscle that, though still subtle, seemed to often draw Mary's gaze whenever her thoughts drifted.

Tomas shrugged. "I guess I'll never know."

"But you said you were close," Mary insisted, drawing a light finger across his undershirt, absently pulling at the strings and exposing the flesh beneath. "If you'd never left Pelsemoria, don't you think you would have ended up together?"

Without thought, more a response to Mary's explorations, the squire let an arm drop around her shoulders, gently drawing her even closer. "I thought about that just after I left. While I was walking north, I realized that, even after my quest was finished and I went home, I would probably end up marrying Cecilia. That's usually how it works, right? Two families are close and have children of similar ages. An agreement is made, and it's understood that, as soon as they're old enough, they'll get married."

"Is that how it works in the south?" Mary asked.

"Usually," he replied. "Cecilia and I were raised together. We were friends from the start, but love was never an issue. If the Emperor hadn't died, then we would have probably married by now."

The young woman looked up at Tomas. "You said that with... resignation," she noted in surprise. "Like it was something you wouldn't have wanted."

Tomas glanced down at Mary, letting himself once again fall into her eyes. "I'm sure Cecilia would have made a fine wife. She was loyal and kind and honest."

"But...?"

Tomas looked back to the stars. "But, there was no fire."

Mary blinked. "Fire?"

"All the stories and plays and poems, they all talk about the flames of love. The passion that can burn between two people. With Cecilia, I cared for her, more than I cared for most. But that was it. Even that one night we were together, there was some passion, but it didn't feel like I thought it should."

"What should it have felt like?"

"That's just it. I have no idea. I want to know, but I do know that what Cecilia and I shared wasn't it. She just wasn't my... I don't know."

Mary looked back at him and tilted her head to one side. "What do you think was missing?"

Tomas closed his eyes, trying to summon a picture. "Strength," he nearly whispered. "My woman would have to be strong; but at the same time, she would have to have a softness, a gentleness. There should be an energy to her, though, a will. Cecilia was always so deferential, so submissive. My ideal woman would have her own ideas." His eyes opened then, and for the first time, in plain sight and knowing she saw him do it, Tomas' eyes traveled Mary's body. "She would have to be beautiful, of course. But her beauty would come just as much from the inside as the outside. She would have to be powerful, but not really need that power."

"Doesn't sound like anyone I know," Mary sighed.

Tomas raised his eyes and looked into hers, turning his face so that only a breath separated them. "I don't know," he said very quietly. "I think I may have found her."

The maid blushed and looked down. "If she's so ideal," she whispered, "then why haven't you taken her for your own?"

The squire was quiet. He studied her face, taking in all the curves and lines, all the subtle shifts of color. The answer spoke in his mind, but he found it hard to voice. Mary looked up and saw the truth in his eyes. "It's because of Cecilia, isn't it?"

He nodded.

"You slept with her the night before you left. She gave herself to you and you left."

"I should have had a problem with that," he remarked. "She felt something when we were together, I think. But I just picked up my father's sword and walked away, and I had no problem doing it."

"Is that why you haven't taken this ideal woman of yours?"

Tomas nodded again. "I'm afraid that if I do, I'll be able to leave again. Not that I will, just that I'll be able to."

"You're afraid there won't be the fire you wanted? The passion?"

Tomas closed his eyes and leaned back. "It scares me a lot more than you'd guess."

Mary reached up and raised and, with a light touch, drew his eyes back to hers. "If this woman of yours is as ideal as you think, then she'll wait."

They lay for a long while, enjoying treats from the kitchen, the night sky, the quiet of the evening, and the warmth their bodies shared. Both Tomas and Mary found themselves more than a little embarrassed by their conversation, so they made an unspoken agreement to change the subject while they lounged together under that opening sky, staring into the flames dancing before them, close but just out of reach. With little else of any significance to talk about, they quickly turned to the paradox of Tomas' current situation. "How could it be," he asked, "that I had left Pelsemoria on a quest to uncover some way the Black Duke might be defeated, and now somehow be in service to him?"

"Fate can put us in places we never thought we'd be," Mary told him. As engrossed as they were in each other's company, they barely even noticed the occasional explosion from the Guild tower.

"I just can't figure it out," Tomas insisted, sliding his arms along hers, enfolding Mary and gently pressing her against his chest. "I leave home with a specific goal, and now I'm pretty much doing the exact opposite thing I planned on."

Mary held her ear to his chest, listening to the harmony of his heart. "Didn't you originally leave home to find Cyras Darkholm?"

"Yes," he admitted as took in the scent of her hair.

"Then you did what you planned to do," she told him, entwining her legs with his. "You found the Trickster Mage."

"And now I'm the squire of the man who killed my father."

The maid started looked up into Tomas distant eyes. "You don't still think the Prince did that, do you?"

He sighed. "He admitted it. I saw... I don't know anymore. I was there. I saw my father lying on the ground, and I saw Rogan standing over him with blood on his sword."

"But you didn't actually see the Prince put his blade into your father's chest?"

The squire looked away. "I just don't know anymore."

"Have you asked?"

"What do you mean?"

She looked into Tomas' eyes. "You've spent all these years listening to everyone who wasn't there. You've believed the Prince was a murderer and terrorist. You've believed King Cylan was a tyrant who wanted to conquer all of Lanasia. Well, you asked the King and learned the truth. Why don't you ask the Prince?"

Tomas thought for a while, then stood, walking to the stone railing of the balcony. The young man looked out on the city he once considered the source of all evil in Arayel, and was now sworn to protect. Mary stood up from the divan, walked up behind him, and wrapped her arms around the young man. The maid put her head against Tomas' back. "You're afraid, aren't you?" she asked quietly. "You're afraid of the truth."

"My father was the bravest man I've ever known," the young man insisted. "He was one of the most decorated soldiers in the Legions. He died defending the Emperor."

"And you're afraid you'll learn he died as something else?"

Tomas shut his eyes.

"There's only one way to find out for sure," the maid insisted. "There's only one man who can tell you."

Tomas turned and took Mary into his arms, holding her as a dying man holds onto life itself. They stood there for a very long time, neither wanting to end the moment. Finally, Mary stepped back. "Go and ask him," she told him. "Now, before you change your mind."

The squire wordlessly took her hand and pressed his lips lightly. He then walked out the room and headed straight towards the quarters of his knight. One of the Archaeknights, a young Sylvu, was standing watch at the door to Rogan and Kyla's suite. Nodding to the warrior, Tomas jabbed a thumb towards the large double doors.

The Sylvu nodded. "He's in there."

"The Princess?" Tomas asked.

"Temple," the Archaeknight replied. "She will be absent another hour at least."

Without another word, the young man knocked. Rogan opened one of the engraved wooden doors, wearing a thick robe and looking as though he had been sleeping.

"Little early for bed, isn't it?" Tomas asked.

"Always try to get a nap in before Kyla comes home," the knight yawned. "She won't let me sleep for hours after she gets back." Rogan turned and walked into the study where he did most of his unwanted paperwork. The room was large and had rows of bookcases lining the walls, each filled to capacity. Scanning them with curiosity, Tomas noted with interest that present in his knight's library were most of the great works of Tramanese philosophy, various histories of the many wars to have plagued Lanasia, geographical studies of some of the most remote regions of Arayel, and more than a few books on art. The squire could not help but show great surprise at the presence of these, many of which were written by men and women of House Eigenhard.

Noticing the young man's attention and surprise, Rogan grimaced. "The family business," he grunted, pouring some cider in two glasses.

"Why didn't you become a great artist, too?"

"Everyone wanted me to," the knight told him, walking towards the large desk that was piled high with reports and dispatches, all marked 'urgent.' "Was instructed by the best my family could find. Never had much love for it, though."

Tomas noted that nearly every form of artistic expression was covered in some form by an Eigenhard. Taking up the glass Rogan had left for him, the squire grinned. "So, what was your thing?" he asked. "Sculpting, poetry, music, painting?"

The knight nodded towards his sheathed sword. "That's my brush, kid. And my enemies are my canvas."

"Does that make blood your paint?" the young man asked pointedly.

Rogan pulled his chair away from his desk toward the fireplace and sat. "All too often, kid. All too often."

"Sort of funny, isn't it?"

"What's that?"

Tomas took a drink from his glass. "That a Noble House known throughout the Republic for producing entire generations of great artists has a member that hates the thought of being an artist so much he became a warrior who doesn't like war."

"Yeah well, if you think that's funny you should see a platypus."

"What's a platypus?"

The knight drained his glass. "It's a furry animal that lives on a few of the islands off the southern coast of Darez. It's like a cross between a duck and a beaver."

"Weird."

"Seen some strange things." Rogan looked up at his squire and raised an eyebrow. "So just how much more small talk do you want to have before we get to whatever it is that brings you here?" he asked.

Tomas sat down in another chair across the room from his knight. Rogan looked over at the face of the young man and saw through the light of the fire the conflict raging through his soul. "You look like you don't want to ask me something."

The squire nodded. "My father," he said quietly.

"Was wondering when you were going to get around to asking about that." The knight leaned back in his chair and looked into the fire dancing before them both. "Are you sure you want to know? He didn't die easy."

"I think I have to know before I can go any further."

Rogan nodded. "Alright then. According to what you've been told, House Calonar went down to Pelsemoria to respond to accusations made against them by the Emir of Tordenia. As far as it goes, that's true. I really can't tell you about what happened when they first arrived in the capital since I wasn't there."

"Where were you?" Tomas asked.

"That's a whole other story, kid. I enter this story after the King had already arrived in the capital. By then, Beraht and Aebreanna had already been working for him for a little while. The two of them left Pelsemoria for a few days and ran into me. I came back with them, met the King and signed up."

"Sounds familiar," the squire snorted.

"Told you, he's got a way with people."

Rogan stood and poured himself and Tomas more cider before sitting again. "Aebreanna and Beraht had been recruited to deal with Tienel Greysoul."

"I thought you were the one who defeated Tienel."

"Eventually we all did. The Greysoul was causing mischief, and Calonar wanted him dealt with. Aebreanna and Beraht had been working for Tienel but changed sides after the fifth or sixth time he betrayed them. The King thought that they'd be best suited to fight him since they knew his plans. I found out what was going on and joined the fun.

"While we were in the city, we found out the Greysoul was going to try and kill the Imperial Family and most of the Elector Lords."

"Why?" Tomas asked.

"He wanted something from the Vaults, and the Emperor wouldn't give it to him. Greysoul made a deal with Theodorico Balshazzar to put the noble Emir on the Redwood Throne in exchange for access to the Vaults."

"Huh."

"It gets better. The Greysoul knew full well that as soon as we found out what he was planning, we'd come after him, so he set off riots in every quarter of the city the same day he planned the assassinations."

"I remember that," Tomas noted. "Fights were breaking out all over the city. School was cancelled and the City Watch was warning everyone to stay in their homes. My father was called to duty to help restore order."

Rogan nodded. "We were so busy trying to help the Legions and the Watch restore order that we almost didn't hear about what was really happening. That's when I met your father. We, me, Aebreanna, and Beraht, were protecting the inn the Calonar family was staying in from a crazed mob; your father led a Legionary detachment that helped us. After the fight, word came to your father about the attack on the Elector Council. So, we made for the Palace. Once we reached the gates, the Praetorians weren't going to let us in, being minions of the Black Duke and all, but your father vouched for us."

Tomas said nothing, he just leaned back in the chair and listened.

"Your father assembled a detachment of Praetorians and led us all to the Council chamber, but by the time we got there, it was too late. The Greysoul had put some kind of spell on one of his cronies. The man burned with a strange blue flame, but he didn't die. He did, however, kill the Emperor, the Imperial Family, and every Elector Lord present. Beraht killed the burning man, and Aebreanna wounded the Greysoul, but not before the wizard killed every Praetorian there, except your father.

"The Greysoul knew he'd won, so there was no point in staying; he also knew House Calonar would take the blame for everything he'd done. The only thing blocking his escape was me, Beraht,

Aebreanna, and your father. He hit us with everything he had and then some. The Council chamber was obliterated."

"I remember," the squire said quietly.

"What?"

Tomas looked up with dead eyes. "I was there. I saw the battle. I heard and saw my father fighting, I saw Tienel Greysoul, and I saw you."

"How?"

Tomas took a long drink from his glass, letting the warm cider offer what comfort it could. "I'd snuck out. When my father left to save the city, I wanted to see. All my life, I'd heard stories about my father's bravery, his strength, his leadership. I wanted to see it. The riots had distracted the Legionaries, so I was able to sneak into the palace. My father had taken me on a tour before, so I knew where the Council Chamber was. I arrived as the Greysoul was killing the last of the Praetorians."

"Did you see how your father died?"

The young man wordlessly shook his head.

Rogan rubbed his eyes. "Wish I hadn't. Tienel blasted Beraht through a wall, almost killed him. Aebreanna was knocked unconscious, which left only your father and me. The Greysoul must have thought I was the worse threat because his next spell was sent at me. Your father jumped between us and took the attack.

"Whatever that damned spell-slinger did, I hope he's burning in Underworld for it!" the knight snapped as he looked into the flames. "This... blackness started creeping all over his body. It slowly ate away his flesh, consuming him from the inside out. Your father was one of the bravest men I've ever met, but the agony..." Rogan's voice failed him.

"I need to hear this," Tomas whispered.

"Kid, no man needs to hear this."

The squire kept his eyes locked on the fireplace. "Please, just tell me."

"He started spitting out his own blood. The darkness started in his middle and ate his entire body, just about as slow as possible, just to extend the agony. By the time his arms and legs had been severed and the darkness was eating his heart, he somehow found the strength to speak. Anyone else, they would have just kept screaming, but your father, he found the strength."

"What did he say?"

A pause. "He told me to finish it."

A single tear rolled down the squire's face. "I saw you standing over him. I saw his blood on your sword."

Rogan nodded. "I couldn't let a man like your father die that way. It was no way for a soldier to go. I put my sword through his chest. As soon as he was dead, the darkness stopped spreading; I guess its purpose was finished. The Greysoul escaped the city. We eventually beat him." Rogan stood and poured himself another glass. "Was a wreck that night. Seeing what happened to your father and all…" The knight swirled the cider in the glass and sat back down, his eyes lost in the flames. "Kyla came to my room and comforted me. We ended up being together for the first time that night. And that set off the Madness. The city was already in chaos because of the riots and the Greysoul's attack. No government, no military leaders, no Praetorians. When Kyla lost control, that just finished the job."

"So that's it."

The knight sighed. "Yeah, kid, that's it."

Tomas stood. "Thanks, Rogan. I needed to hear that."

"I know it isn't much comfort, kid, but he died doing his duty. He died a soldier."

Tomas entered his rooms without a word. Mary jumped up from the chair she had been seated in and ran to him. Seeing the look in his eyes, the young woman just stood there, uncertain of what to do. The squire collapsed to the carpet, tears running freely. Mary knelt and held him, rocking him gently back and forth.

The two of them remained like that for much of the night. Even after Tomas found the tears no longer fell, he still lay on the floor of his sitting room, wrapped in Mary's embrace. It seemed that it was while his lady held him, all the pain and grief that he had held for so long in his soul could finally be released. After so many years, in Mary's arms, Tomas Fidelis could finally let his father's memory rest.

IV

Autumn

Chapter 34

The first day of the Harvest Festival dawned crisp and sunny. Fear and grown amongst the people of the Northern Keep that the growing threat of winter would thwart their beloved celebration. Distant Ulheim already had its wintery mantel, weeks before it customarily did, and ominous clouds were seen lurking behind those harsh mountains. The summer sun had done its best to fight back against the rumbling invasion, but all the people of the Northlands knew this was a losing battle. Winter inevitably must come again. In the past weeks, though, there seemed a respite. The bright autumn wind that had made this past season such a delight for the Northern Keep held strong, and held the ominous clouds back. The sky was bright and clear, a cheerful blessing from the world for the Northlands to enjoy its celebration.

On the command of his most royal majesty, King Cylan of House Calonar, the final Godsrestday of autumn would mark the end of all harvesting, all labors in preparation of the winter to come. To celebrate the completion of their arduous tasks, King Cylan, with his queen, commanded that for four days after the completion of harvest, no man, woman, or child would work. Instead, the people would spend the days of the Harvest Festival with their loved ones in celebration of a successful harvest and to renew their support of one another during the encroaching winter. Even the Calonar House Guard, renowned as one of the most professional and disciplined fighting forces left in the world, were under standing orders that, during the four-day celebration, only the most vital personnel would be on duty, and they were to be compensated with double their normal wages.

Traditionally, the days of games, feasting, and celebration would not begin until the Queen performed the commencement ceremony, invoking the blessing of the gods on the Keep, the Northlands, its people, and the Festival. Due to the constant threats against the royal family, Prince Rogan insisted that all members of House Calonar be escorted to such public events. Despite the gentle protests of the

King and Queen, Rogan had put his foot down. "The royal family will not be risked to a suicidal assassin that might get lucky!" he declared.

Now, on the morning of the Harvest Festival and dressed in a blue long doublet and grey trousers, as dictated by Mary, Tomas was forced to admit that he felt more than a little excitement for the upcoming days. His training was nearly complete and his schedule had been reduced to a predictable routine only occasionally disrupted by bureaucratic tedium. Although peace and joy were the standing orders for the Festival, and keeping in mind the advice of Remm and Beraht, Tomas wore a padded vest under his long doublet and strapped the heavy dagger that had been a gift from Beraht onto his belt.

Tomas regarded his image in the large Khepric mirror Mary had moved into his living room. As far as he could tell he looked fine, a little too dressy for something as simple as a festival, but overall, not bad. He could not help but marvel, as he sometimes did, at the dramatic change the past year had wrought upon him. He stood taller and was heavier in muscle. Not bulky by any measure, but rather solid. His hair was cut close and neat and now had to shave nearly every day. His hands had become callused from weeks upon weeks of weapons training, and his legs and back showed his efforts at horsemanship. The squire could not help but stare at the only two adornments on his clothes: the golden rose on his collar, its pedals in mid-bloom, and the silver emblem of House Calonar adorned his chest. Despite his growing loyalty to the Northlands and is ruling family, Tomas could not help but feel conflicted while staring at the two pins on his doublet.

A thought brought renewed peace to the young man's mind. He could almost feel Alexia straightening his collar and laughing at his foolishness. Looking into the mirror, Tomas felt as though he could see Alexia's opalescent eyes, filled with pride at the sight of her young friend, the life he had made, and happy that he had finally found peace amongst her family. Satisfied that he was ready for both the Festival and his new path in life, the squire left his personal quarters to meet up with his knight.

"The ladies have already left to practice for the closing performance," Rogan said as he admitted his squire. The knight was dressed immaculately, to his discomfort. Like Tomas, Rogan wore a long doublet of royal blue with silver embroidery. They both wore heavy leather belts on which rode heavy Northland daggers. The only real differences between the two were Tomas' hat, this one a deep grey with a bright silver cord, and Alexia's golden rose. In fact, the two men were dressed so alike, they appeared almost in uniform with one another.

"I sense conspiracy," the squire muttered.

"Get used to it," the knight shrugged, jerking his head to the dining table. He sat with a grunt, making another adjustment to the uncomfortable clothes and saying, "We're playing dress-up for the Festival, and women love dress-up. Easier to just let them have their way."

"What is this performance they're so interested in, anyway?" the young man asked, taking a seat and helping himself to food.

"The Sisters of the Lady of Light have this big performance in front of their temple on the last day of the Festival. They dance and sing; supposed to have some kind of deeper meaning, but I never really got it. Isn't your little maid going to be in it?"

Tomas nodded. "She mentioned it but didn't get too specific."

"Or you weren't listening."

"I was listening! Mostly."

Rashid entered without knocking as usual, dressed in his own Festival finery. He carried only a small stack of parchment requiring his prince's approval. Sitting down, the spymaster raised the parchments he had been carrying. "I've got a Guard company assigned to security," he said. "One platoon on duty each day, with all three rotating through the last. The companies have turned in their rosters, each soldier pulling only one half-hour of duty before getting at least six hours off.

"The City Watch will have half their personnel on duty at any one time, with rotations for that half through the day, alternating one day on and one off. Of the seven Archaeknights in the city, four will be assigned to the King and Queen at all times. One will try to keep up with Princess Karen, and the remaining two will be on relief."

"What about the twins?" Rogan asked.

"Aebreanna and I will be with them for most of the festival," Rashid said. "Once the children get tired, they'll be escorted back to the castle to stay with Karen and watched over by the Princess' bodyguards. My people will be on watch day and night."

"I thought everyone was supposed to take the next four days off," Tomas interrupted.

"My people don't take days off," Rashid said evenly. To Rogan he said, "We still need someone to go with the Queen for the commencement ceremony."

"Tomas and I will take care of that," the knight said, hurriedly finishing his meal.

"You still have time. The Queen sent word she wouldn't be ready for another hour or two."

"That's alright," Rogan said, standing and belting on his sword. "We're done anyway."

Tomas, his mouth full of sausage, could not mouth a useless dissent.

In addition to the Queen, there was one other dominant personality in the royal apartments, the young princess, Karen Calonar. Tomas had met the younger of the Calonar daughters a few times, of course, but she always seemed to fade from his memory. The squire's close association with Rogan meant that most of his contact with the ladies of House Calonar was through Kyla. The exuberant princess was a dominating personality, radiating her cheer in any company. Her sister was a sharp contrast.

Karen was a little smaller than average for her age, and had the same deep golden blonde hair as Kyla. Her features were as fair as her mother and sister's, and they all had the same lightness of step. Most obvious of all, of course, were their eyes; both had the sapphire pearlescence of a daughter of House Calonar. And, like her mother, when Karen turned her gaze to you, the sight seemed to examine your very spirit.

The differences that separated Karen from her sister were at once subtle, and dramatic. Kyla was almost two decades her sister's senior, and in the full bloom of her femininity. While Kyla habitually modified the traditional Northland gowns to emphasize comfort and titillation, Karen's sense of style better seemed to reflect her mother's, with an emphasis on propriety and modesty. This was further emphasized in their behavior; whereas Kyla was extroverted to the point of shamelessness, her little sister seemed, if not shy, at least reserved when meeting new people. Tomas could hardly recall the first time he was introduced to the princess, her just curtsying with downcast eyes. In the handful of other encounters, Karen had happily drifted into the background, seemingly uninterested in being the center of events as did her older sister. More often than not, the younger princess of House Calonar seemed content to drift into the background while her enthusiastic sister attracted all the attention.

Now, when Rogan and Tomas entered, Karen stood and bowed, mumbling a greeting. The princess' voice sounded odd to the squire's ears, perhaps more so because the girl spoke so rarely. It was soft and high, as most children's were, but to an extreme. Her words seemed to drift on the air, lighter than the brightest, most distant clouds. She never spoke more than a few words and, even in the months of Tomas' presence amidst House Calonar, still the little princess seemed put off to this newcomer, uncomfortable in his presence, and uninterested in his company.

While Rogan checked with the Queen's imperious maid for an updated departure time, Tomas decided to try once again in his efforts to be friendly with the most withdrawn member of House Calonar. "What kind of card came is that?" he asked, nodding to the large table at which Karen and one of her Archaeknight bodyguards knelt.

The princess mumbled something inarticulate, her Halvan, pearlescent eyes locked on the cards spread across the table.

"It looks like Tahazu," Tomas noted, picking up one of the cards at the edge of the table. It was octagonal, with the image of a Druug stylized on one side and small numbers and symbols printed along the edges. The squire replaced the card, exactly where it had been. "We used to play that in the capital. We even had great competitions at school."

Karen leaned to her archaeknight, a Tramanese woman. The princess whispered something to her bodyguard, who nodded. "Did you have your own deck?" the archaeknight asked.

Tomas realized the question actually came from the little girl, and directed his answer there. "I did. My father commissioned some cards for me, and then on each of my birthdays, he would get me a few more." Tomas stepped a little closer. "We had to be careful, of course, to make sure the cards were legal."

"Legal?" the archaeknight asked, but then Karen whispered something else in her ear and the bodyguard nodded understanding.

Tomas continued. "There was nothing worse than trying to play a game, and your opponent accuses you of having an illegal card."

The princess again whispered something to the Tramanese woman. "That happened to me," the archaeknight relayed. Karen picked up a card from the floor and handed it to Tomas.

The squire looked at the card and quickly spotted the problem. "Ah," he said. "A knight on foot, but he has a charge value."

"I thought it was strange," the archaeknight relayed, "but Uncle Beraht said he could knock down any horse, and he's a knight."

"May I?" Tomas asked, gesturing at the floor in front of the table around which Karen and her archaeknight bodyguard sat. The young princess smiled softly and nodded. When the squire sat, he said, "That's why Uldra have charge values without horses. Humans don't."

"I didn't know that back then," the princess admitted through her bodyguard. "Not a lot of people here play Tahazu."

"You'd be surprised," Tomas objected, picking up some of the scattered cards and organizing them by type, strength, and ability. "When I was in school, a lot of kids picked on anyone they found out played, especially if they secretly had a lot of cards at home." The squire leaned back a bit, his eyes drifting over the cards as much as they drifted through his memory.

"That happens at my school too."

"You go to school? I would have thought you'd have private tutors."

"Those too." The princess reached forward and began building a deck. "But Daddy wants me to go to the same school as everyone else."

Tomas collected a few more cards himself and built a deck.

"Did you have anyone to play with?" the princess asked though her relay while shuffling her cards.

The squire nodded, shuffling his. "Eventually. I noticed my friend Elpidius had some cards, and I told him about mine. We played together and even found a few more." He looked at Karen. "Do you have friends to play with?"

She shook her head slightly, her gaze lowering.

Tomas set his newly-built deck on the table and drew his first seven cards. "Well," he said, "you do now."

Rogan eventually returned with the Queen and cleared his throat. Tomas looked over and nodded. He and Karen were into their fifth round by that point. Although the squire had won the first hand easily, he had changed tact after that, deliberately letting the princess win some, and others making as close as he could. With his knight's summons, he sighed and stood. "Well, I guess I'll need a rematch later," he said.

Tomas turned and was about to leave, when a voice as soft as warm summer rain drifted over. Light and airy and impossibly gentle, the voice said, "Next time, don't let me win."

Rogan, Queen Nora, and Tomas all turned back, surprise clear on their faces. The little princess was smiling shyly, but with a knowing twinkle in her pearlescent eyes. She lifted a small hand and waved slightly.

Rogan and Tomas escorted the Queen to the large fountain standing at the center of the city. A great crowd had gathered for the opening ceremony of the Harvest Festival, with colorful ribbons and bright clothing on display across the squire, and bright laughter and merry-making filling the air. The crowd made way as Nora approached. Her escorts had no need for crowd control, as the people opened a wide lane for their beloved Queen, bowing to her and whispering in hushed tones their reverence for her.

As the trio neared the fountain, the Queen paused. She glanced at Rogan. "Would you go ahead and make sure they're ready for us?" The knight was about to object, clearly uncomfortable at the thought of leaving his queen unprotected, but Nora held up a small hand. "It's alright, Rogan. Tomas and I need a word."

Queen Nora waited until Rogan was out of earshot, and gave him a level stare when the knight was obviously loitering to try and overhear. She glanced around and spoke to Tomas in a very soft tone. "You must hear some truths, Tomas," she said, with the slightest hint of sadness.

"Ma'am?"

"Do you know what a Truthseer is?"

"No, ma'am."

Nora folded her hands into her robe and looked off into the past. "Alexia had many gifts. My teacher was very powerful. She was also very close with Cyras Darkholm and…"

"And?" the squire asked.

The queen breathed deeply. "No, not yet. Soon enough." She then turned back to Tomas and smiled. "Their relationship was not what you might be thinking," she continued. "Although I wouldn't doubt Cyras was attracted to Alexia, my teacher never really thought of the Trickster Mage as anything more than a... friend, of a type. In any case, Cyras often confided in Alexia, and after one such meeting, she introduced me to my husband."

"Sounds like a setup," the young man muttered.

She laughed. "Oh, it was, certainly. I didn't really mind, though. My husband was a very dashing young man. He lived just outside my village, you see, and the adults often spoke of him as trouble, as something to be avoided. He was always a little sad, though. You could tell he wanted to have friends, to be included, but being Halvan meant being outcast. I admit I was already quite smitten by the time I learned of Cyras' manipulations. Alexia and I once talked about it, and she admitted that a large part of my education as a girl was in preparation of becoming the matriarch of a restored House Calonar, one not of Sylvai blood, but Halvan."

"I'd be bitter at being so used."

"I was put out at first," Nora admitted. "But you will learn, in time, the nature of Fate. Although we retain free will, some measure of control over our lives, some events are firmly fixed. My husband and I were Fated to be together, and we already loved each other very much. We were Fated to have children, to lead the people of the Northern Keep." Her eyes, as soft and as distant as the sky, turned to him. "You are Fated, Tomas. The mark of it is on you. I have no doubt Alexia saw this, even as I do." The queen smiled. "This is why you were direct here, Tomas, why Alexia trusted you to find Cyras and Rogan." Her face clouded, just slightly. "In the days to come, try to remember that you are on a Fated path, but your actions, your decisions, are still your own. You choose to whom you give your loyalty, your love." She closed her eyes and breathed in the Festival atmosphere. "Enjoy this celebration, Tomas. Draw strength from it."

The squire felt unease, even glancing about as though to spot some unseen threat. "Ma'am," he said, "if there's some problem, something that's going to happen..."

"I can't see the future," Nora admitted. "No one really can; there's just too many possibilities." She smiled again at the squire, but this time with a hint of something more... wicked. Tomas recalled Alexia having a very similar look. "Remember that, when others try to convince you your path is fixed. You can…" She shrugged. "Just enjoy the Festival, Tomas."

"Yes, ma'am." The squire blinked. "Was I supposed to understand any of this?" he asked candidly.

Nora laughed then, a laugh of genuine delight. "Not yet," was all she said, gently caressing his cheek. The queen turned and moved towards the center of the plaza.

Seeing Rogan had finished talking to Kyla, the squire moved to his knight's side and watched as the preparations for the ceremony were completed. "Interesting family you've married into," he said.

"You should meet my family," Rogan grunted.

"Bad?"

"You have no idea."

"What were you and Kyla talking about?" the squire asked.

"I was just curious where Mary was," the knight replied.

Trying to sound casual and failing miserably, Tomas asked, "So, where is she?"

Rogan grinned knowingly. "Your lady has returned to the castle to begin her preparations for your date today." The knight stifled a yawn.

"Starting to get tired, are we?" Tomas asked.

The knight shook his head slightly. "Sometimes. This life does tend to wear a man down. With men like us, kid, it's not the years that will get you, it's the miles."

Turning back to the fountain, the pair of warriors saw that the ceremony had finally begun. Queen Nora stood in the center holding a small bag of grain and dressed in the undyed robes of the Harvest Mother. The queen had a soft smile on her face as she looked about the gathered crowd. To Nora's left stood Kyla, her own dress as a Sister of the Lady of Light made of such a light material that it seemed the light breeze might cast it away. To the far right stood Cardinal Tain, his crimson robes such a burden to the old man that he seemed at the point of collapse. In front of the three was a simple wooden altar with no symbol of any particular god upon it. Stepping forward, the queen laid the bag of grain on the altar, lifting her gaze to the heavens. "Our labors are through, and we stand together to face the coming winter, secure in the love the gods have for us and their commitment to our wellbeing." As she spoke the words, Nora reached into the bag and spread the grain on the altar.

Her part done, Nora returned to her original spot with Kyla stepping forward. Smiling brightly, her love washing over the crowd and lifting the spirits of all those present, the priestess lifted a small vial of water. "As we look ahead to the cold months to come, we renew our love for one another, for together, nothing the world can do will pull us apart." She sprinkled the water over the altar.

Once Kyla stepped back, the elderly Cardinal Tain moved forward, lifting a small box of incense. "Facing the uncertainty of what may lie ahead, we take these days to feast with those we love, celebrating the life we share and the joys we experience... together." The cardinal lit the incense.

The old cleric stepped back with the two priestesses, all three joined hands and raised them to the heavens. Together they intoned, "May the gods of light shine their love and blessings upon us as we celebrate our harvest." In conclusion, all three lowered their hands and Nora looked about the square. The queen let the tense excitement build a few moments before finally saying, "And now, my children, let our Festival begin."

A wave of cheers erupted from the gathered crowd as the entire citizenry of the Northern Keep set about to make as marry as they may.

Chapter 35

With the opening ceremony complete, Rogan and Tomas escorted Nora and Kyla back to the castle. The queen excused herself and returned to the royal apartments, and the princess called for Aebreanna. The baroness arrived with Mary in tow, but allowed for nothing more than a heated glance between her and Tomas before herding the young woman into Kyla's personal bathing room. With a glance back towards the two men, Aebreanna assured them the ladies would be ready shortly.

Two hours later, Rogan was sprawled on something called a fainting couch, while Tomas perused his knight's collection of books. Skipping past the works on art and artists, having little interest in the subject, the squire skimmed the various titles on history and cultures. He noted having read most of them, the others being tiresome retreads of better works. Finally, unable to hold still, he proceeded to pace. Rogan was used to waiting on his wife, so the extended time meant little to the snoring knight. His squire, however, was on the verge of a breakdown.

"What is taking so long?" Tomas demanded, not for the first time.

"Take it easy" Rogan grumbled from his improvised bed, not bothering to open his eyes. Dressed as he was for the festival, one would think the prince would take care to keep his blue and grey doublet from being unduly rumpled. The knight, however, cared little for finery, and his festival clothes were already getting wrinkled.

"I can't help it," the young man argued.

"Look, just take a deep breath and sit down. Plenty of times when you've got no control; you just have to wait for whatever's going to happen.

Tomas stopped his pacing and threw a confused look at his knight. "What in Underworld is that supposed to mean?" he demanded.

Rogan shrugged. "Don't worry about it," he said. "Mary has this night mapped out. Right now, she and her general staff are finishing their final strategy session."

"You can start making sense any time now," the squire said, throwing himself into a chair.

The grizzled veteran stood and filled a glass with cider, pouring one for his edgy apprentice as well. Handing the drink to his young friend, Rogan sat back down. "I ever tell you about how me and Kyla courted?" he asked.

"A little."

The knight took a deep breath, letting it out explosively. "You'll never know how hard it was," he admitted, sitting back down and staring through time. "Fought her all the way, but I just couldn't win. That woman was determined to have me, and by God, she got what she wanted.

"It was that mission I told you about, the one to rescue Cardinal Tain. Back then, I only knew the King from his reputation. Now, Aebreanna and Beraht, those two are walking, talking clichés for their respective races. You can imagine what I was thinking about them and House Calonar, but as time went on, I learned they really are good people. One of the main reasons I was so quick to join up was that he had those two working for him, them and the others: Esha, Rashid, Cardinal Tain, and the rest. After years of searching for somewhere I could belong and people I would be honored to fight for, I found them in this madhouse," he gestured around to include the castle. "Figured that if the King had patience and kindness for people like Aebreanna and Beraht, then he must be the kind of man I'd always hoped to serve.

"I was determined to prove myself to the King and his people, earn their trust and maybe earn a place here. Did everything asked of me, never questioned and never gave anyone reason to doubt me. And then I met Kyla."

Tomas sat back in his chair, lost in the memories that Rogan was recounting.

"Still remember the first moment I laid eyes on her," the warrior noted. "Aebreanna was introducing me to Esha and Alexia, and the door to my room just flew open. There she stood, the most beautiful woman I'd ever seen. She was dressed in a short red skirt with a white blouse and this red embroidered vest. Her hair was tied behind in a ponytail, and she wore these soft slippers that had ribbon tied up around her calves.

"I still remember that first moment. She'd heard Aebreanna had come back from her mission for her father and wanted to give a proper welcome. This was while we were all in Pelsemoria for that last meeting of the Elector Council. She stood there in that doorway, just staring at me with those big, beautiful eyes."

The young man smiled. "Sounds like love at first sight."

"Well, lust at first sight, maybe," the knight shrugged. "Keep in mind that, at the time, I hadn't had any kind of female companionship for quite a while. Aebreanna had been the first woman that I'd even laid eyes on in months."

"That's one impressive first sight of the fairer sex," Tomas noted.

"Yeah, but Rashid was courting her at the time, and she made it clear she wanted no funny business from me. So, besides her, Kyla was my reintroduction to the female form, and what a form."

"So you two..."

Rogan snorted. "If Kyla had her way, she would have reacquainted me right there on the spot. She ran right up to me, pushed herself right against me. Never took her eyes off me, just looked at me like I was a piece of meat. She asked Aebreanna who her new friend was like I wasn't even there."

"Doesn't sound like you appreciated that."

Rogan took a long drink and shrugged. "Most guys would say they'd have no problem being used by such a beautiful woman. Most guys would've just taken advantage of the opportunity."

"But not you."

The knight stood and set his glass back on its tray. "I took a step back, shook her hand, and introduced myself." Rogan laughed. "That had to be the single most confused look I'd ever seen on anyone's face. You see," he glanced to the door nervously and, seeing it still safely closed, crossed to sit near Tomas, lowering his voice. "I'd never say this to... the King, but Kyla was raised as an only child, and her father spoiled her a little. Her brother had been killed a few years before she was born, and I think they were... I don't know, making up for the loss, maybe. Kyla was used to getting whatever she wanted, whenever she wanted it. The fact that she couldn't have me nearly drove her insane. From that moment on, I didn't have a moment's peace."

Tomas leaned back in his chair. "So, *she* courted *you*?"

"More like harassed," the knight snorted. "She tried every trick in the female book. Tried playing little miss innocent, hard to get, making me jealous, she even tried playing the damsel in distress."

"And none of it worked."

Rogan shook his head. "Nope. After two months of that, Kyla was ready to kill someone. Probably me."

"What finally won you over?" Tomas asked.

"She cried. She broke down and showed me some genuine emotion. Her father had been attacked and wounded. This was before that last meeting of the Elector Council, it's actually why the King wasn't at that meeting Tienel Greysoul attacked. We'd been ambushed outside Pelsemoria, and he'd been wounded. He'd be fine, but it started a chain of events. Her father was wounded in an ambush, Cardinal Tain was captured and tortured, and then me, Aebreanna, and Beraht were all nearly incinerated by the Greysoul. It was a rough few weeks; there'd been a real chance House Calonar could've been wiped out. Kyla put on a brave face, helping tend to her father and contributing where she could. She never let on how much it was all starting to affect her... the toll it was taking. Finally, after the attack on the Elector Council, she just collapsed. Kyla started shaking and broke down in my arms; she couldn't stop. At first, I thought it was another game, but she never tried anything. She just sat there and cried. After that, we talked for hours and really got to know each other."

"And then you got married."

The knight laughed ruefully. "Well, first we had to escape Pelsemoria, recover the Seals of Stalline before the Greysoul, then rescue Aebreanna when he kidnapped her, but yeah, eventually we got married."

"An interesting romance," Tomas noted.

"That's just it, kid: that's the point. No force in the universe can keep a woman from what she really wants. Kyla wanted me, and she got me. It was only a question of how long I could fight. Mary wants you, and she got you. You might as well lose with some dignity and enjoy whatever she has planned."

Any further conversation was cut off as the door and the dangerous pair of Kyla and Aebreanna emerged, their eyes sparkling with mischief. They made an interesting sight, a true study of opposites. Kyla wore a traditional Northland dress: a flowing grey skirt attached to a dark blue bodice on which was embroidered the crossed-diamond sigil of House Calonar, with a very light blue apron tied around her waist with a large bow on the right. Her blonde hair was tied in two long braids and ornamented with blue ribbons to match the apron. The shorter Aebreanna, though, wore a traditional Sylva dress, a single piece of very thin, very sheer material dyed a similar blue to Kyla's dress, that was tied about her waist with a golden cord and flowed down the curves of her body to stop just below the knees. The dress was gathered at her right shoulder with a golden pin, fashioned into the crest of House Calonar. Although the material was opaque enough for Northland sensibilities, it did little to hide the most enticing features of Aebreanna's body, and seemed to match perfectly the golden hue of her autumn skin. Her long hair had become auburn with the changing of the seasons, and the baroness had gathered it in a light bun at the nape of her neck, but seemingly-random locks dangled around her face, artfully curled to highlight the Sylva's beauty and highlighting the autumnal amber in her opalescent eyes. All of this Tomas' brain noticed for future consideration. In that moment, however, his eyes were locked on the young woman standing between them.

With their hands on their hips, the two women threw Tomas a pair of quick winks and, with no preamble or introduction, moved to either side of the doorway, framing Mary between them. Although Tomas had seen his lady so many times before, the young man had never seen her as he did at that moment.

Mary wore a traditional Northland dress. Her skirt was blue, like a spring lake, rippling under a warm breeze. Her white blouse was like summer clouds with the sun shining from behind; the intricate design in swirls that closed in to conceal the parts of Mary that would remain only for Tomas, while spreading out in other places to reveal the soft flesh beneath. Her fitted bodice was like an evergreen forest: ivy swirling around the hills and valley, and tiny blue streams teasing their course around those curves. Her apron of light purple had a bright red bow, tied at her right. A ribbon of flawless white held back the single braid of Mary's hair, tied in a large bow whose ends drifted as though in their own light wind. She wore a collar of very thin, delicate lace, from which hung a small golden charm in the shape of a blooming rose. From her ears dangled the emeralds Tomas had bought for her months ago. Lastly, and most perfectly, the hint of a smile curved the very edge of her lips.

The young woman's eyes were demurely downcast. Fluttering her eyelashes, the maid clasped her hands in front of her waist. "Do I look alright?" she asked modestly.

After a few inarticulate attempts at speech, Tomas could finally summon enough thought to say, "Wow."

Rogan shook his head and sighed. "Like I said."

Chapter 36

The first day of the Festival was traditionally spent with friends and family, playing games of skill, watching displays of slight-of-hand and simple magic, and watching and listening to the songs and dances of the various performers, all under the stern supervision of the Sisterhood of the Lady of Light. On these days, the beautiful priestesses had absolute dominion over the people of the Northern Keep. By their command, everyone would make merry and have joy in their hearts. For those few who stubbornly refused to partake in the joy to be had, they quickly found themselves surrounded. The sweet-natured and selfless sisterhood all wore bright red dresses, unadorned but for the tiny bells they wore around their waists, wrists, and ankles. They carried shepherd staffs adorned with ribbons of all colors, and endlessly stalked the streets. The Sisters hunted for any who doggedly held on to sorrow, misery, or jealousy. These pitiable fools were quickly pounced upon by a giggling, tinkling clowder, tied up in bows and forced to experience joy. For it was the commandment of Kyla, Sister Superior of the Lady of Light that, during the Harvest Festival, all would have cheerful good times, on pain of a merciless tickling.

The three couples, Tomas and Mary, Rogan and Kyla, and Rashid and Aebreanna, quickly separated upon reaching the festival. Promises to meet the following day were extracted from all, but it was clearly understood that each pair wished for time alone. Once Tomas and Mary were finally separated and left to their own entertainment, the two stood for some time by the fountain at the city's center, staring into one another's eyes.

"So," Tomas said after some time. "What do you want to do first?"

Mary smiled and put her arms around her squire, pressing close enough that their hearts could caress, and pulling his eyes down into hers. "It doesn't matter," she sighed. "Whatever you want."

The young man was content for a long time to stand there, with his arms wrapped around his lady. It was with only the faintest regret that Tomas broke the embrace and led Mary, hand in hand, towards the games of chance and skill. The maid looked up at her gallant escort with a warm smile. "And will my lord win for me some great prize?" she asked playfully. "Some fabulous trophy of gold and silver?"

Tomas stopped at a booth run by an older man with a streak of grey in his dark red hair. The squire pointed towards some stuffed animals lined up along the back counter. "How about a trophy of wool and thread?" he replied whimsically. He picked up one of the wooden balls and tossed it in one hand as he glanced over at the game owner. "So, how's this work?"

The red-haired old man smiled knowingly at the young lovers and gestured to the stack of wooden cups. "Very simple, young sir," he said in a voice made hoarse from years of festival yelling. "I will place a ball of red yarn into one cup. I will fool your eyes with the skill of my hands and hide the one cup among four others. You must, in only three attempts, throw a ball and knock over the cup concealing the yarn."

Mary began looking over the stuff animals while Tomas looked at the row of five cups. The squire shook his head. "How often does anyone win this game?"

"This is a contest of skill and perception sir," the game owner replied. "It is not meant for the simple or feeble. Only the greatest of men may attempt this and win."

Tomas was about to ask another question but was interrupted by a delighted squeal from Mary. With a grimace, he noted his lady had taken an interest in a stuffed dragon, not as menacing as its larger cousins, with a large smile sewn into its face and sad eyes that seemed to look up in adorable supplication. Without a word, the game-owner handed Tomas three wooden balls and happily took the young man's money in exchange.

Tomas Fidelis was a young man. He liked to think he was in the prime of life with acute senses and a quick mind. Because of this, he entered this situation with some hope of victory. Mary stood beside him, careful not to disturb the squire's concentration, but obviously eager to win the meaningless prize. Tomas narrowed his eyes at the old man staring back at him, both sizing the other up. The young man squared his shoulders and cracked his neck, allowing not the faintest hint of fear to register in his eyes or heart. A slight grin appeared on the old man's face, showing the contempt he felt for this young challenger.

The slightest breeze pulled at the corners of their awareness, failing to draw even the slightest acknowledgment from either man. A quick nod from Tomas began the contest. The old man's hands flew across the counter with blinding speed, dropping the ball of red yarn and covering it with a wooden cup within a single eye's blink. The squire tried to follow the cup as it danced among its brothers, but everything before the young man became an incomprehensible blur and the beginnings of fear tugged at his heart. Then, with no warning, the cups stopped their dizzying parade, set in a perfectly straight line.

"Five cups, young sir," the game owner said. "One ball. Choose and throw."

Indecision tore at Tomas. He could not deny that his target had been lost in the mad dash across the table. Feeling his lady on his arm, the squire knew he could not fail her. Closed eyes and a deep breath brought a small degree of calm to his warrior's heart. Tomas glanced briefly at Mary, gaining strength from her eyes and smile. Suspending all thought, the squire leapt into action, turning and hurling the wooden missile at its target. His aim was true and the cup was knocked back, away from all others and off the table. But nothing was revealed beneath; the red ball had escaped him.

"An excellent toss, noble sir!" the old man decreed, crossing back to the table and revealing the ball of yarn from beneath a different cup. "But the wrong cup. Two throws left to you sir, are you ready to continue?"

Tomas narrowed his eyes and nodded. He would not fail again. The game owner smiled and dropped the ball down, again covering it before it even hit the table and again beginning the cups on their mad dash around the table. Sweat beaded the squire's brow as he fought to track his goal, struggling against the melee before him. Suddenly, order was returned to the chaos and the cups stood before him once again in perfect formation, four wooden soldiers facing off against a lone squire.

The young man never broke eye contact with one cup, there was no doubt in his mind or soul now. His enemy could hide no longer. Tomas briefly placed one arm around Mary's shoulders, drawing from her the strength he needed to face this trial. Then, rearing back, he took careful aim and released, felling another cup with his attack.

Again failure welcomed the squire, for again there was no ball of yarn beneath.

"Take heart, my boy," the old man said as he revealed the red ball from beneath a cup on the far corner. "Only three cups remain."

Mary had not been looking at the cups. Instead, the maid looked through narrowed eyes at the old man. Something just short of a sneer danced across her beautiful face as the cups once again danced across the table. As Tomas struggled one last time to track the ball of yarn, Mary maintained her frosty gaze on the true enemy of this encounter. When, for the last time, the cups were arrayed before her squire, the young woman lightly placed a hand on his chest. Seeing the fear and indecision ripping at Tomas' soul, Mary smiled and took his hand, drawing the wooden ball from it. "It's alright," she reassured him.

Tomas nodded and stepped back. It was all right, he knew. Mary was not the sort of woman who would place more value in some meaningless stuffed animal than the pride of her young man. The game did not matter, only that they be happy together this day.

On the other hand, Mary did *not* appreciate her Tomas being made to look foolish. The young woman moved in a flash, taking aim and firing with only a blur of her arm. Her aim was as true as her squire's, and her target fell just as surely. Her target, however, had not been a wooden cup, but the old man.

The game-owner's eyes rolled back in his head, back towards the large red mark already blossoming on his forehead, and he fell. With the impact of his unconscious body on the ground, a small ball of red yarn tumbled from his limp hand. "I guess this means I win," she sniffed, taking the dragon.

And so it was that the two young lovers turned away from the contest, Mary with her victory and a glowing smile, and Tomas with the shreds of his dignity and a stuffed dragon looking up at him with a mocking grin.

Chapter 37

Their dinner that night was as pleasant as could possibly
be. Tomas and Mary dined in the same Sylvai restaurant from their
first lunch together. The same waiter served them, bringing them
more treats they enjoyed enormously. Again, they sipped at the
Sylvai wine, *Way'et'ay'nas'a*, as they stared into each other's eyes.
Somewhere in the back of the squire's mind he realized that the cost
of the meal they shared together would put a serious dent in his
wages for the next several months, but as he stared across into those
soft eyes, as he felt the gentle exploration of a foot, he had little care
of it. Nearly any price would be more than acceptable to be with his
Mary.

Like before, Tomas trusted to his lady's knowledge of Sylvai
dishes and let her order. Again, he had not the slightest idea what it
was the waiter brought them, but he still found it delicious. Each bite
was seasoned to perfection and balanced with each other to create
as pleasing a meal as the young man could ever remember having.
The wine again brought an inner sense of peace and contentment,
yet anticipation and courage, which emboldened both Tomas and
Mary. They had not finished even half the bottle of *Way'et'ay'nas'a*
before they found themselves inching their chairs ever closer,
brushing their legs against one another and even occasionally feeding
each other small tidbits of their meal.

The Sylvai were renowned across Lanasia for their knowledge
of love, romance, and seduction, and the ambiance of the restaurant
only confirmed this reputation. The music played by the owner's
wife and two daughters drifted across the open-air restaurant; soft
notes from lute, harp, and drum blended and teased long glances and
lingering touches. Lanterns floated above their heads, casting both
gentle warmth and soft radiance upon the diners, keeping the
encroaching winter at bay. The lanterns were painted in different
colors and each seemed to merge with one of the bright stars visible
that night, blending together to create a multihued ambiance
captured and magnified by Mary's luminous eyes. The tables were

small and the chairs close, encouraging the caress of hands and legs. The very air itself in this eatery seemed to conspire to bring forth romantic desire, and Tomas and Mary offered little resistance.

At some point, dessert was brought to the young couple. Tomas had never seen or tasted anything quite like it. It was somewhat like a sweetbread, but far thinner, as dark as peasant bread but as sweet as honey. Mary ate the delicate treat with a relish that bordered on ecstasy; in all honesty to himself, Tomas took more pleasure in the maid's reaction than to the dessert. "What is this?" he finally asked.

Mary's eyes had rolled back into her head. "Chocolate," she nearly moaned. "From Maka. Traders bring it."

A simple treat from the other side of the world, Tomas marveled. A secret dish whose mystical creation, like silk, was known only to those strange peoples in their distant homelands. Another marvel of this city. But then, Tomas considered the effort to bring something like this chocolate from so far away. The effort, and the cost. The squire chose not to concentrate on just how long he would need to pay for the moments of exquisite joy he was buying for his Mary, instead focusing on her flushed face, heavy breathing, and soft moans of pleasure.

Overall, Tomas decided, it was only the presence of Terry, as Mary had named her new stuffed toy, seated as he was between them on the table and staring up at Tomas with those beady eyes and that mocking grin, that kept their evening meal from being perfect.

"So," Tomas said as they ate their dessert, "is there something special about that ribbon? The one in your hair?"

Mary looked up. "What makes you think?"

"Well, the rest of your outfit is so fancy, and the ribbon is so simple. I just figured it meant something."

"You don't like it?"

The squire shook his head. "It's not that. I think everything about you is perfect. There's just something about the ribbon. It stands out, I guess."

Mary put her tiny silver spoon down and dabbed a napkin at her mouth. "Well, it actually does mean something," she confessed. "About my family."

"You talk much about your family," Tomas noted.

"There really isn't much to tell," she replied.

"You've said that before," he pointed out. "If it has anything to do with you, I want to know. I want to know everything."

The maid blushed. "Well, like I said before, my father was in the Legions before joining the Calonar House Guard. He left the service after I was born, taking over his family farm." She smiled. "Father always said he preferred farming to fighting. That it takes the same skill, the same delicacy, but with farming you create things, instead of destroying them."

"He sounds like a wise man."

"He was. He died about a year after I came to the Keep. Pestilence."

Tomas took Mary's hand in his own. It was clear the young woman still mourned for her father's death. It was an old pain, but still there, and one the squire knew well. "So, where did he serve while in the Legions?" Tomas asked.

"Darez," she said softly. "He was one of the soldiers assigned to Darez."

The squire paled when she said this. "Was he there when...?"

"Yes. When Reydia the Deranged led her uprising of the prisoners, my father was there. He fought during the rebellion, all the way up until the Emperor ordered the penal colony abandoned and quarantined."

"But he got out."

"Oh yes. In fact, he was one of the last men to leave. He was his legion's signifier, he carried the standard, you see, and he refused to leave. My father believed the standard couldn't be taken away as long as any of the soldiers were still fighting."

"He's right," Tomas confirmed. "As long as any part of a legion was still fighting, the standard was supposed to stay on the battlefield. The centurion and the signifier were supposed to be the last ones to leave."

Mary nodded. "That's what my father said. He and his commander stayed, fighting Reydia's followers until the last boat was ready to leave. When my father came home, my mother became pregnant with me, and Father left the Legions to stay home with us."

"My father led that mission," Tomas told her. "He was the one who pulled them out." The young man thought a moment. "So, if my father hadn't saved your father, then you would have never been born?"

The maid smiled. "I suppose not."

"Remind me to include that in my thanks to God tonight."

Mary blushed.

Tomas shook his head. "So how does that ribbon come into all this?"

"It belonged to my grandmother," she said. "She gave it to my mother, telling her to give it to the man she had chosen to father her children. When my father's legion was ordered to go to Darez, she gave it to him for good luck. When he died, my mother gave it to me; she told me I would have to make the same choice someday."

"Well, it's beautiful, Mary. Like you."

"It's just a ribbon," she argued.

The young man shook his head. "Too many people think beauty must be complicated. Too many people think that, for something to be beautiful, like a ring or bracelet, it must be ornate. They think it requires an enormous jewel that's been fashioned into a heart or something. But I don't agree with any of that."

Tomas took both of Mary's hands and enveloped them with his, looking deep into her soft eyes. "Beauty is a simple thing. Beauty is how God created a thing. If an object doesn't have natural beauty, then no amount of crafting will change that. But for something… some*one* who is naturally beautiful, it remains the simple things that create that beauty. Perfect eyes, delicate hands, a soft smile, a gentle soul. These are the things that create beauty.

"The ribbon is beautiful, Mary."

Following their meal, the young couple took another trip to the temple of the Harvest Mother. Tomas and Mary had kept their promise to Ilse, and often returned to visit the sick children. At least once a week, the pair arrived and shared more stories of heroes and epic adventure. At first, Tomas had tried keeping his visits secret, suspecting Rogan would object to such a waste of time. To the squire's great surprise, when his knight did learn of the excursions, he encouraged them.

"The job's not just killing bad guys," Rogan had said. "It's helping people, even if by just showing up."

The stories that Tomas and Mary told the children brought a kind of happiness to the eyes of those kids that was a wonder to behold. In the early weeks, during the couple's initial few visits, there had been such a feeling of sadness among the children; although this lessened over time and with more visits, that sadness had returned with the arrival of autumn. The Harvest Festival was the highlight of the year; none of the young patients had wanted to miss the celebration, but they were simply too weak to go. The Sisters of the Lady of Light had dedicated a few of their number to stay with the children, playing music and games, but the difference was not lost on their young hearts. On seeing the arrival of their favorite new friends, however, that growing sadness vanished in an instant.

As the hours passed, Tomas varied his stories with occasional feats of skill. His juggling act was such a complete disaster that even Mary could not contain her laughter. The squire's attempt to recreate the game that had nearly defeated him that afternoon also brought laughter at his expense, to say nothing of the five coppers he lost to a boy named Brian. Tomas' balancing act was much more successful; he stood atop a bed post on one foot, greatly exaggerating flailing his arms and free leg for the amusement of the children only to show that he was, in fact, in complete control. It was not until he glanced at Mary that he had trouble, as the young woman, with a wicked sparkle in her eyes, drew a light touch along the neckline of her blouse. Seeing this, Tomas slipped and tumbled onto his rear end, to the delight of his young audience.

The maid's attempts to teach basic dance to several of the little girls was much more successful than anything Tomas tried. Despite the protests of the boys, to which Tomas jokingly joined, once Mary began a small dance for them, all were entranced at the young woman's movements. The grace with which she moved and the skill she showed were more than enough to bring cheers from everyone, but most especially from the one she wanted most to please. The young woman ended her performance with an old song that gloried at the beauty of autumn.

At long last, Ilse and Medaka returned. They were a sharp contrast to one another as the Harvest priestess wore, as always, her simple cleric's robes while Medaka wore the same light red dress and bells as did all her sisterhood during the festival. The two holy women gently, but firmly, insisted that the children needed their rest. A chorus of objections very nearly knocked the priestess out of the room, but she remained steadfast.

"Just one more story," a little boy named Kyle insisted.

Ilse and Medaka shared a glance. The Harvest priestess sighed and nodded in resignation. "Very well, one more" the Sister of the

Lady of Light conceded. "But after that it's time to sleep," Ilse added sternly.

"What do you want to hear?" Tomas asked. "Another about the Heroes of Fate? Or how about the great knight Sir Talius Ironheart? How about the tales of the great Republic explorers of the third century?"

"We want a new story!" young Brian declared. The other children quickly agreed.

The squire looked at Mary and smiled. "Alright," he said. "I'll tell you about a beautiful goddess and the evil Umbral that held her prisoner."

"What was her name?" Kyle asked.

"Well, that's just the thing. The knight who quested to rescue her didn't know her name. He didn't know anything about her or where to find her."

"Then how did he know that she needed to be rescued?" Brian demanded. "How did he know what the goddess would look like?"

"Well, he had a dream one night. In his dream, he saw a goddess with long hair and a beautiful face and a perfect smile. In his dream, he saw his goddess trapped by an ancient spell and guarded by a fierce Umbral. In his dream, he heard his goddess call out to him. The knight felt her touch on his soul."

On the squire's story went. The brave knight battled monsters and evil men and ancient traps before finding a castle far to the west that was built on a cloud and surrounded by a dream. The children sat in their beds as Tomas told his tale using all the tricks he knew of the storyteller's trade. Even Mary, sitting off in a corner, could not tear her eyes away from the young man as he told of the brave knight.

"And he traveled through the dream," Tomas said. "All manner of deception and trickery was used by the Umbral, but nothing would stop the knight from finding his goddess. On and on the knight quested, besting many trials and defeating many foes before finally entering the castle and battling the Umbral itself."

The squire grabbed up a broom and pantomimed the fierce struggle which, he assured them all, seemed to last for days. By the end of the titanic struggle, the Umbral was banished back down to Underworld, and his goddess stood before the knight's eyes. Tomas walked over and led Mary to the center of the large room where all the children could see them.

"And there he was," Tomas said. "All his many years of struggle and hardship were over. All the battles he had fought and the blood he had shed had been for this one moment. For now, his goddess finally stood before him." The squire dropped to his knees before Mary. "But he could not look too long upon her," he noted, turning his face away. "Her beauty was such that it would blind a mortal man and burn his soul. But no matter how greatly he pained at being so close to someone so lovely, his heart hungered to draw even nearer.

"'What may I do?' the knight asked, 'to earn your favor?'" Tomas held up the broom in both hands. "'I swear to you on my life and my honor. I pledge my eternal loyalty to you, if only you would command me.' And though it blinded him forever, the knight looked up into those perfect eyes of divine fire. 'I look into your eyes now,' he said, 'knowing it will be the last sight I ever see. For even should I be unworthy to serve you, I may at least live out my meaningless days with your glory forever in my heart.'"

"What did the goddess say?" Brian asked.

Tomas looked into Mary's eyes. "What did she say?" he asked.

Tears stood in the maid's eyes. Somewhat breathlessly, she tried to speak. "She said... she said, 'for now and forevermore, you are my champion.'"

The squire stood and bowed to his goddess to the cheers of the children. The clerics walked forward, adding their soft applause to the joyful cries of their patients.

Despite the children's insistent demands for yet another tale of the knight and his goddess, Tomas and Mary departed, leaving Ilse and Medaka to coax the children to sleep. The couple exited the temple and, noting the silent streets, suddenly realized how late the hour had grown. "I guess we should be getting home," the squire said.

Walking again with hands clasped, the two returned to the castle. Tomas walked his Mary to the door of her room. Upon reaching her home, the maid turned and looked expectantly at her squire. "That was a wonderful story you told," she nearly whispered.

"I liked the ending, personally," he admitted.

"So, what do you think will happen to the knight and the goddess next?"

Tomas looked deeply into her eyes, as though trying to look into her very soul. "I can't wait to find out," he said.

The young woman closed her eyes and turned her head up, waiting for what she was sure would come next. She opened them again in surprise when Tomas took her hand and raised it up, then shivered a bit when he kissed the back of that hand. "Good night, Mary," he said, then turned and walked away. Reaching the end of the hall, the squire looked back and smiled before returning to his rooms for some desperately needed sleep. Mary opened her door and entered her own rooms where her roommates were waiting for an immediate debriefing.

Chapter 38

The next morning, Tomas was surprised to note that Mary was not at her apartments. "She went to practice for her performance at the end of the festival," one of the other maids informed him. "She said she'd meet you outside the restaurant." There could be only one restaurant she meant, so the squire hurried off towards the Sylvai eatery. Even as he approached, the young man easily spotted his lady, this time dressed in green and blue and her hair still decorated with the white ribbon.

The two embraced just as soon as they were able, words being unnecessary at that point. They could easily have spent the entire day thus had not another explosion rocked the Keep. Tomas looked off towards the large tower of the Arcane Order in the far edge of the city. "Is Esha working today?" he asked.

Mary was looking in the opposite direction. "That wasn't Esha," she noted. "They must have started the wizard's show."

"The what?"

The maid took his hand and led the squire off at nearly a run towards the large parade grounds near the House Guard barracks. The expansive field, into which an entire neighborhood could fit with room to spare, was well manicured, with low grass and neatly-maintained shrubbery. Tall stands had been erected along opposing sides of the roughly-square field, and these stands were packed with city residents, all cheering and waving and calling out to friends and acquaintances. The other two sides of the parade field held no stands; instead, one was dominated by the Guard barracks complex, a series of squat buildings and guard towers. The opposite end had a line of tall earthen mounds, beyond which was a sea of tents and pavilions, all bearing the banners of various minor noble Houses. Vendors walked up and down the field, and up and down the stands, selling all manner of wine, cider, mead, sweet treats, and other foodstuffs. Entertainers: jugglers, fire-breathers, illusionists, painted clowns, and other performers delighted the crowds with their skills. There were so many spectators, in fact, that upon reaching the stands, Tomas and Mary were hard pressed to find a seat and view the show. Finally spotting Rogan and Kyla, the two having apparently held seats for them, the young couple dodged and weaved on their way up, nearly leaping from tier to tier to join the prince and princess and somehow keeping their hands clasped the entire time.

Once the two reached their seats and Kyla shared a brief welcoming hug with Mary; Rogan threw a somewhat grumpy look at his squire. "You know, I used to be that nimble, too," he grumbled.

"Have a little trouble climbing the steps, did we?" Tomas asked lightly.

"He's just a little grumpy," Kyla said, snuggling up against her knight. "He was up late last night."

"Any particular reason, your Highness?" Mary asked sympathetically.

The princess giggled. "Oh my, yes! Rogan had a peacock's feather and used it to..."

"So, who's in the show this year?" the knight asked.

"Are you blushing?"

"Shut up, kid."

Tomas could not help but laugh. After several seconds of continued laughter, though, Rogan felt enough was enough. "You think it's funny? Alright, Kyla, tell them what I did with the damned feather."

And she did, in excruciating anatomical detail. Within one minute of the princess' impassioned story, both Tomas and Mary were blushing so brightly their faces both nearly matched the mid-morning sun. While the squire's eyes betrayed only a desire to erase recent memory, the maid's wide eyes held a hint of speculation.

"So, who is in the show this year?" Tomas asked.

Both Rogan and Tomas tried changing the subject. Unfortunately, Mary and Kyla engaged in a lengthy conversation on the various uses for feathers and other accoutrements of the bedchamber. This led to other topics that caused both knight and squire to consider retreat. Finally, a group of grey-robed mages marched onto the field, signaling the show was set to begin, and the mighty warriors were spared the indignity of fleeing from their women. The four friends watched with delight as the apprentice-wizards summoned dancing lights of every color and shot sparks into the air that exploded with a loud crack. "Why are only the apprentices doing the show?" Tomas asked.

"This isn't a show to them," the knight replied as a jet of flame erupted from one mage's hands towards the audience, only to arc back and disappear before any harm could be done. "It's a test."

"Test?"

"The Guild gives tests to its members as they progress," the knight explained.

The squire nodded. "I know. They did the same thing in Pelsemoria. But I was always told the tests were grueling and dangerous."

"Esha stopped all that. When she took over the Tower here in the Keep, she ordered that, instead of those old trials the Guild used to put wizards through, they'd perform for the people of the city."

"I don't get it."

"The whole point of these tests is to gage how much they've learned to control their power. Esha thinks that, since the wizards are in service of the people, the people should be their judges."

Tomas looked out on the group of perhaps a dozen young mages, all wearing the grey robes of apprentice wizards. "So, this is their test?"

Rogan nodded. "If they can do enough magic to impress the crowd, they pass and become full wizards. If they don't, they wait until next year to try again."

The crowd erupted in applause as the group show concluded. Each of the apprentices bowed before stepping back, forming a straight line across the parade field. Tomas was surprised as everyone in the stands stood and turned to face a private section in the shadow of the barracks. Looking over, the young man saw King Cylan and his queen step into the large booth obviously reserved for them. Accompanying the royal couple was their youngest daughter, Karen. The little princess wore a soft blue dress, grey blouse, and white apron with a bow tied in the front, and eagerly ran to the front of the booth, nearly bouncing with delight over the show to come.

Wearily dropping into his cushioned chair, the King nodded to the crowd, waving for them to sit. Four Archaeknights escorting the royal family spread to the corners of the large booth, their eyes constantly scanning the crowd for any sign of threat to their king and queen. Another other two stood behind the King and Queen. Tomas did not recognize most of the Archaeknights, but he did spy Sarah among those standing at the corners of the royal booth.

With the crowd again seated, Tomas saw that Esha had stepped onto the field, her typically burnt and rumpled robes now looking clean and neat. Standing in the center of her apprentices, the archmage raised her staff and bowed to House Calonar. The old king nodded in return, gesturing for the test to begin. Esha turned back and gestured to the mage at the far edge of the line.

A young man, little more than a boy, stepped forward. The mage nearly trembled with fear but resolutely walked up to stand in front of his master, facing the assembled citizens of the Northern Keep. The young man closed his eyes in fierce concentration and raised his arms as he chanted in the musical language of magic. It seemed to Tomas that he could almost feel the mage trying to draw into himself enough power to manifest his will. Subtly at first, but with increasing clarity, a faint green mist gathered around the mage, coalescing around his outstretched hands into a large ball. Sweat beaded the apprentice's brow, and he trembled with exertion until the green ball popped, making only a faint sound. Revealed in the mage's hand was a small flower, a daisy. The young man crossed the field and bowed, handing the tiny flower to Princess Karen with trembling hands.

Stepping back in anticipation, the mage stared at the royal family in near terror. Esha raised her voice, "What says the King?"

King Cylan smiled and looked about the stands. "What says the people?" he asked in a deep but somewhat weak voice.

The response from the audience was thunderous.

The old king placed a gentle hand on his young daughter. "What says the Princess?" he asked.

Karen stared at the mage very seriously, regarding first the mage, then the small flower in her hands. Her bright eyes of pearlescent sapphire, the same as her sister's, seemed as though they could see into the trembling apprentice, holding far more wisdom than a girl of so few years. Even from a distance, Tomas was reminded of how similar Alexia and Queen Nora looked at people with their own piercing gazes. The mage looked on the verge of tears as he waited for the princess' verdict. Finally smiling, Karen cheered the apprentice spell-caster, her applause quickly followed again by the crowd.

"A wizard's entire career resting in the hands of a little girl," Tomas noted.

Mary smiled. "She hasn't been wrong yet. Somehow, the Princess just seems to know when a mage is ready for promotion."

"She has Mother's sight," Kyla confirmed.

The mage turned back to face Esha. The archmage regarded her student seriously for a moment, then raised her staff. Several multi-colored beams of light drifted slowly out of Esha's staff, surrounding the young man. When the light vanished, the grey robes of the apprentice mage he had been wearing were replaced by the blue robes of a full wizard, with a light brown inseam marking him as an Earth Mage. The new wizard looked down at his robes and at the simple, unadorned wooden staff in his right hand. The young man bent down and threw his arms around his teacher with tears of joy running freely. Esha showed no signs of surprise or embarrassment at the outburst of affection, patting her student on the back before gently guiding him back to the line.

And on it went, one after another. Each of the mages took their turn, making various demonstrations of their abilities and waiting for the approval of the audience and the Princess. Only one of the students failed to gain the blue robes they each sought, and that one only failing after passing out during his attempt. Rogan shook his head in regret. "That's a shame," he said.

"Do you know him?"

The knight nodded. "Robert. His family paid for him to come here all the way from Alvaro to study under Esha. He's a good kid, but everybody knew he was going to attempt the test too soon."

"Too impatient?"

"Pretty much. He wants it all, and he wants it now. Esha says he's got some talent, but he'll never be one of the really great archwizards. Speaking of which..." The knight drew Tomas' attention back to the parade field where three wizards all wearing their ceremonial blue robes had walked out from behind the stands. Unlike the newly-promoted apprentices, these adepts had more decorative robes, with runes of bronze, silver, and gold along the colored inseams of sleeve and hood. Their staffs were also more ornate, with runes inscribed and charms of metal, fabric, hide, and feather adorning and individualizing the mystical tools. The three adepts stopped directly in front of Esha, standing equal distances from each other and their master.

"What's this?" the squire asked.

"The next test," Mary replied. "These three are wizards who have appealed to Esha to allow them to advance to the next level."

"Archwizard, right?"

"Right. If they pass this test, they'll be promoted to archwizard and be expected to take an apprentice."

"I thought any wizard could take a student," Tomas noted.

Kyla shook her head. "According to Guild law, only an adept who's proven their mastery of magic is allowed to train another."

"I wonder why."

Rogan shrugged. "Asked Esha a while back. She told me this was one of the few Guild rules she approved of. Said that if an inexperienced wizard tries to train a mage, they could both be put in danger. The mage could lose control."

Tomas nodded. "Makes sense."

On the field, Esha walked up to the three petitioners and stopped before each of them. The archmage carefully inspected them, their robes, their staffs, and even their faces; with each in turn, she looked deeply into their eyes. As the archmage did this, the small Sylva asked each several questions, very quietly, and all in the language of magic. All three must have answered correctly since, as Esha returned to her previous place, the crowd burst into applause. "Did they pass?" Tomas asked.

"Not yet," Mary replied. "First the questions, then the demonstration, then the test."

"What does that mean?"

"First, they have to answer the questions Esha asks them, proving they have the knowledge to advance. Then, they have to perform a spell that Esha names, showing they have the control over magic to advance. Finally, they have to show they have the ingenuity to advance."

"How do they do that?"

The maid put a finger on the tip of her squire's nose. "Just watch."

Two of the applicants walked off to opposite sides of the field, leaving the one in the center standing alone in front of Esha. The lone wizard, a man wearing the light blue lining on his robes of a Water Mage, held his staff casually at the ready. Tomas could see that the wizard's staff was a very pale white. Along the shaft were runes, all a deep black against the pale white. Unlike his compatriots, this wizard had his hood pulled up, with a scarf covering his mouth and nose. Gloves covered his hands, making his gender known only by the way he stood and the way he moved, by the deep timber of his accented voice.

"Is that…?" Rogan asked Kyla.

The princess nodded. "Xathias."

Tomas glanced over at his knight. "Somebody important?"

"Maybe," Rogan replied. "For one thing, he's the only Xeshlin who's ever trained here."

"A Xeshlin?" the squire asked in shock. "Why would a Xeshlin train here? I thought they didn't even join the Guild. I thought they were forbidden from Lanasia, that the Sylvai would kill them on sight."

"Normally," Kyla agreed. "They use magic in a different way than Lanasian adepts. Corrupt; evil. Xathias is the exception. He petitioned my father for sanctuary and permission to study under Esha. When my mother agreed, Daddy said yes."

"Why?" Tomas asked. "Why would a Xeshlin come here? Why would the King and Queen agree?"

Rogan shrugged. "We don't know. One day Cyras showed up with Xathias and met with the King and Queen. Cyras didn't say why he sponsored Xathias, and Xathias himself doesn't talk about it."

"What's more," Kyla added, "Is his gender."

"What do you mean, your Highness?" Mary asked.

"Normally, only females have any magical ability among the Sylvai and Xeshlin. When a Sylvu manifests, his Speaker puts him through special training to limit his ability. Male Xeshlin who manifest…" the princess sighed.

"What?" Tomas asked.

"They're murdered," Rogan said. "Sacrificed to the Dark Empress."

Tomas was quiet, considering the implications. Then, he narrowed his eyes. "I'm assuming Rashid has someone keeping an eye on him?"

"Of course," the knight laughed. "So far, he hasn't shown signs of treachery. He's just a really powerful wizard."

"How powerful?"

"Powerful enough that Esha took personal charge of his instruction. Powerful enough that he took his test to become a wizard after less than a year."

"How long ago was that?" the squire asked.

"Three years ago."

"He only took three years to make Archwizard!?! It usually takes decades, if ever!"

"Like I said, he's powerful and he learns fast."

On the field, Esha spoke a single word in the language of magic. In the instant the Water Mage nodded, the archmage threw something at her student. The small vial exploded a second before it would have hit him and erupted in bright blue fire. Xathias lifted his staff high and barked the words of magic, gesturing at the fire as though forming it.

As Tomas watched, he saw that the Xeshlin was, indeed, manipulating the flames. The fire did not die as it should have. Instead, it flowed around Xathias, responding to his slightest command and twisting into shapes of people, animals, buildings, and even writing. Finally, the Water Mage called the fire to his outstretched hand, pulling it all together into a tight ball before launching it high into the air where it exploded.

Even as the crowd burst into applause, Mary frowned. "Where was the water?"

"What do you mean?" Tomas asked.

"I thought he was a Water Mage," she said. "I thought there would be water."

"The names of the schools of magic aren't literal," he explained. "They're symbolic. The school of water isn't about literally controlling water. It's about intuitive thought."

"Oh. I always wondered about that. So, what are the other schools?"

Tomas thought for a moment. "Well, there's fire, which is the school that studies active magic, the flashier stuff that's easy to see and feel. There's the earth school, which studies building and creating. Wind studies motion and how things change. Life and death magic are the literal ones; they study life and death itself and how to control them. There's also time and fate, except nobody knows how to use them."

"Nobody?"

"Well, there are rumors," Rogan noted. "Some people say Cyras can use fate magic. But as far as the Guild says, they only just recognized fate magic about a century ago."

"What about time?" Mary asked.

"Well, there are stories about a secret sect within the Guild," Tomas said.

"Oh, come on kid," Rogan snorted. "Don't tell me you think the Chronomagi exist."

"They might," the squire insisted.

Mary turned to Kyla. "What are the Chronomagi?" she asked.

Kyla leaned in close to Mary as the two boys continued to argue over their heads. "There have been rumors for years about a group of wizards who learned how to control time. Supposedly, they call themselves the Order of the Chronomage and use their power to change the course of history."

Back out on the field, Xathias bowed to his master and moved away, letting the second applicant take his place, this one a woman wearing the brown of an Earth Mage. "This should be good," Rogan noted, ignoring Tomas' most recent argument.

"What makes you say that?" the squire asked also dismissing the irrelevant discussion.

"That's Jade. She's a Sylva from the Wood who Esha thinks may go far. She's the only one that's ever understood any of Esha's explanations of anything. Supposedly she's even in line to take over the Tower once Esha steps down."

Esha again spoke a single word and the woman nodded. Unlike the tradition for wizards, this geomancer carried no staff, instead using both hands to form the complicated gestures that accompanied the words of magic. As the crowd watched, the Earth Mage knelt and picked up a small stone at her feet. Speaking the words of magic, the woman closed her hand over the stone and concentrated, a bright white light emanating from her fist. When the light passed, the words stopped and the earth mage opened her hand. A small butterfly flew out and off, into the sky.

Again, the crowd cheered the magical demonstration as Jade bowed and moved away.

The final applicant, this one a Sylva wearing the red of a Fire Mage, stepped forward. Mary leaned forward and narrowed her eyes. "Someone you know?" he asked.

The maid nodded. "That's Amatria," she replied. "Her tribe lives near Snowholm, where I grew up."

"A friend?"

"Not really. We knew each other, but she was always more interested in learning about magic than anything else. Even the other Sylvai didn't spend much time with her. I don't even think she has any family."

"Sounds lonely," the squire noted.

"It was her choice really," Mary said. "Amatria made little secret of the fact that she's just about the smartest person around. She's really arrogant, even for a Sylva. It kind of put people off."

The wizard Amatria stood before her master without a hint of humility. Esha smiled as she spoke the single word to her. The fire mage knelt on the grass of the parade field, and Tomas stared in shock as she sank her free hand into the earth. Silence pressed in on the crowd for several minutes before finally the Sylva withdrew her hand from the ground lifting a diamond the size of her fist.

This time the crowd nearly went insane with applause, most standing to properly cheer the wizard's skill. The three applicants returned to their previous places, all three before their master for the final test. Without a single command or gesture from Esha, a grey robed mage ran out from behind the stands, carrying three staffs. "Did Esha make those?" Tomas asked.

"It's part of the test," Kyla explained. "Potential archwizards must build their own staff."

As the crowd eagerly looked on, the mage drove each of the staffs at equal points around Esha. Once this was complete, the archmage nodded and the apprentice ran back to the stands. The three applicants put down their own tools and walked forward, surrounding their master and each standing only a few feet from one of the staffs.

"What's going to happen?" Tomas asked.

"It used to be," Rogan explained, "that two applicants would battle with their magic, and whoever won was promoted."

"Esha changed that," Kyla added. "She didn't think it was right to put colleges against each other."

Mary laughed. "So instead, she pits them all against her."

"What?" Tomas demanded.

Rogan leaned forward. "The object is to grab their staff," he said. "All they have to do is get past what Esha throws at them and claim the staff they built."

"That sounds a little unfair," Tomas noted. "Three against one."

"Oh, it's unfair," Mary giggled. "But only because they don't have more people."

Kyla nodded. "It's not a test of power. It's a test of ingenuity. They don't have to beat Esha; they just have to trick her, to get past her."

Tomas nodded, recalling his own, similar lessons.

The Fire Mage, Amatria, hurled a curtain of fire between Esha and her staff, lunging forward with arms outstretched. The Sylva hit something in midair that was not there but nonetheless halted her flight. The flames lifted into the air and surrounded the Water Mage, Xathias, who had been trying to sneak forward while he thought the archmage distracted; the Xeshlin swore for several moments in the jagged language of his people before using his magic to escape. The Earth Mage, Jade, crossed her arms over her chest and sank into the earth; Esha smiled at this and pointed a finger down. An arc of lighting erupted out of her fingertip, burrowing into the ground. With a squeal, the Earth Mage appeared out of the ground, even further from her staff and her long brown hair standing straight out.

The adepts of water and fire pulled back, conferring with each other. Esha stood with arms crossed, waiting for their next attempt. Amatria spoke the words of magic and called from nothingness a large monster, feathered and scaled, with claws and fangs. Her ally, Xathias, gestured to the monster, and a soft yellow light surrounded it, causing it to grow. The enlarged creature lunged towards Esha, hissing its rage. The archmage raised an eyebrow and gestured almost negligently. The flying monster stopped in mid-air, looking very confused. With another absent gesture, the diminutive Sylva sent the creature back whence it came.

Xathias saw this and narrowed his eyes of burning blood. The Xeshlin marched up to his staff and stood there for a moment. He cast another spell. Esha raised a hand to counter her student's attempt, but was distracted when an Uldra appeared, trying to embrace her. As the archmage back-peddled away from the horror before her, the Water Mage snatched his staff and twirled it in the air.

Esha saw this and smiled, banishing the frightening image. She nodded and watched as Xathias' blue robes exploded with golden light which solidified into a golden band that intwined with the blue inseam of his robes. He had passed.

The two remaining wizards saw this and renewed their assaults, both trying every form of attack and misdirection they could conjure. Everything they attempted was blocked or redirected instantly by the seasoned archmage. Finally pushed to desperation, sweating from the exertion and gasping for breath, Jade squarely faced Esha with a sneer. Esha looked back at her with calm indifference, ready for whatever she attempted.

Jade closed her eyes and took a deep breath. She held her staff in front of her and calmly began speaking the words of magic. The air around Esha shimmered, as though hardening into solidity. At first only a vague bubble, the phenomena around the archmage morphed under Jade's direction. It expanded and straightened, forming a perfect sphere. The sphere divided and shifted, becoming a pyramid outside the sphere. The pyramid divided and shifted, becoming a cube outside the pyramid. Again and again the process repeated, with the construct expanding and dividing and shifting into a great variety of spaces. Esha saw this and, with a gesture, shattered the sphere. But the mystical burst did not translate to the pyramid. The archmage destroyed one construct, only to be surrounded by another, in an increasingly-complex prison of myriad shapes. Esha summoned her power and forced her way through the constructs, needing only a moment to escape, but a moment was all Jade needed.

Esha watched as Jade snatched her staff and raised it high, the golden light appearing around her and solidifying into her robe's inseam.

After the second applicant stepped away, Esha resolutely faced the final wizard. Amatria stood near her staff but well out of arm's reach. She stood there staring at her master and thinking as hard as she could. Esha merely returned the stare, occasionally yawning. Seeing this, the Sylva's eyes widened, and she smiled. Speaking very quickly, she cast a spell.

Esha was surprised when a small flower bloomed at her feet. The archmage did not move, but instead glanced down at it, then back up at her student. The Fire Mage just waited.

The tiny Sylva narrowed her eyes, trying to understand. Sweat began to form at the archmage's brow as she threw repeated glances down at the small flower. Esha bit her lower lip. Amatria simply stood and waited.

Finally giving in, the archmage obliterated the flower with a word and a lance of fire, looking up just in time to see her student grab her staff and receive her golden band.

The audience exploded into cheering. All three had been tested, and all three had passed. The archwizards all walked over to the royal booth and bowed, King Cylan nodding in response.

Chapter 39

The demonstration of wizardry was over. The newly-anointed archwizards, their golden bands resplendent in the late-morning sun, proudly walked off the parade field. Dozens of grey-robed apprentices swarmed the area, cleaning up and otherwise repairing any damaged caused by the magical trials. At the same time, several groups of workmen were quickly assembling wood posts and beams as temporary fencing, sectioning off the parade field. As this was done, the entertainers once again plied their trade, delighting sections of the audience stands with feats of acrobatics, comedy, dexterity, and slight-of-hand. The citizens rewarded the performers with gifts of silver and delighted cheers.

"What's next?" Tomas asked.

Mary leaned her head against his shoulder. "Now that the wizards have shown what they can do, it's time for the warriors to do the same."

Rogan stood then. "Damn! Almost forgot!" The knight kissed his wife and left the stands, heading across the parade field at a jog. The knight made for the large collection of tents across the field from the Guard barracks and the royal booth. Tomas spied a grand array of other men-at-arms, squires, blacksmiths, horses, and others in that area, all intent upon some growing tension. The parade field itself was a chaotic swarm of workers, moving, assembling, and preparing.

"What's going on," Tomas asked.

Mary directed his gaze to the line of earthen mounds bordering one end of the parade field. There, workers were attaching large sheets to the line of earthen mounds; upon each sheet was painted a series of concentric rings. "After the wizard tests, there's the grand tournament. First is the archery contest," she then pointed to an opposing section, "and wrestling." The maid nodded towards and outer ring being marked off, bordering the entire parade field. "There's the footraces, and then the burhurt."

"The what?"

Kyla was waving at a food vender. "The melee," she explained. The princess ordered two small bags of almonds dusted with sugar, offering one to Mary and Tomas. "It's after the other events."

"What are the teams?" Tomas asked, savoring the treat.

"Teams?" Mary seemed confused, also nibbling.

"Southern tourneys have teams for their melee," Kyla explained through a mouthful of almonds. "They take prisoners or something."

"Right," Tomas agreed. "Two teams in battle, and they try to capture opposing knights. After the battle, opposing teams have to pay ransom for any captured men."

"Why?" Mary asked.

"Uh… it's like real combat," the squire tried to explain. "In a battle, if a nobleman is captured, his family will pay a ransom for his release."

"Well, that's not how we do it here," the maid replied somewhat scornfully.

"In the Northlands, we don't have a melee," Kyla explained, "we have a burhurt. Every man for himself, no prisoners." The princess shrugged. "That's how wars were fought up here."

Tomas blinked. "People aren't really…?"

Mary and Kyla laughed. "Of course not!" the maid exclaimed. "Blunted weapons. Any man who falls to the ground is out and the others aren't allowed to touch him."

"Oh."

The archers then took the field for their contest. Mary explained the contest to Tomas as they watched. First came the butts: the line of archers took turns firing at the targets on the earthen mounds. The group was separated into pairs, and the best, most accurate of each continued into another volley with a new partner; the less accurate was eliminated. Over a series of volleys, the line of archers was gradually reduced to only four. "Now comes the popinjay," Mary explained. As they watched, a team of three Uldra under the barked instructions of Remm Stonebearer wheeled out a strange contraption of pulleys and ropes. "A thrower," Mary explained. "Something they invented. It takes a clay target and hurls it into the air. The archers take turns trying to hit it mid-air."

"I thought archers shot at birds," Tomas noted, "ones released for the contest."

"Mother put an end to that nonsense," Kyla sniffed.

Tomas looked to Mary. The maid nodded. "The Queen didn't like the idea of shooting at birds just for a contest. She asked Remm to come up with an alternative."

One archer made ready and nodded to the Uldra. Their 'thrower' convulsed and a large white object leapt into the air. The archer aimed and fired, but missed. The next stood ready as the Uldra reset their contraption, before launching another of the clay targets. On it went, with the archers attempting to hit gradually smaller and smaller targets, being eliminated upon a miss until only one remained, a Sylvu. The master archer moved to stand before the royal booth, where the Queen awarded him with a full purse and a golden arrow. The crowd cheered the victor.

"Next?" Tomas asked.

Mary pointed to the opposite end of the field where several rings of sand had been set up. Into these marched groups of large men. "Wrestling," the maid explained. The contest was divided by race, Humans competing with other Humans, Uldra with Uldra, and Sylvai with Sylvai. The nude, oiled males maneuvered and lunged, twisting and pulling, wrapping and throwing. Over several bouts, through a series of eliminations, three champions, one of each race, emerged. They dressed in loincloths and presented themselves to the Queen, who awarded each a purse and small golden statue.

The footraces came next. A series of contestants, competing in groups of four, sprinted around the course bordering the parade field. The winner of each heat advanced to the next race, until the final four competed and a victor emerged. He stood before the Queen and received his purse and his golden prize.

As the runners had competed, workers had again swarmed the parade field. They furiously adjusted the temporary fencing, until the field was divided into quadrants of roughly-equal size. A palpable buzz was growing among the spectators. Although the crowd cheered for the contestants in archery and wrestling and running, a greater anticipation was building for what was to come.

"The... what was it?" Tomas asked.

"The burhurt," Mary repeated. "The melee."

Kyla sighed. "I just love it when Rogan competes." Her smile was heated and her eyes half-closed as she stared out at the field. A light hand ran along the neckline of her dress and her face grew flushed.

Mary nodded. "He is very handsome in his armor," she admitted, her own face gaining a slight blush.

Tomas raised one eyebrow. "How exactly does this 'burhurt' work?"

"It's actually two parts," the maid explained. "The foot battle is first."

"It's an elimination event," Kyla added, somewhat eagerly, leaning forward as four groups of armored men marched out into their respective sections of the parade field. "Two rounds in each field, so eight smaller foot battles. The winner from each gets the honor of competing in the final event tomorrow."

"Another melee?" the squire asked.

"No, a mounted joust," the princess replied. "The winners from each melee then joust each other, two at a time, until there's only one left."

Mary smiled. "And the winner earns the right to challenge last year's champion. One lance, one pass, winner take all."

Tomas grimaced. "Let me guess who's champion."

"Seven years running and still undefeated." Kyla replied dreamily.

"Nobody can beat him? He doesn't participate in the melee or anything?"

Mary shrugged. "Well, he does participate, but it doesn't matter. As champion, he automatically makes it to the joust. The others have to battle for the right to challenge him."

"Nobody's been able to beat my knight yet," the princess added with pride.

"I don't know," the maid objected. "Markgraf Hans is pretty good. Some people say he might beat the Prince this year."

"Where do I know that name from?" the squire asked in a voice deepening with annoyance and something else.

Kyla whispered in his ear. "He's the one you beat up in church. Hans of House Wurst? He's the one who likes Mary."

"Really?" Tomas replied flatly.

Mary nodded. "He's just about the best there is."

"Look," Kyla calmly noted, "here he comes now."

Tomas noted with a sneer that the fop was, indeed, approaching. The nobleman was mounted on a well-groomed horse, wearing red-enameled armor with his family crest engraved onto the breastplate. Hans reached the stands and removed his helmet, letting his long blonde hair flow freely in the light breeze. Looking up into the rows of seated people, the arrogant twit nodded and smiled a perfect smile at the many young women who said his name and waved dreamily at him.

Tomas crossed his arms over his chest, a low growl rumbling in his chest.

Hans lifted his steady gaze, looking up at Mary. "Well, my most lovely lady," he almost sang. "Have I been so blessed that you have come to witness my victory today?"

"Ah, well..." Mary started to say.

"Of course," the nobleman interrupted. "Dare I hope that you would bless me with a smile and a few cheers as I defeat the Prince?"

By now, Tomas was gripping his arms so hard that he should have felt great pain. He did not, however.

"Lord Hans," Mary said, blushing faintly. "I'm afraid that I will be cheering for the Prince again this year. Loyalty to my employer, you understand."

The young squire's head snapped around, noting the blush and the smile on his maid's face. His eyes narrowed dangerously.

Hans laughed a hearty laugh that caused a few of the nearby maidens to swoon. "Worry not, my lady love. No warrior here has the strength to face me. Even should I not hear your cheers, I shall feel them in my heart."

"That's it!" Tomas snapped, jumping to his feet. "You and me, you...!"

"What's this?" the nobleman remarked with obvious amusement. "The shepherd thinks to challenge such a warrior as I?"

"You got that right!" the squire snapped.

"Very well then," Hans replied. "I shall look for you on the field."

Without another word, the richly armored nobleman turned his steed and returned to the gathering warriors, dismounting and turning his well-groomed horse over to a servant.

Tomas turned to Kyla. "How do I enter this thing?" he demanded.

"You can't," the princess replied while smoothing the front of her white dress. "It's too late for anyone to sign up."

"There has to be a way!" he insisted.

"Nope," Mary sniffed. "The only way for someone to enter late is if they can get a warrior of the Keep to vouch for you to the King. And the Prince is too busy."

The squire looked frantically about, desperate for anyone that might vouch for him. With mixed feelings, he finally spotted someone he recognized. The young man almost sat back down, until he spotted Hans blowing a kiss to Mary. Growling in fury, Tomas charged down the stands, absently apologizing to anyone he stepped on in the process. With grim determination, the young man charged up to the only warrior he knew in the Keep who might vouch for him.

Beraht was more than a little drunk. He was so drunk, in fact, he should not have been able to remain seated on his cider barrel. The dirty and disheveled Uldra was seated next to Rashid, laughing uproariously at something and gesturing across the field at nothing. The spymaster was clearly dividing his time between the Uldra and his two children, the twins seeming to make a great game of waiting until their father seemed distracted before trying to sneak off. They were never successful.

"Excuse me, Beraht," Tomas said.

The barbarian looked about with blurred eyes. "What?"

"Beraht, I need some help," Tomas said.

"Hi, Tomas!" Rashid's daughter, Rasha said as her brother attempted escape.

"Say hello to Prince Rogan's squire, Jalad," Rashid said without looking. His son stomped his foot but returned, waving hi and tensing for his next attempt.

"Help with what?" Beraht demanded.

"I want to enter the tournament, but I need a warrior of the Keep to vouch for me."

Rashid looked up with a raised eyebrow, catching his daughter as she tried to duck away. "Why do you want to enter the contest?"

At that moment, Hans strutted up to the wooden rail bordering the parade field. He sneered as he looked Tomas up and down. "So, giving up before we have even begun?" he asked. "I suppose I should have expected such from a peasant."

"I'll be there!" the squire snapped.

"Excellent! We shall compete, then, for the serving wench. To the victor go the spoils."

Flames wrapped around Tomas' soul. "Wench!?!"

The nobleman turned and gestured back at Tomas with his blunted sword. "I'll look forward to satisfying myself with her almost as much as with you."

With his back turned, Hans missed seeing Tomas leap at him. The squire would have choked the life out of the disgusting noble had Beraht not tripped him. The twins laughed delightedly, even pausing in their game for a moment before making their next attempts.

"Let me get this right," Beraht said with something of a slur as he drank from his horn. "You have a serious hate going for that fop who just insulted your girlfriend, so you plan to ruin the good time everyone in the Keep is having just to satisfy your need for revenge?"

Tomas lifted his face from the turf. "Yup."

"You should do it!" Jalad insisted, punching Beraht's arm.

"Yeah!" Rasha agreed, punching the other.

"I'm in." Beraht tossed his helmet on and rose, only needing the most minimal assistance from Rashid and his children to prevent falling. The Uldra lifted Tomas off the ground and led him to the royal booth.

Princess Karen saw their approach and squealed in delight, leaping from the raised platform into Beraht's outstretched arms. "Uncle Beraht!" she yelled, giving the gruff warrior as strong a hug as she could manage.

"Hey, little axe-blunter!" the Uldra laughed, placing an obnoxiously loud kiss on the princess' cheek. "Been causing your old dad any trouble lately?"

"Yup!" she giggled.

"Good." Tuning to the king, Tomas was stunned to see Beraht actually bow. "I got Llamas here..."

"Tomas," Karen corrected.

"Tomas. He wants to compete."

The old king looked at the squire with raised eyebrows. "Are you certain about this, Tomas?" he asked.

A hearty laugh drifted across the parade field. Tomas threw a hateful look back. "I'm sure," he growled at the king.

Following the look, King Cylan nodded. "Ah. Yes, I'd heard about that." He glanced at Queen Nora, who smiled. "Very well, Tomas, you may enter the competition."

"Thank you, sir," the squire turned to leave.

"Oh, and Beraht?" the old king called out.

"Sir?"

King Cylan looked straight at the Uldra. "I would very much appreciate Tomas making a good showing of himself."

"No problem."

"And Beraht. I would also appreciate no great harm coming to Rogan's squire."

"No problem."

"Beraht, please find Aebreanna."

"But..."

"Beraht, please find Aebreanna."

The Uldra grumbled a bit but nodded his compliance. Karen twisted in Beraht's arms. "Can I go too, Daddy?"

The king looked as though he might object, but Queen Nora put her hand on her husband's and smiled. The father sighed. "Very well, you may go. Beraht, I trust you to see to Karen's safety."

Chapter 40

Together, Tomas, Beraht, and Princess Karen
made their way around the parade field to the collection of tents and
pavilions. Tomas rubbed his hands in anticipation. "So, what do we
do first?" he asked.

"We do like the King said," the Uldra replied. "We find
Aebreanna. She'll keep you in one piece through the fight. Now
where's that Sylva witch when I need her?"

Karen stood up on Beraht's shoulders and looked about eagerly.
"There she is!" she pointed off towards where the Sisters of the Lady
of Light had set up refreshment stands.

"What?" Beraht grunted, still looking about. "Where?"

Karen grabbed his head and turned it in the right direction. "Oh,
there she is," he noted.

As the trio approached, Aebreanna had her back to them.
Despite this, the Sylva suddenly stopped her work and straightened,
shuddering, her priestess bells somehow not singing with the
merriment as they typically did with the movement of the Sisters, but
rather intoning a dark, foreboding song. Looking over her shoulder,
the beautiful baroness sighed and shook her head. "Corrupting the
youth of the Keep again, are we, my good Sir Beraht?"

"Hi, Aebreanna!" Karen exclaimed, waving enthusiastically.

"Hello, your Highness," the Sylva replied, curtseying gracefully.
"I see that my lessons in ladylike behavior have taken firm hold."

The princess shrugged, letting her feet slide off Beraht's
shoulder and seating herself primly on the warrior. The Uldra
seemed not to notice her movements. "Oh, that's for ceremonies
and stuff," she replied. "It's just Beraht."

"You would be amazed how often those very words have
preceded some great tragedy."

"Enough talk," Beraht barked. "We need help."

"Yes," Aebreanna murmured. "And in more than one respect."

"The kid here's going to fight. But we need a cleric."

"I am not a cleric."

"Yes, but you know how to keep a fighter going. Look at all the times you've put me back together."

Aebreanna sighed. "The number of instances being nearly enough to make me weep."

"Besides," the Uldra grunted, "the King said you've got to."

"No, he didn't," Tomas argued.

Beraht turned and punched him in the stomach.

Aebreanna rolled her opalescent eyes. "Although I am not the expert on combat that you are, Sir Beraht, I somehow doubt that disabling young Tomas before the contest has even begun would be the best strategy."

"See," the Uldra insisted. "That's why we need you."

"I could not possibly abandon my duties here," she replied primly, gesturing around the nearly-empty concession station and the bored-looking sisters. "We are far too busy."

"Oh, it's alright," one of the sisters said. "We can handle things here."

The baroness leveled her opalescent eyes at the traitorous sister, her expression promising vengeance.

"Please, Aebreanna," Karen asked, looking at the Sylva through large, pearlescent eyes. The princess seemed somehow to appear as though on the verge of tears, her lower lip even quivering just slightly.

Aebreanna sighed. "Oh, very well. Let us assist this young hero in his first battle."

The Sylva helped Tomas to rise from where he had been huddled on the ground from Beraht's punch. The squire tried to voice his thanks, but Aebreanna silenced him. "Concentrate on regaining your breath," she instructed. "You will have great need of it before very much longer, I think."

Considering his complete inability to speak, the squire chose not to argue.

"Alright," Beraht grumbled, rubbing his massive hands together. "Let's get the kid some armor."

The Sylva pointed towards the cluster of tents where the blacksmiths were working. "I will trust in your judgment for that. Go and procure for our young hero some appropriate armor and a weapon."

The Uldra grabbed Tomas roughly and briefly looked him up and down, then forcibly turned him. Beraht then nodded and turned. "Got it," he muttered.

"And, your Highness?" the spy said, addressing Karen.

"Yes?" the girl replied.

"If it would not be an imposition, please ensure that our good Sir Beraht buys armor and not ale."

"You got it, Aebreanna!" she happily exclaimed, urging her Uldra steed towards the blacksmiths.

"You know," Beraht noted primly as they left, "I had no intention of buying ale."

"Really?" the princess asked in concern.

"Of course not. You drink cider and beer at a festival. Ale is for meals. It amazes me how little class that witch has."

Tomas and Aebreanna made their way to the rows of tents set aside for the burhurt fighters. The spy led her charge into an unoccupied one. "Very well then," she said, "strip."

The squire blushed from head to toe. "What!?!"

Aebreanna tossed her thumb towards the padded undergarments the warriors were wearing under their armor. "You would be well advised to don that," she informed him. "This will minimize the damage to your young body."

"Well, shouldn't you leave?" he asked.

"Why? You plan to enter late, therefore time is of the essence." She tilted her head towards the outside, where the clash of steel, the shouts of men, and the cheers of the crowd all merged into a stormy surge. "The first burhurt has already begun and we have much to do. I can have you changed fast enough to be ready once Beraht returns with your equipment."

"I can't change in front of you!" Tomas insisted.

"Oh, for the Goddess' sake!" she snapped. "I have seen nude males before, and from what I have been told you have at least *some* familiarity with the female body. Set aside your meaningless Human sensibilities and change!"

"There is no way I'm taking my clothes off with you in here!" he snapped.

"Would you feel more comfortable if I removed my clothes as well?" she asked, a hand going to the edge of her short red dress.

Aebreanna blinked at how red Tomas became, choking sounds emerging from a throat strangling against Church upbringing. "I propose a compromise," she said softly. "We are in a great hurry, but I will turn my back while you put on the pants. Once you have finished, I will assist you with the rest. Is that alright?"

Tomas nodded, and the spy turned.

Waiting a few moments, Aebreanna noted. "You know, the air *has* grown chilly."

"YOU LOOKED!!!"

With no further observations from the sinful Sylva, Tomas pulled the padded leggings on and grudgingly gave the Baroness permission to turn. With no further objections from the squire, Aebreanna had him dressed in the padded undergarments so fast that, had he blinked, he may very well have missed it. "Did you apprentice as a seamstress?" he asked as she settled the shirt on his shoulders.

"What gave you that idea?"

"Well, you're so good at getting people dressed quickly. I just thought you must have trained in tailoring."

Aebreanna finished her adjustments and put a light hand under the young man's chin. "I am simply doing what I enjoy most in reverse," she purred.

"Enjoy most? But you're just putting clothes on..." Again, that deep red filled the squire's cheeks. "Oh."

Beraht, with Karen still perched on his broad shoulders, burst into the tent. Tomas very nearly jumped out of his skin and made a great show of standing as far away from the sensual baroness as he could without exiting the tent. The Uldra noted the flush on the squire's cheeks, his state of undress, and Aebreanna's wicked smile. "Where'd she touch you?" he demanded.

"What!?! She didn't!! We didn't!!!"

The Sylva sighed. "I believe that was an attempt at Uldra humor," she informed Tomas.

"How can you tell?" he asked.

"I have an unpleasantly detailed knowledge of Uldra culture. I have, after all, been subjected to Sir Beraht for more than a decade."

"I'm sorry."

"I survive, though some days prove more difficult than others."

Again, in a surprisingly brief amount of time, Tomas found himself seated on a stool with Beraht brutally strapping armor onto him. The squire could not help but notice that, while both Uldra and Sylva had the same commendable efficiency with rapid preparations,

Aebreanna's skills were infinitely more pleasant than Beraht's. Each time the young man attempted some objection to the sheer ferocity with which he was man-handled into his gear, the Uldra would bluntly remind him that it was his idea to compete in the first place. As the barbarian yanked on the straps that secured the squire's breastplate, he continued to coach him on the best tactics to use.

"Fight dirty," the Uldra advised. "Don't be afraid to kick a man in the back or swing at his legs."

"Isn't that dishonorable?" Tomas tried to reply. Although he was still learning how to properly wear armor, it was the young man's opinion that he should, at the very least, be able to breathe.

"Ha!" Beraht laughed, or possibly grunted. "Honor is for stories," he spat, cinching the straps even tighter. "Winning is all that matters."

Aebreanna had been watching Beraht torture the squire for several minutes before finally interceding on the young man's behalf. Reaching up and laying a hand lightly on the Uldra's arm, she sighed. "Beraht, although the Uldra constitution is a thing of legend throughout *Ar'ae'el,* you simply must take into allowance the fact that we poor, weaker races of the world require air to survive." She released one of the straps.

With the sudden easing of the pressure around his chest, Tomas was overjoyed to find life-giving air surging into his lungs. He stood there for several moments, drawing deep breaths, and apologizing to God for his lack of proper appreciation for something so simple, yet so wonderful, as breathing.

Beraht shook his head, snarling down at the Sylva. "If you leave his armor that loose, it's not going to stay on straight. He'll get tripped by his own gear!"

"And if it remains as you set it, he will collapse before a single strike finds him," Aebreanna retorted, jutting her chin up at the lumbering Uldra.

"Uh, guys?" Tomas tried to break in but was ignored.

"What would a Sylva witch know about fighting?" Beraht demanded. "All you shiny-eyed pansies know is singing and dancing!"

"Whereas the only contribution the Uldra have made to Lanasian society has been drunken brawling," Aebreanna retorted.

"What's wrong with drunken brawling?"

"Guys," the squire tried again.

Aebreanna put her fists on her hips. "I often wonder what would happen if the gods were to remove every trace of alcohol on *Ar'ae'el*," she snapped. "No doubt the Uldra would wither and die within moments."

"Oh, how original," Beraht snapped. "Call an Uldra a drunk."

"You are drunk!"

"How else could I stand to be around so many mouse-sized sissies?"

"Guys!" Tomas barked.

Karen tugged on his undershirt. The squire glanced down at the princess, who smiled and handed up his helmet. "You might as well give up," she advised him.

"Must you stand so close?" Aebreanna demanded. "Your breath is fouler than a *Xesh'lin* prison."

"Which you never would have gotten out of if not for me!" Beraht pointed out.

"True," she conceded. "Of course, I would never have found myself *in* one had *you* not gotten me there in the first place!"

"GUYS!!!" Tomas roared.

"What!?!" they both snapped.

The squire gestured helplessly out the open tent flap at the gathering crowd of fighters, all moving towards the parade field. Both Sylva and Uldra sneered at each other but turned back to their young charge. "Alright," Beraht grumbled. "Don't forget, cheat. Cheat when you start, cheat when you finish, cheat until you're dead. If you think you've run out of ways to cheat, think harder."

"Observe your opponent," Aebreanna advised as she straightened the squire's armor. "See how he moves and counter." She held the entrance flap a little wider as the others trooped out, letting it fall in Beraht's face.

The towering Uldra bent and exited the tent, growling down at the Sylva and handing Tomas the blunted sword he would carry into the melee. "As soon as you get in there, somebody is going to square off against you. Don't take him; go for the guy behind him."

"And watch behind you for just such a deception," the Sylva added.

With his head spinning and his heart racing, Tomas nodded at each of their comments. The squire looked out and noted the area that he was to battle in. The arena was bordered with a low wooden rail. Most of the fighters were already within their respective groups, swinging their arms, pacing about, and eyeing the competition. Hearing the horn blast that signaled the commencement, he grabbed the shield Karen was trying to hold up, strapped it to his arm, and charged into battle.

"Don't forget to cheat!" Beraht called after him.

Chapter 41

Tomas entered his ring and paused, scanning the surrounding chaos. A mountain of a man, nearly the size of an Uldra with braided blonde hair and wearing chainmail made eye contact with the squire and raised his sword and shield in the traditional challenge. Tomas' eyes flickered past the giant to the smaller man standing behind him with his back turned. Roaring a war cry, the squire ran straight at the blonde giant. The huge man roared his own cry and counter-charged. At the last instant, Tomas ducked the giant's swipe and spun around him, swinging his own weapon at his true target. The squire's attack landed true, smashing into his opponent's head and knocking him out of the battle.

From where they watched outside the brawl, Beraht, Karen, and Aebreanna cheered the young man's victory. "Yes! That's how you do it!" Beraht roared. "Cheat! That's the way!"

Back in the melee, Tomas barely caught the blonde giant's attack with his shield. Pain shot up through the squire's left arm, and he was forced to back up from the huge man's vicious attacks. "Remember!" Beraht called out. "Deflect!"

Tomas heard and acted in the same moment. When the giant swung his blade downward at the squire's head, Tomas caught the attack with his sword, angling it down and away from him. In the same motion, the young man spun around again behind his adversary and swung his blade twice, landing two strong blows on either side of his enemy's back. When the blonde tried to turn and renew his attack, Tomas pushed his shield into the larger man's face and spun behind yet again, this time landing a blow on the giant's head. The young man watched with great satisfaction as yet another opponent went down.

"Watch behind!" Aebreanna called out.

Tomas threw a glance over his shoulder and spotted at the last instant a warrior in splintmail and carrying a longsword charging at him. Tomas pivoted on one heel and drove his right fist into the on-coming face. The fighter was spun clear around and fell. "That's the way!" Beraht roared as Karen squealed in joy, jumping up and down on the Uldra's shoulders.

From the stands, Kyla and Mary watched in rapt fascination as Tomas defeated one foe after another. Seeing her squire battle so ferociously, Mary noted a flush creeping up her face and her hand tracing along the neckline of her dress of its own accord. With each warrior her man sent to the ground, her pulse sped and her breath shortened. Before very long, the maid found herself leaping to her feet with an increasing number of others as Tomas added one victory after another, her cheers a mixture of delighted joy and an almost feral hunger.

After an eternal instant, a horn blast rang through the parade field, signaling the rest period. Each of the remaining fighters retreated to outside their rings to rest and be tended to by friends while the robed clerics of the Harvest Mother quickly retrieved those men unable to walk under their own power.

Tomas nearly collapsed onto the stool Aebreanna brought him. His breath came in gasps as some invisible vice of lead and hate pressed on his chest. Pain was seeping into every part of his body like an insidious venom. His boots were weighted down with half the mud of the forest, the other half being spread across his face and clothes. "I never thought I could hurt so much," he gasped, dropping his sword and shield.

Between the nimble fingers of Karen and Aebreanna, the squire was released from his armor in moments. The wind that suddenly found his sweat-drenched body was like the caress of a beautiful woman.

Beraht poured cold water over Tomas' head and made eye contact with the young fighter. "Alright, you're almost there. Just you and six other guys left."

"And one Sylvu," Karen pointed out.

"Yeah," the Uldra rumbled, looking over at the lean Walker who showed no signs of weariness. He was tall for a Sylvu, with toned muscles that came not from pampered exercise, but from hard living. sylvai tattoos adorned his arms, swirling in glittering silver as though his blood held the stars themselves. His hair was short-cropped, a single lock of black braid at the back of his head held in place with a steel clasp so polished it gleamed in the sunlight like the purest silver. "That's the one to watch for," he said.

"What?" Tomas tried to ask. "But all the others are so damn strong."

"But the Sylvu is quick," Beraht countered. "All those other guys, they're just as tired as you. But look over there." He pointed towards where the dark-skinned Walker was sipping at a flask of wine. The warrior was handsome and tall for a Sylvu. He had a very thin and well-groomed beard and mustache and his green-dyed leather armor bore no signs of damage. "He isn't even breathing hard."

"I must agree with Sir Beraht," Aebreanna said as she massaged oils into the squire's shoulders. "Longshot is the most dangerous of your remaining opponents."

"You know him?" Tomas asked.

"I know of him. He is a disciple of Khaine. Among the Walkers, he is considered great, perhaps the greatest. He has fought many battles and won many victories. He already won the archery contest today, and is favored for the melee. The warrior is good, and he knows it."

"Which is how you get him," Beraht snapped.

"I don't understand," Tomas confessed. When Karen brought him a large cup of water, the squire greedily gulped it down.

"When you go back in there, go right at him," the Uldra explained. "He'll just stand there with that damned superior Sylvu look, waiting for you. Just before you reach sword length, turn away and go after someone else. No matter what, don't engage him."

"I though the whole point was to take him out."

"Longshot will consider you dismissal a slight," Aebreanna said. "Like so many males, his vanity is his great weakness. Ignore him. Treat him as unworthy of your attention."

"It'll drive that shiny-eyed arrow-shooter crazy," Beraht agreed. "Let the other guys take care of the Walker; you ignore him. He'll go nuts and start to slip. If you're lucky, one of the other guys will take him down. If not, he'll get tired from fighting all of them before having to go head-to-head with you."

Aebreanna began strapping the squire's armor back on. "Do not allow Longshot to draw you into combat until you are the last two standing. He will try, again and again, putting his back to the others in trying to engage you. Avoid him, deflect his strikes, and keep moving."

"Don't let yourself get stuck in place," Beraht advised as he strapped the squire's shield back on. "You're the fastest one left of everybody except the Sylvu. Use that. Dance with them. Get them tired. Let them swing their swords and get mad. You just stay cool and play with them. All the fighters left are good, but they all know they're good. If you play with them, they'll get mad and slip."

Tomas nodded and took the helmet Karen held for him. "What about when it's just me and this Longshot guy?"

"You cannot out run him," Aebreanna said, "so do not try."

"He's a fast little tree-lover," Beraht growled. "But you're stronger. Let him do all the running, you just stand still. The Walker will try to fake you, make you think he's coming in one way when he's really coming in another. Use your shield. Take the hit. He can't put much power in one, and it will take a lot of them to put you on the ground. Wait for your opening; you'll know it when you see it."

"Make your one hit count," Aebreanna added. "Do not expect Longshot to allow more than one, so with one you must win."

Beraht grabbed Tomas' face and looked straight into his eyes. "You hit that Sylvu with everything you've got. You hit him beyond the mountains. Put him down with one blow."

Aebreanna mixed a small pinch of green powder into the next cup of water Karen brought. The final horn trumpeted, signaling that combat would resume. Tomas took the drink the Sylva held to him and downed it in one gulp. Tossing the cup aside, the squire took the sword Beraht offered and pounded a fist on the Uldra's massive chest before marching back into battle. The Uldra glanced at Aebreanna. "What did you give him?" he asked.

Aebreanna lightly smiled. "Just a little something for stamina."

On the field, Tomas stopped as an odd feeling began in his stomach. With no warning, fire seemed to lance up through his throat and into his brain. The squire roared in rage as the very essence of hate speared into his mind, and it seemed as though the essence of evil shot from his mouth and nostrils. Tomas shook his head as his vision went red, and then felt that horrible rage fill his entire body. Looking up, the berserker saw his prey and charged.

Beraht noted all this with a clinical detachment. "So," he said to Aebreanna, "you got any more of that?"

The Sylva jiggled a small pouch. "If you behave."

Tomas barreled straight at Longshot, roaring in fury. The wild Sylvu stood steady as Aebreanna and Beraht warned he would. In the last instant, the squire spun past his apparent target and caught a warrior carrying two shortswords by surprise. Beating the poor fighter senseless, Tomas paused not a moment before leaping at another victim, still roaring. Longshot stood several seconds, clearly confused why the squire had not attacked him. Then an expression of outrage twisted his lean face, and the Walker took off in pursuit of Tomas.

The young man paid as little attention as possible to the stalking Sylvu. Every attack the Walker tried to launch at him was met either by his shield or by air as Tomas departed to engage someone else. On and on it went, Tomas battling each of the remaining fighters and ignoring Longshot. The squire did not stand and fight, as nearly all others did, but would instead feint and parry, spin and back-peddle. As a result, his was the final battle still raging on the parade field. All the other fighters, and the audience in the stands, focused on the running battle going on in Tomas' ring.

With great satisfaction, Tomas sent the last of his opponents spinning to the ground, the last but one. Standing there for a moment, the squire spared a glance to the stands. His eyes traveled along all the people of the Keep watching in breathless anticipation of the final battle. His gaze found the one face for which it searched, and saw that those eyes were locked on him. Turning, a renewed purpose filling his body, the young man squared off against Longshot. No challenge or insult was given by either warrior, instead just a single moment of silent respect before they charged.

The Walker darted in, feinting to Tomas' left before twisting his curved saber and striking at the young man's right. The squire just stood there, letting the strike come in before deflecting it at the last second with his blade. The battle-scarred wild Sylvu leapt and flipped in mid-air, clearly expecting pursuit and surprised to find none. Across the stands, the people of the Keep, to include the King and Queen, sat at the edge of their seats.

Longshot narrowed his opalescent eyes and crouched low on the ground. Nearly hissing his spite, the Walker sprinted back in, dancing to the side and swinging his weapon, catching Tomas on the back. Pain shot through the young man, but his legs refused to let him fall. The Sylvu again leapt out of his opponent's range and again was surprised to find no pursuit. Again and again Longshot attacked Tomas, all the while the young man just defended, never pressing a counter-attack. For every three or four attacks the squire would defeat, one would win through as the Walker's incredible agility slipped passed the squire's defenses. The squire could take little more. Longshot's patience was seeming to win out.

Tomas stood in place, fighting to clear his vision and focus on his opponent. His knees were beginning to buckle, and his grip on his weapon weakening. It would end soon, he realized. More and more of the Sylvu's attacks were getting in. Patience, he told himself. An opportunity would come.

And come it did. The squire saw the Walker approaching, clearly meaning to finish the battle with one last blow. It was then Tomas saw it. An opening. Longshot had raised his arms to strike the squire's head with every bit of strength he had left, and that made the archer vulnerable. Raising his sword, Tomas caught Longshot's attack and deflected it, then spun and slammed his shield into the Sylvu's back with terrific force. Stumbling, the Walker was unable to recover in time to stop the squire's strike before it landed. One strike to the head, another to the shoulder, another to the side; one opening and Tomas spent the last of his strength on a flurry of blows across Longshot's entire body.

Without a sound, Longshot fell. Tomas strode up to him, and the Sylvu struggled to rise to his knees. It remained thus for a moment. The squire was ready to make a last strike, but waited. Finally, the Walker dropped his blade and lowered his head, signaling that he yielded.

Mary leapt to her feet, along with everyone in the stands, cheering the new hero. When Tomas raised his sword and shield high, the cheering got even louder. Beraht, Karen, and Aebreanna grabbed the squire's arms, making sure he did not fall during his moment of victory. They gently escorted him back to the tents to tend his wounds.

Entering the maze of tents set up for the participants of the tournament, Tomas made little protest over the help Aebreanna and Beraht provided. Were the truth be told, he was even glad for the assistance of little Princess Karen, so great was his need. Rogan stepped out from behind a row of tents with a smile on his face. "That was some show, kid," he said after crossing his arms over his chest.

The squire shook free of the helping hands of those around him and straightened as much as he could. "Did you see it?" he asked calmly. "I thought you'd be busy with your own fight."

"Yours took longer," the knight replied. "Everybody else finished before you started dancing with Longshot."

"Nice to know the entire city was left waiting on me."

"Are you kidding?" Rogan laughed. "They were on the edge of their seats. I think you put on a better show than they've seen in years. I never thought anyone could force Longshot into a fight the way you did. I have to admit, I'm impressed. Be proud, kid. You won."

Tomas nodded and entered the tent Aebreanna was holding open. Once inside, the squire promptly collapsed. Beraht and Karen dragged his limp form to a cot. Once there, the young man curled into a ball. "He hurt me all over," he sobbed. "I think he broke parts of my body that weren't even there before."

Given his earlier experiences with Uldra efficiency, the squire was relieved beyond words when it was Aebreanna and Karen who stripped him of his armor rather than the rough-handed Beraht. Once free of his metal skin, it was all the young man could do to keep from crawling back into a ball and welcoming Death. The Uldra picked up the various pieces of armor the females had removed and shoved them all in a sack before picking up Tomas' sword and turning to leave.

"I'll handle this stuff," he grumbled as he also picked up Karen, placing the little girl at her typical perch on his shoulder. "I'll also take the little axe-blunter back to her folks. See you all tomorrow."

Karen happily waved goodbye and urged her Uldra steed forward.

With their departure, Aebreanna was left to escort Tomas back to the castle. The Sylva led her young charge at a very slow pace, often stopping when a bench presented itself to give the squire a rest. Not a single glib remark passed through the spy's full lips during the entire trip. Once the two reached Tomas' rooms, Aebreanna spoke briefly with his new maid and helped the squire to his bed. Once the young man was lying down, the spy began massaging his muscles, never letting her hands stray to any inappropriate areas, but still working to relieve the obvious suffering of her young friend.

"Am I interrupting anything?" Mary asked from the bedroom door.

Tomas tried to rise and protest his innocence, but he could not. Aebreanna shook her head at the foolishness of youth. "Do not worry," the spy told Mary. "I have no designs on him. I was, however, trying to relieve his pain."

Compassion flooded through the maid's heart as she saw her squire lying in obvious discomfort. Crossing the room, she knelt beside Tomas and took his hand. "Is there anything I can do?' she asked softly.

The young man smiled through his agony. "Actually," he grunted, "I think I'm starting to feel better already, now that you're here."

Mary lowered her eyes and blushed.

"As sweet as that notion may be," Aebreanna said, "there remains the practical fact that he will be unable to compete tomorrow without treatment."

"What does he need?" Mary asked.

"I have sent his maid to my chambers for a special oil that will loosen his muscles. Once she returns, you must massage the oil into his body."

"I'm not sure I can," she replied. "I know a little, but..."

"Again, worry not. I will instruct you."

Between the two women, they managed to remove Tomas' shirt and expose his chest. Mary tried to concentrate on her work, but could not help letting her eyes linger. Tomas' torso spoke volumes of his training over the past several months; he was muscled and lean in all the right places. The light of the fireplace danced over his hardened flesh even as Mary's fingers slid over his smooth chest and firm stomach. Catching Aebreanna's knowing smile, the maid blushed and looked away.

"There is nothing wrong with appreciating what is yours," the baroness told her.

Once the oil was delivered, the two women went to work in earnest, rubbing the scented medicine into every corner of the squire's torso. Mary quickly picked up the techniques of relieving Tomas' pain and soothing his tense muscles. Within minutes, the Baroness was standing beside her student, giving minor corrections while Mary herself did most, if not all, of the work.

The relief Tomas felt was obvious from his expression. Never once during his treatment did the slightest protest pass his lips at these two beautiful women rubbing their hands over his exposed chest. His normal feelings of self-consciousness were negated by his absolute weariness and gratitude.

"I think I should be retiring now," Aebreanna noted, cleaning her hands on a towel.

"Are we done?" Mary asked, somewhat disappointed.

"I am. You, however, mush finish. Our young hero still needs his lower body worked on. You may keep the oil. I have more." The spy moved to the door and glanced back, casting a knowing glance at Mary. The Sylva nodded and left, leaving orders with the maid that the young couple not be disturbed under any circumstances.

"Can you roll over?" Mary asked softly.

Tomas nodded and worked to reposition on his stomach. The young woman spread more of the oil on his back and worked quietly for some time, massaging it into every muscle before beginning to work her way lower. With fingers that alternated with perfection, the maid applied pressure where needed and tenderness when appropriate, easing the ache out of her young man's body with a skill the belied her lack of experience.

Mary had come to know her Tomas' typical reactions and was properly prepared for his normal self-consciousness. "If you want me to stop, just say so," she said.

"I'd have to be a priest to want you to stop," he replied.

The young woman smiled. "This isn't making you uncomfortable?" she asked.

"Not at all."

"You looked like you wanted to object whenever the Baroness and I were working before."

"That was before," he noted, closing his eyes. "Aebreanna always makes me a little uncomfortable."

"I don't?"

"You make me feel a lot of things, Mary. But never uncomfortable."

The maid fought to control her quickening breath. "Time for the legs," she informed him, loosening Tomas' pants.

Tomas did not reply, but offered he no objection when Mary pulled his leggings free. Starting at his feet, the maid rubbed more of the oil in. Throwing frequent glances up to ensure her young man was still comfortable, Mary began working her hands slowly up his legs. Never once did she bypass a muscle, no matter her desire to get higher faster, taking great care to ease the pain and tension out of every fiber of his being. At one point, the maid found a thick knot in the back of Tomas' right thigh which no amount of oil or massage could relieve. She was finally content to ease the area around the knot and move on, trusting the squire would not need to be on his feet for any great time during the joust tomorrow.

At long last, Mary found herself nearing the area that held the most appeal to her, and yet caused the most hesitation. "You were magnificent today," she breathed, letting her hands work around the muscles surrounding her final objective.

"I was lucky," he mumbled.

"You were good," she insisted. "Today showed just how much you've learned. Since you came here, you've learned swordplay," her hands drifted closer. "You've learned strength." And ever closer. "You've learned endurance and... hand-to-hand combat."

Tomas snored.

Mary's head snapped up. "You didn't," she grumbled. "You did *not* just fall asleep on me *again*." Her hands tightened into fists as rage replaced the prior feelings. Again, her eyes flickered to her goal, but then they flickered to the tight knot of muscles on the back of Tomas' right thigh. A moment of hesitation was swept away as she noticed her "hero" had started to drool on his pillow.

Tomas screamed as a sudden pain lanced from his leg and shot throughout his entire body. Under Mary's gentle hands, the young man had felt all traces of his aches and pains leave his body and a peace had flooded through him. For just a moment he had feared he may fall asleep under her tender caress. That all ended, however, when his lady had hit a spot that brought tears to his eyes.

"My leg!" he screamed, rolling along the bed in agony.

Mary jumped back from the bed and lowered her eyes as tears started to flow from them. "I'm so sorry," she sobbed. "I should never have tried this alone. I'm just not any good at it."

In the silence of his mind, Tomas was forced to agree. Of course, seeing his lady's tears made that opinion impossible to voice. "No, it was just fine. You were great. I think I'm just a little more hurt than I originally thought."

"No, it's me. I just make things worse all the time!" by now her tears of shining sincerity were flowing freely down her face.

The squire limped around the bed and took Mary in his arms. "Nonsense," he said softly. "Just having you here is the best therapy I could need. You voice is all the medicine I could ever want."

"No, I should have let Aebreanna do this; she's the one with the experience."

Tomas held his lady against his chest, running a hand along her hair. "Aebreanna could never do for me what you do," he insisted. "She could never touch me the way you do. She could never touch my heart."

With her face buried against Tomas' chest the way it was, the squire did not notice the somewhat malicious smile that Mary was having trouble hiding. As they stood there, the young man began to grow uncomfortably aware of just how underdressed he currently was.

"Uh, maybe I should put a robe on," he suggested.

Mary broke their embrace and went to the door. "You're right. I shouldn't stay. I might make things worse."

"That's not... wait, I..." She opened the door and left.

Tomas smacked his forehead with the palm of his hand. "Women," he muttered as he followed. Reaching the living room, he called out before Mary could exit. "Mary, wait! I don't want you to go!"

The young woman shook her head. "No, I should leave. You have a joust tomorrow and I would just keep you from your sleep." Mary looked over her shoulder at where Tomas stood in the center of the room. "Perhaps you should put some clothes on," she suggested as she left.

The young man looked down and realized that he was, indeed, still wearing nothing but a thin coating of oil, and his maid was standing in the door to her bedroom staring at him with a raised eyebrow. "Do you require some assistance, my lord?" the matronly woman asked.

The squire snatched a cushion from the nearby couch to cover himself and gathered together what little dignity he still had. "No thank you, Alice," he replied. "But please make sure that I'm up in time to go to the joust tomorrow."

"Of course, my lord."

Without another word, Tomas picked up another cushion to cover his backside and limped with great nobility back to his bedroom for some sleep.

Chapter 42

Beraht entered the tent to find Tomas already dressed, seated on a stool and ready for his armor. Aebreanna was standing in front of him, trying her best to explain the basics of the joust while she examined his injuries from the burhurt the day before. The towering Uldra had a bag over his broad shoulder containing the squire's armor and a box under his arm.

"What's in the box?" Tomas asked.

"I don't know," the Uldra shrugged.

"Then why are you carrying it?"

"Kyla asked me."

"How long ago was that?"

"A couple of hours," the barbarian shrugged, setting down the bag but holding on to the box. Beraht appeared to be uncomfortable and made several attempts to scratch a spot on his back.

"And you've been holding it the whole time?"

"Kyla asked me," he grumbled as though that explained everything.

"Our good Sir Beraht takes his taskings very seriously," Aebreanna noted, "even when he does not understand them. Or perhaps even more so when he lacks understanding."

"How's the kid?" Beraht demanded, still trying to reach the spot on his back.

"Sore," the kid replied.

Beraht grabbed the squire and roughly checked him, twisting limbs and thumping ribs with a finger. "Ah, you're alright," he muttered in disgust. "Don't be such a baby."

"Baby?" Tomas demanded. "I didn't see you out there!"

Fortunately, Aebreanna had been much more meticulous in her examination of Tomas, and much gentler. "Worry not," she smiled. "Your wounds are minor. You should be more than able to joust today. It would appear that your young lady is quite skilled."

"Yeah, mostly anyway," he grumbled, rubbing the back of his leg.

"What's the matter?" Beraht asked. "You pull something?" The Uldra put his back to a tent pole and rubbed viciously against it, seeking some relief from his torture.

"I have no idea."

"Did you perhaps say or do something uncouth?" Aebreanna asked.

"I don't think so," he replied in a worried tone. "I hope not."

"Focus!" the Uldra snapped. "Don't get distracted!"

The Sylva raised an eyebrow at Beraht's comment. "I am somehow reminded of the pot and the kettle," she murmured. "Something about one calling the other black."

"No time for recipes!" Beraht insisted. He abandoned his tent pole and pointed a thick finger at Tomas. "Alright, here's your strategy. You get on the horse; you point your stick..."

"Lance," Aebreanna corrected.

"Whatever. You point it at the other guy, and you make the horse run forward. Just stay on the horse and you're alright."

Both Tomas and Aebreanna looked at the Uldra with flat stares.

"He's serious isn't he?" Tomas asked.

"Sir Beraht is considered a master strategist by his people," Aebreanna replied.

"Wow."

The three turned when Kyla and Karen entered. The sisters wore identical dresses, matching in colors, the detailed embroidery of their aprons and bodices, and even with matching silver circlets in their braided blond hair. The only difference between the two was the bow each had tied around their waists. Kyla's was tied on her right, while Karen's was tied at the small of her back. "Morning!" Kyla said happily.

"I assumed you would be with Rogan just now," Aebreanna said to Kyla, "presenting him his token."

"I had to get Karen her present," the elder daughter of House Calonar replied.

"Present?" Tomas asked.

"It's my birthday!" the younger happily noted.

"Oh. Happy birthday, your Highness," the squire said. "How old are you?"

"Eleven," the little princess replied.

Kyla walked to Beraht, who wordlessly handed the package over. The priestess smiled and leaned up on the tips of her toes, gently pulling the mountain-man down so she could place a kiss his cheek. "Thank you, Beraht," she said. The beautiful princess handed the box to her sister, who tore it open it with glee.

Aebreanna and Beraht worked to dress Tomas in the jousting armor the Uldra had acquired. The squire glanced over and did a double take when he saw Karen draw what appeared to be a black leather whip from the box. The young princess squealed in delight when she saw the small weapon and immediately tested it with an expert snap of the wrist.

"Now don't forget what I told you," Kyla warned.

"I know," her sister replied. "Only use it in self-defense or on the people I love."

"Don't you mean, 'only in self-defense *but never* on the people you love," Tomas corrected.

The confused look both princesses gave him was answer enough. Karen noticed Beraht still trying to scratch the itch on his back, this time with his waraxe, and reached back with her new whip. With a quick flick of her wrist and the snap of her whip, a look of utter bliss appeared on the Uldra's face. "Thanks axe-blunter," he grumbled.

"You're welcome!"

"I don't know how much more of you people I can take," Tomas noted.

"We are an acquired taste," Aebreanna said.

Tomas was on his third attempt to mount Urge when Beraht, at the limit of his limited patience, took charge and grabbed the squire by the back of the neck. The chestnut stallion snorted in surprise when Tomas was unceremoniously dropped onto the saddle. "Quit messing around!" the barbarian snapped. "Your opponent's waiting."

Tomas was surprised when he emerged from his tent to find the stubborn, belligerent warhorse waiting. Beraht had just shrugged. The squire had feared that this sullen mount would refuse to participate from his enjoyment of thwarting his rider, if not his sullen resistance to work. Contrary to Tomas' expectations, though, Urge snorted and pawed at the ground, looking at the other horses with murderous anticipation. His patience with his inexperienced rider, though, was limited.

The squire scrambled desperately to stay on Urge now that he was finally up there. The warhorse kept grumbling and throwing annoyed looks back at him. Tomas ignored these and took the lance Aebreanna offered while working for a minute on how to organize the weapon and the reins. For a moment, it seemed Urge would leave for the joust whether his rider was ready or not, but Karen soothed the sullen animal. Bizarrely, or so Tomas thought, Urge was deferential to the young princess.

"Remember," Aebreanna advised as Beraht indicated how to hold the lance and shield, "concentrate on holding on for the first pass. Your opponent is very nearly as inexperienced as you, so you need not fear his skill. Simply aim the lance as best you can at the center of his chest and keep a firm grip of the horse with your legs."

"Right. Got it. Why am I doing this again?"

"Cause Hans said he wants to do the axe thing to Mary," Beraht replied.

"No, he didn't," Tomas replied. He then blinked. "Wait, what's the 'axe thing?'"

"No time." The Uldra moved out without a backward glance. Urge needed no prodding, but happily followed behind, heedless of his rider's readiness. The parade field had again been reorganized that morning, with the smaller arenas for the various contests of the day before removed. In their place, a long wooden fence had been set up, dividing the parade field in two. Tomas' opponent was already mounted and waiting at the opposite end of the tilt.

Roderick, the Calonar stablemaster, walked out to the center of the field, holding the banner of his sworn House. Once in place, he looked to one end and Tomas' opponent raised his lance, indicating he was ready. Roderick looked to the squire, who also raised his blunted weapon. The banner was raised, and Tomas and his opponent charged. Both Aebreanna and Beraht noted that he held his lance much too low and the inevitable conclusion resulted. Tomas' lance flew unbroken from his grasp as his opponent's own weapon struck him in the center of the breastplate in a shower of wood splinters.

The crowd cheered the pass as the two combatants returned to their corners.

Tomas reached where Aebreanna, Karen, and Beraht stood. He raised the visor of his helmet. "Ouch," he said. Urge snorted and tossed his head, eagerly pawing the earth.

"What in Underworld was that?" Beraht demanded. "I've seen children joust better than that!"

"Hey, it's my first time doing it!" the squire objected. "Rogan never got around to teaching me this!"

"No excuses!" the Uldra grabbed the next lance and held it low, but level. "Like this!" he snapped. "Tuck it under your arm! Don't let the damned point dip so low! Keep it level! As you close, take aim at the center of his chest with the tip. Don't try to look down the lance, aim with your arm. Just before you hit, push forward in the stirrups and brace. He's going to hit you. Accept this. The key is to HIT HIM BACK!!"

"Sounds simple."

"Most of Sir Beraht's methods are very simple," Aebreanna pointed out. "But one cannot dispute their validity. Focus on what he says and act on the advice."

The squire nodded and took the lance, raising it to show he was ready. His opponent did likewise. The banner went up, and they both charged. When the two combatants collided this time, both lances exploded to the delight of the audience. Urge tossed his head in celebration, prancing back to their side. Once Tomas returned to their corner, he raised his visor and laughed through the pain. "I did it!" he exalted.

"That's right, you did," Beraht agreed. "You notice that feeling you've got right now? That's called victory. Feels good, right? You want more, yes? Well, this time you've got to knock him off his horse. You can't just break the lance. You've got to unhorse him!"

"How do I do that? If I didn't know better, I'd say he was glued to that saddle."

"Aim low. Don't hit him in the chest. Hit him lower, just where the breastplate ends. It'll hurt like the Underworld and give him a damn good reason to fall off."

"Isn't that cheating?" Tomas asked.

"Of course it's cheating!!!"

"I don't know," the squire hedged.

"If you mean to defeat Markgraf Hans," Aebreanna pointed out, "you must win here. To win here, you must do as Beraht suggests."

"But how? I don't think I can aim that well."

The Sylva glanced at Beraht. "This is true. He lacks the skill to aim his weapon in such a way.'

The Uldra's face twisted in a look of fierce concentration. So great was his focus it seemed as though the ends of his great, braided beard started to curl upwards. Then an idea dawned on him, and he pulled a horseshoe from the pile of nearby scrap metal. The barbaric blacksmith twisted the shoe in his hands and snapped a piece off one end.

"I never knew Uldra were that strong," Tomas marveled.

"They typically are not," Aebreanna replied. "I have, however, noted that the strength Sir Beraht possesses is often limited only by his understanding of natural laws."

"Huh?"

Karen tugged on the squire's pantleg. "He can do stuff because he doesn't know it's impossible."

"Oh."

By now the Uldra had broken off the very tip of Tomas' next lance and set the piece of iron against it. Reaching for the waraxe that always rested at this side, Beraht used the blunt end of the weapon to nail the piece of lead to the tip of Tomas' lance.

"Is that not a holy relic of your people?" Aebreanna asked.

"It still works as a hammer," the Uldra pointed out. Finishing the work, Beraht handed the modified lance over to Tomas.

"I don't get it," the squire admitted, hefting the lance.

"You don't have to. Just aim like you did before."

Tomas maneuvered his horse into position, and led Beraht and Karen to the side. "You realize," the Sylva mused, "that if you attached the incorrect amount of weight, his lance could do anything from spear the rider in the leg to kill the horse," she pointed out.

"Then it's a good thing I got it right."

"Let us hope so."

The banner went up, and the opponents charged. The two powerful warhorses covered the distance with blinding speed, and the two lances struck. A shower of splinters and wood chips covered the area, and a warrior fell. Tomas reined Urge in and looked back just in time to see his opponent hit the earth. The squire raised his broken lance in victory as the people of the Keep cheered.

"I told you so," Beraht grumbled.

"Yes," Aebreanna conceded. "Once again I am uncertain whether to be impressed or terrified by your uncanny ability to defy the laws of probability with either incredible skill or the dumbest of luck."

"Huh?"

"She said, 'good job, Beraht,'" Karen translated.

"Oh, thanks."

The spy looked at the younger daughter of Calonar. "That is not what I said."

"But it's what you meant."

"I think I'm dead," Tomas groaned as he lay on the small cot in his tent.

"You are not dead," Aebreanna informed him.

"You're right," he gasped, rising to a sitting position. "Death can't hurt this much."

The Sylva continued her examination of her young charge, concern showing clearly on her perfect face. "Your wounds are not serious, merely painful. You have the ability to continue. You need only the will."

"Give me a few days; I'll work on the will."

"You don't have time!" Karen insisted. "The next joust is starting; you need to be at the lists in less than an hour."

Tomas groaned as Aebreanna gently forced him to lie back on the cot. "I don't think I can," he noted. "I can barely move my arms."

"Druug-shit!" Beraht snapped, yanking the squire back into a sitting position. "All you have to do is sit on the damn horse and hold on!"

Aebreanna narrowed her eyes while staring at the Uldra. "Why are you suddenly so insistent that Tomas joust?" she asked. "Maintaining your interest in anything beyond a few seconds typically takes a miracle."

Beraht looked down at the Sylva with wide eyes of shining innocence and sincerity. "What? I can't root for a friend's new square?"

"Squire," Karen corrected.

"Whatever," the Uldra snapped. "Tomas is a friend of Rogan's which makes him a friend of mine. I just don't want to see him back out now and regret it later."

The Sylva stood there, suspicion plain in her opalescent eyes. Finally, "How much did you bet, Beraht?"

"You know, that's just insulting," he sniffed, smoothing the braids of his long, coal-black beard. "Here I am trying to help the kid and..." the Uldra was stopped by Aebreanna's visible scorn. "Fine!" he grumbled. "Five hundred plebeians," he mumbled.

"Five hundred silver pieces?" she demanded. "On a young human who has never jousted? Who has not the slightest idea of *how*? You bet a small fortune on someone barely out of childhood?"

"You know I'm right here," Tomas reminded her.

The spy shook her head. "Sometimes, your insanity is the stuff of legends. So, who will be claiming your money?"

Rashid entered the tent with a grin on his handsome face. "So, I hear Tomas will be dropping out of the joust."

"And just how in Underworld did you hear that?" Beraht demanded.

"I was snooping," he casually replied with a shrug. "That's my job, remember?" The spymaster rubbed his hands together. "So, should we settle now, or did you want to wait until after Rogan wins?"

Aebreanna walked up to her husband with a seductive sway to her hips and a dangerous smile on her delicate-seeming face. "Dear husband," she said, looking up at him with something mysterious and dangerous in her opalescent eyes. "Did you swindle this mentally deficient Uldra out of five hundred plebeians?"

Rashid's grin got even wider. "Yes, I did. Are you proud of me?" The Sylva ran a hand along her lover's chest, letting it dip further and further down. The spymaster's eyes rolled back in pleasure, until Aebreanna clenched her fist. "Do you believe what I feel now is pride?" she asked sweetly.

"No," Rashid sobbed, nearly doubled-over.

"We will discuss this later," she threatened and released. "Wait, where are the children?"

"They're in the royal booth."

"Return to them," the baroness said in an even voice, dripping with malice.

The spymaster wisely departed.

"Remind me to never make you angry," Tomas noted as he lay back down.

Aebreanna turned and looked at the squire, narrowing her opalescent eyes. "I think my dear husband requires a lesson," she mused. "You will assist me, Tomas."

The young man tried to laugh. "I don't see how. I can barely move."

The Sylva smiled, somehow appearing both sweet and menacing. "Worry not, my young charge. I have a plan that will provide you the proper motivation." She gestured to Beraht and the hair-covered mountain-man leaned far down. The Sylva whispered into his cavernous ear and he nodded, leaving. The spy smiled again and left as well.

A short time later, Tomas opened his eyes with surprise as he saw Beraht carrying a struggling Mary into the tent. The barbarian had resorted to the simple expedient of tossing the slight maid over his massive shoulder, ignoring the many punches and kicks Mary lashed out as casually as one ignores drops of rain. "What in Underworld...?" the squire demanded.

The Uldra unceremoniously dropped Mary onto the cot and jabbed a finger in Tomas' direction. "Tell her."

"Uh, well." words failed the young man. "I, uh... well..."

"Oh my God," Mary exclaimed, noting the bruises that covered her squire's chest. "Oh, Tomas. Why are you doing this? Look at yourself."

"Well," he stammered. "When I saw the way you were talking about Rogan fighting yesterday, I just thought that... well..."

Mary smiled at her foolish young man and put a light hand on Tomas' chest. "Is that why you're doing this? Are you just trying to impress me?"

"No," he insisted. "Well, not exactly. I mean... well..."

A hearty laugh startled them both. Standing at the open flap was Markgraf Hans, pride of House Wurst, flanked closely by Aebreanna. "So, what the noble Baroness of Tressalon told me was true. You mean to quit rather than having to face me."

"Face *you*?" Tomas demanded.

Aebreanna entered the tent and poured herself some wine. "Yes, apparently Markgraf Hans won his burhurt yesterday and his joust just now. You would have jousted against Hans next to win the honor of challenging Prince Rogan. Since you plan to withdraw, Hans will automatically advance."

Hans took Mary's wrist and lifted her to her feet, kissing her hand softly. "So, my lovely lady. It would appear that you are in need of a champion. I assure you that I will win out this day in your name."

Tomas leapt out of his cot, his hands going for Hans' throat. He would have caught the arrogant nobleman off-guard had he not again been tripped by Beraht. "Now, now, youngster," the Uldra sagely said. "You attack him, you go to jail."

Mary was trying to dislodge herself from the persistent Hans, but she was having some difficulty. The maid stopped briefly as the Baron whispered something in her ear that brought a deep flush to her face. "I think, my lord, that you should win before making too many promises. Especially of such a... private nature."

"Kill!" Tomas tried to shout. Unfortunately, Beraht had him pinned under a thick Uldra foot.

"Your choice, squirt," the Uldra sighed, absently rubbing his beard. "Jail or joust?"

"Joust," he snarled. Beraht smiled and helped the squire to his feet. "Hans!" he barked.

The nobleman turned to see Tomas throw one of his gauntlets at the nobleman's feet. The hansom Markgraf raised a well-groomed eyebrow at the challenge. Then, kneeling, he took up the gauntlet. "Very well, shepherd. As you apparently need to be reminded of your place, I will gladly be your instructor. I will see you on the field." He then turned to Mary and leered. "And I will see you tonight."

Again, Beraht was forced to hold back the homicidal squire as Hans kissed Mary's hand and left. The maid glanced at the red-faced Tomas and sighed, turning to leave the tent quietly. Before she could exit, though, Karen took her hand. "Could you take me back to my parents?" she asked.

The maid glanced back at Aebreanna. The Sylva nodded. "That would be best, I think."

Chapter 43

Mary sighed as she and Princess Karen made their way back to the royal booth. Karen noticed this and looked up. "What's wrong?"

"It's nothing," the maid replied. "Just... men."

"Oh yeah," the princess nodded. "Men. My sister and Aunt Aebreanna always say that men are nothing but trouble."

"I have to agree."

"But they also say that men can be fun."

Mary nodded. "But there's always a cost."

"What cost?"

"Well, usually we have to be patient while they go off and act like children."

"I don't understand."

"Tomas is only in this joust to try and impress me. He's just jealous of Markgraf Hans."

Karen stopped and rubbed her feet, obviously tired. Mary saw this and guided them to a nearby bench where they sat for a moment. "My sister says she likes it when Rogan does things for her," Karen pointed out.

"Well, that's the Princess," Mary replied.

"You didn't like it when Tomas got into the burhurt for you?" Karen asked.

"He didn't do it for me; he did it because he was jealous."

"I don't think so," the little girl argued. "I think he did it because of Hans."

"The baron?"

"Yup. Anytime that guy touches you, Tomas gets all red, and Beraht has to stand on him."

"Jealousy. It all comes back to jealousy."

"Not the way he talks. He always says stuff like, 'I'll kill him for treating Mary like that.' And, 'if he grabs Mary again I'll...' What do you think he'll do?"

"Something childish."

Karen giggled. "My sister says she thinks it's cute when Rogan gets childish. She says it makes her hot." The princess looked at Mary. "What does that mean?"

The maid cleared her throat for a moment. "Well," she stammered, "that means that she gets... um, happy. And it means she wants to... hug the Prince, a lot."

"Oh. I thought it meant she wanted to have sex. Does Tomas make you hot?"

"Well... uh…"

Karen put her little hands on her hips. "Don't try to lie," she warned. "Us Calonar girls can sense people's emotions, you know."

"It's not that I get hot over Tomas…"

"Then think about him. Think about him wearing that armor and fighting in the burhurt yesterday, just for you."

Mary thought about it, the images of Tomas leaping into battle after battle, defeating everyone around him, all in her name. His muscles rippling with each swing of that sword, his chest heaving as he roared, the sweat glistening off his... "See," Karen said, "you're getting hot."

The maid's eyes snapped open as she realized she was breathing a bit harder. "I am not!" she snapped, blushing furiously.

The princess put a hand against Mary's flaming cheek. "You even feel hot," she insisted.

"If you say so," Karen said in a tone that clearly said she did not believe.

Seeing that the small princess was rested, Mary stood and led her back towards the royal couple. As the two approached the royal booth, Princess Karen broke free of Mary's hand and ran to her mother's side, happily describing her adventure. Baron Rashid Tressalon was sitting, somewhat surly, in the corner with his two children, who were busily playing with one of the Archaeknights. The King rose slowly and walked to the rail. "Hello, Mary. I hope you're enjoying the show so far."

The maid bowed. "Yes, your Majesty. Thank you."

King Cylan looked a bit closer at the young woman. "Are you alright, Mary? You look a little flushed."

"I am not!" she snapped, then stammered an apology.

"Now who's being childish?" Karen pointed out.

The King raised an eyebrow and then smiled. "I see. Perhaps you would like to join us here. The view is much better."

"Oh, I couldn't, your Majesty."

"Nonsense. I insist." The king turned to Sarah, the red-haired Archaeknight. "Sarah, would you find Mary a chair, please?"

The warrior-woman nodded and left, wordlessly returning moments later with a chair and a cushion. Mary stammered her thanks before taking a seat to the King's left. Before long, Kyla arrived, nearly floating on the air with a euphoric smile on her beautiful face. "Where have you been, young lady?" King Cylan asked in mock sternness.

"Just giving Rogan his token," she sighed dreamily. The princess climbed up into the booth and dropped wearily into the next seat Sarah provided.

Mary leaned in and whispered into Kyla's ear. "Would I be wrong in assuming that his Highness was grateful for the gift?"

"You would not," the priestess giggled. "He was *very* grateful."

The two young women shared a laugh together that the King seemed determined not to understand. As they sat, waiting for the next joust to begin, Mary glanced at Kyla. "What happened to your belt?" she asked.

The King tried to rise, receiving the necessary help from Sarah. "I think I could use some refreshment," he said, not wanting to hear the conversation he suspected was imminent.

"Can't someone bring you food, Daddy?" Karen asked.

"That's alright, Karen. I would just assume get it myself." One of the Archaeknights accompanied Sarah in escorting the king to some nearby food vendors.

Kyla noted his departure and shook her head. "Daddy's always so old-fashioned."

"Most fathers are with regards to their daughters, dear," Nora replied, moving into the King's seat to be closer to the two young women. "Don't forget that your father and I were raised in a different time than you."

"I know, it's just... I don't understand. He's always asking when Rogan and I will give him a grandchild."

"It's the way he is," the queen replied. "I wouldn't change him for anything."

"I know what you mean," Kyla replied, her thoughts obviously going back to her own husband.

On the field, Tomas was again struggling to mount an increasingly irritated Urge. "You're not coming down off this thing once I get you back on," Beraht grumbled as he once again dropped the squire atop his steed.

"It wasn't my idea to get such a tall horse," the squire insisted.

Urge snorted.

"Would you perhaps prefer a Sylvai Pony?" Aebreanna suggested.

"Very funny," he grunted. The squire finished settling himself in and grabbed the reigns.

"Remember all we have said," the spy advised him. "Hans is much better than your previous opponent. He will win if you do not do as we advise."

Beraht nodded, moving around the front of the horse. "That's right. Now, he's good but he does..." the Uldra words were cut off by an oath as he tumbled to the ground.

"Drunk again I see," Aebreanna noted dismissively.

Beraht ran a hand along the ground and felt what had tripped him. A very long and thin metal wire had been tied up in front of Tomas' horse. With a sneer, the Uldra looked around and spotted Rashid inconspicuously moving away from the area, unaware his trap had been discovered. "So that's the game, is it?" he muttered, standing and moving away.

"Hans is arrogant." Aebreanna was advising the squire, uncaring of Beraht's departure. "Use that. He will never suspect you have any ability in this contest, certainly not enough to be a threat to him."

"So, on this first lance, I've got the advantage."

"Yes, exaggerate your movements. Let him think you are worse than you are. Let your lance dip low on the first pass as you did on your first joust. Hans will recognize this immediately. He will want to make an example of you and aim for your head, thinking that your lance will not even strike. At the last instant, raise the lance as you lean forward, catching him off-guard. With any luck, your lance will strike a split second before his, and he will miss."

"What if it doesn't?"

"You will take a lance strike to the face. Ensure your visor is down." She patted Urge on the rump, drawing a please squeal from warhorse, who flicked his tail playfully at the baroness. "Best of luck."

Tomas and Hans squared off on either side of the lists, both raising their lances to show they were ready. Beraht walked up to stand beside Aebreanna and watch. "Where have you been?" she demanded.

"Just making sure your husband didn't do anything to give Hans an unfair advantage," he replied.

"Between the two of you, I am uncertain as to who is being the greater child."

Beraht laughed. "We'll find out in about ten seconds."

The banner went up, and the horses leapt forward. Tomas and Hans closed on each other, the squire leveling his lance but letting it drift low as the spy had instructed him. Hans, however, appeared to be having trouble with his weapon. He could not lower his lance. The nobleman tugged again and again at it as though the weapon was caught on something.

Tomas' lance struck Hans squarely in the breastplate. Urge thundered past their enemy, not caring that even after the nobleman had dropped his lance, it continued to drag along the ground behind. They returned to their end of the tilt, Urge once again tossing his head and prancing in victory. "It worked!" he exalted. "He never even lowered his lance!"

"So it would seem," Aebreanna noted, staring hard at Beraht.

The Uldra was not looking at either her or Tomas, however. He was looking down the field at where Rashid was examining Hans' lance. The spymaster found a very thin metal wire that had somehow been tied to the tip of the Markgraf's lance and the back of his armor. Rashid held up the wire and sneered across the field at Beraht who wiggled his fingers back.

"So, what's next?" Tomas asked.

Aebreanna quickly discussed tactics during the pause Hans insisted on to check his armor. The spy made sure Beraht was included in the discussion, grabbing the Uldra each time he tried to slip away. Clearly, though, the Uldra's attention was not on their consultation.

"Ha!" Beraht roared. "Caught you!" He stomped up to a very peaceful and innocent-looking Rashid. The spymaster was calmly petting Urge's neck while the warhorse eyed him suspiciously.

"Why, Beraht, whatever are you talking about?" the spymaster replied amiably.

In response, Beraht grabbed Rashid's other hand and lifted it up, exposing the needle resting in the palm of his hand. "Thought I wouldn't see it, didn't you?"

"I was just going to practice my sewing," he lied.

"ENOUGH!!" Aebreanna roared. "I have had more than my fill of you two immature, self-centered, egoistical, hormonally imbalanced fools! I will *not* allow your foolishness to further impede this young man's competition. Now if I must, I will see the both of you locked in the dungeons for the duration of the Festival. Am I understood?"

"He started it," Beraht insisted.

"I said, AM I UNDERSTOOD!?!"

"Yes ma'am," they both sullenly replied.

"Good." Without another word, the Sylva returned to her conversation with Tomas, whose face wisely remained neutral.

Beraht threw a look of pure mistrust at Rashid and rejoined his teammates, never breaking his eye contact with his adversary. The spymaster continued to pet the horse. Once Hans appeared nearly ready, the trio broke up. Rashid moved over to Aebreanna.

"Was there something you wanted?" she asked coldly. "I believe you are supposed to be watching the children."

He sank to his knees and bowed at her feet. Aebreanna rolled her opalescent eyes. "Your pathetic attempt at humor will not pacify me this time, Rashid," she warned.

The spymaster kissed the tops of her soft-leather half-boots, making his absolute best attempt at groveling. "Stop that!" she snapped.

Rashid rose back to his knees and kissed his wife's hands. "The time for chivalry is past, I think," she said.

He wrapped his arms around her waist and put the side of his face against her stomach. "This will not work," she insisted.

Tomas watched in utter confusion as Rashid alternated between groveling and worshiping Aebreanna, never once speaking a single word. More and more it became obvious the Sylva was desperately trying to remain angry at her husband but was fighting a losing battle to keep an amused smile off her face.

"Why must you always test my patience?" she demanded.

Finally, the spymaster looked up longingly into her opalescent eyes and spoke. "Because you are never more beautiful than when your eyes flash in anger, when you are ready to strike me down."

"Then I must be positively stunning at this point," she snapped.

Rashid rose to his feet and held her in his arms. "Always. You are my heart's desire, my goddess. You are my everything."

"And you are my greatest pain in the..." her somewhat subdued reply was cut off as the spymaster kissed her, leaning her back against Urge and running his hands along her back. Tomas made a great effort not to notice the Sylva's sensuous writhing against his leg, but his warhorse neighed appreciatively.

"Am I forgiven?" he asked his wife.

"You are most certainly not," she replied, savagely biting his lower lip. "Your apology will be long-lasting and most unpleasant." Aebreanna ran her hands along her husband's lean frame. "Tonight, when we have both the time and the privacy such an apology requires. Now, return to the children."

Rashid moved his face to rest just in front of his wife's. "I am yours for as long as you'll have me, my Sylva goddess," he whispered, again passionately kissing her.

"Uh, guys?" Tomas said. "They're ready, and you're leaning against my horse." Urge agreed, clearly eager for another pass.

"Until tonight, my goddess," the spymaster said as he left.

Aebreanna moved to stand beside Beraht, trying to regain her composure as the combatants squared off again. The Uldra looked down at her and shook his head. "I never did get what you saw in him," he admitted.

"Rashid is much more interesting than any other male I have encountered of any race. His schemes and games are such that even an archmage could never hope to follow them. He is never in a situation in which he does not have at least one contingency ready. You, my dear Beraht, only beat him occasionally because you are one of the few beings who does not try to out think my Rashid."

"Yeah, well, I did beat him."

"In point of fact you did not."

"What are you talking about?"

Aebreanna absently nodded towards Tomas' horse. The animal was obviously taking great pains to stay off one leg. "But I stopped him!" Beraht insisted.

"The first time, yes. But while he was kissing me and had me pressed up against the horse, he used a needle to make the animal lame."

"WHAT!?! AND YOU LET HIM!?!"

"I could not very well let you cheat the first time and not allow him to cheat the second, could I?"

"NO!!" Beraht roared as the banner went up.

Urge only managed to cover half the distance he could in previous passes before Hans struck. Because his mount was stumbling as he tried to run, Tomas was unable to keep his lance steady and so was very nearly unhorsed when the nobleman's lance struck him. Once Hans had laughingly returned to his corner, Tomas turned to move Urge back to Beraht and Aebreanna.

In the royal booth, Nora looked archly at her older daughter. "So, just what exactly did happen to your belt?"

"Oh look," the king noted. "I'm out of cider."

"That was the token I gave to Rogan," the princess replied quickly enough to spare her father another retreat. "He wanted something else, but I didn't have anything besides my dress."

"And you didn't give him the dress?" Mary asked with a mirthful grin.

"Well I tired, but Rogan had to get ready for the next joust."

All three women laughed. The king stared intently into his cider mug.

"I've never really understood that whole token thing," Mary confessed.

"It's a common practice in tournaments, dear," Nora replied.

Kyla nodded. "It always means a lot to Rogan to carry something personal of mine into battle. I guess it's supposed to be for luck."

"More than that," the queen argued. "Much more. For men like Rogan and Tomas, and your father, by the way," she noted and smiled at her husband, taking his hand in hers, "the token means so much to our men. For warriors who hold honor as important as our men do, when their lady gives them a token to carry into battle, it allows them to think they're fighting for your honor. Their winning means winning for you, to prove themselves worthy of you."

"Did you ever give Daddy a token?" Karen asked.

"As a matter of fact, I did," Nora replied. "Right before he fought in a tournament Talius Ironheart was holding, I gave him something he carried next to his heart. It must have worked, too, since he won."

"What did you give him?" Kyla asked.

The look the queen gave her daughter was more than a little naughty and brought a flush to the old King's face.

"Mother!" the princess exclaimed.

Nora shrugged. "Never ask a question, Kyla, unless you want it answered."

Mary looked out on the field where the preparations for the final joust between Tomas and Markgraf Hans were nearly continued. His horse was mending, under the care of Aebreanna and Ilse, who had been summoned with a poultice for the animal. "I suppose I should have given Tomas something," Mary sighed.

Kyla stared at the maid. "You mean you didn't!?!" she exclaimed.

"Well, I didn't know..."

"You have to!" the princess rose and lifted Mary up as well. "Hurry, before they start!"

"But..."

Queen Nora nodded. "Trust her, Mary. It would mean everything to Tomas if you gave him something."

"But what do I give him?" the maid asked.

"Something personal," Kyla replied. "Something only you can give him; something he can carry with him."

Mary nodded and left, hurrying back across the field. As Mary hurried over to Tomas, her mind ran through what she should give him. Suddenly it hit her. If it worked for Princess Kyla, it would work for her. He would be a little angry at first, she knew. After all, the maid's belt would not be the sort of token he would put any real value in. He would try to hide his disappointment, but Tomas would get that look on his face of confusion and irritation. It would probably be much like his face when she told him the name of the stuffed dragon she had won after he failed in that silly festival game, that same mixture of confusion and irritation that made his brow furrow.

In fact, he had that same look when he had hit Hans in church. He always did when he thought he was leaping to her rescue. The maid looked up and saw that her squire was again having trouble mounting his horse. He always did have these noble images of himself, Mary thought. They never lasted much past when he did something silly.

That really was the most adorable thing about him, the maid realized. He tried so hard to fit the ideals of the heroes of yesterday, but he never failed to have that same self-abashed look on his face when it never worked out. He wanted so much to be her knight in shining armor, if only he realized that she had not fallen in love with a knight.

Mary came to a complete stop in the middle of the field as that last thought seeped into her mind. Did she just...? Was it possible...? She continued, somewhat in a daze before stopping just next to his horse. The young man had finally, with much help from Sir Beraht, gotten onto his horse. After only a few confused moments, he had managed to turn around in the saddle so that he could face the front of the animal. "Are you alright?" he asked.

The young woman had as odd a look on her face as Tomas could ever remember seeing. She slowly raised her eyes to look into his. It seemed to Mary as though she was looking at her champion for the first time. There he was, her hero, desperately to stay on his horse. The obvious fear in his eyes made his foolish grin all the more endearing. A laugh briefly drew the maid's eyes across the lists to where Markgraf Hans effortlessly mounted his own magnificent horse, his perfect hair flowing in the wind and not the slightest trace of uncertainty clouding his face.

Looking back up at Tomas, Mary realized what she was seeing for the first time. She saw her squire in armor that would have shined if only he had polished off the large mud stain. As Tomas looked down questioningly, the young woman reached behind and untied the white ribbon that her mother told her she would know what to do with. Letting her long hair flow freely about her shoulders, Mary handed the ribbon up to Tomas. "For you," she said breathlessly. "For my champion."

The squire's eyes widened as he took the token. He held the ribbon in his hand as though it was made of spider web. Licking his lips, he looked down at his lady. "I will win in your name!" he cried, holding the ribbon aloft with his eyes shining.

Mary blushed and ran back to the royal booth, tears running freely down her face. Once back in her seat, Mary glanced at Kyla. The princess was looking at her and smiling. The two young women hugged each other and laughed.

Chapter 44

Tomas tied the ribbon around his right hand with great care, making sure to keep it clean and safe. Aebreanna noticed his care. "Does the ribbon hold some significance of which I am unaware?" she asked.

"Mary just gave it to him," Beraht grunted, struggling to fit the squire's foot into a stirrup.

"I see," the Sylva said. "The warrior receives his token. Very sweet, I suppose."

"It used to belong to her mother," Tomas said, his eyes bright.

"Really?" she asked.

"Yeah, I guess it's some kind of tradition in her family. Her grandmother gave it to her grandfather; her mother gave it to her father."

"And now she gave it to you," Aebreanna added, looking past the horse to where Mary sat with Kyla in the royal booth. The Sylva turned her opalescent eyes up to where Tomas sat. "I hope you appreciate the significance of that gift."

The squire nodded. "It means I'm her champion."

The baroness shook her head. "Not only that, it also... never mind. You will learn soon enough." The Sylva turned and roughly grabbed Beraht's beard, yanking it around and down so the Uldra had to look her in the eyes. "Beraht," she said very slowly.

"Hey, watch the beard," he snapped. "Grabbing an Uldra's beard is like grabbing his..." Aebreanna released the beard as though it was on fire.

"Beraht," she said, wiping her hand off on her sleeve, "I want you to listen very carefully. I want Tomas to win this contest. Do you understand? I want him to win, no matter what."

Understanding dawned on the Uldra's brutish face, like a dawn rising over a jagged swamp. Leering as evil a grin as any god of darkness could manifest, the maniacal barbarian growled in pleasure. "You got it," he said,

Before he could leave, Aebreanna stopped him. "No killing," she commanded.

"Aww."

She held a finger up. "I mean it. No blood loss; no violence. Do not attempt anything that you would ordinarily do. In fact, do the exact opposite. Be stealthy; be subtle; be clever."

"Well," the Uldra shrugged, "It sounds risky, but I'll give it a try."

Beraht made his way across the field and picked up a shovel. "No bloodshed!" Aebreanna called out. The Uldra grimaced and tossed the shovel aside. Reaching Hans' horse, the barbarian paused for a moment. The baron dismissed the approaching barbarian, as engrossed as he was in the sight of the ribbon he had seen Mary hand to Tomas. Finally, taking a long drink from a lead flask tied to his belt, Beraht reared back and punched Hans' horse, knocking the poor beast to the ground.

Aebreanna saw this and sighed, shaking her head.

Hans hit the ground cursing and tried to rise. Beraht stepped over the flailing horse. "Hey there!" he said, breathing as hard as he could on the arrogant nobleman. "Hey, let me help."

Hans could not help but inhale a full breath of the horrid stench Beraht emitted. "Dear God, Uldra! What have you been eating?" he demanded.

"Ho ho! How harsh you are. You should be happy I didn't hit harder. Here let me help you."

As the arrogant nobleman rose, he began swaying. He clearly had trouble standing, and his arms flailed about, in search of something to steady himself. His servants rushed to his aid, struggling against the weight of his armor to keep him on his feet. Beraht turned to leave, pausing only briefly to breathe heavily on the horse. The animal let out a squeal and collapsed, twitching horribly.

Aebreanna stood glaring at the Uldra. "I suppose you think that was clever?" she demanded.

"For me?" Beraht replied. "That was a stroke of genius." He fell.

Tomas stared at his Uldra friend. "Is he going to be alright?" he asked.

"Define alright," the Sylva muttered. "You have more important things to worry about," she said, stepping over the happily-humming barbarian. "Hans is getting on his horse. Goddess knows how, but he is doing it. When you charge, remember you get only one more pass. Two of you will ride out, but only one can return victorious. Concentrate on staying in your saddle. When he hits you, it will hurt like nothing you can imagine, but you must hang on. Aim your lance for the head of the horse."

"My horse?" Urge looked back in concern.

"NOT YOUR HORSE YOU...!!!" Aebreanna paused for a moment, breathing deeply with eyes closed. "Aim for the head of *his* horse. The instant before you hit, close your eyes, brace yourself in the stirrups, and raise the lance. The weapon will impact, and the upward momentum will drive him from his saddle. Questions?"

Roderick walked out to the center of the lists with the House Calonar banner. Hans had managed to remount his horse and now sat, somewhat unsteadily, waiting for the signal to charge and shaking his head to try and clear his vision. "Remember," Aebreanna said, "if you lose, he will ravish Mary nightly as an animal would. Picture in your mind what that would look like."

"I don't think I could," Tomas admitted.

"Allow me to assist." She pulled Tomas low, rising to the tips of her toes and whispering in his ear.

"No," the squire said. "There's no chance. How? With a *what*?! Is that legal? Do legs bend that far? That SON OF A...!!!" He straightened and slammed down his visor. He snatched the lance from a waiting page and raised it high, murder in his heart.

The banner went up, and both men charged, roaring in fury. In the stands, Mary wanted more than anything to look away, fearing the worst for her Tomas, but she was unable. Urge thundered across the field, turning up earth and snorting his rage. All traces of fear left Tomas' heart as his enemy finally drew within reach.

Time stopped. Just as the tips of the two lances passed one another and Tomas could make out Hans' eyes, the world froze. Aebreanna's advice rang in the squire's head. He rose in his stirrups, bracing his legs and raising his lance to target Hans's black heart. Then, without warning, time resumed.

The collision was incredible. Splintered wood flew everywhere, and the world turned white. Awareness returned to the squire, and he looked about in confusion. He realized he was still mounted. Hans, on the other hand, now lay on his back in the dirt.

Tomas looked at the stub of wood that had been until very recently a lance and noted the white ribbon flowing freely from his wrist. Looking out at the crowd, he raised that lance high, bringing a cheer to the throat of every citizen. Urge reared and thrashed his front legs, neighing in a victory cry that rivaled his rider's. In the royal booth, Mary nearly went insane with cheer, screaming her joy, sobbing in relief, and embracing Princess Kyla. Even the King and Queen applauded, though he lacked the strength to rise.

Aebreanna and Beraht joined Tomas and held him steady in his saddle. "Are you alright?" the Sylva asked.

The squire chuckled. "Define alright," he said with pained breath.

She smiled. "Well enough for one last encounter?"

"I have to do this again?" he asked in exasperation.

The beautiful spy nodded back to the opposite side of the field where Tomas had begun. Rogan was moving towards Stick and a lance was being brought forward. The squire saw this and hung his head. "You have got to be kidding."

"Tradition," she explained. "You have proven that you are worthy of facing the champion."

"I'm exhausted!" he cried. "How in Underworld am I supposed to take him on!?!"

"Tomas!" Mary cried, running up to him with tears shining in her eyes. The maid looked up with something akin to adoration. "You were magnificent!" She hugged his leg and kissed his hand. "I couldn't believe how incredible you were! Go get him!" She danced away, bouncing in joy.

Beraht looked at the squire and noticed the silly grin on his face. "So, how're you felling?"

"Pretty good."

Aebreanna shook her head. "Nevertheless, I must insist the clerics tend to him before his final joust. We must give him every opportunity for victory." She waved Ilse over, who took charge of Urge. The warhorse happily went with the young priestess, playfully butting his head against her as they walked.

The Sylva helped Tomas toward where the clergy of the Harvest Mother waited to use their magic to renew his strength. Although this was technically a violation of their oaths, the priests and priestesses assumed their goddess would be alright with it since the Harvest Festival was Her holy time.

Beraht looked around as the Harvest clerics applied their magic to Tomas. "What should I do?" he demanded.

"Make yourself useful for once," Aebreanna retorted without looking back.

The Uldra stood for a moment before an idea penetrated his mind. Grinning that same incredibly evil grin, Beraht went off in search of supplies.

Tomas and Aebreanna returned later, once the squire had been restored by the holy magic of the Harvest Mother. They found Beraht standing by Urge, who had similarly benefitted from Ilse's healing, smiling and whistling a bright tune. "Oh no," the Sylva gasped.

"What?" the squire asked. "He looks happy."

"Exactly." She stood before the innocent-seeming barbarian, glaring up at him with fists on her hips. "What did you do?"

The Uldra just shrugged, making sure not to make eye contact with the fuming Sylva.

"Damn you to the lowest pits of Underworld, Beraht," Aebreanna snapped. "What in the name of the Lady of Light have you done?"

"The kid needs to hurry," Beraht replied with an innocent look that would have worked had anyone else in the world used it. "He'd better mount up."

Tomas moved to climb onto Urge, who nearly trembled in anticipation, eyeing Stick and sounding as though he were muttering. Before the squire could mount, though, Aebreanna stopped him. She stood, staring up at Beraht. Finally, Tomas pushed past her and tried to mount, once again needing the Uldra to pick him up. Once safely in the saddle, he felt something odd. "What's the matter?" Aebreanna asked suspiciously.

"I don't know," he replied. "I feel strange."

"Strange how?"

"No time for that," Beraht said slapping the horse.

Once Tomas was set, Aebreanna noticed the squire shifting uncomfortably. The Sylva stared at her young charge, narrowing her opalescent eyes. "What did you do to that saddle?" she demanded of her brutish companion.

Beraht shook his head. "You know, it really hurts that you don't trust me." He absently kicked a small, empty bucket into a large pile of scrap armor.

"What was in that bucket?"

"Nothing, don't worry about it."

The Sylva's eyes narrowed in thought, then widened and darted back to Tomas. "Oh, Goddess!"

Roderick stepped onto the field one last time. "Ladies and gentlemen of the Northern Keep!" he roared in a voice that probably carried all the way back to Pelsemoria. "I give you our tournament champion, Prince Rogan!"

The crowd cheered as the knight awkwardly waved a hand.

"Ladies and gentlemen, I give you the challenger. Squire and apprentice to the Prince, Tomas Fidelis of Pelsemoria!"

The crowd cheered just as passionately for their new hero.

"As prize for the victor of this contest, the winner will receive, as is traditional for the joust, a kiss from the noble lady of his choice, which will most likely be the same lady it is every year, Princess Kyla!"

Kyla jumped out of her seat and waved to the crowd, bouncing in joy. The princess did not retake her seat until first blowing her husband a kiss.

"Champion," Roland said, gesturing to the prince, "Challenger," this to Tomas. "Prepare yourselves. Once lance, once pass, one victor!" With that, Roland was brought the House banner that would signal both combatants to charge.

The stablemaster stood there, letting the tense excitement build through the audience. Tomas still shifted in his saddle, uncertain what was causing this strange feeling in him. Throwing off the sensation, the squire set himself and signaled ready. Across the field, Rogan also signaled. Roderick paused, looking out to the crowd. In this one moment, both Tomas and Rogan did not see each other; all they saw was an enemy. Neither warrior looked at the banner; they stared at one another to the exclusion of everything else.

The banner of House Calonar went up, and the warhorses charged. Again, Tomas and Urge flew across the field, feeling the same rush of excitement as he closed the gap between him and his target. As one, the people in the stands leaned forward, holding their breaths for the impact.

Time stopped. The world paused for Tomas, letting him set himself and raise his lance. In the instant both lances exploded into wooden fragments, both knight and squire's eyes widened as they sensed Uldra foul play. Many in the audience flinched at the impact, then quickly looked back to see two shattered lances flying into pieces that flew across the entire field.

A gasp ran across the stands. Rogan flew off Stick's back, hitting the ground and rolling, cursing the entire trip. Tomas, though leaning far back in the saddle and appearing to be on the verge of falling, remained mounted. Both Aebreanna and Beraht sprinted on to the field to help their friends.

The reality of what they saw hit the people of the Keep, and all at once they cheered and cried as though their hearts would burst.

Unknown to all but a very select few, at that moment, Tomas Fidelis, the newest hero of the Northern Keep, wanted nothing more than to fall out of his saddle, but he found to his great surprise and dismay that he could not. He kept trying to fall, but for some reason he remained firmly in his saddle. Seeing this, Aebreanna slapped Beraht in the thigh. "You glued him to the saddle!" she accused in absolute disgust.

"What makes you think I did it?" Beraht insisted, looking down at her and holding the limp Tomas somewhat erect.

"Who else would so something so unbelievably stupid!?!"

"Maybe it was a miracle."

"The only miracle here is that your brain actually generated enough clear thought to do this!"

"You know, you really don't have to be so insulting."

"How are we supposed to get him down?" Aebreanna demanded.

Beraht shrugged and let Tomas go, reaching down and releasing the saddle's buckle. Tomas and the saddle fell to the ground with a surprised yelp. "See, nothing easier."

"Except for the minor problem of a saddle attached to his backside!"

"Again, nothing easier," Beraht grabbed the saddle with one hand and Tomas with the other and pulled them apart.

The squire bit his lip to keep from screaming. Only a small whimper escaped his mouth. Despite this, tears fell freely from his eyes. Aebreanna put a hand lightly on the young man's shoulder. "Are you alright?"

"No," he whimpered. "He... that... I..."

"I know; believe me, I know. The Goddess alone knows how well I know."

"But the pain. Oh, God, the pain."

"Something you must acclimate yourself to if you plan to associate at all with an Uldra, I am sorry to say."

"How's Rogan?" Beraht asked.

"Rogan's fine," the knight growled. All three noted with some surprise, all three with the exception of Beraht, that is, that Rogan was still in his saddle seated on the ground. The knight was currently looking at the saddle strap that had obviously been cut. Holding this up, he looked accusingly at the Uldra.

"Oh, I suppose you're going to blame me for that," Beraht demanded.

"You're still holding the knife!" Rogan bellowed.

Seeing this was true, the Uldra tossed the evidence away. "Doesn't prove anything," he insisted.

"Beraht..." the knight descended to a series of the worst curses he could think of while trying to free himself from the stirrups.

"You damned, deformed, despicable, umbral of an Uldra!" As a counter-point to Rogan's cursing, this newest diatribe came from a very red-faced Rashid.

"Where's my money?" Beraht demanded.

"You cheated!"

Beraht held up a small rock. "So did you! A rock in the hoof? Is that the best you could think of?"

The spymaster huffed a bit. "Well, it would have worked with anyone else."

"Then you should have bet anyone else."

"Yeah well, glue on the saddle? What's that?"

"You're just jealous you didn't think of it!"

"Well... yes."

"Ha!" the Uldra spat, throwing away the stone. "Pay!" he barked.

Rashid handed over the large purse, muttering several vile curses.

"Tomas," Aebreanna said gently. "Are you well enough to be presented to the King?"

The squire nodded. "I think I'll manage, but I need a new pair of pants."

"I think we both do, kid," Rogan grumbled, noting his own disheveled state. The knight walked unsteadily and led his limping squire off to the tents. "Tell the King we'll be there in a minute," he said over his shoulder as they limped to the waiting Ilse.

Having quickly cleaned and dressed in his festival clothes and benefitted from Ilse's healing, Tomas now stood several paces before the King and Queen, behind and to the side of his knight. Rogan bowed to the royal couple and moved aside, letting Tomas step forward. With the aid of the Archaeknight, Sarah, King Cylan descended the steps to stand level with the squire. "Tomas," he said softly but in a voice that no one had to strain to hear, "you have proven yourself to the people of the Northern Keep." The crowd cheered as the king ceremoniously placed a crown of gold, fashioned into laurels, onto Tomas' head. "However," King Cylan continued, "it seems to my wife and me that, since you have clearly proven yourself worthy of being the squire to my son, you need more than some ornament as your prize." Turning back, he gestured to the Queen. She stepped down, holding in her hands Steelheart, the traditional sword of House Calonar. "Tomas," King Cylan said once his wife stood at his side, "I have already told you the history of this weapon. It has served three men of my family, and all of them have brought honor to it. Now, the time has come for a new hero of the people to claim it. I ask that you honor my family and my House by carrying the sword of my sons as you journey forth to whatever adventures await you." Queen Nora raised the weapon in both hands towards Tomas.

The young man stared at the simple black hilt, looking past the perfect blade to the family he had once despised with every fiber of his being. He stared at the man he had once called the Black Duke. With more pride than he thought his heart could contain, Tomas accepted Steelheart, the sword of House Calonar. He drew the weapon and raised it high, the flawless blade shining in the afternoon sun as though it were a pillar of fire. The people of the Northern Keep roared their approval of their newest champion.

This done, the squire sheathed his blade, attaching it to his belt and bowing to his king and queen.

King Cylan put a hand on the young man's shoulder and smiled. Stepping back, the old man again let his voice carry to the crowd. "I believe the new hero of the people has one last prize to claim." He and Queen Nora stepped aside.

With a sultry smile and a dangerous sway to her hips, the delectable Princess Kyla advanced on the shaking squire from the royal booth. As she approached, Tomas tried to brace himself against the magic the Sister Superior of the Lady of Light possessed, remembering how it had always affected him. But then, as she drew nearer, the young man noticed an odd thing. Her power washed over him, there could be no question of that, but it seemed lesser somehow. Tomas looked at the princess and saw the same flawless beauty, the same perfect figure, but somehow, wanted more. In his heart, Tomas saw the princess become somehow more common, and yet, more beautiful. As he rubbed his fingers together nervously, he felt the soft fabric of the white ribbon. Looking down, his eyes slid over the soft curves and gentle beauty he now held. Holding that ribbon, Tomas could suddenly appreciate the soft humor, gentle voice, and fiery spirit that had claimed his heart.

In surprise, the young man looked up just as Kyla was rising on her toes to give him a kiss. Without warning, Tomas stepped back, away from the fantasy of so many men. "Forgive me, your Highness," he said while bowing. "But I believe the tradition is that I receive a kiss from the lady of my choice."

King Cylan stepped forward with a confused look on his face. "Well, that is true, Tomas. Of course, every year the winner has asked for..."

The squire turned to his king. "I could never ask for a kiss from the wife of the knight I serve" he declared. "Besides, there is another lady my heart yearns for." He leaned down a bit then and whispered to Kyla, "No offense."

"None taken," she whispered back and walked over to stand next to Rogan.

Tomas turned back, then, to look up at the royal booth where he knew Mary was waiting. Always before, the young man could not help but let his eyes roam across the maid's beautiful body. This time, however, his eyes remained locked with hers. As he climbed the steps leading to his lady, never once did their gaze wander.

Standing there, with the whole of the Northern Keep looking on, Tomas and Mary stood only a breath apart, staring into each other's eyes and awash in the emotions neither tried to fight. The squire ran a light hand along the side of his lady's face, reveling in its smooth perfection. The maid put a hand lightly on her champion's chest, feeling the heartbeat that perfectly matched her own. The two moved their faces closer together, drawing in one other's breath, silently praying they would never be forced to live without each other.

They kissed. With every citizen of the Northern Keep looking on, cheering the couple as they had cheered the victory, Tomas and Mary shared that first real kiss, not of passion or lust or desire. They kissed that first real kiss that held all the promise of a future together. They kissed and held each other and let the world do whatever it wished, for in that entire world, they had found each other.

Chapter 45

In the morning, Tomas woke to find his Mary gone. They had returned to his rooms, intending to finally consummate their relationship, but the squire's injuries made that impossible. The magic of the Harvest Mother wore off by the time they reached the castle doors, and the champion promptly collapsed in near-agony. Mary had helped him upstairs and to the bath, gasping at the revelation of the maze of bruises upon his flesh. She had worked long into the night, massaging oils into his chest and shoulders. Tomas did not even remember falling asleep, only that the night had ended with them in bed, holding each other close.

A knock at the door brought the limping, nearly-immobile Tomas to his door, grumbling at the holiday for having excused his new maid from her duties. Tomas was both shocked and completely unsurprised at the sight of his grinning knight standing in the door.

"How you feeling, kid?" Rogan asked in mock sympathy. "Little sore?"

Tomas looked his knight up and down. The heroic prince stood tall and casually, one foot jauntily cocked to the side and his hands on his hips. He showed no discomfort at Fang belted to his waist, nor of the long tunic and trousers wrapped around his body. Tomas, however, could barely tolerate the horrid weight of his dressing robe.

"Why aren't you dead?" the squire bitterly asked his knight.

In response, Rogan jerked his head to the side. Tomas looked, and saw Ilse. "Need a little magic touch?" the knight asked.

Tomas only sobbed gently and nodded. With a tender hand, Ilse guided him to a feinting couch in his living room. "You will need to strip," she advised. "I can leave or…" The soft-spoken priestess could not finish her sentence before Tomas, his pain far outpacing his modesty, wordlessly dropped the robe and collapsed to the couch.

Some time passed, though how much the squire could not tell. With Rogan's help, Ilse turned Tomas onto his stomach. She breathed deeply and recited soft prayers while slowly moving her gentle hands along the squire's body. The pain floated away. Muscles that tore and cursed and burned relented, smoothed down by the irresistible magic from the priestess. Bruises, cuts, and scabs fell away in the warm radiance of her faith. Time passed, and Tomas was healed.

The squire made inarticulate noises of relief and joy, unwilling to lift his head. Ilse leaned in. "I'm sorry, what?" she asked.

"He said," Rogan translated, "thanks, Ilse."

The priestess patted her patient on the now un-bruised shoulder. "You are very welcome." As relieved as he was to be freed from his pain, Tomas could not be sure, but he thought for a passing moment he noticed Ilse's eyes drifting where they should not have.

Rogan let his squire sit for a little while, helping himself to some cider before finally clearing his throat. "Uh… don't forget there's a little performance we're supposed to attend."

Tomas leapt to his feet. "Shit!" He moved towards the door.

"Might want to put on some pants, first."

"Or…" Ilse countered.

Although this was the last day of the Harvest Festival, still excitement and joy filled the streets of the Northern Keep. Neighbors heartily greeted each other, offering good tidings as they passed. Colorful ribbons and banners swayed gaily in the streets. The new Uldra gaslamps, installed only that summer, burned brightly. From each hung wreaths of sage and lilac, chrysanthemum and crocus. Their color and scent blended together with the treats of street vendors and kitchens, and the laughter of children and adults alike, to lifts the spirits of the entire Northlands in defiance of the imminent winter.

The two warriors made their way through the celebrating crowds at as fast a pace as they could manage. The festival was still in full force in the Northern Keep, and would remain so long into this final autumn night. The people of the city had waited all year for what was, for them, the greatest holiday of their lives. Gifts were exchanged and meals prepared. Everywhere, the apprentice-mages put on small shows of magic and slight-of hand for the delight of the children. Bards from all over the Northlands sang the songs of harvest and family, and telling the most thrilling stories from throughout the history of Arayel. Games of chance were played by all, and every instrument of string and wind was played this day to give the air of the city a joyful din.

There had been festivals and holidays in Pelsemoria. The old Emperor had made a point of having as many holidays in his capital as possible. Though his childhood home had long seemed to the young man to have been the pinnacle of Human society and culture, a realization dawned upon the squire as he followed his knight towards the temple of the Lady of Light. The people of Pelsemoria had always treated their holidays with a kind of pleased indifference. The citizens of the Northlands, Tomas now realized, held more joy for this one celebration than Tomas could remember seeing in any of the people of the capital.

The answer to this paradox struck Tomas like lightning. He noticed a bard, singing of the great joy in harvesting apples. Such a man and such a song would draw only scorn from the wealth and prosperous citizens of Pelsemoria. Here, his crowd praised him and offered what meager coins they could spare. As they walked towards the Temple of the Lady of Light, Tomas spied a house's open window; therein, a father gave his daughter a single present, a doll made of yarn. A Pelsemorian child would toss aside such a meager gift, hungry for more. In another home they passed, the family was gathered around a table, offering a prayer of thanksgiving before their holiday feast. In the capital, a noble family would be outraged at having so little, let alone being expected to offer thanks for it.

Where have I found myself, Tomas questioned as he and his knight made their way to the temple. To what strange place have I come where status and wealth mean so little compared to selfless generosity?

"Problems, kid?" Rogan asked.

"No," his squire replied. "Not really. I was just noticing how different things are between here and back home."

"Different people have different ways in different times, kid," the knight told him. "What may have worked in the capital may not work up here in the Northlands."

"It's not that. It's more that you people seemed to put a lot more joy into your celebrations."

"We don't have the time to have as many up here. Down in Pelsemoria, you people could have festivals every few weeks. Games ran all the time, and the only wars you knew of were hundreds of miles away, maybe thousands. Up here, our lives aren't as comfortable. We don't have the option of throwing a party any time some bad news comes our way. Here, we have to deal with our problems, rather than trying to ignore them or make someone else solve them. Here, we can only have a few celebrations in the year. Here, they mean a lot more."

Tomas dodged between two Sylvai who were lifting a banner up above the street. The squire looked back and noticed that Rogan was starting to have trouble keeping his pace and continuing their conversation. The young man slowed just a bit to let his knight keep up. "You people have the Ulheim Mountains to the west, warlords and bandits to the south, the Gunrsvein to the north, and wild Sylvai all around you. How can you be so happy about something as simple as a harvest?"

Rogan dodged past an Uldra carrying a large stack of crates. "Simple," he replied. "It's *because* of all that the people are so happy. We've made it through another year. Life isn't as safe up here as it was down south. Here, we believe in living life for all it's worth."

The two finally entered the front courtyard to the temple of the Lady of Light. Again, Tomas was impressed by the marble columns and broad steps surrounding the holy place. There was an enormous stage in the courtyard before the temple, with hundreds of townsfolk pressed in to view the upcoming show. "So what are they going to do?" Tomas asked as they fought their way to the front of the crowd. Despite Rogan's status as prince, few of the people, if any, made way for him. The performances of the Sisters were the subject of many stories, depending on the storyteller. They were either a graceful expression of life and service, or a debaucherous exhibition of wanton sin.

"They dance," the knight shrugged. "There's some kind of deeper meaning to all of it, but don't expect me to explain it. I've never understood half of what they do."

"And your wife is Sister Superior?"

"Hey, just because I'm around it doesn't mean I understand it."

The two warriors finally pushed their way to the front of the crowd, standing just feet from the front of the stage. Tomas laughed and shook his head. "Hasn't Kyla ever tried to explain any of it to you?"

"Many times," he confessed. "Many, *many* times. But I've never placed a lot of value in ceremony. Personally, I think if you have something you want to say, just say it. All this 'symbolism' that surrounds most religions... you can have it."

"Not a religious bone in your body, is there?" the squire asked.

"Never had much use for it. Don't get me wrong. I think religion is a good thing. If someone has a spiritual problem, there's no place better to work things out."

"You've never had a spiritual problem?"

"Men like us, kid, we've got two options. Either we dedicate ourselves to a single ideal, be it religion, philosophy, or a country or leader, or we lose all sense of morality and just become stone cold killers."

"So, which did you pick?" the young man asked whimsically.

The knight shook his head. "I didn't for a long time. I've tried fighting for God and country and philosophy. I've tried just wandering and trying to fight the good fight. But it wasn't until I came here that I finally found something that was worth fighting for."

"House Calonar?"

Rogan shook his head and gestured around the plaza to all the people happily chatting with each other in eager anticipation of the celebration to come. Tomas knew what he meant. More than any banner or ideal, it was the people of the Northern Keep who were worth fighting for.

While looking about the city center, Tomas noticed a familiar face. "Beraht's here."

Rogan nodded. "Figured he would be."

"Why?"

"Got a reason for seeing this show," the knight noted in a tone the spoke plainly that they were approaching a private subject.

"You know," Tomas said to change the subject. "Someday one of you is going to have to explain that headband; it doesn't exactly go with the rest of his outfit."

Rogan looked and noted that Beraht was indeed once again wearing the deep purple headband with the red embroidery around his temple. The barbarian stood in the far back of the milling crowd, easily seeing over top of the shorter Humans, and ignoring any hails. Instead, he stared hard at the improvised stage. His helmet rested in his hands and his beard showed signs of extensive care. His broad, ugly face was soft, empty of its usual savagery.

"One day *he* will when he's good and ready. Beraht's not the type to talk a lot about his personal life."

If the knight had more to say, Tomas was not listening. A hush fell over the crowd and all attention focused ahead. From the temple emerged a ling of women, walking softly, almost floating, down the broad steps to the stage below. The young man barely noticed the priestesses, their grace, their charm, and their beauty little more than a blur in his mind's eye. A dim portion of his brain noted the various colors of their outfits, but even that failed to register in his conscious thoughts. Instead, all his focus, his entire soul, locked upon a single face.

Tomas had known his beautiful lady now for longer than he could remember. Had someone asked him at just that moment when exactly he had met his wonderful Mary, he would have been hard-pressed to remember a time when he did not know her. She had become such an integrated part of his life, there was no way for Tomas to imagine without Mary being a part of it.

She wore a dress so vibrant green it seemed as though Wildelves Wood had come alive and joined the performance. The hem drifted around her calves, seeming to have sprouted the ribbons that spiraled down to her slippered feet like ivy. Her bodice was clasped at the young woman's chest, and her flesh emerged from the frilly white blouse like a goddess rising from the sea. Tiny bells were tied to her ankles and wrists, and strings of them were braided into her long hair, creating a perfect symphony that joyously sang at her slightest move. Mary's bright eyes scanned the crowd as she glided across the stage to her starting place, finally stopping once she spotted Tomas. The two stared at each other, and a bright smile illuminated her face.

Accompanying Mary and the four other green-clad young women, four Sisters of the Lady of Light arrived on stage, led by Kyla. Each was wearing short skirts and blouses dyed a riot of brilliant colors. Like Mary, the sisters all had bells tied to their ankles and wrists, but unlike the maid, each of the priestesses had strings of bells tied not into their hair, but around their slender waists. Had the squire been able to take his eyes off his love, he would have picked out Kyla in her white outfit and Aebreanna in her blue, and even Medaka in vibrant purple. The last, wearing red, Tomas did not know. None of it mattered to Tomas; to him, there was only Mary.

An orchestra took up positions around the stage once the dancers were in place. To most of the crowd, these musicians went largely unnoticed. It was a common joke amongst the people of the Keep that the most thankless job in the world was to be a musician for the Dance of the Lady of Light during the Harvest Festival. Despite this lack of acknowledgment, each member nonetheless took his or her position and prepared to give their all for what would be a performance only the priestesses would be congratulated for.

Each of the green-clad young women assumed set positions in a half-circle around the Sisters. The way they stood there, Tomas was reminded of a flowerbed, with the multi-colored priestesses closely set in the center and the green around them. Slowly, very slowly, with music that seemed to float from out of nowhere, Kyla and the sisters moved, letting their flowers bloom. They separated then, each twirling about across the stage, followed closely by a dancer in a green dress. Around the stage the women danced, conveying dozens of messages all at once, only a few of which Tomas could follow. The young man, perhaps, could have seen the overall theme of life and rebirth presented by the assembled cast, if only his eyes had not been locked on Mary.

The squire could not tear his eyes off his maid. The graceful motions of her arms and legs perfectly counter pointed by her shoulders, head, and waist, all seemed to come together to allow Mary to glide across the stage. For all Tomas knew, the world itself had ended, for his entire universe was contained in the flowing hair, slender form, and sparkling eyes of his lady.

As the dance wound up to its fevered conclusion, the women twirling about in a kind of reckless abandon, Tomas was just barely aware enough of the overall performance that he realized it was clearly meant to celebrate life itself. With a deep drum accompaniment, Mary spun her arms and legs in alternating circles, every breath in the crowd speeding to match her movements until finally she and all the other dancers came to a sudden stop, ending the dance as they had begun, in perfect stillness. After only the briefest of pauses, the crowd erupted in thunderous applause, yelling their appreciation as though their hearts would burst.

"Nice dance," Tomas said in a strangled voice as he applauded.

Rogan grinned, his own eyes having been similarly locked on his princess.

Rather than returning to their temple, the women on stage picked up their shepherd staffs and made their way into the crowd. As was traditional, the sisters would not change following the dance of their goddess until the Harvest Festival was concluded, instead once again patrolling the city on that final day. Rogan and Tomas walked up to the edge of the stage to help their ladies down.

The knight playfully grabbed his diminutive wife, kissing her passionately and spinning her about in the air, drawing from his princess a delighted squeal. Rogan held his wife aloft for some time, staring deeply into her eyes. Kyla ran her hands very lightly over her knight's face. They kissed then, not with great passion, but with great love.

Mary was standing at the edge of the stage, looking down at the wide-eyed Tomas. The squire had just as much chivalry in his heart as his knight, if not more so. Holding his arms up, he supported Mary's weight and eased her to the ground, not thinking to let her go even once she was safely on the ground. Noticing his hands still resting on her hips, Mary smiled and stepped closer into his embrace. "I hope you liked our dance," she said in a soft voice that dripped with innocence and emotion.

"We've been working on it for weeks." Putting her hands on Tomas' chest, the young woman looked up into his eyes. Seeing there only pure adoration, she smiled and blushed a little.

Tomas leaned down, moving his face closer to his lady. "The dance was incredible, Mary. You are incredible." The fact they were in the middle of a busy courtyard was lost on the couple, and the young lovers leaned in to each other.

"Hay, kids!" As if from the pits of Underworld itself, Rogan appeared right beside them.

Turning to face his knight, Tomas felt all that love and eagerness turn rapidly into a murderous rage. "God, I hate you," he said in a low, dangerous voice, even as his hand drifted towards Steelheart, belted as his waist. Only then noticing that the King and Queen were standing beside Rogan and Kyla.

"I am sorry to interrupt," Cylan Calonar apologized, "but we must soon return to the castle. Before I left, I wanted to congratulate you, Mary. That was the finest performance I can remember seeing in years."

The maid shook off Tomas' embrace to curtsey. "Thank you, your Majesty," she replied, glowing from the complement.

The old king nodded, never losing his gentle smile. "I won't keep you; I can imagine just how much you two are looking forward to today. But if it wouldn't be too much of an imposition, keep in mind that you are both invited to the banquet in the gardens tonight."

Mary bowed again. "We wouldn't miss it," she replied for them both.

The King and Queen turned to leave, followed closely by two Archaeknight bodyguards. They stopped only to say a few words to the assembled musicians, giving praise to each individually and then all as a group before slowly returning to the castle.

Left once again with some degree of privacy, Mary turned back to Tomas, eager to resume where they had left off. The young man, however, seemed pensive. "What's wrong?" she asked.

"I was just wondering how he got down here so fast," the young man replied. "Rogan and I had to run to avoid being late."

Mary smiled and nodded at one of the Archaeknights, a tall male Halvan who moved with a purposeful stride that spoke of an unending readiness. "That's Fulcan. He can open doors."

"... Can't we all open doors?'"

Mary rolled her eyes. "When a warrior becomes an Archaeknight, his Majesty imbues them with a portion of his power. He gives each one a special ability. Fulcan can create doorways from one place to another."

Tomas looked at the King and his Archaeknights. "And each of them has one of these... abilities? No wonder they're so feared," he noted.

"It takes years for someone to become an Archaeknight," she pointed out. "And they have to prove themselves before even being considered, let alone trained."

The squire's eyes remained for as long as they could on King Cylan. "Is it just my imagination," he asked, "or is he moving a lot slower than normal?"

"He's probably just tired."

Tomas shook his head slightly. "It's more than that," he insisted. "He looks..."

"Old?"

He nodded.

Mary sighed. "Don't forget the King has been alive for four centuries. Even a Halvan gets old sooner or later."

"Too bad we could never see him while he was still in his prime. I bet he had to have been one of the most powerful men to ever live."

"Some would say he still is."

"I don't mean his magic or his command over armies. I mean his charisma, his drive."

Mary gently, but firmly, took Tomas' chin in her small hand and turned his eyes back to hers. "You know," she said somewhat archly, "you were *supposed* to be obsessed with me today."

The squire ran a hand ever so lightly down his lady's face. "No matter what I may be talking about, you are always the most important thing in my heart or on my mind. I was empty without ever knowing it, until I met you. With you near me, I am finally whole."

She melted into her young man's arms, letting the emotion flowing from of his eyes envelop her, carrying her own heart to heights she never knew could exist. "Keep talking like that," she said breathlessly, "and I'll think you're trying to seduce me."

Tomas placed a light kiss on his lover's lips. "It would be only fair," he replied. "You seduced me with your every move, your every breath."

"Oh, come on," Rogan said, interrupting the moment by throwing an arm around his squire's neck. "There'll be plenty of time for all that later; right now, we have a banquet to get ready for."

Chapter 46

With nightfall imminent, the celebration was at last
coming to a conclusion. Final stories were told and games played,
and the good little boys and girls were put to bed. As was traditional,
the royal family hosted a banquet complete with feasting and dancing
in the gardens outside the old Sylvai shrine at the eastern edge of the
city. In most kingdoms, the only guests to such an event would be
the absolute highest ranking of the nobility and most honored of
citizenry. In the Northern Keep, however, it was those citizens who
had distinguished themselves throughout the year for their hard
work and dedication to their neighbors, along with the closest
friends of the royal family, that could attend this party. It was the
highest honor for any person of the Keep to be invited to the Royal
Banquet, there to receive the personal thanks of the King and Queen
for all their hard work, to say nothing of the best meal there was to
be had in the Northlands.

In attendance this year, in addition to the royal family and
Tomas and Mary, were several faces Tomas had come to know over
the last several months, some of which had traveled even from as far
as Velaross to celebrate with House Calonar. Cardinal Tain was
there, along with the priestess, Medaka, once again clad in purple.
Also in attendance was General Killdare, commander of the House
Guard, recently returned from an inspection of the installations
bordering Ulheim. Klug Rainer and a few soldiers who had earned
distinction over the past year accompanied the general to represent
House Calonar's military. Ilse, Rainer's daughter, was also present,
along with Medaka and a few other members of the city's clerics.
Velaera the Sylva seamstress who tailored Tomas' new clothes was
the Uldra gemsmith, Gadrul, from whom the squire had purchased
Mary's emerald earrings. Together, this mismatched pair represented
the Merchant's Guild, the city's merchants, shopkeepers, and
tradesmen. Esha was present, of course, accompanied by the newly
promoted Amatria, Xathias, and Jade as representatives of the
Arcane Guild. Rashid and Aebreanna were there along with Vincent

and another senior House agent currently in the Keep, a woman named Chandra. Even Remm and Beraht were present, doing their best to eat and drink everything in sight.

Despite his objections, Rogan insisted that Tomas accompany him on what he described as his rounds. "If I've got to do it," he growled, "*you've* got to do it."

So it was that the squire grudgingly accompanied his knight around the hedged-in area of the gardens that held the many tables and guests of the banquet, making idle conversation with the dizzying array of people to whom Rogan introduced him. The only concession Tomas was able to wring out of his knight for this parade was that Mary accompany them.

"Why your most royal Highness," Klug Rainer exclaimed, "you honor me with a personal conversation."

Rogan stared at the officer in obvious irritation. "Tell me something, Rainer," he grumbled. "How exactly did you get yourself invited to this party?"

The soldier bowed floridly. "Why, your honored father-in-law personally sent me an invitation, sire. I apparently earned his favor during our battle with the dead minions of Anninihus."

"I see you even managed to get promoted again," the prince pointed out, nodding to the captain's rank insignia Rainer now wore.

Ilse took her father's arm. "General Killdare was lavish in his praise and rewards following the battle, your Highness," the priestess proudly said.

"Indeed," Rainer agreed. "My entire team received promotions and medals. Most of us have also been reassigned to positions of our choice."

"Did you get a new assignment?" Mary asked.

"Father has been made the General's adjutant," Ilse happily said. "No more dangerous assignments or late guard duties."

"What's an adjutant?" Mary asked.

"I assist the General in his duties," Rainer replied. "I maintain his schedule, run errands for him, organize his staff, and generally try to make his life less difficult."

"You know," Rogan noted to the captain, "the common soldiers have another name for adjutants."

"From what I understand, they have a few descriptive names for you as well, your Highness," Rainer noted back.

The small group spoke briefly with Velaera and Gadrul. "The entire Keep is abuzz with your great victory, my dear," the Sylva gushed.

"Don't you mean, my victory?" Tomas asked, confused.

Velaera smiled. "Do I?" she mused. "We did witness many great battles this year, but I must admit to being most interested in hers."

"What…"

Gadrul just shook his head. "She gets giddy when she drinks," he grumbled.

"What was that?" Velaera asked with an edge to her voice.

"Hm? Nothing." The smith moved to a nearby table to pour his companion another glass of wine.

Esha was her normal happy, distracted self, though her students still had an air of pride over their recent promotions. General Killdare made little pretense at mingling, having much the same opinions on the custom as Rogan did.

On and on it went, with most guests making note of Tomas' recent victory in the tournament, through more than a few women showed much more interest in Mary and her victory. Most expressed an almost extreme curiosity over the progress of the young couple's romance, wanting greater and greater detail over their time together. More often than not, the squire found himself deferring to Mary, who delighted in retelling the events. For his part, Tomas stood and agreed with whatever she was saying. The only pause in the parade of meaningless small talk when Beraht pulled him aside and handed the young man a small box.

"Already?" Tomas asked in surprise.

The Uldra shrugged. "You said as soon as possible."

"What is it?" Mary asked.

The squire tucked the small box into his belt. "Just a little project I asked Beraht for help with."

With no further explanation, Tomas continued the pointless parade until finally, after what seemed an eternity of meaningless conversation, the knight released his squire to eat. As Tomas and Mary sat at the royal table, he mentioned to Mary his surprise at their being the center of so many conversations throughout the banquet.

"Does it really surprise you that the people would want to know more about us?" she asked gently as she sipped a crystal goblet of wine. "We did put on a show yesterday."

"I guess," the squire said through a mouthful of roast goose. "It's not every day that a commoner like me is the center of conversation for a group of nobles, city elders, and religious leaders."

"You forgot about the farmers, miners, shopkeepers, and soldiers," the maid reminded.

"What do you mean?"

Taking a small bite of the duck, Mary finished before speaking. "This is the Northern Keep. King Cylan began life as an exile and wandering hero. The Queen was priestess for a small mountain village. General Killdare over there began his military career as a common soldier in the Legions. Esha was the assistant to a warehouse clerk before Cyras took her on as an apprentice. Rashid and Aebreanna were thieves, assassins, and worse before coming here and becoming heroes. Beraht and Remm... well, I'm not really sure. Even Prince Rogan, now a hero of the people and heir to the throne, was once just a wandering mercenary. This is a place where ordinary people come to be extraordinary. Even commoners like me can dream of something more."

Swallowing his mouthful, Tomas looked at his lady. "There is nothing common about you, Mary," he said, his hand lightly caressing her face.

Losing herself in his touch, the maid sighed. Raising her hand to touch Tomas' arm, Mary looked deep into his eyes, letting her breath and heart speed up to match his.

"I don't think I told you how beautiful you look tonight," Tomas said, his voice barely above a whisper. Indeed, Mary was an icon of feminine glory. Her gown was perfectly white, with delicate green embroidery tracing captivating lines along her body. The long sleeves were gathered at her wrists with green ribbons, and flowed nearly down to her feet. Her hair maintained the bells from the dance earlier that day, highlighted by her beloved emerald earrings.

Blushing modestly, Mary said, "Princess Kyla and Baroness Aebreanna are very skilled at enhancing a girl's beauty."

Tomas leaned in to the maid and said, "They only showed you for what you really are, an angel from heaven. I've never known a woman that could make me feel what you do. The only thing I regret about this night is that it has to end."

"Flatterer," Mary said, her face now only a breath away from his.

"Hey kid!" Rogan exclaimed, falling into his seat beside his squire. Having been interrupted yet again, Tomas' hand once again drifted to Steelheart, resting at his hip. If not for Mary placing her hand lightly on his sword arm, it was quite possible blood would have been spilt.

Kyla sat down beside her husband, snuggling up to him and playfully feeding pieces of meat to her champion. "I hope you two are having a good time," she asked brightly.

"We were," Tomas muttered sourly.

"Patience, my lord," Mary murmured into her wine glass.

A soft series of chimes drew the attention of everyone in the park. All eyes turned to see the King, standing with the aid of Sarah, calling for attention by raping gently on his crystal goblet. "Ladies and gentlemen," he said as clearly as he could. "I ask you all now to raise your drinks, as is our custom, to the people of our beautiful city. May we never forget how much we all depend on each other. To the people." The King's toast was echoed by all those assembled.

When King Cylan again raised his goblet, a soft smile played on his lips. "As is also our custom, let us toast the hero of the people and our tournament champion. This year, I have the distinct honor to praise a new champion of the games, and of the people. Ladies and gentlemen, I give you Tomas Fidelis of Pelsemoria."

All raised their drinks and praised Tomas, whose face burned at the attention. Even Mary lifted her glass to her champion, echoing the praise of the King. "Speech!" a familiar Uldra voice called out.

"Shut up, Beraht!" Tomas tried to call out, but the demand was echoed.

Rogan forced Tomas to his feet with a malicious grin. The squire awkwardly waved a hand at the crowd of people that were all staring at him. "Uh... thanks," he said.

"Come on, kid," the knight grinned. "You've got to do better than that."

"You're really enjoying this, aren't you?" the young man demanded.

"I just love that I don't have to do it this year," he smirked.

Tomas' hands went awkwardly to his belt, where he felt the small package that Beraht had handed him earlier. "Well, I did plan to do this later, but I guess now's as good a time as any." The squire took Mary's hand and lifted her to her feet. "Mary, when I left Pelsemoria, I thought God had spoken to me. I thought he had said, 'Go, and find what you seek. Find a way to forever stop the evil of the Black Duke.'"

Laughter filled the park. Even the king smiled gently.

"I realized a short time ago," the young man continued, "I realized that my quest was in error. God didn't want me to leave my home to find a way to stop House Calonar. He did, though, want me to leave for something else. God spoke to me that night, Mary. He told me there was something I needed to find. He told me I would never know peace until I found it. He was right.

"In this entire world, of all the people and the places and the times, I found you. You have become everything to me, and I could never imagine life without you."

By now, tears were standing in the young woman's eyes.

"I'm stalling, I know." Tomas glanced out at the people of the Keep, at the very people he once thought of as the enemy. Looking back into Mary's eyes, he dropped slowly to one knee. "Mary, I do love you. Now and forever, my heart and soul are yours to do with what you please. I may be your champion, but I want more." He pulled the small box out and opened it, showing the golden ring inside that had been fashioned to resemble a simple ribbon wrapped around a small diamond.

"Mary, will you take me to be your husband? Will you be mine, forever?"

The young woman looked down at him through eyes wide in wonder. The tears that stood before now flowed freely. Every man and woman, even the Uldra, stared in rapt anticipation. Everyone waited for Mary's response.

Chapter 47

"Yes!" she exclaimed, enfolding her fiancée in a fierce embrace.

The people cheered and toasted the happy couple. All around came calls of congratulation and praise. Tomas slipped the ring on his love's finger, both of them gasping as a miraculous thing happened. The golden color drained from the ring, instead becoming perfectly white, the same white of the ribbon tied about the squire's scabbard.

"How did you do that?" Mary asked.

"I didn't," he replied. The young man looked across the park at Beraht. "How did *you*?"

The Uldra shook his head and jabbed a thumb at the grinning Esha.

Both Tomas and Mary looked at the archmage and back at the ring in near terror. The Sylva laughed. "Perhaps not everything created necessarily needs to explode," she told them.

Tomas breathed a sigh of relief and bowed to the master wizard. Esha raised her staff and nodded in return.

Mary looked at the ring and back into Tomas' eyes. "It's perfect," she said. "Thank you."

"Thank Beraht. He's the one who made it. I asked him just yesterday before the tournament. I still can't believe he finished it in only one day."

The maid smiled through her tears and led her love by the hand across the park to where Beraht stood, absently kicking a stone. The young woman released her grip on Tomas and wrapped her arms around the thick Uldra's bulging middle. "Thank you, Beraht. It's just wonderful."

The barbarian shuffled a bit and wiped at his massive nose. "Yeah, well... you know... the kid won me a lot of money and I kind of owed him... so... you know."

Again, Mary embraced him and placed a light kiss on his hairy cheek. She and Tomas then made their way back to the royal tables where Rogan and Kyla expressed their own happiness for their friends. Beraht growled a bit and looked around in anger. Remm was leaning back in his seat, looking at his younger friend with a level expression on his ugly face.

"You want to say something?" the younger Uldra demanded, reaching for his waraxe.

From behind the barbarian, Aebreanna reached around and playfully tugged on the end of his long beard. "That will do Beraht, that will do," she smiled.

Beraht slapped her hands away in disgust before looking back at Remm. "Well?" he demanded.

Remm shrugged. "Sylvu," he said.

"THAT'S IT!!!" An immediate fight broke out between the two Uldra.

The minor eruption of chaos did little to dampen the joy at the royal table. Tomas and Mary alternated between accepting the congratulations of the guests and discussing tentative wedding plans with Rogan and Kyla. Eventually, the same orchestra that had performed at the Dance of the Lady of Light struck up a song that had most of the women leading their men out onto the stage.

Kyla stood and tried to pick up her hesitant husband. "If you two aren't going to eat you might as well dance," she suggested. Not seeing the look of terror in Tomas' eyes, nor the mute appeal to change the subject, the princess continued her suggestion while working hard to pry her knight from his seat. "There's no point in coming to one of these parties without taking your date onto the dance floor at least once."

"What a good idea," Mary said, rising to her feet and half-dragging Tomas out to the dance floor.

As the young pair made their way to the center of the crowd, Tomas made one last ditch effort. "You know, I really can't dance all that well."

Taking Tomas hand and placing it on her hip, Mary smiled and said, "Don't worry, I'll show you." Distracted as he was by the placement of his hand, Tomas could offer no further objections as his lady led him through the intimate dance so favored by the people of the Keep this season.

Even as they moved through the steps, Tomas found that the close physical contact with Mary was causing certain reactions that made his dancing even more difficult. Feeling more than seeing Tomas' difficulty, a slow smile crept its way onto Mary's face.

Trying to move his thoughts to a less stimulating course, Tomas decided on pointless conversation. "So, Rogan tells me that Kyla wants you to work in her Temple as an archivist."

If possible, Mary pressed herself even closer to Tomas. "Yes," she sighed, "the Princess has offered me the position."

"So, books and scrolls and quiet halls?" His thumb traced small circles against her lower back, feeling the warmth beneath her gown.

She smiled up at him, her arm trailing up his, to encircle the back of his shoulders. "Also attending meetings with the Princess. Keeping a journal of her decisions. Maintaining the records of the Temple."

"Sounds," Tomas' voice gave out for a moment. The young man cleared his throat and tried again. "Sounds like you're duties will require a lot of time in the castle." He found himself leaning in, closer and closer to his lady love. Some irresistible force had bound them and, even if the squire had wanted to break free, he could not.

"Just like yours," Mary breathed, her mouth opening and her eyes shutting.

As their lips closed in, a sudden thought crossed Tomas' mind. Pulling his head back sharply, the squire looked around with a suspicious gaze, certain an interruption was imminent.

"What's the matter?" Mary asked.

"Where is he? I just know that he'll pop up any second and ruin the moment."

"Who?"

"Rogan. Every time we have a moment, there he is. Well, not this..." Tomas could not finish his sentence. Mary had grabbed his face with both hands and pulled him down, greedily pressing their lips together.

From the royal table, Kyla and Aebreanna were dabbing their eyes and smiling.

"That's the sweetest thing I've ever seen," Kyla said.

"That girl certainly needed to take charge," Aebreanna agreed.

"Hey, they have melon balls," Rogan noted.

Once the couple had broken off their embrace, they stood for a time in each other's arms, their eyes absorbed in each other. "You know," Mary said, "this banquet is probably going to take most of the night. I don't know about you, but I think I'm ready for bed."

"I guess you must be tired," Tomas said.

"No, not really," a hungry look in her eyes. "At least, not yet."

A rather goofy smile spread across Tomas' face as Mary led him by the hand towards the garden exit.

Of course, Fate is fickle. Rogan intercepted the pair as they tried to make their escape. "You two aren't leaving, are you?" he asked with a grin.

Releasing Mary's hand, Tomas gritted his teeth and, grabbing his knight by the front of his tunic, said, "Go away."

Looking past his squire at a blushing and very intense Mary, Rogan grinned. "Sorry, kid. Just don't forget about the council meeting tomorrow at noon."

Taking Mary's hand, Tomas once again tried to leave when a woman's scream shattered the music.

"Now what!?!" Tomas and Mary demanded, both clearly enraged.

With the scream as an opening, the gardens and woods beyond erupted suddenly with warriors, dozens of them, cutting off all escape. It became clear after only the briefest of glances that each of these invaders were frighteningly familiar; a shared look by Tomas, Rogan, Rashid, Esha and Rainer all confirmed that they each recognized the attackers. Pale scrapes of sallow skin clung to yellowed bone, and blank eyes stared unblinkingly from sunken sockets. The stench of the grave pushed in front of them. Breath did not move them, nor the pulse of living blood; instead, only some alien will animated their jerky, unliving motion. In each of their hands were vicious weapons, weapons with hooks and serrated edges and spikes, weapons meant to cause pain and suffering before the release of death.

"What is the meaning of this?" King Cylan roared from his table, rising to his feet.

"Now, now, your Majesty. I wouldn't do anything rash." A harsh, bitter voice came from the edge of the garden. "You all know my familiarity with the secrets of magic, so I wouldn't do anything you might regret later." Out of the trees stepped a tall man, thin and dressed in a mockery of the ceremonial robes of a Guild wizard. Rather than the traditional blue robes of the Guild, his were so deep black that it seemed they absorbed the warm light of the surrounding lanterns and candles, leaving only a hateful cold. The golden runes and colored inseam that should have adorned his sleeves had been replaced with the symbols of death, declaring the spell-caster's devotion to the White Lady. He bore a staff of polished, grey wood, surmounted with a human skull, upon which had been placed Druug horns. The intruder's sunken face twitched and twisted in a vile sneer, and was pock-marked and covered in vile symbols, but Tomas could not tell if they were scars or tattoos.

"Anninihus," Rogan sneered.

Esha stepped towards Anninihus, her staff raised and the words of magic already tumbling from the Sylva's mouth.

"I wouldn't do that, Esha!" Anninihus snarled, a black nimbus curling out of his own skull-tipped staff and surrounding his thin frame, merging seamlessly with the darkness of his robe. "I have complete control of these creatures, and if you do anything to me, they attack. If I command it, they attack. If it amuses me, they attack." The Death Mage's lips spread in a hideous grin revealing yellowed and broken teeth.

"What do you want?" Cylan Calonar asked, his normally soft, friendly voice carrying a hint of steel in it.

"Why your Majesty, you of all people should guess. *You* were the one to exile me, *you* were the one to strip me of my rank and position, *you* were the one to declare me an outlaw, and *you* are the one who will suffer for it."

Lowering her staff, Esha snorted derisively. "Who do you serve, Anninihus?"

"Whatever do you mean, my master?" A sneer replaced the smile, hideous in its complete lack of humanity. Distracted as he was with his gloating, the Death Mage failed to notice the exchange of glances between Rogan, Tomas, Rainer, and Rashid.

"You had little enough power to raise a half-dead cat, you putrid zombie molester," Esha spat. "Your new power is clearly the gift of a superior, more knowledgeable master, so I ask again: who do you serve?"

"Question my power at your risk, my master," the Death Mage sneered. He gestured, waving a hand to a figure standing behind. That person stepped forward, into the light of the lanterns.

"Althaea!" Kyla gasped.

Tomas barely recognized the spy. She was dressed in little more than the barest of rags, drifting across her body and doing nothing to preserve her dignity. Her hair was unkept, and her movements unsteady, as though compelled. Although her body moved the same as Anninihus' other creatures, her face remained her own, and locked into a tortured hell. Tears flowed and her mouth was open, as though to scream, but no sound seemed allowed to escape.

"You dare!?!" King Cylan snarled.

"I do!" Anninihus screamed. "I dare! I will rule your servants! I will imprison them just as I imprisoned this whore!"

"Power given to you," Esha snapped. "Not yours. You are nothing but a puppet! The power is your master's!"

"It's mine!" the Death Mage roared.

"Who do you serve?" the archmage demanded again.

Anninihus laughed then, flecks of spittle flying from his mouth. "The same person who ordered the poisoning of your king."

All eyes turned to King Cylan; he did not look surprised.

"Oh, didn't you tell them your Majesty?" the necromancer gloated. "So many secrets in House Calonar. How ever do you keep them all?"

"What are your intentions, Death Mage?" Cylan Calonar asked calmly.

"I intend to take you and your family hostage, and then I intend to kill everyone at this miserable banquet, making them my slaves." Even as Anninihus strode forward, confident of his victory, Rogan and the others were moving to strategic locations across the gardens. The prince issued silent commands to each soldier and Archaeknight in the gardens through slight nods and barely-seen gestures. The dead warriors, though fierce in battle and obedient beyond death, were mindless; they watched the movement blankly, waiting for their master to order them into action. Only Althaea's eyes tracked the defenders of the Northern Keep.

"And what makes you think I will comply?" the King asked.

"Because I have your younger daughter already," Anninihus leered. "Her and Tressalon's twins."

A flash of anger burst across Calonar's face, and his eyes filled with the crackling blue energy of his magic. Raising his right hand, the King made a gesture at the Death Mage, speaking the words that manifested his power. Anninihus was surrounded by a blue nimbus that eradicated the black and lifted him off the ground; flecks of red sparks stabbed the Death Mage, bringing gasps of pain. "What have you done?" the King demanded in a voice that could have set fire to ice.

A strangled curse was Anninihus' only response. Calonar's power lashed out in waves of pure white light, tearing at the Death Mage's robes and flesh. As Tomas looked on, he saw waves of illusion ripple off Anninihus' skin, revealing what the squire thought at first to be more of the same tattooing, or perhaps scarring. The fallen wizard had carved the runes of power into his very flesh.

"My patience grows thin, Death Mage," Calonar warned. "Speak or I will end your life once and for all."

In response, the Death Mage only looked at Calonar and smiled despite the pain inflicted by the hero's magic. The light in the king's eyes, along with the spell surrounding Anninihus, fluttered and died. Clutching his heart, Cylan Calonar collapsed into his seat. The Queen put her hands on her husband's chest and spoke a brief prayer, restoring enough of his strength so that he could sit up and breathe.

"Your Majesty, do you really think you could muster enough power to harm me, or even light a torch at this point?" Anninihus laughed in derision. "Behold," he declared to the surrounding leaders of the Northern Keep. "Behold the light of goodness and hope in the world. Behold the hero of the people and the bane of evil-doers everywhere. Behold the last of the Heroes of Fate: a weak and useless old man."

"Not quite useless, Anninihus," Calonar said, his breath heavy and his words weak. "You are right that I cannot maintain my connection to the Winds," he admitted through heavy breaths. "But my power was never my magic. Now Rogan."

The command given, Rogan, Tomas, and Rashid, supported by the soldiers and guests, hurled themselves at their enemies. As fast and deadly as the dead creatures were created to be, they could not stand against the skill and rage wielded by the defenders of the Northern Keep.

Hacking viciously at one of the creatures wielding a hook pointed spear, Rogan could not help but laugh. "Well kid," he said, blocking a thrust with his shortsword Fang before beheading the attacking creature, "I bet of all the possibilities racing through that head of yours about how this date would end, this wasn't one of them!"

Ducking under a clumsy swing by a saw-edged broadsword and stabbing Steelheart through his opponent's heart, Tomas grunted as he moved to the next. The mystical blade of House Calonar seemed especially deadly to Anninihus' creatures; any stab, any cut, any significant contact from the venerated sword was enough to sever the magic animating the abominations. "Some candles," the squire grunted, "maybe a little dessert, even some deep conversation. But I never thought I'd be beheading anyone tonight." He beheaded a creature.

"Oh, quit complaining." Rashid dove under a pair of creatures as they swung their battle-axes at him, rolling and coming up in a crouch behind them, using his daggers to sever their hamstrings. "At least the food was good!"

"Trust the spymaster to look on the bright side of things!" Rainer laughed, cleaving one of the creatures in two and using the momentum of his attack to swing his longsword in a complete circle and strike another opponent with such force that its spear broke in two and the monster itself was driven to the ground where the captain beheaded it.

"I'm glad you people are enjoying yourselves!" Tomas snapped, parrying several blows before knocking the creature's blade aside and, spinning around behind it, reversed Steelheart and ran it through the creature's back. "You do realize we're in a fight here, right?"

"Come now, Tomas!" Rashid said, slitting the hamstrings of yet another monster. "Just because you could die at any second doesn't mean you can't have a good time!"

Over the din of the battle, twin roars of joy and fury shattered the gardens. Beraht and Remm, Uldra both, grabbed up their barbarian weapons and barreled into their enemies. No thought or finesse could be seen in any action taken by the two warriors. Beraht wielded his waraxe as though it was weightless, never halting in his attacks against any of the monsters until each was destroyed utterly. The younger of the berserkers moved constantly, never once so much as pausing as he plunged into the thickest fights time and again only to send the creatures flying away or tumbling to the ground in small pieces. Each swing of his massive waraxe would not stop with impact into an opponent, instead continuing through Beraht's target and on into another and another. His weapon was anathema to Anninihus' creatures; it burned them on contact, it destroyed their unholy weapons and devastated their corrupted bodies. Though the barest contact was enough to defeat each monster, Beraht was not satisfied, instead using his unconquerable strength to obliterated his enemies. Time and again the human warriors of the Northern Keep were forced to leap back, away from the Uldra's attacks as Beraht destroyed everything within reach of his short arms.

For every bit of rage that Beraht reveled in, his older compatriot reveled even more. Wielding a greataxe nearly twice the size of a Human, Remm lost himself in the joy of battle, exalting in the glory of hatred for his enemies, the most devout way for any warrior of the mountains to pay homage to the Allfather. Unlike his young countryman, Remm did not take the battle to the monsters, instead satisfying himself with destroying any foolish enough to approach. Time and again one of the dead would launch at Remm, swinging a weapon of horror and suffering; time and again there would be within moments only a spray of gore covering the Uldra barbarian.

General Killdare rallied his Guardsmen and dispatched them into small teams to protect those people who could not protect themselves. The grizzled old veteran moved with a speed and power that belied the grey at his temples, slicing through one monster after another while roaring his orders to the soldiers throughout the gardens. Within minutes of the eruption of battle, Captain Rainer had fought his way to the side of his general, the pair of soldiers effortlessly combining their skills in combat to cover one another and maintain control of their forces. No group of civilians was left undefended. The deadly power of Killdare and Rainer was compounded by the fact that the dead could not reach them. The two men stood shoulder to shoulder, and they were surrounded by a nimbus of soft white. Behind them, sheltered by their skill and their blades, the Harvest priestess Ilse spoke aloud prayers to her goddess. The dead retreated from the white nimbus of her faith, turning away from even the sight of it. Killdare and Rainer took advantage of the priestess' magic, launching one attack after another at the paralyzed monsters. Though outnumbered and facing a horror from the darkest of nightmares, the professionals of House Calonar once again showed their unwavering commitment.

Each dead creature the people of the Keep pulled down found itself stripped of any weapons. Not content with their role as spectators and ignoring the shouted commands of General Killdare to flee, the common citizens grabbed what weapons they could steal from their attackers or fashion from the surrounding items and hurled themselves at their attackers, furious that their celebration had been ruined by the petty schemes of the Death Mage. As numerous and skilled with their weapons as the monsters were, they could not repel the sheer number of the Keep's defenders.

To match the violence of close combat, it took only moments for a magical counterpoint to join the symphony of combat. Esha rallied her three students, forming a small half-circle at one edge of the park. Speaking in the musical language of magic, the four wizards hurled a constant arcane assault on the dead around them, never ceasing in their casting as they worked tirelessly to support the warriors and citizens. Walls of green flame erupted to break up large clusters of the monsters. Small tornados picked the creatures up and tore them apart. Flashes of blinding light distracted attackers at critical moments while the defenders counter-attacked. The entire area was lit with the power of the Northern Keep's arcane adepts as they brought their incredible skills to bear.

Within minutes that seemed to last eons, sweat was rolling down the faces of each of the new archwizards. Despite trembling arms and gasping breaths that otherwise could have interrupted their spell-casting, Esha's students did not relent in their magical support of the battle until the unbearable weakness of their exhausted magic overwhelmed them. Despite their discipline and commitment to their fellow defenders, the strain of their craft eventually proved too much for the younger adepts. One by one, they each collapsed to the ground, drawing in trembling breaths and trying desperately to summon enough strength for even one more spell. First was Jade, unable to support the weight of her own slender body. Then fell Amatria, her Sylvai pride wounded at being unable to continue. Then it was only Xathias and Esha standing back-to-back, staves raised and spells flying without pause until the Xeshlin collapsed also. In the end, Esha stood alone, the light of her magical aura casting shadows through the gardens and her voice calmly filling the battlefield with the song of magic. All three of her students looked up in awe that night as the archmage gave ample demonstration of her true power.

The Archaeknights flowed throughout the area with a grace and teamwork that defied description. The four warriors who had attended the banquet flew across the garden, destroying any of the dead foolish enough to approach the members of House Calonar. Where one would attack, another would defend; where one would strike, another would parry. At all times, Ward, the hulking leader of the royal bodyguards, maintained a zone of absolute safety around the royal family. Never once during the brutal fight did even one of the monsters close to more than twenty paces of any unarmed member of House Calonar, allowing the non-combatants to tend to their weakened patriarch without interruption.

The mystic warriors used their gifts flawlessly. One moved from place to place in flashes of arcane light, constantly appearing behind the creatures for only the briefest instant to destroy them before appearing again behind another opponent. Ward picked up any creature that came within arm's reach and either crushed the decayed body or swung it about, destroying any of its compatriots that had the misfortune to be nearby. The Archaeknight archer let fly an unending stream of enchanted arrows that froze and burned and detonated the creatures. Above all performed Sarah, the newest Archaeknight; with an endless reserve of energy, the young woman leapt from place to place, letting fly with a flurry of punches, kicks, and blade strikes as scores of the monsters threatening her king and queen were destroyed utterly. With the protection of the most elite warriors of House Calonar, the members of that family never felt the slightest hint of fear, knowing that they were as safe as any mortal could be.

As the warriors and citizens of the city went about the business of destroying the invaders, those members of House Calonar who did not live by their weapons sought to help their lord. Nora and Kyla shared a look of mutual concern at the sight of the grey-skinned king. Aebreanna removed her cloak and threw it over him as the queen and princess lowered the trembling old warrior to the ground. "Can I help?" Mary asked, fearful for the man long-thought to be invincible by the people of the Northlands.

"Water," Queen Nora commanded. The young maid scavenged the few water glasses that remained unspilled, pouring them into an empty bowl and bringing it to the side of her King and Queen.

Kyla crossed her small hands over her father's heart and drew upon her own healing powers. "Twelve gold artisans say Rogan kills more than Rashid," she said off-hand to Aebreanna. Mary could tell the Princess was trying to sound calm, to bring a light note to this terrible night. Her eyes, though, betrayed her deep worry.

The sultry baroness sent Mary, escorted by Sarah the Archaeknight, to retrieve her small bag from the far end of the table. "You are, as the saying goes, on," she replied.

"How can you be so calm?" Mary demanded as she handed the bag over to Aebreanna.

The spy put a light hand on her young friend's shoulder. "Losing one's calm rarely serves any useful purpose," she advised. "Do not allow yourself to be overwhelmed. Concentrate on one problem at a time, solve it, and move to the next."

The maid took a deep breath and nodded, trying to block out the sounds of death and destruction surrounding them. "What do we do first?" she asked.

Tables and chairs were overturned or destroyed outright. Fire spread through the gardens, and the screams of the wounded filled the air. The dead creations of Anninihus lunged forward like a wave of moaning death. But that wave crashed against the defenders of the Northern Keep. The Northlanders stood defiant of the initial onslaught, roaring their hatred of Anninihus' terror-tactics. The people threw themselves at the monsters who poisoned their beloved king.

Again and again, the warriors of House Calonar tried to attack Anninihus directly, especially once his mystical battle with Esha intensified, drawing his attention. Soldiers, in and out of uniform, tried lunging at the Death Mage, they tried sneaking around behind him, and they tried hurling improvised missiles at this hated enemy. In each case, the threat was intercepted and neutralized by Althaea. With the infinite skill provided by Rashid's training, she deflected any weapon hurled at her master. She diverted any attack made on the Death Mage, no matter the direction. She opened throats, severed tendons, and sliced arteries. She made no sound, no scream or cry of any kind, just an endless choking sob of absolute misery.

As the battle progressed, it seemed to Tomas that the skill of the dead warriors increased, almost as if they were capable of learning as they fought. Even as in the previous battle with these abominations, the monsters adapted to their tactics, forcing the defenders of the Keep to constantly change their methods, often while attempting to dispatch a single creature. Once the dead force had finally been reduced to a little more than a score, the warriors found themselves having a tougher time putting these last few down; the creatures had even developed resistance to the magic launched at them by Esha and his students. At one point, Rashid became blocked in by three of the creatures, unable to use any of his characteristic tumbling moves to escape. Although his daggers were excellent for sneak attacks and backstabbing, when facing three opponents armed with spiked clubs and barbed scythes, the spymaster could accomplish little. Then, a small Sylvai dagger suddenly buried itself in the middle creature, allowing the spymaster to vault over it and, using it as a shield, finished off all three, sparing only enough time to quickly bow to where his wife knelt helping her family care for the failing king. In response, the beautiful spy spared a moment from her work to throw him a wink and a kiss.

"Those don't count!" Kyla protested.

"Yes they do," the baroness protested, "Rashid actually killed them!"

"But you helped!" Glancing over at Rogan, who was having trouble with four of the creatures, Kyla made a little pout and, with a negligent gesture, set two of the creatures on fire.

"Now that was unfair!"

Kyla just stuck her tongue out at her friend before returning to her father.

The fight drew on. The numbers of the dead monsters were whittled down but not without cost to the defenders. First one, then another and another of the House Guard fell. Each defender was brought down only at great cost to the invaders, but each was a life lost nonetheless. Not a single civilian fell, but in payment of this miracle, the warriors of House Calonar gave up their own lives. When one monster stood over Velaera the seamstress ready to end her life, Gadrul bodily grabbed the abomination, ignoring the repeated thrusts of its hooked blade into his broad torso. With a sickening crunch, the creature was broken in tow and fell limp. Gadrul stood a moment, the gemsmith looking at Velaera, then followed the monster to the earth. The Sylva seamstress sobbed and knelt, her tiny arms clutching at the Uldra.

More small victories were won, but at a terrible cost. The leg of a local baker was severed by a jagged scythe and would have lost his life had not a Calonar Guardsman leapt in front of the deadly weapon, taking the lethal attack but burying his own blade into the monster's head in return. A woman from the Explorer's Guild was grabbed by two of the creatures, but lacked even time to scream before three soldiers barreled into the hideous things, two losing their lives, but not before seeing the citizen was safe. More and more of the defenders of the Northern Keep fell in their desperate attempt to finish off the last of the dead, to protect the people, and a silent vow was made amongst these professionals that not a single person under their protection would fall so long as even one of them drew breath.

Anninihus saw more clearly with each passing moment that his defeat was inevitable. Every spell the Death Mage attempted to cast was countered by Esha. Desperately, he tried ordering his creations to take hostages. Unfortunately for the Death Mage, Rogan ordered Esha to use her magic to open magical doors. The House Guard, under General Killdare and Captain Rainer, threw themselves at the remaining monsters to cover the civilians' retreat. Anninihus tried raising the fallen in the garden, but was again blocked, this time by Ilse and Medaka, combining their faiths to keep the dead at peace.

Anninihus spoke the words of magic, calling the darkness of the night to his hands and, pointing at his one-time teacher, released a spell. Waves of darkness hit Esha and rolled over her collapsed students until the archmage raised her own staff and a bright light erupted from its tip, banishing the Death Mage's spell. In response to the attack, Esha raised her other hand and, casting her own spell, summoned the fire from a dozen nearby lanterns to her hand and hurled the fire at her traitorous student. Anninihus jumped aside, barely escaping the flame and rolling out of the way as Esha's spell detonated a large patch of trees. He rolled on the ground, snarling magical words until he stopped and plunged his free hand into the earth. Esha let out a startled oath in the Sylvai tongue as hands of solid rock erupted from the ground beneath her, grabbing and pulling her down. She concentrated and spoke a single word of power, destroying the hands and gathering the rubble into a spiral around her outstretched hand. Red lightning danced amidst the stones and blue mist swirled around them. The tiny Sylva, mystical words flowing in an endless song from her snarling lips, reared back and hurled the shrapnel cloud. Anninihus swore and fell backwards, conjuring walls of darkness that Esha's orb burst through without slowing. The Death Mage screamed, seeing his own pain-filled death, and gestured as though grabbing something and pulling it over his body.

Althaea leapt forward, taking the attack on her own unprotected body. The stones shattered her. The red lightning cut burning gashes in her. The blue mist flooded her eyes, ears, nose, and mouth, searing her from within. She fell to the ground, writhing and gasping and, at last, weakly screaming. The once-beautiful priestess and spy turned red from her blood pouring from innumerable cuts. Her lustrous hair caught flame and burned to the root. Her porcelain skin charred to smoking black. Anninihus did not spare her a second glance.

The Death Mage looked about the gardens. The last of his monsters was even then being cut down. Seeing his death in the eyes of Rogan who, sword raised and roaring in fury at the invader, charged across the clearing towards his old enemy, Anninihus made ready his escape. "This isn't over, Rogan!" he declared, the black nimbus around him deflecting the knight's sword strikes. "We're just getting started!" With a single word of power and flash of green light, the Death Mage sent Rogan spinning away.

"Say your goodbyes now, brother! My master will see you dead yet!" The air behind the Death Mage rippled and split, and Anninihus was gone.

"Damn!" Rogan roared in fury.

"The children! He said they have the children!" Rashid snapped.

"Esha!" the knight snapped.

"Stand ready," the wizard calmly ordered. Raising her staff once again, the archmage opened a doorway to the royal apartments in the castle. Without a word, Rogan, Tomas, Rashid, and Rainer charged through, finding themselves before the door to Princess Karen's bedroom. Weapons raised, they readied themselves for anything, but when they burst through the doorway, the heroes were greeted by a sight that chilled each of them to the bone.

Dressed only in her robe, the eleven-year-old Princess Karen, surrounded by her stuffed animals and other toys, using the birthday gift recently given to her by her older sister, was viciously whipping a pair of assassins who were huddled in a corner begging for mercy. Behind her, the Tressalon twins were yelling encouragement, Rasha pointing out unprotected spots and Jalad gleefully laughing.

IV

Winter Returns

Chapter 48

The gardens were a disaster. The people of the Northern Keep long believed that the gardens were the living heart of their city. After the assault of the Death Mage and his horrid creations, the once lush gardens with their exotic flowers and centuries-old trees now stood as a battle-scarred inferno. Despite the efforts of the city's defenders to combat the fires that had broken out after the exchange of so much magic and the various torches and braziers and lanterns being overturned, many blazes still crawled uncontrolled throughout the once-beautiful refuge. General Killdare, seeing the futility in battling a fire he had no hope of defeating, instead ordered the City Watch to keep the blaze contained within the gardens until a volunteer fire brigade could be mobilized. Although it broke the hearts of every citizen, they retreated outside the gardens, leaving them to burn. Under the supervision of the clerics of the Harvest Mother, the wounded were taken to the nearby city center in which rested the large fountain and monument that was central to the Northern Keep. It was there the sober priests and priestesses conducted grim triage, separating those who could be saved from those who could only be made comfortable.

In the midst of this travesty, though, lay a sight that would strike worse than any other that night. King Cylan Calonar, surrounded by his Archaeknight bodyguards and representatives from every Temple and Church in the Keep, lay on a stone bench, looking as feeble as his age suggested he should. The old hero was breathing and responding to the treatments by the clerics around him, but it was clear his strength was failing. The king had lost consciousness during the battle, and was unresponsive to any treatment, mystical or mundane. Once Anninihus had been defeated, the Archaeknights had carefully lifted their master and carried him out of the gardens to where Queen Nora and Princess Kyla could pour every bit of magic they possessed into the failing king.

"Is everyone out of the gardens?" Rogan demanded when his team returned from the castle.

General Killdare barely glanced at the prince. "We don't know," he growled in between cursing orders organizing the citizens who were pouring into the square to lend aid. "The fire's spreading too fast and we can't risk..." The veteran's words trailed off as he became aware of how pointless they were. The moment Rogan was told there may still be people in the growing inferno, he was moving, his squire close behind.

The two reached the living wall of ivy and roses to find it replaced with a living wall of flame. "There!" Tomas barked, pointing to where a tall statue had fallen across the wall, creating a small bridge. Knight and squire were across and into the burning gardens in a second.

The heat was unbearable. Trees were screaming torches. Hills were bonfires. The high-arched bridges had collapsed and now were burning islands on the gentle streams. The air was a living thing, forcing into their lungs to cook them from within. Any exposed flesh seared. Their throats closed, their eyes blurred, and their pace never slowed.

"Make it fast!" Rogan said through gasps for clean air. The knight pointed to the left as he moved right, indicating with a sweep of his arm for them to make a quick loop of the banquet area.

Tomas hurried. He blinked away the soot-stained tears and forced his chest to take in the smoke for any air it held. He kicked at bodies, looking for any that might still live. He did not bother with Anninihus' creatures. They were better consumed by the flames. The roar of the dying gardens overwhelmed most sound. The ash and smoke obscured the eyes. Still, the squire would not relent in his search. But then, a strange calmness came over him.

A serenity drifted from the back of his mind. Somehow, the warmth of this feeling even cancelled the burning air around Tomas. The squire closed his eyes and welcomed this newfound comfort. He no longer heard the outraged snarls of the fire, nor felt spiteful embers spit upon his body. Instead, a new feeling washed over his form; it was as though he stood in the sea, just as he had as a child, when his mother and father took him to play in the waters of the Nassinal Sea. He felt the tides gently pushing and pulling, moving with an energy, a life, that was undeniable.

Tomas opened his eyes and saw. The smoke and ash and flames were no obstacle. He saw through the strange tides in which he swam. He saw the dark shadows of the fallen, grey and brown and lifeless. He saw flickering blues and greens of the dying gardens. There, he saw the fading white of a survivor. The squire hurried to that light and picked it up, carrying the wounded Guardsman back to the improvised bridge.

Rogan was there. He saw his approaching squire only when the young man was almost open him. The knight blinked through his watering eyes, and then saw the soldier in Tomas' arms. "How…?" he was about to say, but then blinked again. The golden rose pinned, as always, at the squire's collar was glowing. This light was matched in Tomas' eyes. "Alexia!" the knight gasped.

"I can see," Tomas said, as surprised as Rogan.

The knight paused only the briefest moment. Then, he grabbed the wounded Guardsman and helped move the soldier outside the inferno, to where a group of waiting clerics took charge of him. Knight and squire then looked at each other and nodded. "Ok, let's do this."

The two heroes went back in. Tomas led them to one survivor after another. They lifted the man and carried him back to the clerics, and then went looking again. They kept doing this. Ilse eventually arrived and wrapped wet cloths around their faces, saving her magic for the wounded and pouring more water on the men each time they emerged with another wounded person. This continued, and they rescued many.

"We're almost out of time!" Rogan yelled over the roar of the inferno as they carried one more wounded Guardsman out. Indeed, their searches were taking longer. Fewer and fewer wounded could be found, even with Tomas' granted sight. The fire was still growing, and the gardens' light was nearly dead.

"What about the fallen?" Tomas yelled back as they lowered the groaning man to cobblestone street.

The knight shook his head and looked back into the burning gardens. "One more pass!" he ordered, and led his squire back in. Tomas scanned as quickly as he could, but saw nothing living. They ran through the gardens, around the ruined banquet. Finally, at the far side, the squire spotted two more, two last, faltering lights. "You take that one!" Rogan roared, pointing to the left, "I've got this one! Meet at the bridge!"

Tomas nodded and sprinted to a small clearing, to a body already blackened. It was woman, the squire abstractly noticed, though only barely, now. He knelt and pulled the body into his lap. "Are you alive?" he yelled over the roar of the surrounding flames.

The eyes fluttered open and a short gasp hissed through cracked lips. He reached through the strange tides, towards the body and felt a strange sensation, like cool water poured into his skull. The water was that of the sea, pushing gently with a changing tide. He let the water flow out, into the body, though how he did this, the squire had no idea. "Althaea!?!" Tomas recognized the former spy and priestess, though how he knew her he was unsure. There was something in her, some presence of self, that seemed to flood back into her destroyed body.

"Tomas?" she whispered. Her eyes, the only part of her body unscathed by Esha's mystical attack, Anninihus' abusive mastery, and the burning garden, rolled up and recognized him. Pain filled those eyes, rolling back through the pulsing current connecting their minds. He sensed her agony. He felt the horrid violation of her slavery to the Death Mage. "Please," she croaked. And he understood.

Tomas drew Steelheart and pressed up, into her torso. She stiffened in new, temporary pain, but then relaxed into his embrace. Her eyes went dull. The flicker light when dark; finally at peace.

The squire looked up and saw Rogan. The knight was standing only a breath away, looking down. He said nothing, only nodded. Tomas set Althaea's body down and the two warriors left.

They threw themselves back through the same empty bridge that had granted them access. Gasping and rolling on the ground to smother the heat that clasped to them like lovers, the knight and squire had escaped the burning gardens barely in time. Soft hands grabbed them. Cool water was poured over their faces. A comforting warmth, a sharp contrast to the dire heat of the inferno, washed through Tomas' lungs, pushing out the smoke and steadying his heart. The squire blinked and looked up. Ilse was kneeling beside him, her hands on his bare chest. The priestess' eyes were closed as she whispered a prayer to her goddess and filled Tomas' body with her magic.

The very instant the squire was healed, Ilse turned to Rogan. She tore his tunic apart with startling strength, baring the knight's flesh, and lay her hands upon his chest. A soft light shined, seemingly from

432 The Northern Keep

under Ilse's fingers. Rogan gasped and shuddered. Looking up at the priestess, he nodded his thanks.

Tomas blinked and finally noticed that his head was cradled in Mary's lap. She was the source of the blessedly cool water pouring over his face. He said nothing, only breathed deep and let his lady pour.

The city square was an apparent madhouse. Demands for supplies competed with calls for clerical support from multiple directions. Anyone with medical training, from the clergy of the Harvest Mother to midwives and herbalists employed their respective crafts. Poultices were applied, makeshift litters transported moaning and screaming soldiers. Youths were tasked with gathering discarded weapons and armor, removing them from any hindering placement. The clerics of the Harvest Mother applied their magic. The priests of the Adamic Church eased the dying on their way. The sisters of the Lady of Light comforted the wounded. All of this gave the initial sight of insanity, and yet the chaos was meticulously organized by the sharp commands of Princess Kyla.

The Sister Superior of the Lady of Light and jewel of House Calonar managed the crisis like a seasoned military commander. Patients were triaged. Clerics were assigned. Any person standing still for even a moment fell under her pearlescent gaze and was put to work. Supplies were called for and dispersed efficiently. Litter-bearers were organized and moved like an ant colony. Even when Rogan and Tomas returned, their clothes and faces showing their close conflict with the blazing garden, the princess spared her husband barely a glance, determining his need was not immediate, and continued her work. Anyone who was not in need of care or caring for the fallen were relegated to Rogan for assignment and, like the prince himself, ejected from the plaza.

Following his wife's example, Rogan put his people to work. The guests of the banquet were escorted back to their homes by the City Watch which, under the growled commands of Remm Stonebearer. General Killdare and Captain Forthright organized the House Guard, who moved to seal the city and begin a detailed search of every possible hiding place for more of the monstrous invaders. Rashid's agents began a meticulous inspection of any available evidence. Beraht left for the dungeons to interrogate the assassins they had taken prisoner. Esha gathered her students and, imbuing them with enough of her strength to return to the Tower, ordered an immediate mystical search for the Death Mage.

Tomas took a moment as Rogan was barking orders. He leaned against one of the new Uldra gaslamps, relieved the strange system had yet to reach the gardens for fear of what might have happened. A soft sob drew his attention. Sitting alone on a nearby bench was Velaera the master dressmaker. The matronly Sylva had drawn her legs to her chest, wrapping her arms around them, and lowered her head.

Tomas sat beside her, putting his arm around her quivering shoulders. He said nothing.

"That fool," the tailor sobbed. "That stupid, careless, *male*." She leaned against Tomas, her grief washing over him as she clutched to the young squire. "Why?" she demanded of nothing, or perhaps of everything. "Why did he have to…?" More tears and more shaking and more questions flowed. Velaera demanded why their time together was so short. Why the Death Mage had to kill him. Why he had to die to save her. There were no answers.

Hours passed in moments. Tasks were completed and tasks were assigned. The work continued. Velaera's grief quieted and her breathing steadied. Tomas waved over a pair of Guardsmen, instructing that they help the master tailor home. He sat for a few moments, forcing down his own storm of unanswerable questions before standing and seeking out his knight. Rogan and Tomas found themselves on a set of benches a few yards from where Kyla was finishing the triage for the dead, dying, and wounded. Both warriors felt tired to their very bones. "I didn't think there was anyone in the world who could bring that man down," the squire noted wearily, his eyes going to the castle. "Let alone with one spell."

Rogan grunted. "There are people who may be able to, but Anninihus is definitely *not* one of them. There was something else at work."

Tomas glanced at his knight. "Are you sure you're not just letting your feelings for him influence your thinking?"

"Remind me to hit you once I've rested."

"From what I've heard, Anninihus was never that powerful," Tomas pointed out, wishing to keep the subject away from just how weary he felt. "How could he defeat an adept as powerful as King Cylan Calonar?"

"One of many questions I intend to cut into that scrawny bastard."

They were quiet then. They were past exhaustion, but unwilling to leave for bed when everyone else was hard at work. So, they sat and waited for another call to action. Tomas glanced at his knight and whispered, "Rogan."

The prince of the Northlands glanced at his squire.

"Althaea…"

Rogan nodded. "Do you want to talk about it?"

"I…" Tomas could only shake his head, unable to put into words the storm in his heart.

"Nobody will understand," the knight said. "Nobody can understand." He glanced past the city center, where the glow of the burning gardens cast an ominous red into the western sky. Rogan had ordered the new Uldra gaslamps extinguished and their fuel cut to prevent any possible catastrophes. This cast the city in darkness, save for the evil glow of the dying gardens. "She died in the fight," he said then. "Her body was consumed by the fire." The knight looked into his squire's eyes. "That's what everyone will assume. Most people won't ask about it. It's up to you if you ever want to say different."

Tomas nodded. A thought occurred, then. "My father…?"

The knight nodded. "Pretty much the same, kid."

A messenger ran up and breathlessly relayed a summons from Queen Nora. Rogan and Tomas stood.

Chapter 49

"Why is he suddenly so weak?" Cardinal Tain was asking Queen Nora as Rogan and Tomas arrived in the royal apartments. All seven Archaeknights in the city, to include those who fought in the gardens, were deployed within and around the suite. They faces spoke of grim determination and a silent feeling of defeat. Their king was dying, and they could do nothing.

The Queen was preparing a potion of some kind with the aid of Cardinal Tain. Somewhat to Tomas' surprise, Mary joined the men as they arrived, having been assigned by Kyla to aid the Calonar matriarch. The maid was retrieving ingredients from Aebreanna's bag at the Queen's instruction. Mary offered Tomas only the most passing greeting, her own face grey with worry over the failing king. She passed the men and moved to the Queen's side, handing pouches and bottles as directed.

Nora, not even looking up from her work, whispered something.

"I'm sorry, Nora," Tain said, "but my hearing isn't what it used to be."

"It isn't sudden," she answered. "He's been growing steadily weaker all year. He's been using his magic to maintain what strength he had. I've been supplementing. The battle drained his last reserves."

"Is that true?" Tomas quietly asked Rogan.

The knight silently nodded.

"Why didn't you tell anyone?"

Rogan sighed, trying to rub the weariness out of his eyes. "Couldn't. For centuries, the only thing keeping the Druug and the Inquisition and the Xeshlin, and every other bad guy in check was their fear of House Calonar, especially *him*. Now, with the Emperor dead, the Legions disbanded, and so many nobles fighting among themselves for the Redwood Throne, the only thing keeping Lanasia from erupting in all-out chaos was the fear of the last surviving Hero of Fate." Rogan looked at Tomas. "Why do you think we never bother arguing against the whole 'Black Duke' thing?" The knight shook his head. "The mythology of Cylan Calonar has kept the darkness in check for decades. Maybe longer."

"No one man is that important, Rogan," Tomas insisted.

"Yes, he is. He's the last of the Heroes of Fate, kid; the only one left. Tienel Greysoul, Fak'Har, Anninihus, Ravana, even Kelinva and her Invasion, they were all defeated by the Heroes of Fate. When they started dying off, it became House Calonar. The only reason we've had such a success rate is that each of these problems come at us one at a time. The day the world no longer has Cylan Calonar scaring the bad guys into submission, that's the day they come at us all at once. That's the day the world will burn."

"Is that why you don't want to be king?" the squire asked quietly.

The knight said nothing, his gaze staying on King Cylan's unmoving form. Then, "there are a lot of reasons I don't want to be king, kid. I have so many reasons, I've lost track of them. But to answer your question; no, I'm not afraid that I won't be able to do as good a job as the King. I *know* I can't. I'm not a wizard, a holy man, or even a wise man. I'm a fighter. But there's also..." He closed his mouth sharply.

Tomas looked at his knight. "What?" he demanded. "Also, what?"

Rogan glanced at his squire and then looked to Nora. The Queen somehow seemed to know, to hear her son-in-law's unasked question. She glanced up from the barely-breathing King, looked at Rogan, and nodded. Sighing deeply, the knight rubbed his weary eyes. "Do you remember, back when we first met, do you remember what Cyras said about a prophecy?"

"Kind of," the squire shrugged. "Cyras said a lot of..."

"Bullshit?" The knight chuckled. "Call it what it is, kid. Cyras Darkholm talks a lot of crazy." He looked around and pulled his squire aside with a jerk of his head. Seeing they were out of earshot, he spoke quietly. "They call him the Trickster Mage for a reason, kid. Most of the crazy act is just that: an act. He likes to confuse people, to keep them off-balance. The thing is, I've never once heard him tell a lie. Everything he says is truth, just never *all* the truth."

"Ok," Tomas sighed, "so what was the truth I missed?"

"A long while back, I don't know exactly when, there was a mystic in Otyilia named Darrell. He went under some kind of possession or trance or something, and spoke a prophecy. Now, must 'prophecies' are just vague nonsense, but this was wasn't. It said, *exactly* what was going to happen, in detail."

"You've seen it?"

The knight shook his head. "Only bits, small bits. Cyras won't let anybody see the whole thing. He's the only one with the complete prophecy. He's trying to stop it from coming true, so every now and then he appears, tells us to do something, then disappears again."

"What is it?" Tomas asked. "What's he trying to stop?"

Rogan sighed again, hesitating. "Ramalech," he whispered. "The rise of the Demon-god."

The squire gasped, the name of evil sending shivers down his spine, to his very soul.

Rogan continued. "The prophecy says that, after a series of specific events, the Demon-god will escape Underworld and return to Arayel. Remember that thing with Tienel Greysoul ten years ago? That was one of the events." He nodded towards the cluster of clerics working their magic on Cylan Calonar. "This is another. Cyras told us that the death of Cylan Calonar is one of four major events that will precede the rise of Ramalech."

"What are the signs?"

"The thing with Greysoul was one. The death of Cylan Calonar. Something Cyras calls, 'the Inversion;' we don't know what that means. And lastly…" the knight looked his squire in the eyes. "The return of Kelinva, Dark Empress of the Xeshlin."

"The end of the world…" Tomas breathed.

His knight nodded. "Or near enough to make no difference. That's what we're up against, kid. That's the secret. House Calonar is trying to stop the return of the Dark Empress, and prevent the rise of the Demon-god she worshipped."

"But, how? Why?" A thousand questions flooded the young man's mind, but Rogan held up a hand.

"The answer to all of that is, 'we don't know.' Cyras isn't telling us much, just giving us warning when one of the big events is starting."

"But why not…?"

"Again, the answer is, 'we don't know.'" Seeing the Queen motioning to him, Rogan gathered himself up. He paused a moment and looked back at his squire. "If you want to rethink your place here, I'll understand. We know we're going to have to fight what's coming. And, when the time comes, we'll probably have to do it alone." He sighed and moved to his mother-in-law's side.

"He's wrong, you know," a gentle voice came suddenly from behind Tomas. Spinning around, his hand automatically going for Steelheart, the squire was relieved that it was just Aebreanna, still garbed in her light, flowing banquet gown. The baroness had disappeared for most of the evening, with reports coming in that she had gone to her children. Now, she stood silently in the royal chambers, her gaze on the King.

"Who's wrong?" Tomas asked.

"Rogan. He fears the King's death because it means leadership will pass to him. He knows of the imminent battle against Kelinva and her Demon-god, and thinks he will fight alone."

"But there're others," Tomas insisted, glancing around. "House Calonar, the Guard, allies in Velaross and Ironheartshaven."

Aebreanna shook her head slightly. "Allies are plentiful in easy times," she argued. "In crisis, they are often elusive. You so love the stories of the Heroes of Fate, how often did they stand alone, not for some sense of heroic stoicism, but because they were abandoned by their so-called allies?"

Tomas thought. "Most of the time," he admitted.

The Sylva nodded. "When the battle comes, House Calonar will almost certainly fight. And it will almost certainly fight alone. Rogan fears this, not wanting to lead so many to their deaths."

The squire thought a moment. "But, you said he was wrong."

She nodded again. "Rogan questions his ability to lead, comparing himself to the King. He has the needed skills, and the most important skill of all: he listens." The spy looked closely at Tomas. "What he needs are those close to him, loyal to him, who can offer their support. I suspect the Queen believes you will be one of those."

"Me," Tomas asked. "Why me?"

"Everyone knows Cylan Calonar is one of, if not the most powerful adept in the world, and that his fighting skills were once unparalleled. Everyone also knows that his wife is one of the most powerful clerics in the world, but what a very select few in the world know is that Nora Calonar is also a Truthseer."

"The Queen said that before," Tomas noted. "What is a Truthseer?"

"When Nora focuses on someone, she sees their true nature and destiny." The sylva turned her opalescent eyes on him. "Alexia also had Truthsight. You may have noticed the power of their gaze."

Looking over at the Queen, who was holding her husband's head in her lap and speaking softly yet sternly to Rogan, Tomas nodded. "I guess that would explain why they both seem so... disconnected."

"Correct. Whenever the Queen looks about, she sees possibilities and destinies. That was how the King knew Rogan was the right man to become his heir. For centuries, the women of House Calonar have all shared this ability to some degree. Somehow, when Nora wed the King, Alexia granted her Truthsight as well. The Queen has it, as does her younger daughter."

Tomas started, thinking back to his overly-brief time with Alexia. More implications crashed upon him. A thought occurred to the squire then, a terrible thought that froze him where he stood. "He knew, didn't he? Before Rogan and Kyla got married, and before he became sick, the King knew. That's why he named Rogan his heir. Cylan Calonar has been alive for centuries; the only reason he would be so insistent that he get an heir and that Rogan build a base of loyal friends is because he knew he was going to die."

Aebreanna nodded her head mutely, a single tear running down her cheek. "A gift from Darkholm," she said through clenched teeth. "The Trickster Mage visited about twelve years ago. They were locked in the King's study for days. When the King came out, Darkholm had vanished, as usual. From that day forward, the King has been quietly making plans for the day he would be gone. The next year, we found Rogan."

"So, what do we do now?" the squire asked.

"I have no idea. We try to save the King and find the man responsible for this, I suppose."

Rogan, his faced grayed and worn, approached the small group. "I take it," Aebreanna said, "the prognosis is not good."

"And getting worse," the knight confirmed.

"Beraht's coming," Tomas said, gesturing to the approaching Uldra.

"Tell me you've got good news," Rogan growled.

The mountain-man laughed a cruel laugh, the braids of his long beard split in a malicious grin. "I convinced those bastards to talk," he said, rubbing the butt of his waraxe. "Nobody threatens my little axe-blunter."

"What did they say?"

Beraht laughed coarsely again. "Well, they started with, 'Oh god, please don't. I beg you, have mercy.' You know, the usual stuff."

Rogan rolled his eyes. "We're pressed for time here Beraht. We can't give Anninihus the chance to regroup; we've got to get him."

"Sorry, Rogan, but you know how much I love my work. The assassins were planning to meet with their boss north of town. After a little convincing, they finally told me where Anninihus is hiding."

"Which is?" the knight demanded.

"Heath Dannah. He and his buddies are hiding in the ruins of Heath Dannah."

Rogan nodded. "Alright." The knight thought a moment, then straightened. "Aebreanna, you stay here with the kids. Make sure Remm secures the city and get Kyla and Nora anything they need."

The baroness shook her head. "Rashid can handle that. You will need my aid in the coming battle."

"Fine." the knight grunted. He looked at Tomas. "Go get Esha. Tell her what Beraht found out and that we'll need transport. Then go get your things and tell Roderick to ready our horses for combat." He rubbed his shoulder. "Also, find Ilse and have her and a group of clerics meet us as well; we'll need to be restored before we go. Everyone meets up outside the northwestern gate."

Tomas jerked his head in the direction of the Guards barracks. "Do you want me to get some backup?" he asked.

The knight shook his head. "No time. The Guard is damn good at their jobs, but it takes them forever to do anything. You and Beraht get our gear."

"What are you going to do?" the Uldra asked.

The knight nodded towards where Queen Nora and Cardinal Tain were trying to aid the King. "I'm going to have a talk with the Cardinal. Anninihus is a Death Mage; we'll need protection. This time, we finish him for good."

Chapter 50

There was neither moon nor clouds, casting the world in a dim, colorless void. The few trees were little more than dark fingers rising from a grey earth. The low hills surrounding them looked like rumples on a blanket, hastily thrown over a fresh corpse. Innumerable large stones, boulders really, were scattered about the countryside as though some giant had idly scattered them centuries ago. The land seemed dead, like a haunted steppe of shadowlands.

Esha had opened a mystical doorway into this hellscape, and Rogan had led them through. They brought all their weapons, armor, and equipment, as well as a team of warhorses. Upon their arrival, Aebreanna had set off to scout, leaving the warriors behind to prepare themselves for battle.

Tomas muttered something under his breath as he tightened the straps of Rogan's breastplate. His knight glanced down, "Problem?" he asked.

The squire only glanced up from a troublesome buckle. "You kidding?" The young man threw a nervous look to the surrounding lands. "Now would be a great time to tell me all the stories I've heard of Heath Dannah aren't true."

"Your stories likely are not," Esha replied quietly. She did not glance up from her detailed inspection of the many pouches sewn into her belts. The archmage had set aside her customary wrinkled and burn-scarred blue robes. Instead, she had donned a linen smock under a wool kirtle. The leather belts were wrapped around her waist and across one shoulder. "In fact, whatever legends you have heard of Heath Dannah almost surely underreport the truth."

The squire had at last set the buckle correctly and picked up the leather belt and scabbard holding Fang, his knight's arming sword. "Seriously?" Tomas demanded.

"Seriously," his knight replied. "The Cursed City. Gateway to Underworld. Home of the Damned." He looked squarely at his squire. "Probably all true."

"The last outpost of our *Im'peri'a*," Esha added, rubbing a strange oil onto her staff. "The furthest boundary of our expansion." She glanced at Tomas. "And the first community to fall during the Disaster of Nassinalia. Next to the city itself, of course."

"Uldra don't come here," Beraht rumbled. The towering barbarian was settling his massive scalemail armor over his impossibly thick torso. "Druug neither. Nothing living comes here."

Tomas took a moment and looked around. There were no animals, no sounds. The dark sky above was clear of birds. Deer and rabbits avoided this cursed place. There were no settlements. Even the wild Gunrsvein would not risk entering this borderland to the realm of the dead. Everything that must know the touch of the White Lady shuns the ruins of Heath Dannah.

"An entire city gone in less than a day," Rogan said, signaling Tomas to belt on his sword.

"'The day when all the Doorways to Underworld opened,'" Tomas quoted the famous epic poem *Tragedy of Nassinalia*. "'The day when the Umbral were freed to torment the living.'" He set Rogan's sword belt and glanced at him. "Just stories, right?"

The knight shook his head. "No, not just stories."

Esha stood and settled her own equipment. "A single column of refugees returned from this place. They never spoke of what happened to them, except to repeat, 'Ramalech lives,' again and again."

"And we're going into that ruin?" Tomas asked, handing Rogan his helmet.

The knight took it. "Beats being bored," he half-joked.

Tomas shook his head and turned to his own armor. As a squire, he had not yet earned the right to wear full plate and carry a heraldic shield. Rogan had offered to wave the tradition, but the young man insisted on obeying the forms. Instead, Tomas wore a breastplate over a simple chainmail shirt, with gauntlets, greaves, and the spagenhelm common to the Calonar House Guard. He would carry no shield, trusting to Steelheart. As the squire checked his own equipment, he glanced about, wanting to change the subject. "So, why does Aebreanna hate Cyras Darkholm so much?"

Rogan glanced at Tomas. "What makes you think she hates Cyras?" he asked.

"Well, when we were talking, she mentioned Cyras' name and the look on her face said that if something bad happened to him she wouldn't exactly shed any tears about it."

"That's putting it mildly," the knight snorted. "Aebreanna would probably be more likely to do something unpleasant to Cyras herself."

"Why?"

"That's a personal question, kid. Why don't you ask Aebreanna?"

"I get the felling she wouldn't want to talk about it," Tomas muttered.

"I tell you what," Rogan said, "when we aren't about to go into battle with an insane Death Mage in one of the most cursed places in Arayel, ask me again."

Nodding, the squire finished his preparations even as Aebreanna returned. She was caked with mud and had bits of vegetation clinging to her.

"What did you find?" the knight asked.

Aebreanna moved to a nearby creek and quickly cleaned off the worst of the grime. "Anninihus," she replied grimly, "Among others. He has sought refuge at the edge of the ruins. I doubt, even in his near-madness, the Death Mage would risk entering the city proper." She threw a wicked glance at Rogan. "He seems quite upset."

"How upset?" Tomas asked.

Checking the many small Sylvai blades she had belted across her body, Aebreanna glanced over at Tomas. "Well, he was raving a bit, your name featured rather prominently."

"Good," Rogan grunted.

"Sadly, I fear his mercenaries are not his intended defense, though." She put on a vest of studded leather dyed a mottled black and grey. "When I found them, he was drawing arcane symbols into the ground with green flame."

Rogan looked questioningly at Esha, who had been scanning a very small book. The archmage looked to Aebreanna. "Can you recall what the symbols looked like?" she asked, looking up from her book.

The spy used a stick to draw some intricate designs into the ground.

Looking at the symbols, Esha grunted and turned back to Rogan. "A variation of a summoning spell. He is likely trying to raise whatever is within the ruins."

"What kind of creatures could he raise here?" Rogan asked of Beraht.

Stroking his braided beard, absently picking out the crumbs of his last meal, the Uldra glanced up to the dimly-glittering stars. "Could be anything: ghouls, ghosts, restless dead. It's a cursed place, lots of things for the Death Mage."

"Plus the Umbral," Tomas added.

"What?" Rogan demanded.

"When the Disaster finally subsided," his squire replied, "the Umbral were all supposed to be pulled back to Underworld. But the legends say that's what makes Heath Dannah so cursed. Some Umbral stayed, trapped there."

"Great," Rogan said without much enthusiasm.

"Do not distress," Aebreanna said. "I have taken measures."

"What measures?" Esha asked.

Reaching into her vest, the spy pulled out a flask. "I laced Anninihus' materials with this. As soon as he tries using his materials for casting, he shall be most surprised at the result."

"What is that?" Tomas asked curiously.

"Khepric fire," Aebreanna replied. "It has an unfortunate tendency to blow up for the slightest reasons."

"How did you get close enough to spike Anninihus' tricks?" Rogan asked.

Pulling a small twig from her lustrous main, deep auburn with streaks of white in anticipation of winter's arrival, Aebreanna smiled a wicked smile. "My skills are not inconsiderable."

"How many guards?" the knight asked.

"Ten, not counting whatever Anninihus can summon."

"I thought you took care of that?" Beraht growled.

"My knowledge of death magic is not great," the spy replied. "While I believe that he cannot launch any traditional offensive magic at us, his necromantic powers may remain unaffected."

"Well, what good are you?" Rogan demanded lightly.

Aebreanna raised an eyebrow. "In the future," she replied primly, "send Esha on reconnaissance, and I will be content to carry the stick."

Esha looked up again from her book. "How many times must I tell you?" she sputtered indignantly. "My staff is one of the most powerful of its type."

"Alright, alright," Rogan stepped in, eager to get moving. "We all like your staff, Esha; it's very nice." He looked to Aebreanna. "How far," he asked.

"Ten minutes. More, for silence."

The knight, shifting in his plate armor, grunted. He moved to Stick, the warhorse pawing at the earth and snorting his eagerness for the violence ahead. Tomas helped his knight to mount, Stick only grunting a little at the added weight of his armored rider. Before armoring Rogan, both he and his squire had outfitted the warhorse in his own wargear. The large rings of the beast's mail were covered underneath by a quilted grey coat and above by another, but this one of royal blue. At the front was sewn the overlapping diamonds that were the sigil of House Calonar. Seeing Rogan settled into the saddle, Tomas handed up his knight's shield and turned to his own eager warhorse.

Urge wore a similar armor as did his sire. The same coats of grey and blue offered insulation against the mail, and an identical sigil adorned the front. The sullen animal's normal resistance to work was abandoned, much like it had been for the joust. But in this case, Urge's enthusiasm was like Stick's: intense and deadly. Tomas mounted his warhorse, for perhaps the first time, Urge offered no resistance, no comical obstruction, but seemed in fact to help the squire up. The two settled into one another and Tomas looked to his knight, nodding.

Chapter 51

At first glance, the ruins of Heath Dannah did not seem especially ruinous. The cobblestone streets showed little damage. The buildings, though missing wooden doors and glass windows, still stood. Decorative columns still lined stately boardwalks, statues to forgotten leaders looked out on peaceful plazas, and even the raised amphitheaters seemed ready for another performance. Even Pelsemoria, only a decade into its abandonment, show worse signs of neglect. The Disaster of Nassinalia occurred nearly two thousand years ago, as did the death of this city and yet, as Tomas and his friends rode slowly in, they could find no trace of violence.

This illusion did not last long. Upon entering the paved streets of Heath Dannah, its strange truths began revealing themselves. Trails of an unearthly slime coated the walls of every building, as though the stones themselves wept alien tears. This bizarre material glowed a silent blue, casting an even, sickly light over the city. There was no heat from this light, no sound, and no reason for its existence. Curious, Tomas reached over to touch the slime, but Aebreanna intercept him, grabbing his wrist in her small hand and shaking her head emphatically.

They moved on, and the horror of the ruins grew. Within the houses and shops rested furniture, counters, even toys. These all appeared as though brand new, waiting for new residents. The columns they rode past, resembling any from the great cities of the old Sylvai Empire, should have borne engraved images of past glories, victories, and achievements; these monuments, however, bore images of torture, of riotous madness, of insidious torment. The statues to long-dead Sylvai watched them, the strange slime dripping from the buildings also ran fresh like tears from the eyes, and the stone mouths were open in soundless screams. The heroes drew closer to one another, even their mounts trembled at the soul-deep horror around them. Still, under the leadership of Stick and Urge, the party pushed deeper into the silent terror of Heath Dannah.

They slowly made their way through the glowing, silent ruins. For centuries, tales spoke of treasure, of powerful secrets and hidden wonders to be found in Heath Dannah. Many adventurers, bearing that critical mixture of bravery and foolishness, had tested the ruins. None had ever returned. Still, every generation had its stories of wealth and glory to be found by anyone willing to risk the dangers of this haunted place, rewards that tempted fools. And now, Tomas and his friends were the fools.

For a quarter of an hour, they skirted the edges of Heath Dannah. They saw more than enough to dissuade exploration, but still they followed Aebreanna's guidance. They did not care for hidden treasure or powerful secrets. They lusted only for vengeance. Anninihus had attacked them, and now their beloved king was sick, possibly dying. These warriors would bring justice to the Death Mage.

Aebreanna motioned for a halt. She nodded ahead, to an amphitheater. The tiers of seating looked as new and unspoiled as though it had finished construction only that morning. Yet, tiny streams of glowing blue flowed down them like tiny, otherworldly waterfalls. These streams flowed together, to form an insidious pool in the orchestra, the great circle in which actors, acrobats, musicians, and poets once performed. This pool now churned as though some great beast of the sea dwelt within, just out of sight. The skene, the raised platform and backdrop, stood still, ready for speeches and debate. Now, however, it housed a Death Mage and his mercenaries.

"Will they be a problem?" Rogan quietly asked.

The spy shrugged. "Standard. Mercenaries from the southern Velaross duchies. Typical scum, cheap and worthless."

"Alright then," he grunted. "Let's do this."

Aebreanna dismounted and sneaked around the edge of amphitheater. The group spread out. Esha dismounted as well and followed Aebreanna into the theatron, the tiered seating. Beraht, his Uldra waraxe in hand, moved around behind the skene, in cover of its shadow, waiting for the attack. Rogan and Tomas, armed and armored, prepared to charge from the front atop their powerful warhorses, who snorted and pawed and trembled in anticipation. The mounted warriors drew attention to themselves, moving in the open and allowing the others to surprise from the sides and rear.

Tomas took a moment to study his targets. Like Aebreanna had said, they were mercenary scum, clad in a variety of equipment and armor in varying states of disrepair. For the most part, security was not a high priority for these men, as most of them were sleeping, drinking, or playing dice. They had gathered to one side of the skene, the raised stage. None seemed eager to join Anninihus, who stood alone at the center of the skene. Instead, the mercenaries had retreated to ground level. These would be the targets for Rogan and Tomas.

"I can't believe these guys consider themselves soldiers," Tomas muttered.

"Believe it, kid," Rogan replied in a low voice. "For the most part, any moron can pick up a weapon and call himself a soldier. Just keep in mind that, as soon as you think your enemy can't hurt you, that's when you die. Always assume your opponent is better than you."

"Well, why don't we go find out just how good these guys are?"

Grinning maliciously, the knight squared himself, drew Fang, and charged. The warhorses cleared the distance in an instant, their armored coats offering no hinderance against their powerful legs. Rogan thrust, taking one man in the throat. Tomas ran a second through and kicked the dead man off Steelheart. Stick and Urge sped through and past the clustered, confused mercenaries, rearing and turning to charge again.

Rogan's skill with the sword, legendary in and around the Northlands, was on full display that evening. Three of the mercenaries, hoping to outflank the knight, moved to opposing positions, encircling him. Rogan allowed this. The mercenaries, obviously having worked together before, moved in as one, the first falling quickly as Rogan deftly parried a thrust and replied with one of his own, only barely piercing the heart of his target before he pulled the blade clear and, reversing it, plunged it into the attacker from the rear. The final mercenary, seeing an opening on the knight's left, lunged in, bringing his shortsword down with tremendous force. Stick was ready, though, and lashed with his rear leg, catching the mercenary in the chest and ejecting him dozens of feet away, gasping and spitting blood.

The man tried to keep his feet, but feel. He rose but stumbled back, tripping on the low stone barrier between the theatron and the glowing orchestra. The mercenary kept his footing, dancing a bit to remain standing, but had stumbled into the alien light of the pooling blue slime.

At first, nothing happened. The rippling slime still glowed blue. The mercenary's iron-shod boots did not even sink into the slime. The man looked up, though, terror in his eyes. Soundlessly, with barely any disturbance in the pool, the man dropped down as though some platform beneath had suddenly opened. The mercenary could manage only the barest beginning of a scream, but that alone spoke of his mindless terror at what lie beneath.

Seeing this, everyone, friend and foe, jumped back, the battle for a moment halting against the terrifying unknown of that glowing pool. This pause, though, lasted only a moment. Most of the mercenaries retreated up onto the skene. Only two had courage enough to remain on the ground, and these two lunged at Tomas. Lacking Rogan's swordsmanship and experience in combat tactics, the squire was having a slightly harder time of it. He parried the attacks from one assailant, but could not disarm him. At last, the squire bodily pushed the attacker back and turned Urge, the warhorse lashing out even as his sire just had, but with both rear legs, crushing the man's chest. Even as the first man died, Tomas had to parry a clumsy swing from the second. Worse, the squire was splitting his attention between this attacker, and the merc on the far side of the amphitheater who was raising his crossbow and taking careful aim at him.

The mercenary's eyes tensed in preparation to fire, but in the instant before the crossbowman could, those same eyes widened in disbelief and shock as Aebreanna flipped from the tiered seating, slamming into the mercenary and hurling him into the rippling pool. The man screamed and tried to scramble out, but like his comrade, he was pulled down by some unseen evil. Aebreanna gave the doomed man not a single glance, instead spotting two mercenaries trying to rush her. Using her momentum, the Sylva rolled across the benches and spun around completely, putting her back to the oncoming men. Just as the two mercenaries raised their shortswords to strike, the beautiful spy, in one fluid motion, drew two Sylvai blades from her belt and jabbed them into the chests of her attackers.

Several of the mercenaries, seeing in which direction the tide of battle was turning, thought to escape during the confusion of the melee. Their hopes were destroyed, however, when Beraht emerged from the far side of the skene. The Uldra barbarian twisted his braided beard into a hideous grin, joyous that he could once again release the bloodlust that boiled within his entire race. The first two must have hoped to overwhelm Beraht, but the Uldra laughed at this as he intercepted the first sword strike, catching the small Human's arm with one hand before swinging his waraxe into the chest of the attacker. Spinning away from the second mercenary in the same movement that had finished his initial target, the barbarous mountain-man barreled into the small group of remaining mercenaries, crushing one man's head with an overhand swing of his boulder-like fist, and lopping off another's head with his waraxe. The remaining three turned to flee but had no chance of escape as Beraht threw his weapon into the back of the mercenary in the middle. The Halvan to that man's right gasped and twisted away from his dead comrade, accidentally tripping off the skene and falling into the glowing pool. He vanished as did his friends. The final mercenary found his courage and turned, thrusting his sword towards Beraht's middle. The barbarian just slapped the tiny Human blade aside and swing his fist down, crushing the screaming man's skull.

Anninihus watched the deaths of his mercenaries with a casual indifference. Once the last of the men were cut down and the heroes all turned their attention to him, the Death Mage grinned evilly and spoke a single word in the arcane tongue. In response, the ground all around the amphitheater writhed and the glowing pool of blue slime rose as though Underworld itself meant to force its way into Arayel. Damned creatures long dead clawed their way to the surface, hissing their spite at the living and glowing with the evil blue slime that trailed behind them like the corrupted robes of evil clerics. The air all around the champions of the Northern Keep became suddenly alive, if such a term could accurately apply, as dark mist crept out of every shadow and coalesced into nightmarish warriors, each wailing with the pain of damnation. The wails of the murdered dead and the damned alike filled the minds of the heroes, wringing from them tears of pain and cries of terror. It took every scrap of courage they possessed not to throw down their weapons and flee.

"Did you know he could do this?" Tomas screamed over the horrible wailing.

"He *can't* do this!" Rogan insisted.

"Well he just did!"

"Esha, do something!" Aebreanna insisted.

The archmage appeared at the highest tier of the theatron, raising her staff and calling to its tip the light of the stars overhead. Gesturing with her free hand, the Sylva launched bolts of pure light, hitting one creature of damned unlife after another. Powerful as the archmage's magic was, though, it could not destroy every horror clawing out of the darkness of Heath Dannah. Without pause, Esha targeted the largest groups of the monsters, desperately trying to keep them from overwhelming her friends.

Several of the mockeries of life hissed and leapt at Beraht, their empty sockets glowing with the blue fire of Underworld. The Uldra saw this and stood his ground; grimly swinging his waraxe again and again, felling them as quickly as they could attack him. Never once did the barbarian surrender ground to his enemies. They leapt upon his massive body, first one, then two, and more. On and on they pushed and pulled and stabbed and slashed. Beraht did not scream, but instead growled and snarled his defiant pain.

Rogan and Tomas fought side by side. The nightmares surrounded them and drew grey blades that glowed with a sickly blue light. Rogan blocked each of their strikes with his shield and countered when he could with Fang. Tomas, having no shield, was forced to use Steelheart for his only defense, allowing more and more of the damned to attack. Tomas fought through tears and gritted his teeth against the growing pain. Each unparried slash, each barely-dodged stab, brought blood and a flash of freezing pain. Stick tossed his head against the creatures, forcing them into Rogan's field of attack, and Urge lashed with his steel-shod hooves.

"We've got problems!" Tomas barked.

"Hang on kid!" Rogan yelled. The knight slashed again and again at the creatures. In every instance, his blade would pass through the ghostly mist his opponents seemed to be made of only to have it reform with no damage. "Esha, we could really use something flashy right now!!"

"I am somewhat engaged," the archmage's voice was calm, but strained. Several monsters of bone and claw were dragging themselves up the tiered benches towards the Sylva. Esha launched her mystical attacks, but for every two or three of the creatures she could destroy, another four would take their place.

A saber made of glowing blue nightmares cut through Rogan's armor, slicing straight into the knight's left shoulder. "Dammit!" he swore. His counter strike found nothing but phantom mist. "Esha! How do we stop these things!?!"

"Anninihus!" the Sylva barked. One of the skeletal creatures reached the archmage and slashed across her back with its sharp claws. Esha screamed in pain and collapsed to the ground, barely able to send a flash of yellow light into the monster's chest before it could finish him. "Break his concentration!" the archmage yelled through clenched teeth.

Rogan and Tomas, both hard pressed and bleeding, spared brief glances to where the Death Mage stood. Anninihus was very still; he held his skull-topped staff of pale wood high with his eyes closed and his spells pouring endlessly from his mouth. Beads of sweat glistened on the villain's brow. He seemed oblivious to the fight, to the whole world.

Both knight and squire knew they had no chance of bypassing the horrors surrounding them. Their adversaries were simply too fast. "Aebreanna!" Rogan barked. "Take him!"

"I am blocked!" the Sylva yelled. Indeed, she was surrounded on all sides by a horde of the rotting dead. The creatures, who may have been Sylvai or Human or any other race, responded to Aebreanna's dexterity with sheer numbers. She tried to leap, only to be blocked by a wall of living death. She tried to tumble, only to be intercepted. She was reduced to slashing with her Sylvai blades, causing no damage and little distraction.

"Beraht!" Rogan roared. "Save Aebreanna!"

The Uldra had been engulfed by his own damned horde of moaning nightmares. The barbarian had tried attacking, tried pulling at them, but still more and more of the creatures appeared and clambered up his massive body. His great Uldra waraxe was the only weapon amongst the heroes that had any effect on the nightmarish creatures, dispersing them with each swipe. But there were far too many. They overwhelmed the mountain man, clambering atop his legs and his arms. Finally, he had been pulled to his knees, near to exhaustion. When Rogan called out, when he spoke those words, a new rage filled the Uldra. With a thunderous roar, with a cry of war and hate and unwavering determination, Beraht stood. No matter the creatures pulling at him, no matter his wounds or faltering strength, the barbarian let loose with a roar that could shatter the mountains themselves. And then he leapt.

Beraht launched himself up, across the amphitheater, towards the tiered benches on which Aebreanna was trapped. The Sylva looked up and saw her friend's descent, and responded. She leapt herself into the air, holding out a diminutive hand. Beraht, his entire face covered by the clawing monsters trying to blind him, reached out his own massive hand. The two met, mid-air. Aebreanna's whole arm seemed to disappear within Beraht's boulder-like fist. The Uldra twisted and pulled, and his Sylva friend was hurled away from her attackers.

Beraht crashed into the tiered benches, crushing innumerable monsters beneath his great bulk. Aebreanna used the momentum and advantage her friend had given, and flipped in the air to land gracefully upon the opposite side of the amphitheater.

In her hands was a mercenary crossbow. "Charge it!" the baroness snapped as she took aim at Anninihus and pulled the trigger.

The bolt shot out, and Aebreanna tossed aside the spent crossbow without seeing whether or not her attack hit. The bolt flew, crackling with the arcane electricity Esha imbued it with an instant before finding its target. The bolt lanced into the pouches lining Anninihus' belt. The contents of those many pouches exploded, sending the mage reeling to the ground, desperately stripping off his belt and throwing it away. Without the Death Mage's spells, the phantom attackers rose, roaring in fury at being denied their living victims. Across the amphitheater, the monstrous creatures sustained only by Anninihus' magic and concentration roared their impotent fury. Then the glowing pool angry thrashed. A great wind that could not touch the living howled through the amphitheater. The dead and the damned were pulled up into a horrific cyclone. They were drawn back into the pool and what lay beneath. The cyclone unfelt by the living rose and crashed down, into the pool, which vanished itself.

And then, all was calm.

Chapter 52

Tomas nearly collapsed in relief, both the squire and his mount panting and trembling in relief and near-exhaustion. The pain of his many cuts was searing, and he feared poison. "Not done yet, kid," Rogan said grimly

With all the nightmarish creatures he had summoned dealt with, Anninihus likely realized his doom was at hand. The villain finished away his burning belts and dove for an opening in the back of the skene.

And then a ribbon of magical lashed out and seized Anninihus. He was pulled up and back, tossed to the ground with mystical flames eating at his clothes. Batting the flames away, the Death Mage looked up and spotted his old teacher Esha, standing near Aebreanna and leaning heavily on her staff, already preparing her next spell. Anninihus called on his own magic with words and gestures. Pointing his staff at Esha, the Death Mage let tendrils of pure darkness race towards his enemy, but as the spell reached the archmage, a flash of bright white light destroyed the tendrils. With a sneer, Anninihus spotted the small amulet his old teacher wore and sensed the protective magic of Cardinal Tain.

Both wizards stared at each other. They were exhausted and both knew it. They panted, nearly in unison, and each leaned heavily on their staff. Their magic was weakening, with little of their reserves remaining. What tipped the balance of this engagement, though, was that Esha had friends.

To his right, Beraht made his way towards the Death Mage. The mighty Uldra walked on shaking legs. He bled from countless wounds. He kept shaking his head to force his vision into clarity. He kept a firm grip upon his massive waraxe, but still the weapon swung low, its weight pulling the Uldra to one side.

To the Death Mage's right came Rogan and Tomas. Just as wounded, just as weary, the Human warriors also made their way up to the skene. Tomas felt as though he would pass out at any moment. His strength was almost gone, and he knew it. Loyalty alone kept him at Rogan's side, and the squire had no idea what kept his knight moving.

Then, Rogan charged, burning the air with his curses.

Anninihus spotted this and gestured at the knight, throwing a ball of liquid flame at his old enemy. Rogan lifted his shield, likely assuming the strange hardening Remm had placed on it would offer ample protection. But the Death Mage's latest attack was not mystical, it was chemical. The liquid flame latched onto Rogan's shield and hissed its way into the metal. The knight flung aside his shield and resumed the attack. The Death Mage called to what remained of his magic, this time destroying the stage at Rogan's feet. The knight hit the ground hard but picked himself up and raised Fang, ready to cut down the monster before him. In desperation, Anninihus raised his staff in both hands over his head to try and stop the fatal blow. Rogan swung down and broke the Death Mage's staff.

There was a flash of blinding light and an explosion louder than any thunder ever heard. An invisible force roared out, blowing through the ruins, destroying everything and sending everyone to the ground. When the blinding light cleared, Tomas and the others wearily picked themselves up, shaking their heads despite the pain and looking about. Anninihus lay on the ground desperately trying to clear his vision and rise to his feet. Some distance away, Rogan lay still on the ground with the hilt of his broken sword still in his hand.

Tomas roared in fury and flung himself at the Death Mage, ignoring the pain lancing throughout his body. Just as Anninihus was able to rise to his knees and focus his sight, the Death Mage saw the squire standing over him with Steelheart's tip at the villain's throat.

"Yield, Death Mage!" the squire rumbled. "No staff, no spells, no tricks. You are beaten."

Anninihus looked up at Tomas in disdain. "Perhaps *one* more trick," he snarled.

The Death Mage launched his magical attack. Tomas spun Steelheart. The mystical attack reached the blade and there was a strange jolt in the squire's arm. The ball of fire extinguished midair, as though it were a candle blown out. In the same motion, Tomas swung the blade of House Calonar in a wide arc, separating the Death Mage's head from his shoulders.

A moment of absolute silence descended on the group of heroes, each of them frozen in place with an overwhelming shock of what they had just survived. They looked at one another as though they could not believe. Finally, Beraht, looking about the amphitheater, raised his waraxe and bellowed in victory.

Chapter 53

"How is he?" Tomas asked.

Beraht looked up from where Rogan sat, stripped of his armor and propped against a section of wall. "He's alive," the barbarian shrugged. "He'll need a cleric."

"I think we'll all need a little religion when we get home," the squire tried to joke.

"Just help me up," Rogan grumbled, wearily raising a hand for assistance.

Tomas helped his knight to his feet, keeping him steady until his vision cleared as much as it could. Rogan still held in his hand the ruined hilt of Fang. The squire noticed the look of regret on his knight's face. "Did you hear that Remm is reforging my father's sword?"

"Yeah, so?" He then glanced down at the hilt of Fang. "Ah." He nodded. "Yeah, there's just a lot of history in this sword." The knight stuffed what remained of his weapon into the improvised bag carrying his damaged armor. "I guess it's time to go," he noted.

Aebreanna was inspecting Anninihus' body, trying to gain whatever information the corpse might be able to provide.

"Anything?" Tomas asked.

"Oh, yes," she replied, "a great deal. She stood and cleaned her hands with a bit of the Death Mage's cloak. "I know, for example, where the necromancer has been for the past year or more. I know where he studied in the time Esha could not track him, and I even know what he had for dinner tonight."

Tomas stared at Aebreanna a moment. "I really don't think I want to know how you learned all that from a dead body."

The spy just shrugged.

Rogan was standing over the body of Anninihus, staring down at it with a blank expression on his face. Tomas glanced at his knight. "So," the young man said. "You've got your revenge."

The warrior grunted. The two friends turned their backs on their fallen enemy and went to check on Esha. Beraht walked over to the body and looked down at it. He then relieved himself on the Death Mage's remains.

Esha was rubbing her eyes, from the weariness of casting so much magic in such a short amount of time to say nothing of the wounds she received. "Are you going to be alright?" Rogan asked.

"Eventually," the archmage replied.

"Can you get us back to the Keep?"

The Sylva nodded and slowly rose, leaning heavily on her staff. "If you will give me a few minutes to prepare myself, I will do so." She walked away from the others.

"So, what else did you learn from Anninihus?" Tomas asked Aebreanna.

"Well among other things, he was based out of Tordenia," the spy replied.

"How do you know that?"

"The clothes he was wearing. They were sewn with a type of wool that comes from the sheep raised just north of Tordenia. Also, he had Iris Histrioides in one of his pouches." The Sylva held up a small green leaf with white dots on it. "These only grow on the islands off the Tordenian coast. Added to the fact that all his money is from the Western Empire and there you have it."

"That's a lot of evidence," Rogan noted.

Aebreanna nodded. "Too much. Whomever Anninihus was serving, that person desired that we learn his point of origin."

"Trap," the knight grumbled. "And we already know Emir Balshazzar has something to do with what's going on." Rogan straightened. "There's just too much happening," he said. "Too much we don't know. We need to get back to the Keep and make a plan. I need to talk to the King."

"If he can answer," Aebreanna reminded.

"He's the only one who can tell us what's going on. I don't know all that many inhumanly powerful wizards, but the King is either friends or enemies with all of them. Someone gave Anninihus this power boost. If whoever our mystery guest is wants Cylan Calonar dead, then hopefully the King'll know who it is."

"And if he doesn't?" Tomas asked.

Rogan took a deep breath, looking up at the cloudless sky. "We need to get in contact with Cyras," he finally said. "I think it's about time he gave us some straight answers."

"About that prophecy?" the squire asked.

"About everything. He said there'd be an attack. He said we'd go to Tordenia and meet with Balshazzar. But he didn't say a damned thing about the King getting poisoned!"

"You are surprised?" Aebreanna sniffed. "The Trickster Mage cares for nothing and no one."

"Maybe," Rogan grunted. "I'm sick of being manipulated, and I want to know just what in Underworld is really going on."

Upon their return to the Keep, Ilse and a collection of the city's clergy were waiting. The Harvest priestess once again employed her healing magic. Kyla, Medaka and the sisters of the Lady of Light brought them food and water. Cardinal Tain and a few Adamic priests performed a purification, cleansing them of any residue of Anninihus' death magic or the taint of Heath Dannah. This done, Rogan gave orders to the garrison commanders that all guards be doubled until further notice. Once ensuring the city was secure and being returned to health, Rogan and Tomas visited the royal apartments where the Queen assured them the King was alive, though exhausted. "Until he recovers, you are in charge, Rogan," she said.

"You're the next in line," the knight objected.

Nora held up her hand, cutting off any other arguments. "I must take care of my husband, Rogan; you are Regent until further notice, and that is final."

With the King still incapacitated, Ward, leader of the Archaeknights, reported in to Rogan, requesting instructions. The newly-elevated Prince Regent ensured that all Archaeknights drop whatever they were doing and return to the Keep. "Every seer and fortuneteller in the world is saying things are about to start getting really interesting," he explained. "We're going to need all your people here as soon as possible."

Ward, his graying hair and wrinkled eyes betrayed by the rippling muscles that even his leather vest could not hide, held up his hand. "Her Majesty has given me orders, Prince. If, at any point, the King is rendered unable to rule, you are to receive the full loyalty of the Archaeknights. No explanation is necessary. Simply tell us what you need done, and it will be done." The grizzled veteran gestured to the blue and silver, crossed diamond sigil tattooed across his left eye.

"Once an Archaeknight accepts the crest of our lord, we abandon the need for explanations of unusual orders."

Once Ward had left to coordinate with his warriors, Rogan sent Tomas away, insisting that the squire get some rest. "Just be sure to be at the conference chamber at noon tomorrow... I mean noon today," he reminded.

The simple pleasures in life bring a person the most joy. This fact became plainly obvious to Tomas as he sat in his bathing tub, letting the steaming water draw the weariness out of his body. There are so very few perfect moments in a man's life. Inevitably, they are always interrupted once the person becomes aware of just how content he has become. It thus came as very little shock to the young squire when he heard his maid, Alice, enter unobtrusively.

Now I know why all this pampering annoys Rogan so much, the squire thought. Without looking back, Tomas said, "I'm alright in here, Alice. I don't need any help, so feel free to go back to bed. I'll make sure to let you know if I need anything, but I'll most likely just finish my bath and try to get some sleep."

Hopefully that will buy me a few more minutes of peace, he prayed.

The squire listened as the matronly woman left and heard the door to her room close. The young man sat in the steaming water for another few minutes before rousing himself enough to go to bed. He drained the bathing tub and put on his thick cotton robe before crossing his apartments and opening the door to his bedroom.

Suffice it to say, the sight of Mary, clad in nothing but her radiant smile and illuminated by the fireplace, came as something of a shock. She slowly, very slowly, rose from where she had been reclining on the large bed and crossed the carpets to stand quietly in front of her lord. Tomas could only watch as his lady love, moving with a delicate grace, rose onto her toes and pressed her lips gently against his.

Moving together as one, instinct overriding any hesitation, the couple held each other and allowed their kiss to deepen. After a time, they broke their embrace but remained standing pressed very close against one another. Tomas ran his hand lightly across his love's face, tracing it down her chin and neck. The squire kissed her shoulder, letting his lips and tongue trace the smooth perfection of her flesh. Mary sighed and kissed her champion's neck. She put her hands on his chest and slowly parted his robe, pushing it off his shoulders and to the floor. With delicate hands, the young woman traced the very tips of her fingers along the new scars her squire had earned during his latest battle - scars that Ilse's cleric magic could not fully heal.

Tomas circled behind Mary, tracing his hands along her arms up to her shoulders. The squire gently pushed aside her long hair and ran his lips across his Mary's shoulders and the back of her delicate neck, bringing shivers of pleasure that ran through her body and into his as he pressed against his love, enfolding her in his arms.

Mary turned wrapped her arms around his neck. The two kissed again, pressing their bodies together with increasing passion. When Tomas and Mary broke this newest embrace, the squire lifted his love off her feet and carried her to the bed. He gently put her down there, letting his eyes travel along the perfection of her body before staring deeply into her soft eyes. He kissed Mary again and lay down beside her.

The two held each other, kissing and running their hands along each other's bodies. After a perfect eternity, Tomas rolled above Mary, resting on his elbows and looking down at lady. He ran a finger along her cheek and kissed her again. "I love you," he whispered.

"I love you," she replied.

They kissed again and embraced. Their embrace lasted long into the morning. The weariness the two should have felt left them as their love was expressed finally in this way of man and woman. Their love was consummated forever as the two gave their hearts and their bodies to one another for all eternity.

Chapter 54

"I don't give a damn about the problems you've been having. I want to know why you didn't know this attack was coming!" Rogan had quickly managed to work into a near-fury.

As the meeting had progressed, Tomas frequently caught himself looking about in frustration at their lack of progress, taking in the details of the room to relieve the headache that added to his already sour mood. The circular room had obviously been built to bring about a sense of calm, with a high ceiling and wide expanse. Had the shutters to the three large windows not been closed against the foul weather approaching from Ulheim, one could have seen a significant portion of the Keep. Three fireplaces set around the tower radiated a comforting warmth allowing the members of the council to forgo the thick clothing that was becoming increasingly prevalent with the onset of the Northlands winter. The large circular table, at which the council members sat with various reports and dispatches from across the Northlands scattered before them, was set in the center of the room, made of polished hardwood, and had the sigil of House Calonar in its center. Had the situation been otherwise, Tomas would have found the Council Chambers extremely comfortable.

The meeting of King Cylan's Advisory Council was not going exactly as the squire had expected. Being such a dedicated student of history, Tomas had visions of each member speaking in turn, using eloquent words and convincing evidence to arrive at a conclusion upon which the entire council could agree. Instead, tempers ran high, and one member would frequently shout down another mid-sentence. Arguments broke out between two or more members that would frequently divert from the business at hand. The frustration everyone was feeling due to the ease with which their king had been poisoned and an attack been made drained each council member of their civility and professionalism.

At first, Tomas had assumed the Advisory Council would include only a few very select people. Once Rogan had called the meeting to order, though, the squire could not help but marvel at the large group who made up the King's most trusted allies and counselors. Rogan was there, of course, acting as he often did as leader of the Council. As the heir apparent, the prince was in overall charge of the government. As such, it was his final authority that made decisions on the day-to-day governance of the kingdom. On this day, with the King incapacitated, Rogan was not seated in his usual spot, to the ruler's immediate right; instead, the prince was seated in the royal position itself. It was not the knight's first time in that unwanted chair, but it was clear from the way Rogan slouched in the large upholstered seat and scowled through his clasped hands that the stress of the past day was further souring his mood.

In place of Queen Nora, to the left of the King's position, sat Kyla. The princess, Tomas had been told, rarely spoke during the meetings. Her official position was as a representative of the non-Adamic religions of the kingdom, having taken over that responsibility after the departure of Alexia Calonar. Despite her frequent lack of contribution, Kyla was always in attendance with her husband, working tirelessly to soothe Rogan's temper and help the prince to maintain the calm that is so vital to the proper governing of any kingdom. The princess was having little success on this day, however; her own concern for her father's failing health disrupted the calming effect she ordinarily had on not just her husband, but the entire council.

To Rogan's left sat General Killdare and his aide, Captain Forthright, together representing the Calonar House Guard. Both soldiers arrived to the meeting displaying several wounds from the battle the night before in the gardens. Although having been treated by the magic of the Harvest Mother clergy, both General Killdare and his normally whimsical aide were noticeably sore and weary. It was only the general's strong military bearing and frequent nudges from Forthright that kept Killdare from snapping at the questions from the other Council members over his control of their defense forces.

Beyond the soldiers sat Esha, who was studying notes spread out before her and oblivious to nearly everything else. The tiny sylva needed extra cushions on her seat so as to sit at a more equal level as the others, appearing almost as a child dining with the adults. Sitting with the befuddled archmage sat the newly promoted archwizard, Xathias. Despite Esha's frequent lack of attention, she was still required to at least attend as a representative of the Guild, providing whatever information was asked, but otherwise not contributing much to the discussion.

Rashid and Aebreanna were seated past Esha. With them was Rashid's second, Chandra. Tomas had not yet met Chandra, but could easily see why she made such a good spy; her eyes and hair were nondescript brown, and her somewhat tanned complexion could easily allow her to pass for very nearly any Human race. In fact, it seemed to the squire that every aspect of Chandra's physique and personality were designed to allow her to blend in and disappear. The spy's gaze seemed to be everywhere at once, constantly scanning the group with an obvious analytical and even suspicious air.

Seated at the far side of the table from Rogan was Sora, ambassador of the Sylvai who lived in Wildelves Wood and longtime ally of House Calonar. Although not technically sworn members of House Calonar's military, the Speakers and their Walkers were so closely allied to the King and his family that they always had a representative at the Council and never once failed to respond to any request for assistance. Sora sat in her chair restlessly throughout the meeting; it was clear to Tomas the old Sylva was uncomfortable surrounded by so much stonework, tolerating it only due to her strong loyalty to the alliance.

Seated next to the Speaker was Ward, leader of the Archaeknights, and the red-haired Sarah, their newest member; Ward had not taken the illness of the King well, his weather-beaten face showing lines of sorrow and self-recrimination. The large warrior sat in his chair with his shoulders slumped, rarely looking up or engaging in any debate. Despite the assurances of faith from every member of the council, the Archaeknights as a whole, and Ward in particular, felt as though they had failed in their sworn duty.

Continuing the circle was Tomas himself and Cardinal Tain, whose late-night efforts tending to those who had battled Anninihus and his forces showed on his old face, for he could barely find strength enough to stay seated upright. Tain had been a member of the council for decades, never failing in what he considered a sacred duty to serve the people of the Northern Keep and their king. Although any lesser man would have long since retired and enjoyed his remaining years in peace, the cardinal swore that, for as long as his heart still beat, he would never fail in his service to the Northern Keep or House Calonar.

Completing the circle to the side of Kyla sat the colorful pair of Remm and Beraht, Remm acting as representative of the City Watch, and Beraht in his capacity as House Calonar's ambassador to the Uldra clans. Tomas had been assured by his knight that the Uldra were a frequent source of unexpected wisdom. Beraht, he had been told, possessed the bluntest gift for common sense Rogan had ever encountered, often seeing the flaws in any complex plan, and offering a counter proposal that cut through any nonsense to the heart of any problem. Remm, the squire had learned, was one of King Cylan's oldest friends, having sworn centuries ago the greatest oaths of loyalty an Uldra was capable of. Although none of the council members were certain, there were rumors that a connection of some kind existed between Cylan Calonar, Remm Stonebearer, and Cyras Darkholm. Although the two barbarians appeared to pay little attention to the council proceedings, the observations they made belied this, revealing they were more observant of what occurred around them then any would have thought.

Rashid had felt insulted by Rogan's questions of the intelligence surrounding the attack since his agents were responsible for alerting the council of any potential threats. The spymaster rose from his seat and barked, "Come on! I told you months ago that my people had been compromised and it could be possible for someone to make a surprise terrorist attack on the Keep."

"This wasn't some damn terrorist attack!" the knight snapped, also standing, "someone has poisoned the King!"

Ever-ready to come to her husband's defense, Aebreanna focused her opalescent eyes at the prince. "Rogan. Rashid has done everything possible to keep you informed of possible threats; but so long as his group remains compromised, we have no way of telling the difference between genuine threats and diversionary rumors."

Rogan reoriented on the new target. "It's your damn job to know the difference!" he barked, jabbing a finger at the sensual spy. "The whole reason Rashid was empowered as the King's intelligence advisor was to identify potential threats and nullify them before they can explode into an all-out crisis!"

"Don't blame my people for a breach of security!" Rashid roared, slamming his fists into the table.

"Watch what you say about security, spy-guy," Remm muttered into his cider mug.

"How did a poisoner get to the King?" Rogan demanded of the Uldra.

"It wasn't while he was in the castle or the Keep," Remm insisted. "I've had this place locked down since Cylan was crowned."

Rogan turned to Cardinal Tain. "Have you identified what type of poison was used?"

Taking a deep breath, the elderly cardinal opened his heavy eyelids. "*Kay'ay'eil'nas,*" he said. "The clergy of the Harvest Mother are certain. They have attempted every known antidote and treatment."

The Speaker Sora spoke up then. "No mundane antidote will work. *Kay'ay'eil'nas* is an enchanted poison used by the *Xesh'lin*. It is difficult and dangerous to create, but effective."

"How long does it take the poison to work?" Rogan asked.

"That depends on how it was enchanted. The poison can take as little as a day, or as long as a year. I have even heard of some very rare *Xesh'lin* alchemists capable of brewing *Kay'ay'eil'nas* that takes a decade or more to kill."

"So we have no idea how long ago it was done," Rashid noted, dropping back into his seat. "Or how to heal the King."

"Only the one who brewed the *Kay'ay'eil'nas* will know. The poison can be remedied, but the antidote must be as specific as the poison."

Beraht laughed. "It's too bad we don't have a spymaster to find the poisoner."

"Don't push me, hairy," the spymaster threatened darkly.

"And what have the Uldra done to uphold their end of the alliance?" Aebreanna demanded.

Sora raised her arms in an attempt to quell the fighting. "Gentlemen and ladies, instead of recriminations, perhaps we should instead turn our efforts towards what actions need now be taken."

"We need to find who poisoned the King," Tomas insisted. "Whoever it was, he'll know the antidote."

General Killdare knocked on the table and stood, signaling he wanted to speak. "Perhaps the question of who the assassin was should be tabled for now. No matter who it was, he was most likely hired or ordered to do it with little motivation other than pay. Rather than wasting time and resources trying to find someone we really don't need to find, perhaps we should find the person ultimately responsible. If anyone will know an antidote, it'll be him."

"Xaemus," Aebreanna said. "His name has been mentioned of late, and he would possess the skill to brew the *Kay'ay'eil'nas*."

"Could this Xaemus sneak past your guards?" Tomas asked Remm.

The Uldra grunted and nodded.

"You know," Aebreanna said checking her fingernails, "it really is a shame Xaemus was not killed when we had the chance."

Beraht jumped out of his chair. "Alright, look woman...!"

"Enough, you two!" Rogan said. "Xaemus doesn't serve just anyone. If he's working with someone, that person must have a lot of resources. It seems likely Anninihus was working for the same person." Rogan turned to Esha. "Would that explain his power boost?"

"Indeed," the Sylva archmage replied. "The *Xesh'lin* mastered death magic long ago, and they are the only ones who continue its use. My former apprentice could have learned much from their priestesses."

"Remember Lady Ombretta?" Tomas pointed out. "And Esha says he went to Davenor."

Rogan grunted. "There's definitely some connection between Anninihus and the Xeshlin." He looked back to Esha. "Any chance you could track Xaemus?"

"No," the archmage replied, barely looking up from her notes. "The *Xesh'lin* have always been resistant to arcane locating, and Xaemus especially so."

"Why bother with him?" Tomas asked suddenly. "Granted this Xeshlin may have been the one who poisoned the King, but I think General Killdare is right. If we find who he's working for, wouldn't that be more important? Wouldn't whoever hired Xaemus know the antidote?"

Aebreanna shook her head. "If the monster of Davenor poisoned the King, he alone will know the secret." She paused. "And a search for him would consume time we cannot spare."

"Any luck contacting Cyras?" Rogan asked. "If anybody could find Xaemus..."

"He has not responded to our calls," Esha said.

Rogan turned to Rashid. "What about the bodies? Did you learn anything from the assassins, creatures, or mercenaries?" he asked.

The spymaster shrugged. "Like I said before, the mercenaries were all from the south coast of Velaross, most likely the duchy of

Damaris or Remigis. The corpses looked like they could have come from anywhere."

"And Anninihus came from Tordenia after a brief stay in Frostfront," Aebreanna added.

Remm took a large drink form his mug and, wiping his mouth off with his flowing, unkempt beard, said, "The assassins were definitely from the west. One of them even had Balshazzar's crest branded onto his shoulder."

"Balshazzar," Rogan mused, then looked over at Rashid. "That's another name we've been hearing a lot lately."

Rashid nodded, "The Emir has been a vocal opponent of House Calonar for a lot of years now. If anything happened to House Calonar, House Balshazzar would benefit most."

"Excuse me again," Tomas said, raising his hand, "but why would the Emir of Tordenia hire assassins and rogue wizards?"

"After the death of the Emperor ten years ago, along with the loss of most high-ranking nobles in the Republic, only four men were left with strong claims to the Redwood Throne," Aebreanna answered, "Cylan Calonar of the Northern Keep, Theodorico Balshazzar of Tordenia, Nicalos Georgios of Medesorna, and Edmondo Parano of Daivic. House Georgios has no interest in rebuilding an empire, and the Paranos lack the support. But Balshazzar..."

"And the only thing keeping House Balshazzar from using its wealth and power to force their ascension is that they're scared witless of the King," Rogan added.

"Who has now been poisoned," Tomas added.

"The Emir is looking more and more like a strong suspect," Ward noted grimly.

Rashid leaned back and steepled his fingers. "Balshazzar won't know the antidote, but he might know how to find Xaemus."

The squire stood up, laying his fists on the table. "Then what are we waiting for?" he demanded. "Let's take the House Guard and go ask Balshazzar a few questions."

Rogan raised his hands. "Calm down, kid. If we invade the Emir's lands with an army at our backs, then smaller groups would see it as a threat and ally with Balshazzar. We can't afford to set off a full-scale war, and our invading would do just that."

"Not to mention the large group of mercenaries that were gathering near Crossroads," Captain Forthright reminded.

"And the conflict over Jarek," General Killdare added. "Frostfront has rejected our treaty proposal. They've spent all summer building an army. When the snows melt, they'll march."

"The mercenaries," Rashid mused, leaning back again. "Reports of their movements were relayed by Althaea." The spymaster looked to Rogan. "Who was being controlled by Anninihus."

The prince breathed deeply and nodded. "We can't trust anything she reported. There's no telling when she was corrupted."

Killdare shook his head. "We can't trust anything we think we know about the mercenaries." Rainer handed his general a small dispatch. "And there's more bad news," he added, giving Rogan a flat look. "Vagris escaped."

"WHAT!?!" the prince of the Northlands was on his feet, his fists clenched in rage.

"The report just came in this morning," Killdare said. "The wagons were attacked at the edge of Wildelves Wood. Everyone was killed, including the other prisoners. There were dead mercenaries on the scene as well, but Vagris was missing."

"Why didn't we get a report on this?" Tomas asked.

Rainer shook his head. "The Sylvai who investigated were occupied all summer with something they call 'incursions.'"

The squire looked to his knight. "More Lamashti."

"Anninihus," Rogan growled, sitting back down. "He freed Vagris and kept the Sylvai distracted, unable to report back." His eyes grew distant. "He was coming north already. They want him to command the mercenaries."

"Which will make them infinitely more dangerous," Killdare agreed.

"What do we do?" the squire demanded falling back into his chair. "We can't chase after Balshazzar when an army might be camped at our border, especially one commanded by Vagris."

Rogan turned to Tain. "What's the Church's stance in all this?" he asked.

The Cardinal cleared his throat several times before finally answering. "I'm afraid there just isn't enough evidence. And with the escalating conflict between Alvaro and Frostfront, the Holy Knights can't abandon Church lands. Frostfront might invade. I'm sorry, Rogan, but until you can get definitive proof, Holy Mother Church and her knights cannot contribute to any actions." The old man smiled then. "Of course, we have always made it our policy not to interfere in internal conflicts, so any actions you take will not be opposed either."

"So you can't back us, but you won't block us either."

"I am sorry, Rogan, that's the best I can get from the Lords' Cardinal."

"What about the Speaker Circle?" the knight asked then, turning to the elderly Sylva.

Sora straightened in her chair. "My instructions in this matter are quite specific; the Speakers and Walkers cannot become involved in a foreign confrontation. Your information on the source of the Lamashti incursions was useful, and we hope that, with the Death Mage neutralized, these will halt. However, with the ongoing threat of mercenaries in our Wood, and now the added complication of their being under the direction of a Bellonar, we must conserve our limited strength."

"The Uldra will help any way they can, Rogan," Beraht declared. "Just as soon as you give the word, an army of clansmen will hit whatever target you name. The clans are ready with a path through Ulheim, if you want to go to Tordenia."

"We need more information." Rogan rubbed his temples. "We need to verify the mercenary threat, we need to know what Balshazzr is up to, we need to know where Xaemus is, we need to know who boosted Anninihus... we need... more."

"I can send more people," Rashid said, "but if Anninihus could coop Althaea, he could get anyone. Until I can verify my people, any intelligence we get is suspect.

Ward spoke up. "My Archaeknights are all trustworthy, but we're warriors, not spies."

"It's starting to look more and more like one of us is going to have to personally go to Balshazzar's lands," Rogan said. "He's our only real chance of finding Xaemus and getting the antidote." He chuckled softly, almost to himself. "Cyras said I'd need to go to the Western Empire." The knight then looked at his squire. "Feel like taking a trip kid?"

Tomas grinned. "Definitely," he said.

"Uh, Rogan," Rashid said hesitantly. "You do realize that, with the King incapacitated and the Queen having named you regent, you have an obligation to stay here."

The knight turned back to his friend. "You're right. I do have an obligation. I'm obliged to keep this kingdom and its people safe, and I can't do that by sitting here and waiting for an attack that may never come. The best way to keep this kingdom safe is by being proactive.

"Beraht, tell the clans that Tomas and I will need that safe route through Ulheim. It won't be easy with winter on our heels, but at least the Druug won't be active. Sora, meet with the Speaker's Circle; tell them about Vagris and warn them the mercenaries are likely to get a lot more organized. Ward, whatever Archaeknights are in or around Tordenia are to meet us there. I want backup, just in case."

Ward nodded. "I'll see to it."

"Rashid, make sure nobody knows that me and Tomas are coming," the knight said then. "The last thing we need is a special welcome. Remm, nobody gets near the King. Alright everyone, that's the plan. Tomas and I go to Balshazzar and find out what he knows. Rashid, Remm, Aebreanna, and Kyla keep things quiet here. Tain and Sora seek aid from their respective groups while Beraht rallies the Uldra. General Killdare, make sure the Guard is ready to move, just in case."

Seeing nods and understanding all around, Rogan stood, signaling the end of the meeting.

Chapter 55

Winters have always been harsh in the Northlands. The people had long since grown accustomed to the sudden fury their homeland could unleash. The storm that hit the Northern Keep that night, however, caught everyone by surprise. Howling winds tore through Wildelves Wood, and snow so thick a person could barely breathe in the open fell upon the city. Knowing full well the strength of winter, the people of the Keep could only seal themselves within the safety of their homes and wait for the storm to end.

"This is not natural," Esha informed them from her tower. It had long been the custom of the Keep's most essential personnel to have Esha's communication crystals nearby in case of a sudden crisis. Now, on the third day of the fierce storm, Rogan ordered the Advisory Council to convene by way of the crystals and Esha's magic. "This storm was summoned."

"There is no one of my order who can track the origin of this storm," Speaker Sora offered. Her people had been the hardest hit. With the horribly powerful winds screaming through their Wood, no Sylvai village had been left unbroken. Since the second day of the storm, the Speakers and their people had sought the safety of the many caves throughout the forest.

"Is there any way to stop it?" Rogan asked. He, along with Tomas, Mary, and most of the others living within the castle, had gathered in the council chambers to confer.

Sora shook her head, the magic of her crystal-transmitted form giving the Speaker a bluish hue broken only by the glow of her opalescent eyes. "The force is too great. Whoever summoned this storm must have begun so months ago. Its fury is simply too great. Even the one who created this could not undo it. We can only wait out the storm."

"I believe I have a theory as to the identity of our mystery attacker," Esha said from her tower.

"Enlighten us," Rashid muttered.

"There are only a handful of adepts in the world with the power to affect the weather of *Ar'ae'el* to this extent."

"I think I've got this list memorized by now," Tomas said ruefully.

Rogan threw his squire an annoyed look.

King Cylan shook his head weakly. "I would have sensed Cyras' power had the storm come from him. It did not. Nor did it come from Tienel; I am as familiar with his power as I am my own." The King shifted in his large chair, breathing heavily against the weight of the thick blanket draped over his lap. Queen Nora had been able to restore a small measure of his strength, though only by pouring her magic into his failing body.

"That leaves Fak'Har, the Lords Cardinal, and the sorceress Vara," Esha said, ticking them off on her small, ink-stained fingers.

"I can assure you all that the Lords Cardinal had nothing to do with this attack," Cardinal Tain said.

"That only leaves Fak'Har or Vara," Rogan noted. The knight turned to Esha. "What do you have on either of their locations?"

"Fak'Har is impervious to my divinations. His power far exceeds my own."

"Besides," the king added through heavy breaths, "he has little reason to attacks us."

"Are we sure, your Majesty?" Rashid asked. "His motivations have always been mysterious. We've never known how or why he does anything."

The old king nodded. "True. However, as familiar as I am with the sense of the Trickster Mage's power, I also have a... passing familiarity with the Shadowed Mage. I don't think he's the adept we seek."

"That leaves Vara," Tomas said with a slight shudder.

"How about it, Esha?" Rogan asked. "Could Vara conjure something like this?"

"Yes," the archmage replied. "Most certainly. Her power is strongest regarding the natural world and its forces."

Tomas snorted. "Are you kidding? If she could suck the souls from all the firstborn children of Velaross, this storm would be nothing."

"That was a thousand years ago," Aebreanna pointed out. "And I am fairly certain those tales have been exaggerated."

"Would you want to take the chance?" Cardinal Tain asked softly. "Her villainy is the source of many stories in the Holy City. Her magic is infamous, and her evil unquestioned."

"Is there any way to know if it was Vara?" Tomas asked.

Esha shrugged. "We could ask her."

Rogan grunted. "Any chance of pinpointing her location, Esha?"

The archmage frowned. "That is an interesting question, and a suspicious coincidence. When I first realized this storm had been summoned, I made an attempt to locate each of the adepts I named before. As usual, Cyras Darkholm and Fak'Har were impossible to pin-point. I sensed the King here in the Keep, of course, and Tienel Greysoul is not on *Ar'ae'el* at all. Vara, however, I located almost immediately."

"Why is that strange?" Tomas asked.

"She is of comparable power to the Greysoul," the Sylva replied. "She has the power to shield herself from my divinations. She cannot be found unless she wishes to be."

"Which suggests she wishes to be," the king added.

"Where is she?" Rogan asked.

"Ulheim, in a cave near the Parent Mountains."

"That figures," Beraht grunted.

"Why?" Tomas asked.

The Uldra stood and unfolded a large map of Ulheim. Amidst those great mountains, the Uldra map had marked the scattered villages of the mountain-peoples, as well as those areas of known Druug concentration. In the exact center of Beraht's map was the Allfather's Throne, the mightiest of all mountains, homeland of the Uldra, and, so the barbarians believed, the home of their god himself. Beraht traced a massive finger west, from the Northern Keep, into an unmarked region of Ulheim. "The Parent Mountains are forbidden," he noted, pointed to a pair of mountains standing alone in a large valley. "No Uldra go there." He looked at Rogan with a hard stare. "No Druug, either."

"But why?" Tomas insisted, standing and studying the map.

Beraht shrugged. "Bad land," he grumbled. "No growing, no hunting, no mining." Again, he looked at Rogan. "And the Druug are scared of the place."

The prince-regent sighed. "Well, that's a pretty good indicator," he grumbled.

"Do we have any choice?" Tomas asked his knight.

Rogan looked to the King.

The old Halvan shook his head. The king turned to Beraht and Remm. "Are there clans that can provide help?" he asked.

Remm nodded. "One or two. But like the youngster said," he nodded towards Beraht. "Nothing near the Parent Mountains."

"No help for it, I guess," Rogan said. "Tomas and I'll set out as soon as the weather clears. We'll head into Ulheim and have a talk with Vara. Once we find out the who and the why, we'll move on to Tordenia and have a sit down with Balshazzar." He looked to Remm and Beraht. "Let the clans know we'll need a route as close to the Parent Mountains as they can manage." Rogan thought a moment. "Once we're in there, we might as well head straight for Tordenia, tell the clans we'll need a route south."

"Unless there's anything else?" the king asked. None of the council members had anything to add. Esha deactivated the communication crystals.

Rogan gestured for Tomas to wait. Once the chamber was clear, save for himself, Kyla, Tomas, Aebreanna, and the King and Queen, he turned to Queen Shera. "I have to ask..."

She nodded. "One year."

"No more?"

"No more." The Lady of House Calonar laid a soft touch on her husband's hand. He smiled at her. "And he will get weaker with each day."

"Who knows?" Rogan asked.

"Those in this room. The family. No others."

Rogan passed his eyes over Beraht's map. "One year. Vara's cave, through the Endless Sands, Tordenia, track down Xaemus and get the cure, back here." The knight rubbed his eyes. "It'll be close, even if there's no distractions."

Mary had been waiting outside the council chamber. When Tomas emerged, the couple smiled at one another and went to Rogan and Kyla.

Mary bowed. "Excuse me, your Highness," she said to Rogan. "Since you and Tomas won't be leaving for a while yet, we were hoping you could help us with something."

"What is it?" Rogan asked.

Tomas and Mary smiled brightly.

Beraht tugged at the ceremonial blue and grey uniform that strained against his massive chest. "What's the point of this again?" he demanded as Aebreanna helped him belt a ceremonial sword around his broad gut.

The beautiful spy sighed and rolled her opalescent eyes, now azure with the onset of winter. "The ceremony has been explained to you more times than I could possibly count."

"Yeah, well I still don't get it. If the two of them are together, then what's the ceremony for?"

Rogan stepped up, wearing a full-dress uniform he could only tolerate on the most important of functions. The medals and ribbons adorning the bright blue sash tied across his torso looked to be so heavy it was a wonder the prince could stand straight. No doubt the unnecessarily tight overtunic and stiff leather boots helped him remain erect. "This is a betrothal ceremony. It's for the kids, and it will only take a few minutes. Once it's done, they'll be allowed to have children and own property together and hold all the rights that any married couple has."

"Then why don't they just get married?" the barbarian growled, as Aebreanna tugged the thick Uldra belt against his expansive middle. The Uldra was wearing a dark blue surcoat embroidered with the silver regalia of House Calonar and looked as though he might rip apart the offending garment at any moment.

Satisfied with the belt, Aebreanna used a step ladder to reach the mountain-man's collar, a dark grey tunic that required enough material to clothe a platoon of Guardsmen. She sighed, pulling the ruffled folds of her gown clear of her feet to maintain footing on the ladder, even as she tried to adjust Beraht's collar. "They want to wait until Tomas and Rogan return from Tordenia so their families can be brought to the Keep," the Sylva explained. "This way they have some moral justification for all the physicality they have been engaging in outside the Church-sanctioned artifice of wedlock."

"Huh?"

"They want to be engaged so the Church won't have a problem with them sleeping together," Rogan translated.

"Oh." The Uldra took a better look at his friend. "You look like a girl in that outfit," he said, trying to laugh but lacking the air.

"Have *you* looked in the mirror recently?" the knight snarled.

The Uldra turned and looked into the large mirror set against the far wall of the waiting room. For a moment, Beraht stood perfectly still and stared. He then nodded and reached up with fists clenched in fury.

In the instant Beraht had clearly decided to remove the offending costume, Aebreanna was there. The impossibly nimble spy, in defiance of her voluminous blue gown, leapt from the step ladder, attaching to the lumbering Uldra's shoulders, and began beating him about the head with a wooden stool. "You will not, I repeat, *not*, ruin the children's special day with your barbarian antics!" the beautiful Sylva ordered, punctuating her words with repeated blows to her comrade's thick head. "You will wear the costume, you will not speak, and you will try not to breathe. Am I understood?"

"Why should I?" the righteous warrior roared, still staring into his reflection and all but ignoring Aebreanna's blows.

Rogan crossed the room and looked up into his old friend's eyes. "Because it's for Tomas and Mary, and it would mean the world to them."

Beraht growled a bit, but relented. "Fine." The Uldra reached up and grabbed Aebreanna around the waist with one massive hand, delicately placing her on the floor.

The Sylva shoved her elbow into the back of Beraht's knee, prodding him as one would a sullen ox, out of the way of the tall mirror. She examined herself, making minor adjustments to the blue gown with its many layers of white lace. The garment was caught at her waist by a golden belt, little more than a golden thread, the ends of which dangled stylishly to lose themselves in the lace around her legs. The Sylva's neckline was very low-cut, offering, or really encouraging, a generous view of her decolletage. With winter suddenly thrust upon the Northlands, her luxurious hair had turned to nearly luminescent white, a change Aebreanna highlighted with strings of pearls woven into her mane. At the lowest point of her gown's neckline, she wore a silver pendant, the crossed-diamond heraldry of House Calonar.

Kyla entered the waiting room. The princess was dressed to match Aebreanna, and the two made a perfect complement to one another. Kyla's light blue gown matched the style of Aebreanna's darker blue. Her mass of blonde hair was highlighted with a silver circlet, itself adorned with pearls matching those woven into

Aebreanna's mane. Like her Sylva friend, Kyla also wore the emblem of her House.

Tomas noted this from the chair in which he sat, though only occasionally. He alternated sitting and standing, pacing and adjusting. He was dressed in his own formal uniform, a copy of Rogan's, with identical sashes and ceremonial swords. The only real difference being that Tomas' chest was not as yet encumbered with rows of medals as Rogan and Beraht's were; only the symbol of House Calonar and Alexia's golden rose, its pedals lightly open, adorned the squire's uniform with a pair of small medals, to mark the warehouse battle and the defeat of the Death Mage. "Hey, when do I get a bunch of fake medals?" he had demanded lightly, trying to hide the tremor in his voice.

"When you impress enough fake people," Rogan had grunted.

"Is everybody ready?" the squire asked anxiously, and not for the first or even fifth time.

"We are," the knight grinned. "It looks like you're about to pass out, though."

"Well, this outfit is a little tight."

The knight crossed to his squire and made a pointless adjustment to his collar. "Just remember," he said sagely, "this was all your idea."

"Actually, it was Mary's idea."

Rogan nodded. "Let that be a lesson to you, kid. Anytime you give in to a woman's desires, you're actually giving in to a lot more than you think."

Kyla crossed the room and looked her husband in the eyes. "Excuse me?" she asked sweetly, but with a chill that mocked the winter storm outside.

"Uh, nothing dear. I love you."

The princess wrapped her hands around her champion's sash and pulled him down to her, a feat that caused the prince considerable duress given the clothes he was wearing. "Uh huh," she said in a growling purr before kissing him.

A page entered and announced that everything was prepared.

"Alright," Tomas said. "Let's do this."

Rogan and Beraht escorted Tomas down the short aisle of the castle's chapel. At the altar stood Cardinal Tain, the old cleric having risked the foul weather to make the trip all the way to the castle, insisting that no one else would conduct the ceremony. The men took their places arrayed before the altar and turned back to the chapel entrance where Sarah and Ward, the two attending Archaeknights, ceremoniously swung the doors open. Framed in the center and being escorted by the King himself stood Mary, dressed in purest white with a veil seemingly woven of the clouds, and a crown of fruiting holly. Following behind as the two began the slow march forward were the Queen with Kyla and Aebreanna. Nearly dancing ahead of the bride-to-be, Princess Karen and Rasha Tressalon spread rose pedals across the aisle. Behind them, surprisingly sedate, marched Jalad Tressalon, bearing a cushion upon which rested a crimson ribbon.

Tomas' breath, what little he had, ended as he stared at his lady love. His heart beat in unison with her delicate footsteps as she and the King walked to the altar before he turned her to face Cardinal Tain and moved to stand behind her with his wife and daughters. The benediction by the fatherly holy man was given and the two young loves clasped their right hands together. He told them to love and cherish one another as he tied the crimson ribbon Jalad had brought forward around their wrists. The light of the candles danced across the embroidered golden flames on the ribbon, and sparkled off the small golden charms tied to either end, one a sheaf of wheat, the other a sitting cat.

Cardinal Tain smiled softly at Tomas. "Tomas, speak the words that will bind you forever."

The squire cleared his throat nervously and looked deeply into the eyes of his one and only love. "Mary," he began, "my heart has called to you for as long as I have lived. You give me strength and hope, and I will love you always. My life and all I now own, or ever will, I give to you. I pledge myself to you and only you, now and forever."

The cardinal turned and smiled at Mary. "Mary, speak the words that will bind you forever."

The woman looked at her lord and love with a soft smile on her lips while her young heart beat a rhythm of love. "Tomas. I have dreamed of you without knowing you. I have missed you before meeting you. I promise myself to you, body and soul, that I might hold you and love you always. I pledge myself, now and forever, to you."

Cardinal Tain raised his hands towards the heavens and closed his eyes. "I call now, on all the spirits of light. I call on our Lord, the

Creator, and all the powers of good and love across the world to witness this joining of souls and ask them to bless these two for all their days." The old priest opened his eyes and lowered his arms. He grinned at the two young lovers with a knowing twinkle in his wrinkled eyes. "Tomas. Mary. Share the first kiss of your love. Kiss and know that you are one."

The squire lifted Mary's veil and looked deeply into her eyes. "I love you," he whispered.

Mary looked up at her lord and future husband. "I love you," she replied, letting all that she felt for him flow through her eyes and into his soul.

They kissed. They kissed to the cheers of their friends and to the accompanying beat of their hearts, that now and forever after would beat as one.

Chapter 56

The sun finally broke through the thick clouds at dawn the following day. The storm that had beaten against Wildelves Wood and the Northern Keep was gone as though it had never been. Only the thick snow banks gave mute evidence of the severe weather. The champions of House Calonar waited another five days, to allow returned sun to melt enough of the heavy snow to allow travel.

Nearly every member of the Advisory Council stood waiting in the courtyard, wishing to send the heroes off properly. There had been no question. The weather had cleared and the roads were passable, but no one knew for how long this would hold. Rogan and Tomas would leave immediately. They understood just as Kyla and Mary understood. Everyone understood their duty, despite what their own preferences might have been.

The main doors to the castle proper opened, showing Rogan and Kyla, standing arm in arm beside Tomas and Mary, also arm in arm. Kyla and Mary stood on tiptoe and gave one last, parting kiss to their heroes before gently pushing them down the steps. Well wishes and pats on the back were given from each member of the council, Cardinal Tain invoked God's blessings for their trip, and Remm gave both heroes the traditional Uldra punch in the stomach for good luck. Stick and Brute, along with three pack horses, stood in the center of the courtyard, the warhorses snorting in their own eagerness to begin the quest. Rogan and Tomas mounted and drew Talon and Steelheart in salute of the King and Queen, who watched from a balcony above, as Stick and Brute reared before marching out the gates.

Kyla, eyes full of unshed tears, whispered to Mary, "I hope this takes less time than usual."

Looking at her princess, Mary asked, "Any particular reason, your Highness?"

"I'd like Rogan to be here for the birth of our first child," Kyla replied.

The young maid looked to her friend. "Did you tell him?"

Kyla shook her head. "It would have only distracted him, and this mission will be dangerous enough. Let Rogan be surprised when he comes home."

"If they come home," Mary said, tears once again threatening.

The princess took the maid in her arms. "They will come back to us. They always do. They always must."

The trip through the city was pleasantly uneventful. Rogan had feared word of their departure would have gotten out to the common people, drawing them to the streets to cheer their heroes on to their newest adventure despite the cold and the snow. The knight's relief was short lived, however. Even as the two heroes passed through the city gates, they were greeted by the appearance of two familiar faces standing, one somewhat impatiently, at the edge of the Wood. Shaking his head in annoyance, Rogan reined Stick in. "Aebreanna, Beraht, just what do you two think you're doing?"

The lithe Sylva along with the lumbering Uldra stood beside their respective mounts. Aebreanna's was a white Sylvai pony, small and graceful, with tail and main exquisitely groomed. Beraht's was an impossibly massive Uldra draft horse with a shaggy brown coat. Seeing at last the approach of their friends, the pair mounted and moved up beside the Humans. "Well," Beraht explained, "me and Aebreanna here were thinking that you two might need a little help."

"I was wondering why you two weren't there to see us off," Rogan sighed.

Shrugging lightly, her ample curves as usual enhanced by her every movement despite the thick, fur-lined cloak she wore, Aebreanna smiled gently. "There was little point to our saying good-bye once we had decided to join you."

"Aebreanna, you know where Tomas and I are going. We'll be lucky to get through without a fight," Rogan argued.

Again, the spy shrugged. "If the danger is so great, then you will most definitely need our assistance."

"What about the twins?" the knight asked.

"Rashid remains in the Keep, and he knows how important it is I still do my part; he understands."

"Besides," Beraht said while digging deeply in his cavernous nose, "if you plan to go through Ulheim, then you'll need me; nobody knows that part of the world like me."

Rogan shook his head. "God help us, we're relying on the memory of an Uldra."

"What?" Beraht asked innocently.

Again Rogan shook his head. "I suppose it would be useless to try and order you two back to the Keep?"

The Sylva and Uldra gave Rogan identical looks at the possibility of his giving them an order. "That's what I thought," he grumbled.

By now, Tomas had a large grin on his face. "Well then, I guess we should move on, now that we're all here."

"What did I do to deserve this?"

"Do you really want an answer to that?"

Tomas and His Friends
Continue their Journey in:

The Western Empire

ABOUT THE AUTHOR

William Price Jr is a teacher of writing and literature. Having published numerous short stories and poems, he still searches for truth amidst his many made up stories. He lives in New Hampshire